NB

Eight Dogs Named Jack

And Fourteen Other Stories
from the Detroit Streets and Michigan Wilderness

Praise for *Eight Dogs Named Jack*

"Joe Borri demonstrates a brilliant sense of both time and place, of the city of Detroit and the deep woods of Michigan. He writes with grace and flair and distinction. He makes the whole state seem like an enchanted and magical place."

> — Pat Conroy, bestselling author of *The Great Santini*,
> *The Lords of Discipline*, and *The Prince of Tides*

"Joe Borri is a screaming talent coming out of America's heartland. The setting may be Michigan, but Borri's search is the heart of America, and he's found some gold in some very dark places. *Eight Dogs Named Jack* is a riveting collection of rapid fire stories by a writer who knows his characters and makes you sweat along with them."

> — Jack Epps Jr., screenwriter, *Top Gun* and *Dick Tracy*

"Joe Borri's tales of life in Detroit and Michigan's great up north are gritty, sensitive, captivating, and often shockingly graphic. His characters embody the close-knit, first-generation East Side Detroit neighborhood where Borri grew up and take us back to places sweetly familiar and faintly dark, through rough rites of passage and lessons learned large along the way."

> — Patty LaNoue Stearns, author of *Cherry Home Companion*
> and *Good Taste: A Guide to Northern Michigan Cuisine*

"Joe Borri's characters jump off the page. I dare you to start one of his short stories and put it down without finishing the read. They're quirky, edgy, and always, always intriguing. *Eight Dogs Named Jack* is an explosive start for a literary star in the making."

> — David Alexander, Humanitas Prize nominee for *Anya's Bell*

Eight Dogs Named Jack

And Fourteen Other Stories
from the Detroit Streets and Michigan Wilderness

By Joe Borri | Illustrations by the Author

Published by Momentum Books, L.L.C.

2145 Crooks Road, Suite 208
Troy, Michigan 48084
www.momentumbooks.com

ISBN-13: 978-1-879094-79-6
ISBN-10: 1-879094-79-7
LCCN: 2007922424

For Maria,
who makes coffee strong
and life beautiful.

"Myths are public dreams; dreams are private myths. By finding your own dream and following it through, it will lead you to the myth-world in which you live. But just as in dream, the subject and object, though they seem to be separate, are really the same."

— The Vitality of Myth
Joseph Campbell

" ... and he observed the law more punctiliously; but still there was about him a suggestion of lurking ferocity, as though the Wild still lingered in him and the wolf in him merely slept."

— White Fang
Jack London

"You talkin' to *me?*"

— Travis Bickle in Taxi Driver

Table of Contents

Honest John

Richie was an odd kid, relatively happy, but given to certain moods. Visceral memories of some in his extended family—the things he saw and the things they did—remained for years, particularly those that involved the real characters. Fat Uncle Fredo, who weighed 400 pounds and would squeeze Richie's hand unmercifully; Rossi, who had one eye that never looked quite at you; Guido, who had to shave three times a day; Sal, who could swallow his tongue and turn his eyelids inside out. Some of the men were fringe wise guys, never without a hustle, always selling something. And though they often flashed a wad of bills as big as bagel, no one really knew exactly what it was they did to get all their money.

Richie's father, Lou, was a Detroit policeman. The family lived in a quaint, well-kept duplex in Copper Corner, a section of Detroit's East Side so named because of its heavy population of cops. The idea these white men held was to live as far from the inner city as possible, but still satisfy the archaic residency laws required to work for the City of Detroit. Richie learned by example of how to go on in society. Never take what wasn't yours, stand up straight, and look people in the eye. The rest would take care of itself. But he grew up in a peculiar environment—he had lineage with one foot on the other side of the law. One of these men—and Richie's unabashed favorite—was his mother Ada's cousin, John.

Richie called him Uncle John, even though he wasn't really his uncle. When Richie, or Ada, or just about anyone else mentioned John, Lou would roll his eyes and give a little shake of his head. But because he was so well liked, Ada chose to see things as she wished, as did the rest of the family.

Lou was a different story. Lou knew all about guys like John. John's "real" job was at Ford Motor Company. An electrician, he was high up in the union, though no one ever saw him go to work. And it was common knowledge that if John tried to wire a light switch, he might start the house on fire. It would be an understatement to say everyone loved him—even Lou did, he just did so with a critical heart. He had seen the way John got people to do things for him, things they would normally *never* do, and he vowed he wouldn't let that happen to him or anyone else he held dear.

Richie, however, adored John—the kid hung on every word he said—which made it an appropriate yet funny thing that the boy—a mere seven year old—would be the very one to give him such a lasting nickname. John always made a big deal out of Richie. Whenever he'd see him, John—his round face stuck with that crooked, white-toothed smile, brown eyes squinting into sparkly slits—would lean down, put out his thick hand and talk to Richie like he was a real person, not just some bratty kid.

"How's doing Richie?" he would say, and Richie would take John's hand and give it a big shake. And then he would pretend Richie had superhuman strength and that he was crushing John's hand, the way Fat Uncle Fredo always did to *him*. That always cracked Richie up, watching the faces John made when they shook.

"Hi, Uncle John," he'd say.

After he "recovered" from having his hand crushed, John would rustle Richie's crew cut and pat him on the back. Richie was always happy after that, because he knew John would tell him a joke and slip him a buck or two.

Most of Richie's days were filled fighting off the nuns at St. Jude's Elementary, where he was working through the minefield that was second grade with Sister Veronica presiding. The nun was an evil, broad-shouldered woman just shy of six feet with ringlets of oily, jet-black hair. She looked like a man in a habit, and on more than one occasion she pummeled Richie with her huge fists for not standing straight in line. That all stopped when Lou called the convent and told the principal, *"That crazy bitch touches my kid once more, the barrel of a shotgun's going to go up your ass, too."*

Richie hated the nuns at his school and pined for the day he'd no longer be subjected to their torments. Thankfully, summer was upon him and he had three months of freedom until having to battle his third grade teacher, Sister Imelda. That was the summer Richie gave John his nickname.

★　　★　　★

In July 1968, Richie's family held their annual Fourth of July picnic at Heilmann Park, a six-block-long run of ball diamonds, grass fields, and tennis courts. Fifty or so of his family—cousins, aunts, uncles, and grandparents—sat on folding chairs or played bocce amid picnic tables festooned with red, white, and blue bunting. While the food cooked, a few of the ancient Dagos in white tank tops played *morra*—odds and evens—furiously throwing their fingers out, alternately swearing or rejoicing at the outcome. The smell of grilled sausage and charcoal wafted through the thick heat. Richie scanned the crowd, ignoring Fat Uncle Fredo—testing the strength of a folding chair he sat on and fanning his huge face—calling him to come shake hands.

A car horn's drawn-out honk caused everyone to turn their heads, trying to find the source of the pain in the ass interrupting the serenity of their party. Lou was helping his cousin, Nicolo, cook sausage and peppers on a fifty-five gallon drum that had been converted to a huge grill. A long, black Lincoln pulled up to the curb, a pricey sore thumb in a sea of Pontiacs and Chevrolets. Uncle John—late to the party as usual—got out and waved to the crowd. He was dressed in a pair of plaid Bermuda shorts and a mismatched madras shirt he wore untucked. A collective cheer rose up, and he raised his hands above his head like a prizefighter. In his right hand he waved a flapping American flag.

Richie smiled watching John stop and kiss all the aunts and shake hands with the uncles, the men slapping their thighs, pointing at his ridiculous attire. He slid his dark sunglasses onto the bridge of his forehead and tickled a few of the nieces and nephews, some of the younger cousins, too. Richie waited patiently.

John walked through the crowd like a politician working the polls. When he saw Richie's dad, he put his hands up like he was under arrest. Lou didn't react, but then finally couldn't help it and let himself smile. He shook his head at John, and the two wrapped each other up in a protracted bear hug. It made Richie feel good, seeing his dad hug Uncle John like that. He wanted his pop to love John as much as he did.

Richie studied John's face as he scanned the crowd. Then he made eye contact with him and out came those crinkled eyes, the grin growing impossibly broader into that dazzling Hollywood smile. No matter how hard one tried to resist him, John had the ability to make the person he was talking to feel better than they did before. He stood in front of Richie and gave him a warm handshake.

"How's doing Richie? Here, happy Independence Day," John said. Richie took the flag and then John's fingers rustled through his stiff hair and he felt the weight of one of his gold nugget rings tap his scalp. "Hey Richie, let me ask you, 'cuz I know you're a big baseball fan. Who's going to win the World Series this year?" He bent down, his hands on his knees. Richie could smell the scent of Canoe aftershave and Dial soap.

"I sure hope it's the Tigers," Richie said, excitement pouring out at the prospect of his hometown team winning it all. John's face remained stoic.

"They came close last year, didn't they? Say, who's your favorite player—wait—I bet I know … *Norm Cash*. Am I right, is it Stormin' Norman? It is, isn't it?"

Richie's eyes widened at the apparent clairvoyance. "How did you *know* that?"

"Just a feeling, Richie, just a feeling … I'm friends with him, you know."

"For *real?* Do you think you could maybe get me his autograph?"

John smiled, and his face seemed to take in the request in little pieces.

"Sure Richie. Sure—*for you?* Sure thing!" Richie looked up at John's face, the twinkling slits of his eyes reflecting dots of sunlight. "You know what? They're gonna do it. The Tigers are *gonna win it all* this year, Richie! Mark my words. I can *feel* it."

Richie's eyes grew even larger, and John picked up on it.

"You really think so Uncle John?"

He was slowly becoming convinced his uncle had a mystical ability to see into the future. John's face moved toward him until it was inches away from the boy. And it seemed right there, Richie could see all the way into the man's soul.

"Have I ever lied to you, Richie?" John asked.

Richie thought about it. Uncle John had never told him anything but jokes and funny stories that made him laugh. It never occurred to him that the man would lie about anything. Why would he?

"No, you're real honest, Uncle John … you're *Honest John!*"

John looked at Richie a second and blinked, and with it his face changed. He exploded a loud, resonant belly laugh. It was so *rat-a-tat-tat*, the rest of the family turned to see what was so funny. Lou especially watched the curious interaction between John and his youngest son. John held his gut with both hands, rearing back and laughing even louder like some Dago Santa Claus.

"Honest John! That's great. Oh, I love that! Hey, did you hear that? I'm *Honest John*—hear that everyone? Say it loud, say it proud. *You're looking at Honest John*—hot damn, Richie you are something!"

Lou watched the whole time from afar. "Yeah, you're something, too, Johnny," he said under his breath. He looked at the smoldering white coals in the bottom of the grill, where lost peppers and sausage sputtered, focusing on the heat. Nicolo turned the sausages and checked the blackened skin of the red and green peppers. He poured beer from a bottle of Stroh's over all of it. The hissing snapped Lou from his trance. Flames shot up through the grates from one pepper that fell on the white embers.

"Honest John … funny. From the mouths of babes," Nicolo remarked.

"Yeah. Nicky, pour a little more in the corner—got a real hot spot starting there."

★   ★   ★

The nickname stuck, and every time thereafter, it became a kind of ritual John seemed to need for validation. Except now, John would seek Richie out before anybody else in the family, even the eldest patriarchs. He'd get down real low near Richie's young face, put his hands on his knees and ask, with mock seriousness, "Richie, would I ever lie to you?"

"Nope."

"And why not?"

"Because you're Honest John," Richie always replied.

And then John would stand up, proud as the head bull, and say the same exact thing every time, as if he were trying to convince himself of it.

"Yes I am."

Then he'd slip Richie a couple of bucks. And always there in the background was Lou, watching—the whole time, ever watching—with a cop's cynical eyes. For the time being—mostly because of the innocence of his son's adulation for John—he decided to let it go.

Somehow, the Tigers ended up winning the championship that year, beating a far superior St. Louis team after an inauspicious start. Detroit became only the third team to win the World Series after being down three games to one as the Tigers beat the Bob Gibson-led St. Louis Cardinals in seven games. The victory helped heal—a start, anyway—the riot-ravaged heart of Detroit. More importantly, the win left Richie with an indelible memory of Honest John as a soothsayer of epic proportions—an Italian Nostradamus, as it were.

"But Dad, Honest John *told* me they'd win. He knew. He *felt* it," Richie said.

Lou exhaled. He looked at his son's big eyes, eyes that only saw good in people.

"Richie, it was a *guess* … did he ever get you that autograph of Norm Cash?"

"He told Mom he's working on it."

"Uh-huh," Lou said.

In November of 1968, while out scouting for real estate one day, John drove by a recently vacated meat store located in the middle of good foot traffic. The butchers—Italian immigrants and brothers—had been found hanging from meat hooks, their intestines spilling out of their midsections.

John got the place real cheap.

So it was that Honest John's Ice Cream came to be. The store was on Gratiot Avenue, south of Eight Mile Road, located between a Sears and a strip of specialty shops that housed only one restaurant. Better yet, there wasn't a Dairy Queen or Tastee-Freez in sight. Honest John's would be the only ice cream parlor for four miles either way in that stretch. The place was going to be a gold mine.

A huge neon sign, one that looked as if it would last forever, was mounted on top of the white brick building: HONEST JOHN'S ICE CREAM in blue and red letters on a rectangular white field. A blinking ice cream cone broke the horizontal plane of the sign. The interior of the block letters was lined with blue neon, and to Richie it was as beautiful as anything he'd ever seen. Riding there with his father, seeing the sign lit up, he felt a small sense of pride overcome his whole person, as if he alone were responsible for the success of some celebrity's newfound fame. Lou looked up at the sign through the top edge of the windshield, and his lips managed a faint grin.

"Oh man ... can we come back to see it when it's really dark, at nighttime, Dad?"

"I'll be a son of a ... looks pretty nice. Respectable even." Lou felt his son's eyes. He turned and there he was, smiling at him. He quickly looked away. "Yeah, we'll see. We'll bring your mom and your brother and sisters, maybe. We'll see."

He parked the car at the curb down the street from the store.

The place was as clean as an operating room—all white linoleum and smelling of Pine-Sol. There was a long chrome counter with red and silver padded chrome stools mounted to the floor. Chrome napkin holders were arranged on the counter. Sparkling chrome edges and surfaces entranced Richie as he took it all in. The room felt cooler than the air outside. The storefront glass was crystal clear, revealing the cold fall day as if there were no glass at all. Highboy tables with stools filled the open space. The order board on the wall even had an official-looking logo on it. Someone had drawn a caricature of John, with a disproportionately large head stuck on a tough little body, dishing out ice cream. The cartoon-John held the scooper like a gun and a white comic balloon shouted, "The best ice cream in all Detroit, *honest!*"

The drawing didn't look at all like him, but it made you laugh.

Before they had a chance to go looking for John, there stood the real article, looking out of place in grey slacks and a black silk shirt amongst the canvas of red, white, and chrome. But his eyes twinkled the familiar, smiley way, and his thick arms stretched out proud and wide, waiting for his favorite little cousin.

"There's my boy—Richie, who am I?"

"Jeezus," Lou groused.

"You're Honest John," Richie said.

"Yes I am. It's official now isn't it?" John said, clapping his hands together and going after Richie's hair. "Set 'em up Turk. *Turk!* You guys like Rocky Road?"

"When did you become such an ice cream expert, Johnny?" Lou asked.

"Everyone loves ice cream, Louie. Turk, *come on,*" John called out.

He turned his back to them and motioned behind. Lou looked and saw no one there. Then from behind a wall emerged Turk, the single worker in the place. He wore a white apron and took his position standing behind the ice cream counter. The wiry man's eyes shifted at the sight of Richie's father. As if from thin air, Turk produced two waffle cones stacked high with ice cream. He presented them to the father and son. Lou locked eyes with Turk as he took the cones.

"Well? What do you boys think?" John asked.

Richie attacked his cone and was nearly halfway through it before his dad had even made a dent in his. Lou kept looking at Turk, the ice cream losing its firmness, eyeing him as if trying to decide what it was about the man that seemed familiar. Turk looked down and smoothed his oily dark hair, before wiping his hands on his apron.

"John, I gotta piss, OK?" Turk stated, more than asked. "Need a piss break—"

"Hey, *mamaluke!* The *kid*," John said, tilting his head in Richie's direction.

"Sorry. So, can I go?"

"Yeah, make water," John shrugged. They watched Turk disappear into the back.

Lou placed a hand on Richie's shoulder and walked him to the large window facing the street. They sat down, looking out at Gratiot Avenue. The sidewalks bordered a sea of endless traffic. Hippies walked by, stopping to hug one another, giving the peace sign. Some were spinning around in circles, arms outstretched, looking skyward or making faces at one another. Richie wondered what could make people that happy. One of them stopped and looked in the window at Richie and his father. A kid with ratted-out red hair wearing a tie-dyed shirt with the message, FAR OUT in balloon letters, stumbled around aimlessly. He pulled his dirty yellow corduroy jacket closed and stuck out his tongue at Lou before flashing peace signs at Richie. He pressed the Vs his fingers formed against the window. Richie studied the red fingertips on the glass, forming halos of condensation around each tip.

"Peacenik," Lou said. Richie made a peace sign back at the redhead.

"Is that like a peacock?" Richie asked, looking at the spaced-out kid on the other side of the window.

"Not really. Hey, Johnny, keep an eye on Richie—"

Before Lou could get rid of the kid, John was in front of the store. They could see him yelling at the kid, and Richie watched the hippie put his hands up. The kid shot John the peace sign, too, but John lunged at the kid, moving faster than Richie thought possible.

"Richie, turn your head," Lou said, trying to cover his son's face.

But he watched John throw a slap to the back of the guy's head and the hippie fell headlong to the sidewalk. Richie felt sweat form on his neck. His Uncle John was screaming something, then he kicked the kid in the butt. The scrawny youth skidded to his feet, by now having realized a peace sign wasn't going to work with this angry, stocky man. He ran away down the sidewalk. The door chimed as John walked back in.

"That went well," Lou said to John.

"Hophead. Between the hippies and the eggplant, I gotta keep an eye out," he said, smoothing out his shirt. He saw the look on Richie's face, and the eyes went crinkly again. "Hey—do I got *something* to show you!" He glanced over at Lou. As his smile returned, Richie watched the smile fade from his father's face. There was a little Rocky Road smudged in the edges of his father's enormous, black mustache. He looked at his son, then stared at John.

"What's that, Johnny?" Lou asked, wiping his mustache clean.

"It's downstairs." He snapped his fingers. "Richie, you come, too."

Whatever it was John had down there, Richie was now dying to see it. John put his hand around Richie's neck. "When we come back up, I'll have Turk get you a triple cone of Superman. It's the best darn Superman in the whole city. Not even Sanders or Twin Pines can top it."

He was strutting. Lou stood between his son and John. His posture went straight.

"What are you gonna show us, Johnny? Tell me first," Lou asked, his voice suddenly devoid of friendliness.

"Quit your worrying, Louie. Jesus, just come on. Ain't gonna bite you."

Johnny led the two behind the counter. Richie looked at the frosty tubs of ice cream, steaming in their cardboard cylinders. He had never been behind the counter of any store, let alone an ice cream parlor. The thick, textural richness of the ice cream and the different colors swirled in his mind, and he wished he could sample every one.

Turk was on the phone near the back wall, whispering the names of football teams. He looked back, shifting about and rubbing his jaw. He smiled at Richie as the three walked toward the counter, but Lou got him to stop his smiling with one well-placed glare. Turk's face went bloodless, and he turned his back, putting the receiver closer to his mouth.

They walked past a tall woman in fishnet stockings who was talking on another phone while filing her red fingernails. Lou gave her a sideways glance. The woman had high, bright-red hair, green eyes with too much green eye shadow, and rouged-up orange cheeks. Her chest was excessively large for her small frame. She winked at Lou, who smiled politely then punched John hard in the arm. He mock-grimaced.

"What? She's just a friend, Louie boy … a really, *really* good friend."

"Why do you have two phones in this place, Johnny?" Lou asked.

"So I can always be reached. You know, for the union stewards and stuff—

forget about all that," John said. Lou took a look back at the redhead one more time and muttered, *"Minchia."*

They came to a locked steel door at the very back of the store. John smiled devilishly at them as he went through the two deadbolts that secured it. Lou looked around nervously, as if he were expecting someone to jump out of a corner and shout *"Boo!"* A cord ran through two eyelets screwed into the wall. John yanked it, and a single light bulb hanging from the ceiling lit up. Richie couldn't see the bottom of the stairs from where they stood.

John whistled an old Italian tune as the three walked down the creaky, wooden steps. The place smelled like damp earth and rotting mushrooms. The light from the dim, swinging bulb cast an amber blush to the dead air in front of them. When the three got to the bottom of the stairs, John flicked on another light. It took a second for their eyes to adjust. Then Richie noticed a glare coming from the corner. The cavernous basement was empty and black with the exception of four red and yellow cans of gasoline stacked next to whatever was causing the glare.

"Is that what I think it is?" Lou asked John. "Is it?"

"Stradivarius. Supposed to be anyway. Who gives a shit, still nice, huh?"

John blushed when he said it. He winked at Richie and pantomimed playing a violin. It was a funny thing to see and Richie cracked up, but Lou wasn't laughing.

"Jesus, Johnny. You *show* me this … don't show me this."

"What? I'm just holding it for a guy. Five hundo just for holding it."

"What's in there?" Richie asked, crossing the distance.

His father stood still, looking at the glass case. His hand reached out but Richie was already gone, standing in front of it. John left Lou's side and stood next to Richie. Protected inside was an antiquated violin seated on a bed of crushed, burgundy velvet. The glass was so clean, Richie felt he could reach through it and touch the wet finish of the instrument's spruce and maple body, even pluck the strings if he liked. He had never seen a violin in real life before; nobody in his neighborhood could afford one.

Lou walked over to Richie and placed his hand on his son's shoulder. Richie looked up and saw a look in his father's eyes he'd seen only twice. It was anger, and when it came his dad's face became flushed and his chest puffed and his arms flexed. His eyes turned into squid ink and his thick eyebrows became one, transforming his face into a caricature of its handsomeness. Lou turned and faced John with great deliberation. John looked both ways, walking backward like a trapped rat seeking an escape route where none existed.

"Don't you ever do this again. In front of my *son?*" He lowered his voice but put a finger onto John's sternum. "Are you *fucking* crazy? What the hell is wrong with you?"

John's face turned flat. "Louie, c'mon … the kid—"

"*God dammit John!* Can't ever be happy with what you have, can you?" Lou's voice rose back up, and his large chest looked as if it might disengage from his frame. Richie couldn't understand the rage his father was displaying. It seemed like another person had jumped inside his dad's body and took over the controls.

"I'm only holding it. It's five, Louie. *Five hundo,*" John said, the cheerfulness in his voice a distant memory. Now he sounded like someone pleading to a judge to spare his life. Lou just shook his head and waved his hand at him.

"And don't *Louie* me! You hear? Don't you ever think you can Louie *me!*"

His eyes stayed on John as he addressed his son. "C'mon. We're going home—right now, Richie. Say goodbye."

Richie walked over to John.

"Thanks for the ice cream."

John looked down at the frightened young boy. His eyes tried to crinkle, but it wasn't there.

"See you, Richie. I'll get you that Superman next time. Next time, OK?"

"Sure."

"Good luck with the ice cream parlor … *Honest* John," Lou said.

He took Richie by the hand and led him up the stairs. Above them, the light bulb swayed in lazy circles, and their shadows moved against the wall as though they had lives of their own. Richie looked over his shoulder as they ascended. His nose hurt as he tried to stop the tears from coming. John was standing there at the bottom of the stairs as if he'd been punched in the gut. Then the sight of him disappeared and Richie managed a small wave, but he couldn't see if it was returned.

The drive home was quiet enough that Richie felt the need to cough once to test the air. His father's eyes seemed as though they'd lost their ability to blink. Richie didn't want to look at him. *Maybe I've done something to make him angry*, he thought. He looked out at the grey fall day, and the huge elm trees created black abstract images against the whitish sky. Richie saw black people of all ages teeming in small groups—most were laughing, some dancing with transistor radios to their ears—shuffling past storefronts on the crowded sidewalks. There were a few white people, but those who walked amongst the blacks gave a wide berth, often treading on the grass median to avoid them.

Most of the black people wore high Afros and brightly colored shirts and pants; plaid coats and high velvet hats—clothes that Richie never saw at his school or on anyone in his neighborhood. The clothes were cool looking to him, but seemed almost like costumes. Some older black couples walked the sidewalks holding each other close, while others pushed strollers as they window-shopped. The older ones seemed different than the younger people around them; quieter and slower moving.

Lou's '60 black Bonneville cruised south, slowly along Gratiot Avenue, and a couple of the people walking looked at the car. Richie watched the sign above Honest John's grow smaller and smaller as they drove away from it. They came to a stoplight and he stared out the window at a young black kid. The boy was about his age, maybe a year younger. His red nylon coat had a tear in the sleeve, and his mouthful of white teeth seemed fake against his dark skin. The boy playfully pointed an imaginary gun at Richie and held it on him. Their eyes met. And then the boy laughed and pretended to shoot him with a raised thumb and outstretched index finger. Richie smiled nervously and shrunk back into his seat, dropping his head below the window frame until all he could see was the top of the boy's hair.

They were less than three miles from their modest home on Seven Mile Road—a sturdy brick duplex—but this neighborhood they drove through looked entirely different, as if it had been airlifted from a war-torn country and dropped there. The houses had an unkempt look and the lawns were weedy, pockmarked with patches of dirt showing through. Windows were broken and some cars sat on the street without tires, their tie-rods grotesquely twisted, while a few others rested on cinder blocks.

"Look at all of them. Gratiot Avenue. Can't stop 'em I guess," Lou said in the manner of talking to himself. He looked sideways at Richie and grumbled something unclear. Richie took a peek at his father's face. His dad turned on the radio. "Build Me Up Buttercup" was on, and Lou tuned it in better. Richie loved the song and let the melody form in his head. He closed his eyes a second and remembered the smell of the basement in the ice cream parlor and the way the richly colored body of the violin looked like a figure eight. The image of Turk's nervous face and the redhead in the net stockings and how her body was shaped like the fiddle and the smile his dad wore and the shame on Honest John's face, all of it merged together until he blinked his eyes open to see the grey sky again. He started quietly singing the song, testing his father's mood.

"Why do you build me up? Buttercup baby, just to let me down … "

Richie swayed in his seat a bit. The humor usually present in his dad's face—the quality that made men want to be around him and women so attracted to him—was replaced with a somber aura that was trying hard to put down stakes.

"*God dammit,*" he whispered.

He shook his head with a tight-lipped grin and just a little of the warmth returned, worming its way back into his dark expression. He started singing along with Richie,

"Build me up, Buttercup don't break my heart … "

Richie relaxed, feeling that whatever had made his dad angry regarding the fiddle was gone now and probably wasn't his fault after all. Lou pulled Richie over close to him and hugged him tight. He held him like that the rest of the way home and while it confused Richie, he loved the medicinal smell of his father's cologne and the security of his embrace.

Honest John's Ice Cream was indeed a gold mine. John made money hand over fist, even in the fall and winter months, which seemed illogical to everyone. Whoever heard of an ice cream store selling big in the winter? It would've been great to see how the place did when the city got really hot in July and August. John never got to find out. The place burned down in mid-May of 1969, the cause given as a mysterious electrical fire, a mere six months after that opening weekend. When Ada told Lou the bad news, his one-word reply mystified Richie.

"Shocking," Lou said.

John took the insurance money from the fire and opened a barbecue joint a mile south from the burnt ice cream parlor. Honest John's Barbecue Emporium turned into a healthy, profitable business after only six months of operation. Richie and his dad went to the grand opening, accompanied this time by his mother. On the car ride there, Ada checked her makeup in the rearview mirror.

"I hope he has better luck with this one. Shame about that fire," Ada said.

Lou glanced over at her. Richie watched the exchange from the backseat.

"Oh, will you stop. It was an accident. The wiring was bad," Ada said. In the encroaching silence, she turned to Lou. "Well *what,* then?" she demanded.

"Hey, I didn't say anything over here," Lou replied.

Red, white, and green balloons floated in the lobby, which was crammed with many men in hats and leather jackets. Most saw Lou and turned to head back by the bar—a couple even nodded to the group and hastily ducked out of the restaurant. Lou put his hand on Richie's shoulder, and suddenly the smell of damp earth and mushrooms came into his head.

The memory vanished, replaced by a smoky smell of hickory and rich sauces. Dago music came out from the speakers as they approached the coat check. The red carpeting offset the black iron tables and red vinyl padded chairs throughout the restaurant. People filled their plates with ribs, chicken, and potatoes in the adjoining dining room. John greeted Richie with a huge grin and those twinkling eyes. His belly was bigger now and he had grown a bushy mustache, which didn't suit the boyishness of his face. A different pretty girl stood near him, a blonde this time but with just as much makeup as the redhead. She was hanging on John's arm, and Richie could see a black line where her boobs came together, and he wondered what happened to the fiddle. Ada looked at Lou, her face flushed. As Lou shrugged at his wife in a "What-are-you-looking-at-me-for?" look, John nonchalantly pulled himself from the blonde and came over. The woman put a hand on her hip and fixed a look at him. When John didn't come back, she flipped her hair and went to the bar. Ada turned to her cousin and stared at him.

"She's just a friend, Ada," John explained.

"Johnny." Ada shook her head and left with two of Richie's aunts to the restroom. John's spine went slack until Richie appeared in front of him. Upon seeing his little cousin he straightened up, looking like a cripple cured by a tel-evangelist.

"Richie, my boy! Hey—fellas ... listen up," he motioned to the loose group of men. They put their drinks down, stilled their cigars and cigarettes and looked his way. Lou crossed his arms and studied the carpeting. The chatter quieted down.

 John turned back to Richie.

"Richie, would I ever lie to you?"

That beautiful violin flashed in Richie's head, and he felt a wave of nausea.

"No."

"And why not?"

"Because. You're Honest John," Richie said plaintively.

John looked down at him. A collective groan and errant laughs rained down from the group behind him.

"Yes ... yes I am."

Some of the shine left John's smile as he looked across the room at Lou. He met John's gaze and shook his head with a wry smile. John stuck his hands up in mock arrest, but there was no playful gesture in return from Lou. John let his hands drop, nodding. He smiled at Richie and started to say something. Instead, he made his way to the bar, where all the men in hats and leather jackets greeted him. Richie watched the magic come back to John's face as he slapped the backs of the men. He looked at Richie and raised his glass.

"To my nephew, Ricardo: May you live a hundred years. *Cin-cin. Alla salute!*"

The men clinked glasses and said their *salutes*, but Richie turned away from it, led by his father's guiding hand to the waiting chafing dishes of ribs and potatoes.

It was after 10 p.m. when they drove home. Richie put his fingers to his nose and smelled barbecue sauce. He licked his fingers and tasted the sweet, hot flavor. He let out a big yawn and his lids felt heavy.

"I thought the food was tasty," he heard his mother say. "The ribs especially."

Richie watched her profile in the dark, a navy blue silhouette staring at his father. The streetlights lit everything in the car with a turquoise flare.

"Yeah. Pretty good. Lots of characters in the joint, huh?" Lou said.

Richie watched the back of his father's head. His mother face still aimed at Lou.

"A friend, he called her," Ada said.

Lou *tsked* the air, and she shook her head. "Oh, Richie—I have something for you. From your uncle," Ada continued.

Richie rubbed his eyes and pushed himself into the space between the headrests of the bench seat. His mother handed him something.

"What is it?" Richie asked, taking the eight-by-ten envelope from her.

"Here, put a little light on the subject," Lou said, and clicked on the dome light.

Richie unwrapped the red string and opened the flap. Lou glanced in the rearview mirror and locked eyes with his son.

"What is it, Rich?" He saw the boy's eyes widen.

"Cool! He got it, Dad! He got it just like he said he would."

Richie held the glossy color photo in the air between his parents. On the field of Tiger Stadium stood Tiger legend Norm Cash—a bat yoked across his broad shoulders—the navy, Olde English D regal and crest-like on his crisp, white uniform.

"*Maddon'*, let me see that ..." Lou said.

He plucked it from Richie's small hand, and with one eye on the road, examined the photo. The handwriting looked shaky, hastily written and the word "Norm" was practically unidentifiable.

"Richie—"

"What's it say?" Ada asked.

Lou stared at the photo. Glancing at the rearview mirror, he could see the joy on his son's face.

"Go on. Read it to us," Lou said, handing it back to him.

The boy swallowed. "*Hi Richie. Any friend of Honest John's is a friend of mine. Best wishes, Norm Cash,*" Richie's voice rang out in the quiet in the car. "*See* Dad? I told you he'd get it." He felt dizzy, examining the smiling face of his baseball hero. Lou clicked off the dome and Richie watched the photo go dark.

"Yeah, you were right. You gave Johnny one heckuva nickname," Lou said.

Richie's eyes adjusted to the dark. He squinted at the signature and grazed his fingers across it. It didn't even smear. It was permanent. He smiled at it all the way home.

The Wild

A guy just doesn't wake up one day and say, "From this day forward, I think I'll go by Carmine 'Sausages' Burmanzini," or "Know what? Instead of Ed, call me 'Eddie the Snake.'" Quite the contrary. The nicknames of street gods are coined by others, usually inspired by a physical attribute, the result of some notorious act or in many cases, both. These titles are earned, the men they belong to often knighted by a combination of street mythology and urban legend. Anthony Bernardo Marcazzi, a man from Detroit's East Side that others would seek out when a cold heart was required, was no different. Except he earned his moniker at a very young age.

Since kindergarten in 1948, Anthony Marcazzi's nickname had been Little Tony. Not because he was a junior to his father, but because of a diminutiveness bordering on dwarfism. He was fifteen inches long and weighed four pounds at birth, even though his mother had carried him to full term and gained sixty-eight pounds in the process. Some say the reason he was undersized as an adult was that like a lot of the Dagos back then, Little Tony didn't eat enough meat. His protein intake was minimal, consisting of a diet laden with starches; breads, pasta noodles. The meat he ate was limited to sausage and the occasional breaded veal.

It might've been he just got stuck with *the shorts*—that's what the Sicilians called it. If one of the New Dagos—the name the cops gave to the offspring of the immigrants—grew to be above five-nine, he was a giant. God forbid, if he had the misfortune of possessing lighter hair and somehow passed six feet, his mother's integrity might be questioned. So it was that a couple more generations of marrying non-Sicilians would need to occur before any adult man in those families ever passed seventy-two inches.

Little Tony wouldn't have to worry about either of those things. His black hair looked like bear fur and he'd never pass five foot one. Growing up to become a man of even close to average height just wasn't in the cards. And he knew it. Even as a seven-year-old he knew it. He was two heads smaller than the next shortest kid in his first grade class, a trend that didn't change until he dropped out of school. Whatever savagery lurked inside him wasn't suited for the classroom. Eighth grade was it for him. He claimed he dropped out so he could help his father, Big Tony Marcazzi, with his cement business, but no one believed him.

Big Tony wasn't really that big. Maybe five-six in street shoes, albeit powerful with squat muscles that were dense as stone. He only received *his* nickname after it became apparent his boy would always be smaller than him. Most of his business was new sidewalk work and driveways, as well as tearups of the same. The tough Michigan winters demanded hearty cement, and he was as good as any of the concrete guys around in knowing when to add sand and not overdo the water. Big Tony knew that if the mix was wrong, the first good frost would reveal stress cracks and heaves, mistakes in a word-of-mouth business he could ill afford.

Work picked up for Big Tony after he started paying a modest monthly stipend to the Pomanzano family. It had taken two cups of sugar in the gas tank of one of his trucks to finally get his attention. He didn't read English very well, so Father Spicuzzi, one of the priests in the neighborhood, had to interpret the first warnings he'd received—written in the wet cement of the sidewalks he'd laid. The words didn't scare him, but the sugar spoke a language he understood fluently. It cost him $350 to have the gas tank flushed and the engine fixed. The next time Pomanzano's muscle came around, Big Tony handed over an envelope without being asked.

The collector looked inside and smiled, telling him, *"D'ora innanzi, lei è sicuro il mio amico."* From now on, you are safe my friend.

And he didn't have to worry about those kind of men again, not for a long time. As a matter of fact, Marcazzi Construction got so much work after his first payment, Big Tony needed to hire two men just for mixing and rough troweling. He stayed involved in the physical labor, though. Big Tony enjoyed busting up and removing old cement. He also liked the horses and the numbers, so most of his profit found its way back to the Pomanzanos anyway. Big Tony tried to put enough aside for the kids and the groceries, but was often short for things like equipment, materials, and paying his help on time.

While his business was flourishing, Big Tony knew he needed to help his son get some direction. It was clear to him the kid was not cut out for school. He just didn't have it. He understood math well enough, but he couldn't commit to put in the study time for everything else. More disturbing, though, was the boy's temper! Whether it was a brewing Napoleonic complex, or just being born with a mean streak, Little Tony's anger issues actually scared his father. *What's the kid so mad about?* he often thought. *None of us are very tall.* Either way, Little Tony's temper had become the talk of the neighborhood, and he was only in eighth grade. Big Tony had to get him on track before he did something terrible again.

The first *something terrible* happened while he was a third grader at St. Juliana's.

And while it was just the *first* incident, it may as well have been all of them; every terrible thing he would do rolled into one great ball of ferocity. Yet neither Little Tony nor his father had any way of knowing just how dramatically fighting back would later impact their lives.

Like all the Catholic schools at the time, St. Juliana's required hymnal sessions every morning inside the church, located a block away from the elementary school. Father Barzini, who was also the musical director at the parish, would line the kids up in single file lines—one of girls, one of boys—to return to school. And because they lined up according to height, Little Tony always stood at the front of the line.

A week of mild temperatures that January had created sloppy conditions, as well as great packing snow. Father Barzini instructed the third graders to walk back to school on the clean sidewalks without breaking lines. More importantly, he implored them, in his broken English, "Boys, no throw the snowballs. Some-one a could get hurt."

In fact, the parish had sent out a memo to parents that because of a recent snowball-throwing incident—a girl had suffered a scratched cornea—a one-week suspension would result to any student caught doing so thereafter.

Little Tony hated winter for that very reason. Winter brought snow and snow brought snowballs, and he made a convenient target. On that particular day, lining up to walk back to school, Angelo Ciccarelli and Jacky Talerico spotted him—the perfect bull's-eye. Angelo decided to test his strong arm with a well-formed snowball. Being the two tallest boys in the class, they always occupied the very back of the row. Looking over the tops of other kids' heads, Angelo lined up the short boy's coarse hair.

Using Jacky as a shield, Angelo took a quiet step forward and rifled the white missile. The direct hit behind his ear caused Little Tony to fall headlong to the sidewalk. He suddenly had a burning headache before all went black. When he opened his eyes, he saw the sky above and everything else in a twinkling, green-blue negative. Though none of his classmates saw who threw it, they had a real good idea. None had enough courage to break line and help Little Tony get off the pavement.

Father Barzini's back was to the boys, so he had not seen anything, even though he stood just four kids ahead of Jacky and Angelo. He never even heard the snowball fly, so busy was he scolding Eva Paccini over the immodest length of her uniform skirt.

When Little Tony got up, he shook himself and glared to the back of the line. His vision was slow in returning, but it was still good enough to see Jacky and Angelo trying to keep their laughter in check, as if nothing had happened. Tony's face burned and flushed fire red. He walked over to the curb and scooped up snow, unconcerned with perfection. He dipped the hastily made spheres into the slush by the curb, the icy water numbing his stubby fingers. Then he passed his frightened classmates and made the long walk to the rear of the line to confront his giant tormentors.

After finally getting Eva to agree to have her mother, Loretta, the very sight of whom caused every male parish member and even some of the priests to foster impure thoughts, lower the hem of her plaid skirt, Father Barzini started leading the children back to school. So as the priest walked to the front of the lines on one side of the children, Little Tony trudged to the back on the other side, each shielded from the other by the double row of boys and girls.

The last thing Little Tony remembered hearing was Father Barzini calling out, *"Anthony Bernardo Marcazzi, where didda you go to young man?"*

With wet hair and red ears, Little Tony stood before the two culprits, both laughing at what they assumed was the puny kid's false bravado.

"Who threw it? Own up or you're both gonna pay."

His face was raw. His cheekbone was scraped from where it hit the cold cement, and a gash on his forehead touched the widow's peak of his thick, black hair. He offered them a look at the slushy iceballs to show he meant business. Jacky pushed his hand away and Angelo had simply heard enough. He went by the nickname "Mustache" for the dark upper lip he already sported as an eight-year-old.

"I threw it. So what, runt?" Angelo said.

Jacky Talerico stepped up. "You won't do anything, little shrimp. You're a shrimp."

The other kids in line watched, waiting for Little Tony to get his beating.

None of them dared look sideways at Angelo or Jacky. Especially Jacky. Irrespective of his size, they wanted no part of him because of his lineage.

Jacky Talerico was the namesake and favorite nephew—godson to boot—of one of the few truly "made" men in the neighborhood, Jack "Black Jack" Talerico. Even as third graders, kids *knew*. They'd seen the looks on their fathers' faces when the name Black Jack was spoken; it was usually accompanied by a quick sign of the cross.

Little Tony was treacherously close to breaking an unspoken law. Kids like Anthony Marcazzi needed to just take their ass kicking and get through another day. That was how it worked. Leo Barrasso knew. The slow, lazy-eyed boy who more than had once felt the sting of Angelo's and Jacky's comments and fists stared at Little Tony, urging him to turn around and walk back to the front of the line. Leo tried to reason with him.

"Don't. It's not worth it. *Believe me.*"

And maybe that's what set Little Tony off; a poor, kicked-around kid like Leo was trying to give *him* advice on backing down.

Little Tony never replied. Instead he lunged as if fired from a circus cannon with fists thrust forward. The ice balls found the faces of the boys and scraped their mugs with jagged surfaces. The two toughs had no choice but to put their hands to their noses and eyes, instinctively dropping to their knees.

That's when Little Tony pounced.

To a passing cop, the roles of bully and bullied would've appeared reversed, as the tiny boy attacked the two cowering, larger kids like a hyena delivering death bites to wounded lions.

He first applied a vicious kick to the ribs that made Angelo scream in agony. Angelo tried to cover up, but the smaller boy kicked through his hands, the years of living with his smallness infusing him with sudden, crazy courage.

Jacky Talerico wasn't spared either. By the time Father Barzini made his feeble attempt to put a bear hug on Little Tony, the nephew of Black Jack had already received two kicks to the face. A mailman dropped a stack of catalogs and ran across the street to help subdue Little Tony. For this good deed, the postal worker received a bite to the hand that broke the flesh. Jacky was left with a gash over his left eye that later scarred over, and as an adult, would be the only flaw to detract from his otherwise handsome face.

Father Barzini's recounting of the incident to Monsignor O'Grady, the principal of St. Juliana's, was that Little Tony Marcazzi—unprovoked as he recalled—had smashed two slush balls into the faces of Angelo and Jacky before assaulting them. The vicious attack was bad enough—the scrapes on the boys' faces would take weeks to fade. No, what was more disturbing to Father Barzini, what caused him to *beg* the Monsignor for an unprecedented two-week suspension, was the *joy* the lad seemed to take in administering the beatings—that and the wicked kick to the testicles the old priest had received.

Despite the protestations of the boy's father, Monsignor O'Grady had no choice but to suspend Little Tony for the full two weeks, if only to appease the Talerico family. The Talericos were vain people, and Jacky's father, Enrio, was incensed until his dying day that the little Marcazzi kid had marked his beautiful boy with that sagging crease over his left eye. Jacky, however, found it made him look tough and later wore it as a sort of colophon to announce his willingness to throw down with anyone, thus avoiding further risk to his remnant good looks.

As sometimes happens in bullying, the beleaguered, after emancipating themselves, become friendly with their former tormentors. As such, Little Tony never had any problems with Angelo, or even Jacky again—not directly anyway. Jacky later even came to his defense when a fist fight broke out during a basketball game against St. Juliana's rival, St. Jude Elementary.

By eighth grade, Little Tony, while not growing vertically, had matured and thickened up. He'd inherited his father's strong legs and upper body. And he was quick, too. On the basketball court, where it seemed lack of height would be a disadvantage, the boy turned it into an attribute. Now nearly fourteen, his speed and dexterity made him a formidable point guard during a short-lived hoops career. For a while, many thought he might be able to be a starter in high school. That prognostication ended after the brawl, when he punched St. Jude's star center, Don Manetti, in the jaw, knocking the lanky kid to the floor. Throughout the game, Little Tony had complained to the refs that Manetti had been elbowing St. Juliana's center all day with cheap shots in the paint.

Little Tony's battered teammate was none other than All-League center Jacky Talerico.

None of Little Tony's bravado impressed Jacky's uncle and godfather, who watched among the booing fans from the stands with his young son Paulie on his lap. It sickened Black Jack to see the little shit playing alongside his nephew, the very shrimp who years earlier had spoiled the boy's perfect face. His appetite for vengeance was whetted, however, seeing retribution about to be unleashed.

While Little Tony was being restrained by his coach, St. Jude's Manetti, having risen from the floor, circled to his side. Manetti planted his foot and was set to throw a right at the unsuspecting point guard's face, when Jacky Talerico ruined it for his godfather by stepping in front of the intended sucker punch. He jammed his palm into the kid's nose, putting Manetti down on the floor for good.

Black Jack shook his head, donned his lime green Borsalino, and led Paulie out of the gym.

Before it was cut short in the third quarter, Little Tony had one hell of a game going against St. Jude's, with five steals, fourteen points and ten assists. That seemed like a lifetime ago, the last time Little Tony felt even remotely like any kind of kid, now beginning to feel as if he were the husk of a young man wrapped around the possessed, trapped soul of an old warrior.

Dropping out of school after eighth grade, he found working for his father satisfying. He loved the physicality of the job, swinging the sledge and the hatchet to bust up concrete. He could trowel and finish as good as any of them, too, and was starting to develop a nose for the business. But what had made his father happiest was that his son had seemed to quell a little of that temper, harnessing it at least.

Little Tony enjoyed helping his dad, working in a man's world. And even though it was a bit of a schmuck job, he could still sell swag on the side. Big Tony had no idea his son had been pulling in thirty-five bucks a week selling stolen cigarettes to the old German who owned Fairway Drugstore in Grosse Pointe. He would turn sixteen soon and had been out of school nearly two years. The physical nature of the cement business had caused him to develop sizeable back and shoulder muscles on his stunted frame. His upper body was tightly packed, and his waist remained narrow, giving him a broad V shape atop tree-trunk thighs. He had transformed himself into something resembling a kind of handsome beast.

The day his life turned sideways, he was helping his father lay seven squares of sidewalk in front of Cantaro's Market. Big Tony had temporarily been without his two laborers because of an inability to pay them. He planned on bringing his men back when he got out from under the juice he owed resulting from a spate of unlucky long shots that failed to win, place, or show. The Cantaro job had to be done by the weekend if he was to still take the family to Bob-Lo Island—the floating amusement park located in the Detroit River. Little Tony always looked forward to the elephant cars and ringing the bell with one swing of a sledgehammer. He felt too old for the place, but when he tired of the island's conviviality, it presented a nice opportunity to scrap with the blacks and hone his pugilistic skills.

Big Tony was hammering out the last stubborn corner on a square of concrete, when the handle of the hatchet he was using broke in two. For years after, it would be debated; had the hickory on that hatchet lasted just four more swings, might Little Tony have taken over his father's cement business and lived a relatively normal life?

But the handle did break, and with it, any chance of life ever being normal again.

"*Lei lo slut sporco!* Anthony, go down Vesprini's and get poppy a new hatchet. Tell Pete put it on the books. I pay next week. Only if he ask, though, *capiece?*" Big Tony regarded the snapped hickory handle like he'd just found crab lice while standing at the urinal.

"*Minchia!* Brand-new *accetta … whore sporco grande!*"

Little Tony removed the kneepads he was wearing and stretched the hamstrings of his short legs. He laughed at hearing his father call the hatchet a filthy whore in Italian.

"OK, Pop. I'll be right back."

The young man practically skipped to the store, anxious for any reason to go to Vesprini's Hardware because Pete's daughter, Divina, would be working the register. Divina Vesprini was always nice to Tony, even in grade school when the other girls ignored him. She had large, doe eyes and a curvy figure better suited on a Playboy bunny. Her face was the prettiest he had ever seen, and her deep olive skin exuded an exotic quality he found exhilarating. Once, when he was twelve and she thirteen, he'd watched her at the outdoor pool at Heilmann Park. Her orange bikini was stark against her brown skin. He'd been watching her for a long time that summer. Divina had walked to the candy machines, and he followed. When he came upon her, she was adjusting her bathing suit top and he caught a flash of her breast, snow white against such bronze skin, as if her tan had been sprayed on. She had looked up and saw him there, staring. "See something you like, Little T?" she had asked, perfect white teeth smiling.

He stood there dumbly until finally muttering, "Sugar Babies," pointing into the vending machine. "I forgot my money on the pool deck. Bye Divina!" He covered his crotch and limped back to the pool, feeling warm and strange in ways he never imagined possible. He had been unable to shake the intoxicating vision of her. It was a hard fantasy to hold on to.

Little Tony rolled up the sleeves of his white T-shirt, accentuating his tanned, rock-hard biceps. He dropped and did twenty quick push-ups, making the veins in his arms as big as earthworms. He worked some spit into his hands and smoothed out his hair, dropping a curl off his forehead. He paused to look in the storefront windows of the shops he used to pass on his walk to St. Juliana's. Mrs. Camatarro smiled at him from behind the counter of her deli. She was missing two bottom teeth, and had errant, wispy black hairs growing from her chin, giving her a simian look. She had always been sweet to him though, so he overlooked her homeliness. Back in his grade school days, she would slip him a few slices of hot *capocolla* and fresh bread for his walk home from school, telling him it would make him grow tall one day. He clicked his teeth as he walked by and recalled the flavor of bursting peppercorn seeds in his mouth.

He continued on past Alinosi's Pastry Shoppe, stopping for a moment to look at the tin Vernor's Ginger Ale sign mounted next to the entrance. As a fourth grader, he used to jump and try to touch the top of it, but it had been consistently out of his reach. Finally in sixth grade, he had grazed the top of the smiling, red-headed gnome with his fingers. He had liked standing under the sign while he ate his rolled-up *capocolla,* watching the pretty schoolgirls. And sometimes, if the sun was just right, Little Tony could look at his own shadow and it seemed to rise up, well past the top of the sign, high above the little gnome's grinning face.

Clouds were overhead, and the absence of his shadow made his memory fade and return to thoughts of Divina Vesprini's chest. She had developed earlier than most of the girls in her class and was the type who loved the attention it brought. Little Tony's mother called her kind *troppo facile* (too easy), but he didn't believe it, nor did he care. Looking across the street, he saw the yellow arrow outlined in red that pointed below: VESPRINI'S PRO SPORTS & HARDWARE. He stood before the entrance, checked his hair in the window once more then walked inside.

Divina leaned against the counter and popped her gum, wearing a vacant look. Her eyes lifted and she smiled as Little Tony strutted in.

"Wow, look who's here. Long time no see, Little Tony! Gonna take your father's nickname away with all those muscles. Where you been hiding, T?" Divina asked.

"Here, there, you know. How's school?" His chest puffed up reflexively as he stood in front of her. His eyes wandered to the top of her blouse and fixed on the deep crack her cleavage created. She saw where his glance was directed but did nothing to shrink from it, even leaning forward to further expose herself. Then her eyes shifted, causing Little Tony to turn his head.

Black Jack Talerico emerged from the aisle holding two hockey sticks in his huge hands. His young son Paulie walked at his side. Paulie was a big kid for his age. At ten years old, he wasn't a whole lot shorter than Little Tony. Black Jack wore his signature green Borsalino. His wise guy peers had told him for years how stupid he looked in it, the lime green color suited more for one of the "Micks from the Grosse Pointes," but Jack didn't care what they thought. He knew he was one good-looking bastard, handsome enough to pull off any accoutrement in his wardrobe, so he obstinately continued wearing the ugly hat at all times. He liked the way it looked against his hair, hair so black it shone blue when the light hit it just right. Black Jack straightened as he took in the sight of the coiled, short cement worker.

Little Tony looked briefly at Black Jack and nodded hello. He felt a metallic taste in his mouth, and a cold sweat formed on the back of his neck. It left him quickly though, and he decided out of respect it would be wise to greet him more appropriately.

"Hello, Mr. Talerico ... " Black Jack raised his chin in response. Little Tony turned his attention to Black Jack's son. "Hey, Paulie. Still playing ball?"

"Tony!" Paulie shouted. He ran up and hugged Little Tony's chest.

"Had twelve points against Queen of Heaven last week," Black Jack said.

Rustling the kid's hair, Little Tony was surprised at the odd smirk Black Jack wore. He tried to ignore it, but it made him hesitant to want to shake his hand at all. Instead, he patted Paulie's back and nodded goodbye. Walking toward the tool aisle, he fought back a peculiar pain in his head that hadn't been present in years, knowing it was best that he just buy the hatchet and return to Cantaro's so he and his pop could finish the sidewalk.

"See ya'—" Paulie called out. "I made all four of my throws, Tony."

The kid's voice made him stop.

Little Tony had helped Paulie with his free throw mechanics during his brief stint one year earlier as an assistant coach for the boy's Catholic Youth Organization team until he got banned from the league (he choked a ref over a missed charging foul, an offense he felt cost his team of nine-year-olds the game). He hadn't seen Paulie since being disbarred.

"That's great, Paulie. Way to go. You're really getting tall," Little Tony said, wishing he hadn't spoken. He walked away from them, and was nearly around the corner when Black Jack abruptly spoke up.

"Yeah, *Little* Tony. *He* is getting tall."

Little Tony slowed his pace and looked over his shoulder. Black Jack tipped his green hat and smirked at him. His voice amplified, "Be taller than you pretty soon ... " Then softly, " ... little shrimp. He's a shrimp, Paulie."

Black Jack grinned, nudging his son. Paulie didn't laugh at all, more confused than anything. Black Jack raised his hands to Divina, waiting for her to revel in the joke, too. She managed a weak smile and the slightest *tsk*. She kept her eyes cast down on the register.

But Little Tony saw her *smile,* and in his mind it equaled a laugh *at him.* It was the only spark he needed for his temper to glow white-hot.

He turned the corner, stopping to catch his breath. Little Tony found himself in front of the hammers and for a moment forgot why he was in the store. Everything seemed to float off the shelves, and his legs wobbled. Seeing the wood mauls jogged his memory, and he was aware of the nearby axes and handsaws. He spotted a hatchet—the last one—and swiftly removed it from the metal rack. Lifting it, he saw a tag that read, AMES, INC—RESTOCK #128. He felt the hatchet's weight with both hands. Walking around the corner Divina waved to him, but seeing Black Jack's green hat through the front window as the man walked outside, he ignored Divina's wave and looked down at the edge of the hatchet. He rubbed a thumb against its flat blade. A dull pain in the back of his head began to pulse, but he kept it at bay.

The sound of metal being sharpened pulled at him. He made his way through the sporting goods aisle. His fingers traced over hardball and softball bats,

Rawlings gloves and hockey equipment, too. He felt a pang of regret seeing two basketballs. A thin coating of dust covered them, and he dragged his finger through it as he passed, exposing orange trails in the pebbled surface.

At the counter where the keys were cut and skates sharpened, a grinding wheel whirred and he found Pete Vesprini hunched over it, working the chrome blades on a pair of black leather hockey skates. On the corner of the counter stood two red, circular racks holding key blanks of every kind. Little Tony ran his hand through them, creating a wind chime effect.

The grey stone wheel threw tiny orange sparks from the dull skate blades as Pete expertly sharpened them, angling the long blades this way and that. Little Tony looked at the amber sparks, mesmerized at how collectively they formed a cloud of bright energy, and he got lost in their brightness. Pete looked up, feeling the boy's presence.

"Well hello Tony … Little Tony? *Minchia*, the muscles on you! What's with the hatchet?" Pete finally waved a hand in the space between them. "Yoo-hoo? Tony!"

"Oh—hey, Mr. Vesprini," Little Tony reddened. "Pop's putting in seven squares at Cantaro's, and the handle broke on his. This one's kinda blunt. You mind?"

He handed the hatchet to Pete. Pete rubbed his calloused thumb on its edge and looked at him. He put the hockey skates aside. "You're right. But it's for the cement. Really don't need it to be sharp."

"Well, I know. Can you do it anyway?"

Pete looked curiously at him. "Sure. Sure Little Tony, I'll put a little edge on it for you. Tell your pop to bring the other one back. I'll see we credit his account once Ames makes good to me. They're real fair about that kinda thing. Besides, your pop can use the money, right?" Pete added with a smile.

Little Tony stared at the hatchet blade, enthralled by it.

"OK. I'll sharpen it right quick," Pete said.

Pete started the wheel spinning again. He turned the hatchet blade against it.

"Thanks," Little Tony said. "That's the last one you got. Just so you know." He watched the dull blade shine as the point of a million sparks jumped from its edge, seemingly reaching out for him to join them. He shook himself and looked away.

"Lucky you, got the last one. I'll tell my brother to restock. Thanks for letting me know."

Little Tony looked at the large skates Pete had set aside. His own feet, even in muddy work boots, looked as though they belonged to a ventriloquist's dummy.

"Whose skates?" Little Tony asked, already knowing the answer.

Pete turned the wheel off and tested the blade of the hatchet again with his thumb. He nodded in satisfaction and handed it back to Tony.

"Sharp as a pimp's suit now. You say something? This hearing aid's going to shit." Pete strained an ear at him as the wheel wound to a slow drone. Little Tony looked at the hatchet blade. Light glinted off the new edge. He peeled off a razor-thin metal shaving and could smell the burning steel. The blade was hot to the touch.

"The skates … pretty nice ones. They're CCMs, right?" Little Tony asked.

"Oh, the skates. Black Jack just bought 'em for his kid. Don't know what he's feeding that one. See the size of his hands? Like a big puppy! He'll be a six-footer I bet." And then it was as though Pete realized to whom he was speaking, and his expression changed. It was compassion, the last thing Little Tony wanted. "Tell your pop I said hello and not to be a stranger, OK? He's always welcome here."

Pete picked up Paulie Talerico's size 9 skates and turned the grinding wheel on. The sound hurt Little Tony's ears. Pete went to work on the blades. Little Tony tried not to look back, but he couldn't help it, fixating on the size of the skates throwing a tail of sparks.

Divina Vesprini finished ringing up Old Lady Kalaschefski, a ninety-one-year-old, mean-as-a-snake Polish widow who stubbornly refused to go to a nursing home like her daughters wanted her to. Little Tony waited in line behind her.

"Have a nice day, Mrs. Kalaschefski."

The old woman grumbled as Divina unsuccessfully tried to hand her a receipt for a bag of thistle. Little Tony put the newly sharpened hatchet on the counter. Divina startled at the sound, then turned to him and smiled mischievously, watching the old woman leave. She directed a heavy-lidded stare at him, her large eyes clear and beguiling.

"Ol' bitch will live to be a hundred and fifty. So how's doin' T? Ain't seen you at the basketball games in so long." The words came out as a moan from her full mouth.

"Been busy. Laying concrete with my pop." He looked at her. "Need to get this back." He heard a sudden coldness in his voice that even he didn't recognize. Now that it was there, he welcomed it from whatever hollow place it had been hibernating in.

"You're getting really *big* muscles T." He shrugged off the compliment. "Do you want to pay for this now?" He saw how she looked at his biceps, and when he twitched one, she flinched.

"My pop said to put it on the books," he replied. "He'll get it next week."

She looked away and opened a ledger next to the cash register. She noted the item with a red pen and frowned. "Getting a bit high, T. Uncle Reno gets funny if the bill's above two hundred. Just tell your pop, OK? Business will pick back up. Just mention it to him, OK?" she asked, lowering her voice.

"It's not that." He lifted the hatchet off the counter. "We got lots of work. He'll pay. And your father said there's probably going to be a credit anyway because the other one broke, so—"

"Oh, right—I didn't mean anything, T—"

"Pop will pay it off after Cantaro's is finished. So tell your uncle that."

"No, it's fine, T. I was just saying ... "

There was a pressure in talking to her that he felt wounded by, like he had been trapped in a snare, chased into it by an inexplicable hatred. He stared at her, refusing to look anywhere now but directly into her eyes. She even leaned forward, to let her blouse open up more, but he wouldn't take the bait. He stared and her eyes were circles. He resisted her cleavage until he was past the brown irises and into the black pupils, and he swore he would keep focusing there to avoid giving her any kind of satisfaction ever again.

She suddenly lifted her head upward, as if she'd just spotted a bat on the ceiling.

"Hey T, I'll be up at Assumption Grotto for the teen dance on Saturday. You should try to go if you can, you know—if you can make it. I'll save you a dance. A nice, *slow one.*"

She dropped her head and some hair cascaded across her forehead. She brushed it away from her eyes and stared straight at him, moving closer.

"Just don't squeeze me too hard with those big muscles, OK?"

But his expression remained unchanged—still flat and cold. In his peripheral vision, he noticed her fingers playing with the button of her blouse. An image of white breasts and brown aureoles against severely tanned skin came and went from his mind. He fought throbbing hormones and a tingling in his groin, staving her off with added coldness.

"I don't really dance," he said, holding the hatchet like a tomahawk and walking away.

Her mouth was still open as he left the sanctuary of the store, the pitch of Paulie's dull skate blades growing razor sharp fading as the door closed behind him.

Years later, he would drift back, wishing he would have stayed and talked to her longer. Perhaps telling her he'd love to meet her at that dance. His mind had wandered as he walked away, imagining what the contact of her olive skin, the heat of her breath, and the brush of her lips on his would be like. How it felt to be desired. Maybe even confess to her the onset warmth of excitement that pulsed through him when she had commented on his physique, how it all had caused his mind to foolishly project the vision of them enjoying a visit to a tropical climate.

Maybe if she hadn't smiled at the joke Black Jack made at his expense. Maybe if there had been just a little bit of something akin to sticking up for him. Maybe then he wouldn't have been transformed into this pulsating fissure of rage.

But none of those maybes had happened.

While he had been inside the hardware store, God chased the clouds away—the blue in the sky seeming hyper-real—so that now he walked into a new, blinding wave of sunlight with a desultory gait. He practically forgot the hatchet that he was gripping without effort, and at the same time, gripping so tightly that his knuckles went white.

The wind blew healthy gusts, and his eyes watched tiny dust devils pick up pieces of litter and carry them off. The sudden change in lighting bothered him, causing a headache and a momentary vision of things seen in a bright green-blue negative. The sun was so blinding he had to shield his eyes just to see at all. As he made his way back to Cantaro's, he crossed the street, passing The Fantasy Lounge bowling alley, remembering the time he'd rolled a 240 game.

The four-block walk back to his waiting father would take only a few minutes, so he decided to slow his pace and try to cool off before his dad saw him this way. He found himself again in front of the window of Alinosi's. Through the clean glass he watched a baker throwing pizza dough high into the air. The baker nodded to him as the spinning dough whirred above his head in a lazy, misshapen figure eight. Little Tony saw a reflection in the window that looked familiar—a spot of lime green—flashing behind him across the street. It gave him a foreboding churn in his gut, as if this was all leading up to something over which he had no control—and yet all the control in the world.

A voice shouted, but in the wind, it traveled to him like a demon's song. "Little Toneee … look at you over there. Look like a little boy staring in a candy store. My Paulie's bigger than you. Little shrimp … "

There was Black Jack Talerico, standing at a bus stop with his stupid green Borsalino set at its jaunty, stupid angle, his freakishly tall son Paulie at his side. He was still carrying the two hockey sticks. Little Tony tried to keep his mouth shut. He knew his father needed the hatchet. He walked briskly down the street, acknowledging neither Black Jack nor his taunts.

"Yeah, run little boy. Whatsa matter, your ears short, too, *Little Tony?* Didn't you hear me?" This time the voice was stronger and more challenging.

So this time Little Tony stopped.

He turned and looked across the span of asphalt, some twenty-five yards away at the sight of Black Jack holding little Paulie's hand.

"I heard you, Mr. Talerico. That's not very nice is it, 'specially in front of Paulie?" Tony shouted.

A police car drove past. It slowed down and the cops looked at Black Jack. He gave them a subtle nod. They waved and continued on. Black Jack chuckled and adjusted his Borsalino. He rested the hockey sticks against the brick wall behind him and took out his wallet. He removed a ten-dollar bill.

He waved the bill around in his big hand.

"Here's a sawbuck *Little* Tony. It's all yours if you can make me stop talking, tough guy. *Little* tough guy, can you make me stop busting your balls? Gonna kick *me,* too, you little shrimp? Can your foot even reach my *stugots* from down there?"

"Why are you teasing Tony?" Paulie asked, tugging at his father's belt.

While Paulie pulled on Black Jack, Little Tony kept his eye on that wagging green bill. He watched Black Jack slap the top of his son's head, getting him off his leg, the whole time his left hand raised level with his lime green Borsalino. That ten-dollar bill waving at Little Tony—he could almost see the crosshatching of Hamilton's portrait. He heard the relish in Black Jack's voice, the same emphasis as in the store when he'd called him that name: *Little* Tony.

He was squinting to keep his eyes on the father and son, fighting a pounding headache, wishing he were somewhere else—in another country even. He rubbed his temple with the hatchet handle. The odor of the sharpened metal and the woodiness of the hickory stung his nose.

"See the little shrimp over there, Paulie?" Black Jack mocked.

Little Tony felt outside of his own body, floating level with the metal Vernor's sign. He studied the logo—the gnome—its grinning face, and suddenly instead of a red-haired dwarf, the gnome favored *him,* as if redrawn by an invisible artist. He blinked at his caricature, and then watched *himself,* perched from that vantage point, standing on the sidewalk below. Watched as he took a step toward Black Jack, focusing a last time on that flapping ten-dollar bill, stuck in that big left hand. Reviling it like a waving enemy flag. He could count the black hair on Jack's knuckles. Whenever he would retell the story, he insisted he was only trying to scare Black Jack, just trying to get him to shut the hell up.

And then Little Tony's hand was empty. The hatchet flew across the street, through the air with the efficiency of a javelin, never tumbling in anything but a perfect, splendid arc. The whirring noise it made was frightening. As it left his hand, he knew it was a terrible thing to do; yet he couldn't wait to see what would happen next.

Cochise couldn't have thrown it any better.

The blade made contact just above the anterior deltoid of Black Jack's left shoulder, lopping off his arm at the very point of entry. The sound the arm made as it hit the ground was one that Paulie would never forget. The only eyewitness other than the three of them—a passing courier—described the sound to a reporter as " … a sack of flour falling from a garage."

The ten-dollar bill fluttered away like confetti, unnoticed as the wind blew it down the street. Paulie screamed an otherworldly shriek when Black Jack's severed arm flexed once, rolling over on the concrete sidewalk like a dying serpent.

No one was more surprised than Black Jack to look down and find his own arm lying on the ground, still clothed in the sleeve of his linen jacket. That is, except Paulie. Little Tony felt bad the kid had been there to see the tragedy. It was a moot point now as he watched Black Jack twitch and then drop to his knee, screaming like a little girl.

"How about that, Jack?" Little Tony shouted, the anger turning all he had just seen into a wash of fluorescent green bile.

He was still not quite sure he could trust his vision; Black Jack's severed arm was somehow lying on the sidewalk next to him. From Little Tony's point of view, the blood—pulsing with every heartbeat from the meaty gash—looked like spilled black ink as it spread across the bright concrete. Black Jack was on both knees, clenching his shoulder, trying to stem the gushing blood.

"*Daddy! Daddy!*" Paulie sounded like a siren as he screamed.

Black Jack turned ashy, fighting shock.

"Get help, Paulie … you little bastard, Tony! *You cut off my arm!* You're worm food—*your family's* worm food. I'm dying. Don't let me die!"

Black Jack continued to wail, and rolling like he was on the sidewalk, in such terrific pain, he resembled someone demonstrating how to put yourself out if you were to catch on fire.

Little Tony tried to think of something to say, given the direness of the scene.

"Touch my family and I'll cut the other one off," he shouted as loud as he could, and then he thrust his small hands into his pockets. He took off—not running, though—leaving Paulie and Black Jack's screams dying in the wind.

Little Tony was four blocks away from the incident, standing in front of Bosco's Party Store. He leaned against the wall, sucking down a grape Nehi. His small hand shook as he drank the soda, a purple mustache wetting his lip. Sirens echoed dimly, gaining volume. First a speeding ambulance, followed closely by two squad cars, flew by and he waited for the noise to fade. He swigged some more of the grape pop and choked on it, the soda mixing in his throat with snot and tears. He closed his eyes, and for a moment, the image of Black Jack's dismembered arm left him, and there he was, on the basketball court, flying through the lane as a high schooler, scoring with cutting moves, leaping over men so much taller than he.

And there, on the court, he was teaching Paulie how to set a hard pick.

And there, in the stands, was Black Jack Talerico, clapping with ease, the way men with two arms are able to do, even as he threw him the evil eye—the *malocchia*—the way Black Jack always had since that day Little Tony had kicked his godson in the face.

And there, somewhere tropical now, was an older version of him, in a honeymoon suite, adoring the lovely Divina *Marcazzi's* nakedness. Her doe-shaped eyes closing as the young bride peeled off her orange two-piece and presented him with olive skin glistening with Coppertone, the vision so tacit he could smell the cocoa butter. All those years of feeling small faded as he enjoyed the whiteness of her protected flesh, offset by tan lines delineating the three previously sacred areas from the deep gold that was the rest of her body, the difference so stark to appear as though she wore an ivory bikini.

Then he blinked.

Blinding sunlight hit his eyes. And after he squinted the pain away, he realized he was alone. He walked back to Alinosi's, tasting the now tepid Nehi. He stood below the Vernor's sign and stared into the painted-on eyes of the red-haired gnome, finally seeing the irony in it.

Two police officers alternated between consoling Paulie and taking witness accounts near the ambulance. Paulie screamed as two paramedics loaded Black Jack into the EMS vehicle. Little Tony heard nothing but white noise. An oxygen mask covered Black Jack's face and there were many tubes feeding into his right arm. A paramedic held something long wrapped in gauze that he placed onto a bag of ice, and almost as an afterthought, picked up the lime green Borsalino off the sidewalk. Both were loaded up along with Black Jack. Little Tony watched the whole scene as a voyeur would, draining the rest of his grape pop. Someone by the ambulance pointed at him—Divina Vesprini maybe—and though he was sure they were all screaming, no sound came from their mouths.

He offered neither chase nor resistance to the two approaching police officers who were initially startled to see him standing there. They dropped their notepads and ran toward him with shiny, snub-nose .38s drawn, aimed directly at his head.

"I swear I'll shoot you where you stand. Don't try to run, you crazy little Guinea," the lead cop screamed as he sprinted toward Little Tony. "Christ, he's just a kid," the officer added.

Little Tony didn't run. He simply set the empty soda bottle on the ground and placed his hands over his head and waited. The sense of sound returned to his world, as if someone had turned the knob to a hidden stereo back up to full volume.

And when the cops spoke again, he heard fear there. The lead cop breathed heavily, sweating for no reason. He looked at Little Tony, seeming to feel the need to finish his initial thought, "Not that it'll matter. You're a dead Wop now. D-E-A-D. Do you know who that *is* over there? Do you know *who* you did *that* to? Crazy greaseball."

Tony just smiled at him and nodded. Didn't even realize he did it until the cop shrank away from him. The other cop produced a pair of chrome handcuffs that sparkled in the sunlight. The world seemed different now. Even when the other cop said, "Jesus, he thinks it's funny. Believe the balls on this one? Another New Dago trying to make his bones. Animals."

They were cautious of him when they cuffed him; hell, they even seemed *afraid*.

When the cops spun him around, before his face scraped against the brick wall, he noticed a tall shadow the sunlight had cast from his own body—the former Little Tony's body. Tony the Hatchet—the new nickname Anthony Bernardo Marcazzi would carry from that day forward until the day he died— saw his shadow now reach all the way past the very top of the Vernor's gnome.

And the sight of it made him smile.

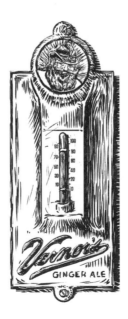

I'm from Detroit

Standing on the partially finished deck of the cabin, Roman Materra rubbed at the temples of his greying hair and closed his eyes, trying to let the sound of the woods calm the beating of his heart. Starvation Lake was in front of him, a glacial lake of spectacular beauty, spring-fed so prodigiously that if you listened closely, the trickling of ice-cold creeks and streamlets could be heard. A drake loon made a mournful cry trying to locate his separated mate, and with that stirring echo, Roman felt the stress disappear for a moment—a sudden serenity, a little better now, but still there just beneath his skin.

The conversation with his builder, Sherman Armbrewster, regarding completion of the cabin weighed heavily on him. It was going to happen soon.

Sherman was on his way over.

There had been problems all along, but in the finishing phase things had really taken an ugly turn. Roman came up to find the interior, directed to be done in tongue-and-groove knotty pine, was knotty *poplar*. Instead of refusing shipment, Sherman decided to put the poplar up anyway. There was more; a pair of matched, side-by-side peaked windows near the top of the cathedral ceiling was off by two inches and finally, the plumbing and electrical was double what Roman had been quoted. All of it led to the crux of the issue; an unpaid balance of nearly $8,000.

So now Roman had a problem. A $7,726 problem to be exact. In 1978, that was enough to buy a loaded Seville and still have enough for a weekend in Vegas. He knew the builder was trying to get over on him. And one thing about Roman Materra that was true in 1978—that remained true until the day he died—was that *no one* got over on him. Ever. No matter how big or tough they thought they were.

Sherman Armbrewster didn't know that, though. And so he had other ideas.

Roman wanted to build a cabin up north so he and his only son, Nick, would have a place to go together. His son was still in college, but he loved the woods, and Roman wanted to make sure the kid had a spot central to all the places he hunted. The family joke used to be that Nick had better find a squaw for a bride because he spent so much time in the woods. More than that, Roman wanted a respite from the dealings in Detroit that took so much out of him. He was getting older and felt blessed to have survived several close calls with "friends" from New York and Chicago. His rep was that of a tight-lipped, stand-up guy—traits that contributed to his longevity.

In the mid- to late-'70s, property in Michigan's Lower Peninsula was still easy to find on the eastern, Sunrise Side of the state. The western side had Lake Michigan frontage that was and still is as expensive as oceanfront sand in Hawaii, and that's a fact. All the rich bastards from Chicago drove the prices through the roof, forcing most working-class folks from Detroit to look to the Lake Huron side for their little piece of heaven. And that was fine with most of them. It was more the Detroit style anyway, raw and wild, devoid of any haughtiness—blue-collar vacation property. Nothing fancy.

Roman figured he had finally found his piece on Starvation Lake, twenty-seven miles southwest of the area's largest town, Alpena, a port city off Lake Huron. His buddy Vito Marsico had a nice lot up on the lake. Vito had been hounding Roman to look at a lot five spots down from him that he heard might come up for sale. Roman told Vito to keep an eye out. Sure enough, Vito's real estate agent, an oily, ex-Mennonite from Fairview named Dwight Yoder, left a message at the pro shop of the Bella Fiori County Club for Roman to call him ASAP.

Calling Bella Fiori a country club was like calling a Motel 6 the Beverly Hilton. The track had eighteen holes and a clubhouse/bar/grill/pro shop. Most of the "members" couldn't golf worth a shit, unless your idea of golfing was nailing a stripper in the bushes behind the twelfth hole. Or burying bags of stolen watches in the sand traps on the par fives. And God only knew how many weapons littered the bottom of the water hazards.

Roman was at the club three times a week, and he actually played golf there, too. He had an office behind the banquet room, right above the pro shop, which was little more than a ten by fifteen foot room offering gloves, balls, and a few hot drivers lifted from a Dunham's sporting goods store.

He saw the message from Dwight Yoder after a round of especially bad golf that was only salvaged by two things: a birdie Roman made on the thirteenth with a six-iron he hit stiff to one foot of the cup, and an errant shot from a parallel fairway on the eighteenth that struck his playing partner, Luca Calamari, square in the onions. Watching Luca rolling around on the grass was worth the 103 Roman had carded. He nearly pissed himself seeing his rotund *paisan* chase after the accountant-type who had misfired his drive, madly wielding a four-iron, swinging it machete-style at the poor bastard.

A month earlier, Dwight and Roman spoke on the phone for the first time:

"Roman, I think you're going to be a land owner. I've got a lot on the newer side of Starvation. Oh it's one hundred feet of sugary sand frontage—"

"Cut to the chase. How much?"

"Only eleven thousand."

"You're outta your fucking mind. Call me when you come to your senses."

Roman hung up before Dwight could reply.

That went on several more times, except each time Dwight called, the lot he had previously offered was sold. And with each *new* lot, the price was higher, generally in increments of $500.

Roman dialed up Dwight.

"Dwight, what's the good word?"

"You might want to jump on this one. Before you can stop me, let me tell you, it's got electric set up already and there's a well been dug on it. Man from Bay City got laid off, couldn't keep the lot. Sixteen thousand," Dwight said.

"*Maddon'!* Sixteen large? That lake got gold in it?"

"Could say that, yes. What do you want to do?"

"Aw shit, will they take twelve?" Roman asked. He heard Dwight chuckle softly.

"Eleven thousand sounds like a bargain now, huh?" Dwight said. "Tell you what—*I'll* take fifteen-five. Firm. I own the lot. And I know I can get sixteen, easy. Let me know by tomorrow morning."

This time, Dwight hung up before Roman could answer.

So Roman begrudgingly paid the $15,500, in cash of course, just like everything else he bought. He was pissed he'd paid so much, but was heartened when a week later, Dwight called back to offer him $16,500 to buy the lot back. Soon the task commenced to find builders in that area of northern Michigan, ones who were not the best, but not the worst either. Vito tried to convince Roman to follow his lead; have a gang of Detroit craftsmen go up there and do it up right.

No way, Roman thought. Vito liked things to be neat and perfect, mostly because Vito wanted things nice for his wife. Roman did not. The cabin wasn't going to be a palace by any means. It was going to be a hunting and fishing cabin. Nothing pretty, and no broads allowed except in the summertime. Other than that, it would just be the guys and Roman's Nick. He didn't want his wife or sisters-in-law mucking things up with any fancy stuff. Besides, with all the Indians and welfare types in the area, you couldn't leave a "dream home" for that crowd to come through and steal your shit. He knew that if you left the place modest, those people didn't feel the need to do much more than break in, maybe drink your whiskey and eat your food. That much he could live with.

Sherman Armbrewster had a hazy past, not that Roman cared. He was kind of in a hurry, and the main reason he picked Sherman was because a local farmer said he was quick. The farmer also warned him to be careful, though. Sherman was a formidable man. It was thought he was from Cleveland or Toledo, where he'd had some success as a prizefighter. At six foot five, he weighed close to 300 pounds, with a nest of dense hair as black as burnt wood and a Fu Manchu that looked painted on. His features were thick, and his appearance was made more troubling by deep-set, smallish eyes better suited on a mink. One story was that, after agreeing to throw a fight, he let his ego get the better of him and decked his opponent, putting him into a two-week coma. Underestimating the heat from the promoter he'd reneged on, Sherman's nascent boxing career was over. Later he resorted to collecting debts for a local bookie before making a break, but not without pocketing a week's worth of receipts.

Sherman fled Ohio, supporting himself by working odd handyman jobs as he wandered into Michigan, past Monroe, through Flint and Frankenmuth. He migrated to Bay City where he spent two years as a carpenter's apprentice before settling in the town of Besch, a sleepy little Mennonite enclave north of Standish.

The big man made an immediate impact on the local carpenters and tradesmen in the northeastern Michigan city. He had become a skilled, hard worker who talked a good game but was known to drink a little too much for the Mennonites' liking, given their strict abstention from alcohol. Still, the tradesmen found that if they could keep Sherman focused, things usually turned out.

Eventually he hung his own shingle, opening Armbrewster Construction. Sherman picked up most of his work from folks below Flint who had money to spend. They all wanted the same thing: a summer home in that area of the northeastern Lower Peninsula. And so the business situation reversed; by using local tradesmen on his projects and acting as the contractor, Sherman built up not only their trust, but also a very successful construction business within just four years. And although the opening of Armbrewster Construction added another builder to the area, there was plenty of work to keep everyone busy.

Not being particularly enamored with the fruits of the outdoors, namely the pursuit of game and fish, Sherman took on a larger work schedule than his competition, constructing homes well into deer season. The others, who hunted not only out of a sense of tradition but as a need to put venison in the freezer, would shut down their operations for the entire month of November, letting Sherman stock up on the impatient downstaters who wanted their resorts built yesterday.

After a few seasons of ingratiating himself with the local craftsmen and lending institutions, Sherman gradually started low-balling his competitors' bids, finding clever and certainly unethical ways to bury the inequities down the road. From buying cheaper grades of lumber from mills south of Zilwaukee and other inferior materials, he'd more than make it up on the back end of the projects. He recouped and beefed up his profits by sabotaging the construction with excuses ranging from needing more labor than he initially budgeted to blaming the work of the local subcontractors, the men who originally befriended him. After all was said and done, he usually came away with nearly ten percent more than the highest bid from his competitors.

Sherman's physical size intimidated not only the other builders but also those people whose very homes he was building. Since most of the problems started far into the job, the client was hamstrung, usually having to just swallow hard and write the check for the extra "work" instead of trying to find another builder to complete their cottage.

Most of the men Sherman used were honest, simple Mennonites too frightened to deny him when he offered them work. They usually got paid what he promised, though occasionally he would short them by fifty or a hundred bucks. If they complained, he'd crack his huge neck, rolling it side-to-side, then ask them if they were questioning his math. To a man, they'd wilt under the threat, walking away with their straw hats in their hands. Sherman never checked his addition the whole time he worked up there and knew that no man could ever make him.

So, shrugging off the farmer's tepid warning, Roman hired Sherman. And now Roman had a problem that had beset the other downstaters before him who had been tricked by Sherman. While the money was the key to Roman's displeasure, he was more disappointed he let himself get hoodwinked. Vito had told him that he'd never heard of Armbrewster Construction. Sherman had built only two cabins in the immediate area. One was for a Milquetoast retiree whose complaints sounded plain whiny. The other victim was a nattering widow, a royal pain-in-the-ass who had probably sent her husband to an early grave. Roman rationalized both at the time, deciding to give the huge man the benefit of the doubt. He regretted it now, of course.

And besides, Sherman's estimate had come in more than three grand lower than the bids of the two other builders. That was dough Roman could make work for him in other ways. He should've known it was too good to be true.

Starvation Lake wasn't unknown to Roman. He and his brothers, along with Vito, had been coming up there since the '50s. Back then, property was really cheap and the terrain harder to navigate. Land was plentiful because the highways were shit, and you had to really work to get to the good hunting spots. They'd forged many memories of successful hunts and had their share of comical moments as well.

One of Roman's favorite stories was when the Baggarelli brothers went up there with their girlfriends for a weekend tryst.

Carl and John Baggarelli were married to sisters. Under the guise of a fishing weekend, the brothers headed north, telling the wives not to buy anything for the Sunday birthday dinner the two sisters were throwing for their mother, Farfella, because Carl and John would be bringing back walleye fillets for the party of twenty-seven.

On their way out of Detroit, the brothers picked up two strippers they were banging regularly at a little love-shack Carl kept downtown, right above Puma's Bar. The four of them drank a case of Stroh's on the drive up I-75 North, to the adjoining rooms they'd reserved at the Dew-Faull Inn, a motel just south of Alpena. The weekend consisted of drinking and screwing, and more screwing, so much so that it wasn't until after the brothers dropped off their girlfriends that they remembered their creels were still empty. Knowing that their wives had a party of more than two-dozen hungry Sicilians waiting at home for a walleye dinner, the brothers made a hasty stop at Alcamo's Market.

"If they don't got walleye, just get perch," John said. "Tastes close enough."

"Got it. Leave it running," Carl replied.

They got to the party just in time and to the delight of their wives held up the fillets, which they craftily transferred into their Coleman cooler. The grill was lit and the Chianti and *grappa* was flowing. The brothers were golden, as everyone commented on how delicious the fish tasted. Until their mother-in-law Farfella, sharp as a tack—and who spoke very little English—made a fateful comment:

"*Ci è il branzino in Michigan?*" Farfella said.

The already suspicious sisters glared at their husbands. "It's walleye, Mama," Rita Baggarelli replied. "Wall-eye."

"Branzino! *Questo è il branzino!*" Farfella insisted.

"No Mama, the boys caught walleye. There's no *sea bass* in Michigan. That's walleye Mama's eating. *Right,* Carl?" Rita asked her husband.

Carl, who had the worst poker face of all the boys on the East Side of Detroit, began to stammer, looking for help from John, whose expression could've killed.

An inspired Carl snapped his fingers. "I spilled salt all over 'em," he offered.

It didn't fly.

Years later, when the brothers were urged to discuss the incident at deer camp for the amusement of others, Carl would say the reason he'd bought the sea bass was because it was cheaper than the walleye. To which John would invariably reply: *"You stupid* mamaluke! *Tell me again how paying alimony to those two dumb bitches is cheaper than buying the walleye I told you to in the first place?"*

Roman thought of how his friends had helped furnish the cabin with their generosity. Construction of the place had started slow, with Roman and his Nick working on some of the landscaping. It was hard for them to get there during the week, but from time to time they'd show up on a Friday and stay at a motel through Monday or Tuesday. It wasn't uncommon for Roman to be inside talking with Sherman when his son would interrupt. That was how the fireplace of the cabin ended up in the corner of the great room:

"Pop, there's a guy out here, says he's got a fireplace," Nick said.

"Send him in."

The truckers would usually come in, all of them the same type; quiet, shifty, nervous-looking guys, who just wanted to get the shit off their trucks and get on with delivering the rest of their haul.

"Where do you want it?" the man asked.

"Wait—this is a corner fireplace. Ours is going to be in the middle of the room," Nick protested.

Roman put a hand up to his son. "Sherman, chimney up yet?" he called out.

"Maybe next week," Sherman replied.

Roman looked at the man. "Put it in the corner."

And that's the way it usually went—slightly warm gifts arriving from downstate.

All the humor of those memories evaporated now, simmering into a misery-laden soup as the thought of confronting the Goliath roiled inside Roman's gut.

There was a low rumble and gravel crunching as Sherman's truck pulled up. Roman readied himself, trying to stand as erect as possible to make himself bigger than his five-foot-eleven frame. He lit a cigarette and watched the pickup dip down and then bounce up as Sherman extracted himself from the front seat. That was in sharp contrast to seeing what hopped out of the passenger side. Having to jump from the seat to the ground was Jimmy Leff, a walking lawn jockey and Sherman's unofficial sidekick. He sidled up, walking beside Sherman, his gait fast and clumsy, kind of a feckless skip.

James "Pokey" Leff was a dim-witted local who had been abandoned by his mother as a young child. He was raised by the Amish but left his adopted family during Rumspringa, the time when all Amish teens are allowed to go off into the world and decide whether to stay in the Amish faith or to join the devilish world of the English. Pokey chose the latter after tasting whiskey and getting his pecker smoked for the first time, in that order.

After leaving his family, Pokey found work at a farm, spending his money on liquor and pulp novels. One night, at what had become a favorite haunt of his—Ma Deeters in Luzerne—Pokey's and Sherman's lives crossed. Sherman had laughed watching the little man's attempts at coupling with a local party girl two heads taller than he. After being sent packing from the drunken tramp, Sherman hoisted Pokey up and set him on the bar. He bought him a couple of shots and the two had been together ever since.

He worked as a laborer for Sherman, mostly doing menial tasks, site clean-ups, and even some rough carpentry. He hung on Sherman's every comment and danced around him, a stunted sycophant in the way the goofy little dog was in the old Warner Brothers cartoons to his big, bulldog buddy:

"Hey Sherman, that's a good one, Sherm!" or *"You're hilarious, Sherm! That's a scream, Sherm! Sherm, you could've been a comedian!"*

The two were inseparable, and Roman couldn't stand the little puke.

Roman was leaning against the house by the corner of the unfinished deck. Sherman lumbered toward him, and with each step Roman swore he could actually feel the ground shake.

"How do Romey?" the man bellowed in a voice so deep it never ceased to startle Roman.

Pokey laughed hard and zipped the plaid coat he was wearing all the way up to his chin, giving him the appearance of a forty-one-year-old head stitched onto the body of a ten-year-old boy.

Although he was nearly a foot below where Roman stood, Sherman's tiny eyes were almost even with his when he got next to him. The steps groaned as he walked up to join him. He leaned a massive foot against one of the posts the porch railings would eventually be attached to, and stretched his arms wide as he looked out at the lake.

"One hell of a view, huh Romey?" Sherman said.

"Hello, Sherman," Roman replied.

"Hey, Roman," Pokey said.

Roman ignored him.

Sherman sighed and looked at Pokey. "Poke, why don't you go check out the shore. See if there's any fish down there."

Pokey compliantly hustled away from the deck toward the shoreline.

"Sure thing, Sherm. I'll be right down there if you need me, Sherm."

Roman watched the diminutive Pokey looking into the water.

"How's he work on rabbits? Does he retrieve 'em for you?" Roman asked.

"That's funny. Pokey's a trusted employee. Does a lot of grunt work."

"Does that include wiping your ass?"

Sherman smiled at Roman; sharp incisors framed his top teeth, giving his grin a fox-like quality. He tapped a tin of Copenhagen until it was tight and packed a ridiculous amount of the moist tobacco between his lower lip and gum.

"Another funny line," Sherman said. When he spoke, the loose snuff floated into his mouth, looking like someone had marked between his little teeth with a black pen. "So Roman, let's have the money. Can't finish your place without the money."

Roman looked out at the lake. Pokey waddled around by the water's edge. Just then a fish jumped, leaving rings on the surface at the point of reentry.

"Hey Sherman, didya see that? Was that a walleye, Sherm? I think that was a walleye!" Pokey hollered.

Sherman exhaled and spit near Roman's feet.

"I already paid you everything you asked for Sherman, and yet my place remains unfinished. I even overlooked the knotty poplar you accepted."

"Looks the same as pine. A little greyer, no big shakes. You owe me close to eight grand. $7,726 to be exact. Tell you what, let's make it an even $7,800."

Sherman smiled, and when he did his face looked like an ermine with blood on its fangs. He turned his table-sized back to Roman and paced to the front of the deck. He looked at the ground below, sloping gradually to the lake, and rested his boot on a post.

"I don't think so," Roman said.

Sherman stood there a moment, and Roman could see his huge shoulders rise, like he was laughing. He turned around and removed the Copenhagen can from his pocket. In his gnarled hands, it looked like he was playing with a bottle cap. He scooped out the last of the dark tobacco and added it to his burgeoning lip. Then he ceremoniously let the empty tin hit the ground below him. It rolled down to the lake, to within three feet of Pokey, who looked like a puppy trying to catch minnows.

"Gotta be careful by the end of this deck here, Roman. We don't get a railing nailed on soon, you may fall off. Maybe get hurt. Or broke. And all them Dee-troit Guineas you know won't be able to put you together again." Sherman squinted, his black eyes shrinking impossibly smaller.

"I'll be at the County Depot tomorrow at eight a.m. Be there with my loot. Not a penny short. $7,800."

He walked up to Roman and got his face close, stooping a bit to make sure their eyes met. Roman held back the urge to gag at the smell of the leviathan's breath. Behind him, he heard Pokey's footfalls as he ran up from the lake.

"Everything OK, Sherm? Did you get the money, Sherm?"

Sherman kept his head straight, but his eyes flinched a second as Pokey's question broke the silence and his intended impact of the moment.

"Go get in the goddamn truck, Poke ... we're done here." Sherman rose to full height and walked down the stairs. As he passed, he said, "Roman. Don't make me come looking for you." He walked toward the truck without looking back.

"You *will* finish this cabin," Roman said, bracing himself against the post. "But I've paid you my last dime."

Sherman stopped in his tracks and turned around to face him. There was a pile of leftover fieldstone in front of his truck. He placed his size 15 boot on top of it. A stone at the bottom, shaped like an oversized bushel basket, stood out. His massive hands grabbed each side. A soft grunt escaped as he lifted it, raising it high over his head.

"That's gotta weigh over two hundred pounds, Sherm!" Pokey squealed.

Sherman stomped over toward Roman, walking much like Frankenstein. Roman held his ground, ready to dive off the deck when the stone came his way. Instead Sherman turned toward the lake and walked in the direction of the shore. When he was ten feet from the water he hurled the boulder into the lake. It created a white geyser that exploded high into the air.

He panted as he turned toward Roman. Walking past the porch, he went back to the giggling Pokey, who by now sounded like a hyena jacked up on amphetamines. Sherman breathed heavily. He grinned at Roman from the open door of his pickup.

"Big bills, Romey," he said.

Roman stood on the porch and looked at his hands. They were shaking so hard he had to put them back on the post and grip it just to steady them.

Keep it together, he thought, as Sherman drove off.

Roman looked at the dissipating ripples created by the boulder Sherman threw. Watching the disturbed water settling to return its surface to glass, he found comfort in knowing that, even as impressive as the superhuman feat had been, its impact would soon be gone forever; a distant memory swallowed whole by an entity, created by a force far more powerful than any man. And the concept of how great strength can be consumed by great will infused him with a certain resolve. The calm water fortified that resolve, not unlike the very springs that fed the lake. He was prepared now for what he had to do, and he planned on doing it with a cold, cold heart.

The County Depot was an oversized, outdated train station a local businessman had purchased at an auction in Gaylord and hauled to the corner of Starvation Lake Road and M-65 North, where he later converted it into a diner. It had ten tables scattered about and three booths stuck along a sidewall. The business had been in operation for twenty years, and the owner kept the place going not merely for profit. The Depot served as a gathering place for farmers and locals to meet and commiserate about the upcoming crops or lack thereof.

Roman was dressed in a long coat when he arrived that next morning. He walked past handfuls of farmers occupying three nearby tables. He faced a group of six that were having breakfast, choosing a smaller table at the back corner of the restaurant. There was a window to his left, and a bureau to his right. The space was cramped. He slanted the table on an angle in such a way that his back was to the wall—like he was sitting behind a desk. He had good sightlines from there. He left two chairs across from him for Sherman and the inevitable Pokey. He looked out at the large windows facing east that took up a good portion of the front of the restaurant. It was 7 a.m., and he felt relieved sitting so far from the entrance; it was perfect.

The waitress smiled at him from the register. She held up a coffee pot and nodded. He'd eaten there in the past, even before Vito had bought his place, and she'd been his waitress once—real friendly, too. Her cheerful voice seemed prying at times—typical when the locals meet someone new—but she was a looker, a wild ride for some lucky soul. Roman smiled back and she gave a little wave, buttressed by a shake of her solid rump.

He looked outside and watched the sun try to invade a sky whose color could only have been dreamed up by a master of light. Azure hues streaked with unseemly rays of yellow turned the limitless blue to turquoise in random patches. It made him wish he could be on a boat or just about anywhere else in the world to enjoy it at that very moment. Anywhere except here.

"Haven't seen you in a while," the waitress said, suddenly upon him. He stared for a moment longer, taking in the wonder of the eastern sky, causing her to finally look out the window, too, carafe at the ready.

"Beautiful, isn't it?" Roman said.

"What's that? Oh, the truck." She looked back at him, apparently lost at his question.

"I meant the sky."

"*Really?*" she said, with a vacant smile. "Hey—I was *kidding*. You get used to it living up here."

He grinned. She smiled, and he noticed the red impression of a wedding ring on her bare finger.

She started to pour. He handed her a ten spot.

She looked at him, amused. "What's this for, handsome?"

She pocketed the bill. Her compliment gave him pause, and for the first time he noticed she was twenty years younger than him.

"A guy's coming to meet me here—big guy. I need to talk to him about something very important. Private. I'd like you to come over to the table. He may not be alone. That doesn't matter, though. Just get them whatever it is they want to drink—no food, though. And leave us be until they go. Can you do that for me?"

"Do you want me to call the sheriff?"

"No. Let's not," Roman said.

She smiled. "Are you like a special agent or something?"

"Nothing that glamorous," Roman said. "Just business."

And he knew by her face that if he wanted her, it wouldn't be a problem. He wasn't the cheating kind, and he also knew not to shit where he ate. So, despite her curvy figure, he'd be taking a pass. For the County Depot was mere miles from Starvation Lake, and with the cabin, he planned on being a regular soon enough.

The RC Cola clock on the wall read 7:35. The clock jogged a visceral memory, and he thought about a time years earlier when he'd sat in this very spot during bow season, laughing with his brothers over breakfast, talking about a nice buck he'd killed. Back then there wasn't a man alive who frightened him. He didn't fear anything but God. Of course, he'd never come across a behemoth like Sherman Armbrewster.

Lying awake in the motel the night before, he'd thought about calling his brothers to come up north to back him up. But he realized this was something he needed to do alone. They were all younger men with younger children, and they had more at risk than he did. He had a large life insurance policy and a stash of more than $100,000 that his brothers knew the whereabouts of, so if anything happened, his wife and Nicky would be taken care of. Of course, that wasn't the main reason he needed to do this alone.

Roman hated the feeling of fearing anything but God.

The bell on the restaurant's door shattered his daydreams.

Pokey led the way. Sherman lumbered after him followed by a tough-looking man Roman had never seen before. Nor had he counted on. Pokey motioned toward Roman's table and the three took their time coming over. Roman took a sip of his coffee and kept his eyes on Sherman. Sherman took the chair across from him and Pokey grabbed the other one to Sherman's left. The new guy, a brooding, dark, six-footer with a permanent scowl and a terrible scar across his left cheek, grabbed a chair and started to pull it around to Roman's side of the table when the waitress intercepted him.

"Hon, would you mind sitting next to your big, strong friend?" She took the chair and set it next to Sherman, so that all three were on the other side of the table. The man looked at Sherman, who nodded yes. The man sat down. Sherman smiled at her directness. "Thank you. Little easier for me to serve you this way." She looked straight at Roman and fake-laughed. "Now what can I get you good-looking men?"

"How about a date with you, sweetie? I don't think I've had the pleasure of seeing you before." Sherman's attempt at smoothness fell miserably short.

"How about let's start with coffee?"

She winked at Sherman, who removed his hat.

"And your friends?" she continued.

Pokey twitched excitedly. "Coffee smells great. Doesn't the coffee smell fresh, Sherm?"

"Another coffee ... how about you?" she asked the third man. "You're a quiet one." The extra man had been staring at Roman since they arrived. He tipped his head at her and she stepped away.

"OK then. Two coffees." She glanced at Roman and walked away. The third man kept staring at Roman.

Sherman tilted his head, watching her ass. "I think she's sweet on you, Romey."

"Hiya, Roman," Pokey said. His eyes were bright.

Roman looked stone-faced at Pokey. Then he turned his attention back to the third man and met his glare. Pokey frowned and played with his fork.

"You I don't know," Roman said. His blue eyes were impassive.

"Name's Snook," Sherman answered for him. "He followed me up here from Lodi. Ran into some trouble back there. Him and I go back. Snook swings a *real* good hammer."

Snook smiled, revealing teeth that never had a prayer of coming in straight.

"Speaking of hammers, got my money?" Sherman stared at Roman, enjoying it.

The waitress returned and gave Pokey his coffee. Sherman took his cup from her hands with his large paw and let it linger there. She smiled at him.

"Back for your orders in two shakes," she said.

Then she disappeared through the swinging doors into the kitchen. Roman looked at the table of farmers behind Sherman and his cronies. The men, all sporting the long beards of the Mennonite, gave furtive glances at him.

"My money," Sherman said.

Roman cleared his throat. "Well, the way I see it, there's still some work to be done. I got two windows lined up about as even as Marty Feldman's eyes. The chimney's not capped yet. The walls in the two upstairs bedrooms need to be taped and the lights hooked up. Gas lines to the furnace still aren't plumbed. Add all that to the fact I already paid you what you quoted me, plus an extra G note in bullshit charges, I'd say you need to finish the job just to make things *square*. It's you who owes me."

"Is that right? You hear that Snook? Man owes me nearly eight thousand and doesn't want to pay up. What do you think about that?" Sherman slouched in his chair like a tired bear, as if waiting for the bees to bring the honey to him.

Snook moved a little, showing a bit of the scarred cheek to Roman.

"Stupid shit. That's what he is." Snook's voice was uneven. "I know where he lives. Took a big smelly crap in his toilet just last week. He's a *stupid shit*."

Pokey snorted, "Stupid." He kept chuckling until Sherman stopped him with a look. His squeaky laugh cut off as he sipped his coffee. He held the mug with both hands.

"That's right, Snook. Something only a *stupid shit* would do. Roman, looks to me like we're done with your place. Just give me the money and you won't ever have to worry about a thing. Like walking normal for instance." He turned his ursine head. "Where the hell that sweet-assed waitress run to?" Sherman searched the diner.

"Sweet-assed! Like to swing from those big boobies of hers, huh, Sherm?" Pokey said. He reached into the air, his little hands squeezing imaginary breasts.

Roman stared at him, and this time Pokey shut up, but his posture changed, and he actually returned Roman's stare, trying to look tough. Roman took a slow swallow of coffee and with his left hand, set the mug down. He wiped at his mouth and rested his arm on the table in front of him, his left hand an inch from Sherman's own.

His right hand was never there from the start.

"You know Sherman, I've been thinking; *you know* you can kick my ass. And *I know* you can kick my ass ... "

Sherman grinned and nodded in agreement. Snook tilted his head.

"But you know what?"

"No, Romey. Tell me. What?" Sherman replied, his tiny eyes retracting into the shadow cast by his overhanging brow.

"I don't think I'm gonna let you kick my ass today," Roman announced, allowing the hint of a smile to sprout on his face. "No. Not today."

Sherman actually giggled. "Snook, Poke, hear that? Roman's not gonna *let me* kick his ass today. Now why's that Romey? I can't wait to hear." He leaned in.

"Well, because instead, what I thought *I'd* do today, was kill your little midget here, and as an added bonus, clip this *stupid shit* you brought along—Scarface—I'll kill him, too. But not *you,* Sherman. No, see, you—I'm just going to blow your *balls off.* After that your kneecaps. That's called a *tri-fecta* where I come from."

Sherman grinned, but Snook sat up rigidly, the man's smugness waning. Sherman remained undaunted. This wasn't the first time he'd had a death threat made against him. He tilted his head at each of his nervous pals, and smiled. Then he turned his gaze back on Roman and his mouth became a canine grin.

"Oh *really?*" Sherman asked, his small eyes twinkling into raisins.

"Yeah. Really. Think I'm shittin' you? Take a look under the table. I've had it pointed at your *martello* from the moment you sat down."

Snook and Pokey immediately looked under the table to see the barrel of a sawed-off, semi-automatic Beretta 12-gauge resting inches from Sherman's crotch.

"Either one of you assholes blinks, he'll be peeing from a pussy and you'll be next. Get up slow and get the fuck out. Both of you."

Sherman's face lost all of its blood, but before he could say a word, Snook and Pokey were gone, the bell at the door ringing like wind chimes in a tsunami. Sherman's big head dipped under the table and when he shot back up, he tried to push away from it. Roman lunged for his wrist, clenching what felt like a limb from an oak tree. He somehow drew Sherman toward him.

"Wait a minute, Roman! We can talk about this ... " Sherman stammered, and for the first time in his life, he looked like any other man.

"*Now* you want to talk," Roman said, pulling him even closer.

"Roman, I'm sorry—this is a big *mess*. Let's make this right, OK? Roman please, we're even ... it's a mess *Roman!* We're even. Roman look—"

"No. *You look,* motherfucker, we're real far from even." Roman's voice never rose above a steady whisper. "Here's the way it's gonna play out, you big lump of shit: You and that little munchkin, you're going to be back at my cabin on Monday morning—sun-up. And *when* you get there, you're gonna work your asses off until it's finished."

The farmers at the table behind Sherman were all turned in their chairs, staring at Roman. He narrowed his eyes and it was enough to make them go back to their coffee.

"All I want to see is asses and elbows flying. Then when and if—and this is the biggest *if* of your worthless fucking life—*I say* all's well, you're going to go back to your little cow town and never do another job around here again."

"Wait. I've got projects coming up! Bids I've won—you can't stop me from making a ... " Sherman tried to continue, but Roman's eyes said clamp it, so he cut himself off.

"I ever find a window broken, a mark on the clapboard, so much as a single *blade of grass* out of place, I'm coming to finish you. I'll do it for fun, do you hear me? Do you under*stand* me, *Sherm?*" Roman's eyes never blinked when he spoke, and he felt the old feeling return, and it felt good.

Sherman's legs shook and the saliva in his mouth turned dusty tasting.

"Wait a minute, now hold on ... what if someone else were to do something—you know, vandalize you? I can't be responsible for these welfare Redskins up here." His lips trembled when he spoke, so Roman waited to respond, because he liked seeing it.

"Then I guess you better pray no one messes with me. See, maybe I didn't make myself as crystal clear as I might have, when you and I first met. *I'm from Detroit.* Do you understand what that means, motherfucker?"

Roman kept his eyes steady, and Sherman nodded yes.

"Now get the hell out of here before I change my mind."

He released his grip on Sherman's wrist. The huge man rose from the chair, knocking it backward. A stain spread on his faded jeans that he was slow to cover up with his hat. He looked ashamed, and though Roman saw it, he decided to let it go.

The farmers and other patrons stared at Sherman as he looked around the restaurant. When he saw the waitress, he trotted out with a quick gait, his hat over his crotch. He nearly ripped the door from its hinges as he exited, setting off an alarming chime from the bells. Roman watched him leap into his waiting truck, Pokey in the middle and Snook driving. Sherman never looked back; instead he screamed directions and pointed ahead with urgency. Snook, however, did look back. Roman waved daintily at him, causing the corners of Snook's mouth to take a downward turn. He floored it out of the parking lot.

Roman smiled at the farmers and other patrons. They quickly turned from him. He steadied his left hand and picked up his coffee cup. It was cold, but he needed it.

"Let me warm that up," the waitress said, filling it. She was looking at him the way all the women used to, when he and his brothers would walk into the dance clubs in Detroit, back in the day, when they ran wild. "What did you *say* to them?" Roman took a protracted sip and got up, careful to conceal the sawed-off shotgun underneath his long coat.

"I told him you were spoken for. He was crushed." Roman handed her a twenty. "Thanks for your help this morning."

He smiled and walked toward the door.

She looked to check that no one was listening and stopped him. He could smell her perfume. "I was wondering ... feel like a few laughs? I'm free tonight."

She sounded hopeful. He looked her in the eyes.

"You'd wear an old man like me out." Roman smiled and walked out.

The sound of hammers and circular saws reverberated through the pines as Roman got out of his Cadillac. He had to park on the side of the road because of all the vehicles in his two-track driveway. He carried a green metal thermos of coffee as he walked toward his cabin. Above the roofline, a mason balanced, carefully setting the cap on the chimney. Other tradesmen worked so quickly you would've thought they were building an ark. A plumber installed a brass fitting on a spigot near the side door, while another put pipe dope on the threads of the well cap. The man looked up and seeing Roman, spun the cap on with a flourish.

When Roman came around the corner near the back deck, arriving at the very spot Sherman had threatened him two days before, he watched a carpenter size a board on the newly erected, sturdy top railing.

"Hold that mullion steady," Sherman yelled.

Roman responded to the voice, looking up toward the peak of the cabin.

"I'm trying, Sherm! I'm trying my best, but it's *heavy* ... "

Roman looked up to the cabin's peak and saw Sherman standing on a scaffold that looked too small to support him. Pokey was on the inside of the cabin as the two struggled to reset one of the misaligned windows. Sherman wrestled with the frame, then his body changed, the way one does when they feel someone watching them. He instinctively looked down and seeing Roman, his face crumpled into a mess of lines.

"Oh hey, Roman. Re-aligning this pesky window. Uh, I made a checklist and we'll be out of your hair by Wednesday, Thursday at latest. How's Thursday?"

"Thursday's *fine* Sherman, but take your time. And thank you very much for your effort." Roman took a step toward the water and stopped. He couldn't resist. He looked up at the pair. "How's it going up there, Pokey? Doing OK?"

Pokey looked at Sherman, confused. The builder nodded at him.

"Uh, well ... fine, Roman. Going fine," Pokey replied.

"Place is coming along nice—going to be *real* nice," Roman called out.

Roman walked past the carpenter who was still busy on the deck. The man checked the railing with a level and pounded it once before checking it again. He seemed rushed, hammering and pulling on the posts, testing them for strength as well as making sure they were square. Roman passed within a foot of him. The man tried to hide his face as Roman walked by. He slowed his pace, but kept walking. As he passed the man he spoke. "Do a good job now. I never forget a face ... *Snook*," he said, just loud enough.

He continued down the slope to the shore. Snook watched him walk away, hammering nails into the railing with even more fervor.

Standing on shore, Roman poured himself a mug of black coffee from the thermos. The noise of the workmen dissipated, giving way to the wildness of the lake. He sipped at the coffee and ruminated on its bitterness. Steam rose from the cold, clear water of Starvation Lake, and the resident loons appeared like silent bombers, flying twenty feet over his head, the sun affecting their white-spotted breasts and greenish black heads with iridescence. Roman listened to the low pulse of their wing beats.

He looked skyward to watch them plummet toward the surface of the water, the male skidding behind his mate, creating a roostertail. The drake rose on his feet, flapping his wings furiously, the whole time singing the song of an insane animal, intelligible only to its own kind. Roman watched them skip across the watery dance floor and only then did he close his eyes, as if trying to create a snapshot. He let the sounds of hammers and saws fade out for good, surrendering to the tranquility created by the trickle of the feeder springs and the cry of the avian lovers.

Switching the Lumpy

I t started with the channel locks. Sonny had bought a case from his brother, and on a whim, he'd spread them out on a table marked at four bucks a pair.

They were gone by noon and a light went on in Sonny's head.

In 1958 he diversified. Solomon "Sonny" Aravakian owned Aravakian's Gallery, an East Side jewelry store in Copper Corner, off Seven Mile and Hayes, that now sold everything from Hummels, Lenox, cameras, and luggage to power tools and maple syrup. You could find almost anything there. Sonny's idea was, while the ladies looked at the trinkets, the husbands, bored as they often became during any kind of shopping, could migrate to other parts of the store. From a business standpoint, it was genius.

As Sonny featured more and more varied inventory, it became apparent that while still his hallmark, jewelry would never be the singular draw it once was. Soon the other items in the store outsold it. Money was money, so he gave the people what they wanted. By 1960, ladies' handbags and onyx chess sets imported from Mexico stood alongside racks hanging with pearl necklaces, gold chains, and pricey watches.

The jewelry was in the back of the store, housed within long glass display cases. The store was always humming—people had to take numbers to get waited on—and Sonny needed all ten salespeople, as they moved plenty of merchandise. Saturdays were busiest, and waits of an hour were not uncommon, especially in the weeks before Holy Days and Christmas. Sonny's studio was in a small room off the back. There he repaired rings, watches, and other items. He kept a workbench set up with a jeweler's vise and propane torch on a stand, its blue flame burning perpetually.

He enjoyed placing the stones into different settings than were displayed, customizing what he kept on hand at the customer's ever-changing whims. A good deal of his work was upgrading existing settings with newer, better gems. Sonny was a true artisan at that.

His real gift may have been his personality, his ability to make everyone feel taken care of, and he charmed them all, men and women alike. Everyone thought they had a special relationship with Sonny. If one were ready to buy a crucifix for their nephew's first communion, and was fortunate enough to see Sonny peeking from the archway of his studio, they'd point his way and whisper to the salesperson,

"Sonny told me to let him know before I pay … "

Having heard the rejoinder ad nauseam, the salespeople would still dutifully call Sonny over. And he'd sashay over to the sales counter, smile and shake the customer's hand, always asking how their family was first. He would then casually ask the salesperson, *"How much are we charging here?"* Upon hearing the *ridiculously high cost*, Sonny would shudder in horror, apologizing for his salesperson's mistake. *"She didn't know who you were!"* he'd say. Sonny would make a big production, giving a disgusted wave of his hand, invariably knocking off a ten or twenty. What the smiling customer didn't know was that he'd built a graduated mark-up into everything, so the "discount" never cost him a dime. But they would leave feeling like they had been treated *primo*.

Sonny, half-Italian, half-Armenian, was before anything else a street rat. He'd fought for everything he'd ever got. He and his younger brother, Garbis, were the only two kids left in the family—a pair of infant twin brothers died in a house fire when their old man fell asleep smoking and their mother had also perished trying to save the boys. Their old man turned drunk and goofy after the tragedy. They moved into a flat near Gratiot, but his father had become violent against him and Garbis.

Sonny got out of the house first, learning the jewelry trade from the ground up. He started by hawking stones for Hasidic Jews who worked in Oak Park, a Jewish neighborhood just north of Detroit where gold, loose gems, and diamonds were sold. At sixteen he was a natural at it, and by the time he was twenty-two he'd stashed more than fifty grand in cash throughout the cellar of his grandmother's basement.

The Jews, sympathetic to his plight, took to him and taught him a true lesson regarding quality. "Everyone *loves* diamonds," they said, "but not everyone *appreciates* them." Sonny grew to despise selling the good stuff to those who couldn't truly appreciate what they had. He just didn't feel it was right for some dumb bastard to wear a stone whose worth he could not differentiate from a lesser one. Now looking out at so many of the clueless shoppers in his store, like the arrogant Mrs. Ruffalino trying on earrings—she didn't know an aquamarine from a blue topaz—he thought of his mentors' sage advice. He returned a wave from Pat Pizzaro. How many of the diamonds in the tennis bracelets he'd purchased for his wife and secretaries were worthy of his loutish personality? *Ignorance is bliss,* Sonny thought.

Regarding metallurgy, gold is pretty much gold, strictly sanctioned by way of its weight and karat stampings. Sonny didn't mess with it as the fake stuff was too easy to spot, mainly because it made people's skin turn green. Gemstones were a different story. Many of his stones were real quality cuts and beautiful in color, especially if you knew what to look for. Several of the diamonds, however, were nothing short of frozen snot; fuzzy stones full of inclusions, pockets of trapped gas, and loaded with more charcoal than a Hibachi. A decent stone passed off to look like a quality gem was called a "lumpy," as in lump of coal. And Sonny's thought was, if you didn't know better, you *never* knew better and you didn't *need* to know better. So when it came to the profit on diamonds, Sonny did real well. That's because Sonny knew diamonds. And most of his customers? Well, they didn't know shit.

The two men had just come from the harsh sunlight, entering the palpable darkness of The Golden Canary. Carmine and his main running buddy, Garbis, squinted as their eyes adjusted. As always, a crowd gathered quickly around Carmine. His voice had the quality of a baritone strained through a chainsaw. Now, as he bragged about a recent score, his hands gestured, and there were twinkling lights from a pinky ring that flickered, making the effect more entrancing.

"So this Kike, he says—get this—he says, 'I'm from *New York*' and Fat Rocco tells him, fuckin' Fat Rocco, he says, 'Oh yeah? I'm from *Detroit*.' That's beautiful. That smug Christ killer—bet your Dago ass he ain't ever heard *that* before. *Fuck.* Let him go back there, the Kike fuck," Carmine said to anyone who would listen, and that was everyone. Behind the bar, Al Nicoletti, the owner of the Canary, listened impassively.

"You use that word too much," Al said. "Makes you sound ignorant."

Everyone got quiet waiting for Carmine's response.

Carmine fixed a pained look on Al, and asked, "What, you mean *Kike*?"

Garbis threw his head back and laughed hard. Everyone else did, too. Al just shook his head and waved a hand at them.

Carmine "Sausages" Burmanzini straightened his hat. He made sure he always looked good. He was a clothes horse by anyone's definition, with a closet of more than thirty-five suits, forty pairs of shoes, and numerous hats, belts, pocket squares, you name it. But his weakness was jewelry. Carmine wore all types of gaudy baubles and bangles: stickpins, tie tacks, cufflinks, whatever suited his fancy. But his obsession for diamonds practically bordered on the feminine. He loved the stones more than he loved his kids, his friends, his wife—even his girlfriends. So it was no big surprise to anyone when he strutted into the Canary that Thursday afternoon in the late summer of '65 wearing a pinky ring with ice on it as big as an acorn.

He put his arm around Garbis Aravakian. Garbis worked as an auto supply trucker and fenced stolen goods as a second job. Carmine and him were tighter than an accountant's rosebud, ever since the two ransacked a Sunoco station when both men were just fifteen. After Garbis' old man posted his bail, he beat him senseless about the head, leaving a permanent knot below his hairline. Carmine found Garbis on his front lawn and moved him into the Burmanzinis' basement. At trial, Carmine took the rap for the crime. The judge didn't buy it—both did six months in juvie together—but Garbis never forgot the gesture.

The Canary was a brick letter T. And while architecturally it was nothing more than a rectangle with two ells for the restrooms, within its lithographed-wood paneled walls, the clientele felt as if they were in the palace of an aristocrat. A jukebox and a single pool table served as entertainment. A little kitchen behind the bar was home to a short order cook who prepared burgers, sandwiches, and soup. From time to time, businessmen stopped there for simple lunches, but mostly it was a place for the neighborhood guys to get away from the wives—and from the cops who weren't on the take. Men could meld into the background and get out of the daylight for a while. The owner kept it dark, and the patrons found comfort in it.

A ruddy-faced drunk at the end of the bar cried softly, moving his lips constantly, as if tasting a bland meal. He blew his nose into a dingy handkerchief, occasionally mumbling, barely above a whisper, "Why, why were you such a whore, Louisa?"

As if on an island, a diminutive, fifty-three-year-old businessman worked a crossword puzzle with an ink pen between bites of a club sandwich. Wearing black horn-rims, he marked up the paper workmanlike, oblivious to everything around him. He nursed a Drambuie and occasionally looked heavenward for answers.

Most of the regular crowd was there: Frank Mirabelli and two of his ten brothers; in the background were Rico Mancini, Cy Cirrico, Babe Bommarito and the usual clutch of wannabe wise guys who couldn't quite make the team—guys who just liked getting on them some of whatever lawlessness the hoods were wearing. Many among them had wives, girlfriends, or both, but none ever dared take either into the Canary. It would have been like bringing a movie camera to a bachelor party—it just wasn't done.

It took all of one minute being inside the bar to see that its upkeep, mood, and décor were the farthest things from Al Nicoletti's mind. The joint was so dark that, aside from the regulars, only a veal calf would have felt comfortable there. For music, a temperamental Wurlitzer sat against a wall. Al had it loaded with Sinatra, Martin, and Bennett, plus a handful of Julius LaRosa tunes thrown in for good measure—the Italian crooners being, according to Al, "the only guys who can sing worth a shit these days."

Al was one of only 334 men to survive the sinking of the *USS Arizona*. His face looked like someone had sculpted a handsome man from clay, then before firing the masterpiece, squashed it down with their fist, compacting the features by an inch or two. He'd forged his folks' signatures and had been on the ship as a wiry sixteen-year-old when the bombs hit. He'd swam through rooms of water, gulping air for hours—hours of liquid blackness with his mouth sucking any available oxygen from the three inches of airspace between the water filling the ship and the ceilings—bumping the bodies of comrades out of his way. And since the day he was rescued from that watery tomb, Al couldn't care less if anyone disagreed with his choice in music, or anything else for that matter.

Carmine earned his nickname from the massive size of his fingers, which were described in various colorful ways ranging from logs to stumps to pony cocks. But when Frank Mirabelli looked at them one day and remarked he'd like to throw Carmine's digits onto a griddle and fry them up with some eggs, "Sausages" stuck. Carmine was a thick man with a slow walk and a brooding stare. While not handsome in a classical sense, his presence commanded attention, and he attracted the wannabes like a cliff drew lemmings.

He loved mirrors and always dressed impeccably, even if it was to go unload a truck, or hang with the boys. His thought was, you never knew when a snazzy dame was going to drop onto your lap, so you better look good all the time. This credo didn't endear him to his wife, Dorothea, but since she'd grown as big as a house, he figured *too damn bad*. He would bang anything with tits and a pulse.

"Ladies, how's everyone doing?" Carmine bellowed, his voice sounding like it originated from an oak tunnel. "Al, set these ugly bastards up and get me a Manhattan—and lean on the son of a bitch for a change, will ya'?"

His left hand went into his pocket and reemerged with a wad of bills that looked as thick as half a sub sandwich, held together by two red rubber bands.

"Carm—*you? Rubber bands?*" Babe remarked.

"Hey, gotta find me a bigger money clip," he mumbled and the laughs followed.

As Carmine peeled off a fifty, the sole light hanging over the pool table danced on the rim of the big diamond set into his pinky ring. Skinkles of light flickered like pale white fireflies in the smoky bar, darting across the patrons' faces and shirts.

"*Maddon'!* Hey everybody, look: Carm robbed Liz Taylor," Frank Mirabelli hollered, letting out a wolf whistle as he grabbed Carmine's meat hook of a hand and inspected the pinky ring.

Carmine smiled, his eyes brimming with haughtiness. He glanced at the faces of the men, who clamored around from their scattered places in the bar, as much for their free drinks as to admire the mountainous diamond in the setting he wore on that pinky, which looked like a Vienna sausage covered with black hair.

"Just got it back from Sonny. Did he do a beautiful job or what? That's called a *floating* setting. The prongs are hidden, so the rock isn't messed up by all that fuckin' gold. Sonny—that guy's an *arteest*. Mike-fucking-angelo," Carmine gushed.

Garbis watched him showing the ring off, and his posture wasn't one of a man exuding pride for his brother, but of concern.

"You really like it, Carm? Sonny do a good job for you? Did he do good?"

"Did he? These *mamalukes* are gonna need sunglasses if they keep staring. It looks different now that I see it in the setting. Bigger, if that's possible. Fucking *arteest!*"

Carmine had scored the three-carat rock as his take in the aftermath robbery of an attempted shakedown of a Hasidic Jew near Eight Mile Road and Greenfield. The unlucky fellow, Janko Rosenvieg, a transplanted, stubborn jeweler from New York, had made the mistake of thinking he was special.

Janko's hope was to widen the berth of his father's expanding diamond business. His first month in town, he'd found the local jewelers in the area eager to buy the fine gems he offered, especially the clear diamonds he and his father had imported from South Africa. He'd even rented a little apartment nearby and was considering bringing his wife and their newborn son to join him.

One day, as Janko was closing a deal on a mess of sapphires with two gemologists, Hasidic Jews like himself, a short man exceeding 350 pounds came through his door, needing to turn sideways to enter. It was Fat Rocco Vozza. Rocco's three-chinned face was pocked with acne scars and carbuncles, and the marks creased into black pits as he smiled at Janko. Janko nodded hello and instinctively glanced at his display cases of loose stones. He stayed on Fat Rocco, eyeing him with skepticism. The two jewelers' faces went scared, and before Janko could stop them, they were at the door.

"Gentlemen, I thought we had a sale? These won't last long ... " he called out.

"We'll get back to you," the older of them yelled from the hallway.

Janko *hmmph'd* as the bell on the door jingled to a halt. He glared at the large Sicilian.

"Something I can show you, sir? A gift for a lady friend, perhaps?"

Fat Rocco said nothing, spinning a mobile of delicate paper doves Janko's wife had made him. Finally after a minute of silence he spoke.

"This is a dangerous business, especially here in Oak Park. The eggplant could rob you, or you could have an accident or something unfortunate. Got to be careful. Been a lot of robberies around this area, but not in this here strip, not yet anyway. Police can't protect you, that's a fact. So it's three hundred for now. That's what it is. Three hundred." He said it without rancor. "That's cheap."

"There are no solicitors allowed here friend. Did you not see the sign?" Janko admonished him, pointing to a sign taped to the door.

"I'm not your friend yet. Three hundred a month. That's the arrangement."

Fat Rocco pressed forward, a step closer to him. But Janko was used to the extortionists in New York who tried to put the arm on his people. Perhaps proprietors here rolled over too easily for these Detroit toughs.

"I've been warned. But guess what? *Forget it.* I'll pay you nothing. Leave my store and never return. Good day, now."

The fat man smiled. His eyes creased into black holes bordered by eyebrows zigzagged with fight scars that had ruined their symmetry.

"OK, Himey. That's the way you want to play. But I'm gonna tell you something once; you ain't from here, and *this* is the way it is. You'll still make your fucking money. Stinking Christ-killers, all the same, the whole lot of you. We're gonna make ours with or without you, see? You be careful."

"I don't scare easily. Understand, I'm from New York."

Janko's voice skipped, but he stared at Fat Rocco without flinching. Rocco walked a step back from the door, and put his hairy hands in his pockets. He looked down as if deep in thought, then cocked his head in amusement.

"New York, huh? Congratulations. I'm from Detroit."

The fat man laughed a little, then walked out of Janko's suite.

The next night Janko was locking up when a man wearing a ski mask, a man with huge fingers—that's all that Janko could recall when he came to—stuck the barrel of a revolver in his ear and walked him back up the stairs. Two men followed close behind.

"This is how we do it in Detroit," the man had told him.

The New York jeweler had no choice but to empty his safe and give the thugs what they wanted. The other two cleared out everything; his diamonds, his sapphires and a pile of emeralds, along with the one stone Janko hated losing more than any other: a single, nearly flawless, round diamond that he had buried in the middle of the emeralds.

"Please, at least leave me the emeralds," Janko begged.

The man with the gun laughed once before knocking Janko on the head. Janko didn't call the police. He also didn't pay. A week later he was back in New York.

Carmine was given first choice of any of the stones, and when he saw the size of the glimmering diamond nesting amongst those greenies, he was in love. It was cut in a classical round shape and looked like it possessed a soul, the light radiated so brilliantly from within. The thing was nearly colorless, which only added to its fire. The first call Carmine made was to Garbis. He wanted his friend to get his brother Sonny to work some of his magic.

Garbis watched Sonny examine the stone as they stood in his studio. He'd told him to really create something special for his best friend Carmine, the man he loved—if forced to admit—more so than him, his only brother. Gripping the big diamond with special tweezers, Sonny lifted his glasses and cupped a jeweler's loupe into his eye.

"Make me proud Sonny," Garbis said.

"You got it, kid. Brother, she's a *beaut.* Gotta be an E, maybe even a D in color. Look at the dazzle on it, Garbey! It's a hard VVS, maybe even a VVS1, a two at the worst … the cutlet's good—I mean spotless, got one little inclusion near the girdle, that's it, though. Man, and the *table!* The table on her is cleaner than an Amish girl's *hoo-haa.* Carmine really scored something here … oh yeah, she's every bit a VVS1."

Sonny looked up at his younger brother, the loupe still in his eye socket for effect.

"When I'm done with this, it'll be a masterpiece that showcases what God creates from his om-nip-O-tint artistry." He smiled, revealing a gold cap in the corner of his grin.

Garbis stared at Sonny for a full second with souring eyes.

"Just make it look fucking *good,* OK Sonny? Forget all the flowery jewelry talk—the table, the stinking cutlet, the girdle—save that shit for the broads. Just make it look good, you hear me? This is *Carmine* I'm talking about."

"Sure, OK." Sonny's smile faltered a bit. "You got it, Garbey."

"And no *funny business,* Sonny, I mean it. It's for Carmine."

Sonny stared at Garbis, and seeing his look, he nodded repeatedly.

"OK, Garbey, I know. I know what he means to you. Sure, don't worry. It'll be *magical.*"

Garbis nodded at Sonny.

"I know it will, Son, I know. It's just that, it's for Carmine." He smiled. "I know you'll do a bang-up job." He reached out and touched Sonny's cheek. "Call me when it's ready, brother."

"Sure thing, Garbey." Sonny watched Garbis smile at the cute, big-busted saleswoman he'd just hired and followed him with his eyes as he left the store.

For all the bullshit he talked, Sonny had a great eye for his craft. He appreciated diamonds, and he knew them very well. Diamonds had afforded him many of life's finer things: expertly dyed black hair, a new Cadillac every two years, his Florida condo in Lemon Bay, and recently, his own personal golf cart at the Bella Fiore Country Club in the northern Detroit county of Macomb.

Then there were the ladies.

A notorious bachelor, Sonny was often able to nail just about any wayward housewife or divorcee he wanted for little more than giving her an upgrade on a stone—for no charge of course. That is, if she took the bait. And taking the bait was usually confirmed by accepting his offer of "a closer look." A *closer look* entailed peeking through a jeweler's loupe for a magnified view. That sounds benign enough, but to look through a jeweler's loupe with any kind of knowledge demands guidance by a trained eye, which for Sonny, required standing *very closely* behind the woman.

He would press himself gently into the lady, his arm lightly touching hers as he held her steady to inspect the stone in question. He'd compliment her perfume, the feel of her skin, and depending on the lady's reaction, he could measure how receptive she was. But it was the look she gave him after *the look* that told him if he was in. They brushed their hair aside, lowered their head and stared. Then all he had to do was seal the deal.

He would set up a lunch meeting at his favorite soul food restaurant in Detroit, conveniently located near the King Hotel, so as to deliver the article in person, but off-site. There was always good jazz flowing, and if the lunch went well—and it usually did—it was a quick jaunt up the back stairs of the King to room 23, for which Sonny had his own key. He'd bartered unlimited use of the room with the manager, Liam Callahan, an Irishman with a weakness for crucifixes and bracelets, the only caveat being Liam needed a minimum one-hour heads-up in case relocating a "tenant" was necessary. Tenants of the King consisted of heroin addicts, traveling salesmen, and high-priced hookers. The hookers were set up in rooms by their regular johns, mostly executives of The Big Three who called Liam at odd hours of the night to satisfy their predilections.

Outside on the floor at Aravakian's Gallery, as salespeople flitted about, showing religious pendants to widows and engagement rings to potential grooms, Sonny fretted. *Why must Garbis have to be so serious all the time?* he thought. He massaged his tired eyes, and looked through the doorway that led to the displays. There stood Mary Ellen Nardoni, looking at an opal-encrusted brooch. She caught him staring and blushed, giving him a little wave. He smiled and closed his eyes. She was only thirty-two, and being more than twenty years her senior, he'd never expected to have a chance. Mary Ellen loved opals. So throwing in a matching pendant on a pair of earrings had proved to be the icebreaker.

She was a lot younger than the ladies he was used to. At fifty-three, Sonny didn't trust his pecker to respond the way it once had, a sad fact most of the women nearer his own age understood. The only spoiler in the memory of their tryst was that Mary Ellen stuffed her bra. He did his best to hide his disappointment as he pulled two foam falsies from the confines of her black silk brassiere. But opals were a dime a dozen, and she was a real firecracker.

Sonny put the loupe back to his eye. Looking through it, he could see again the fire that radiated within the diamond Carmine had looted. It was truly breathtaking. His mind drifted immediately to the only other thing of beauty that could steal his breath away: Gina Bertuzzi. And as hard as he tried to drive away the vision of the full-figured, dark, buxom beauty, he simply could not. Gina would be coming in Tuesday to discuss the upgrade on a ring her husband, Otto, had given her to commemorate their twentieth wedding anniversary.

Otto Bertuzzi, fifteen years older than Gina, commissioned Sonny to make the ring, telling him to go on the cheap. Otto was a stingy, old school Wop from Palermo who still had his communion money. Sonny always felt a woman like Gina deserved something much more befitting her ample gifts than the ring that smelly old Dago had him make. Over the years, she had talked to Sonny about resetting the ring, believing that her long fingers dwarfed it. She was a tall, large woman who felt she could pull off a bigger diamond with a more dynamic setting. While the original stone Sonny had put in the ring was a decent size—a round two-carat number—it was a shade yellow and loaded with flaws. He told her maybe one day down the road, they could work something out for an upgrade.

That day had come last week. And now her anniversary ring sat next to his vise.

Gina had patronized the store on and off for years, and she always accepted Sonny's shameless flirtations with a welcome smile or a touch on the arm. She'd been a fashion model before her kids were born and was still stunning. She'd grown an ass, but Gina possessed Sonny's absolute enough-to-make-him-weak-in-the-knees-feature on a woman—an exceptionally large bustline. How Sonny loved his "sweater meat," as he fondly referred to it. It took something beyond a full D-cup to really make him crow. And Gina had a chest that made Jayne Mansfield look like Mia Farrow.

Occasionally she'd wear a loose-fitting top, so Sonny always made a point of showing her the cocktail rings in the lower cases, necessitating that she bend down, affording him open glimpses of her loaf-sized gifts. He wanted to squeeze them in the worst way, and he knew that *she knew*. Despite her great beauty and the fact that she was married, lately she'd started giving him a *kind of look*, especially when he asked her how Otto was doing.

Presently, Sonny picked up Carmine's stone with his tweezers, taking another glance at the diamond's table, the inner center of the largest facet, where all the fire and magic originated.

"Look at you ... so beautiful, so pure, so *perfect,*" he whispered to it.

There was only one tiny inclusion—barely noticeable—off near the girdle, a tertiary angle to the side of the cut, some trapped gas perhaps, located far from the interior of the diamond. The gem was as close to flawless as Sonny had ever seen. He looked over at a small array of gold ring settings, any of which were ready for Carmine's thick, size 13 pinky. Sonny eschewed the 10-karat settings, instead opting for several cast in 14-karat, a brighter gold. He finally settled on a wide band with an open back, a floating setting that allowed light to enter from all sides. Carmine's ring would shine like a beacon. And Garbis would be proud.

An image of Gina flashed in Sonny's mind, nothing more than a snapshot, of her unclothed, sultry, and milky-skinned. He blinked it away, but as he looked down at Carmine's fiery diamond, he sighed resignedly as a piece of the fantasy remained.

Carmine was a pain in the ass when it came to his boasts. No one had screwed more broads, and no one's dick was bigger, and no one could drink more, and blah, blah, blah, but everyone loved him just the same. He was a load of fun, and truly, in a fight or doing a job, there was no one you wanted watching your back more than him. One true story had him fighting his way out of The Dizzy Duck, an all-black pool hall on the corner of Westmoreland and Cass, with nothing but a broken cue stick, the whole time bleeding from his abdomen.

It all started when Carmine—then thirty-five and two weeks before his wedding—tried to pay only half what he owed to Lester Moorehouse, a big black pimp, for *services rendered* that Carmine found completely unsatisfying. "That snaggletooth *puttana* of yours dented my hammer," he'd complained. Later in the retelling, Carmine would say, *"I'll take thirty-six stitches in the gut over a dirt nap anytime."*

After a half-hour of watching Carmine play eight ball with an old timer, Lester finally approached him. Lester swiped the cue ball and suggested that based on the soulful clientele of The Dizzy Duck, and the fact that Carmine had not only gotten his nut off but was the only "Dago Guinea" in the vicinity, maybe he should reconsider the amount of his debt and just pay the whole twenty bucks. Lester's bodyguard laughed.

They didn't know Carmine.

Carmine smiled at Lester, disarming the men in the act of setting his stick down, so as to get out his wallet. In one quick motion, he broke the stick over the head of Lester's associate, then poked Lester in his sizable gut with what was left of the cue. He followed that up with quick whacks to each side of the pimp's honeydew-sized dome, looking like a man swatting at flies. Carmine thought he was home free, until he realized Lester—not nearly as fazed by the knocks to the head as he had anticipated—stuck a metal file deep into Carmine's side, just missing his kidney.

"Guinea mofo—you leaving here in a roll of carpet time I'm done with your eye-*tallian* ass," Lester said.

Knowing only survival, Carmine grabbed Lester's balls right through his sharkskin pants and squeezed until he got his attention, which was immediate.

"Let go the shiv, you big *melanzana*," he told Lester, squeezing just enough. Lester complied.

"C'mon. Let's dance you and me," Carmine grimaced.

He walked Lester toward the front door, holding him by his crotch the whole time. The file stuck out of Carmine's side, throbbing with each step he took, but preventing his guts from spilling out. He swiped at the patrons trying to stop him with cue sticks and saps, deflecting their weapons with the half-a-cue. He shrugged off their attacks like a bear being driven from a kill, gripping Lester's *stugots* harder each time they tried to block his escape.

"Tell your fellow eggplant to back off or you'll be a eunuch," Carmine warned.

"*Back off, motherfuckers!*" Lester screamed in agony.

Carmine got to the front door and let go, leaving the pimp squirming in a crumpled sharkskin heap at the bar's entrance.

That was the kind of man Carmine was. And he let everyone know about it. You only had to ask once and he'd show you the scar. Of course, over time the tale expanded. In the retelling, there had been, *"Fifty spades in the joint,"* and Lester was, *"Six-nine and four spins."* The shiv transformed into, *"One of them paratrooper knives."* The payoff to the story was a now Bacchanal sex act, described as, *"A Carmine sandwich: me, two colored broads, and this wetback midget with a pair of juggies you could set your beer on."* They always begged to hear it again.

Everyone embellished their stories, but Carmine had a gift for it. The men's boasts were all rooted in seeds of truth, and perhaps that was why they loved hearing the same tales over and over again—to remind them of their own growing legacies.

Garbis leaned on his hip, his right arm draped around Frank Mirabelli's neck. He stood a mere ten feet from Carmine. He was delighted at the response Carmine's ring was receiving. The crowd wouldn't stop talking about it as he showed off the gaudy stone, wiggling his hairy pinky.

"That's a rock, Carm. *Minchia*, look at the shine on that, will ya? Like it's on fire," one onlooker commented.

"Looks like a damn crystal walnut," Al Nicoletti mused.

Carmine grinned at that, taking great joy in dancing the light onto the faces of the other men who sat at the bar. The sparkling distracted the little businessman. He ignored his half-eaten club sandwich and put aside his crossword to stare at Carmine. The little man squinted through his horn-rims as Carmine let the prism skip off the man's retinas. The man smiled and Carmine threw him his hardest look. Still he continued to stare back.

"Sun in your eyes my little friend?" Carmine asked.

"I'm from Flint, just passing through—heading to Ohio. I couldn't help but notice your ring. That's a rather large stone," the little man remarked.

"Three full carats of what they call a VVS1, my friend."

The elfin man grinned and nodded his head slightly.

"Did you say a *VVS1?* That's highly unusual for a stone of that size, especially for a pinky ring. Very rare—expensive."

"You're a smart man. A fucking Alice Einstein."

The rest of the group chuckled while they sucked down their free 7 & 7s.

"May I?" the little man asked, his petite hands held palms up in question.

"What for, you wanna buy it?" Carmine quipped.

"I dabble in diamonds," the man admitted.

Carmine looked at Garbis. "Believe the stones on this guy?"

Garbis nodded, smiling at his *paisan.* "Go on, Carm, humor him," he replied. "Show him the masterpiece my Sonny created for you."

Carmine mugged and put his hand out. "Be my guest," he said.

The little man made no effort to accept Carmine's enormous hand. Instead, he produced a jeweler's loupe from the breast pocket of his suit coat.

"Would you mind removing it?" he asked.

He took off his horn-rims and stuck the loupe mindlessly in his left eye-socket. Carmine found the comfort in which he wore the loupe unsettling. Garbis' face went pale as well, and he stepped closer, his arm still around Frank Mirabelli's neck.

"OK, yeah," Carmine said, struggling to pry the ring from his fat pinky. He gave it to the man, who felt the weight of the ring. He smiled, nodding at Carmine.

"Nice setting. Fourteen-karat, that's good—bright. Bright gold for a bright stone."

"You could tell it was fourteen without seeing the stamp?" Garbis asked, but the little man didn't answer. He was all business.

Carmine's head bobbed and weaved. He watched the man examine his ring.

He held it up to the dim light, rotating the ring this way and that. He frowned once, *harrumphed* and *tsked* several times. With each dismissive sound Garbis and

Carmine traded looks. The other men huddled around, too. Garbis took his arm off Frank's neck, and pushed through the small crowd, stationing himself next to Carmine.

"Very nice color … hmmm … very pale, very *nice* … " that made Carmine smile broadly, his dark eyes playing to the crowd.

"Yeah, you already mentioned the color," Garbis said.

The little man finished his appraisal, holding the ring out to Carmine.

"Very nice indeed … for a *faux gaz*," the little man said.

Carmine's smile faded to a thin sneer.

"Fawww gazz—you mean a *fugazi!*" Garbis said, pronouncing it, *phew gay-zee*.

"A lumpy!" Carmine interrupted. "You saying this is a *lumpy?*" He snatched the ring back from the man and forced it onto his finger. "*Lumpy!* What the fuck—you're a funny little man."

"No, not really. I just know diamonds. *Faux gaz* is French slang for a bad diamond. Means, um, trapped gas, like gas inclusions. It's still a *nice* stone. There are other colorful sobriquets for it … snot, zirc. Lumpy," the little man smiled, chewing on it. "I've heard that one, too. Whatever jargon you prefer, it's the best one I've ever seen."

"*Lumpy*," Carmine muttered. The crease between his eyes grew deep enough to stick a quarter into.

"Easy, Carm," Al said from behind the bar.

"Easy *my ass!* This little frog just called my rock a fucking *lumpy!*" He waved his pinky at the men. "This look like a lumpy to any of you? Well? Does it?"

There were murmurs from the small crowd. The little man shrugged and returned the loupe to his pocket. He put on his thick horn-rim glasses and shrunk back to his crossword puzzle, as if the exchange between Carmine and him had never occurred.

Al laughed and fussed with the reception of the fuzzy picture on the black and white set, twisting the rabbit ears into a tangled wire sculpture.

Carmine sneered at Al while taking Garbis by the forearm. He walked with him a few steps, still clearly pissed at the besmirching of his gem. The clan of wannabes and hangers-on quietly took their free drinks to the other side of the bar, avoiding Carmine's wrath.

"Believe that little turd? I'll give *him* trapped gas. The fuck does he know, huh? Lumpy. No self-respecting Kike would hide a lumpy in a sack of greenies—am I right?"

"Right as rain. That little munchkin's just trying to get over on you, Carm."

"I mean, you heard Sonny—all that VVS1 talk when we picked it up. I mean, 'the fire, the clarity,' he babbled on and on. Wouldn't *stop* babbling."

"No. He wouldn't." Garbis shook his head. "Besides, Jews don't sell lumpies."

Carmine looked closely at his friend. "That's what I just *said* ... "

"Right." Garbis stared vacantly at the ring. "Carm, I got to run some bets over to Joe and his brothers then swing by Vicarro's to move a couple hundred cartons of smokes. I'll pick you up on my way there. And *oh!* Mirabelli just tipped me off on six cases of scotch he pilfed from O'Hara's Pub. Said they're mine for ten bucks a case—Dewars and Glenlivet. You want in?"

"Glenlivet?" Carmine said, his rancor gone for the moment.

"Take a ride. C'mon, come with me."

Carmine looked at the back of the little man, who continued eating his remaining club sandwich. He thrust his large hands into his pockets.

"Count me in. I love that Glenlivet—shit's like mother's milk." He shrugged. "Think I'll hang around these goons 'til you get back. Take your time."

Garbis tapped him on the shoulder and grabbed his coat.

"OK, 'bout an hour, Carm." He waved at the group and walked out. "Bya' boys."

Frank Mirabelli approached Carmine. He cleared his throat and smiled.

"Still a helluva rock, Carm," he said, placing his arm around Carmine.

"Goddamn right it is!" Carmine shoved Frank away. "Little fart. What's he know?"

Frank put up his hands. Carmine bumped past him and leaned on the corner of the bar, watching the little man eat. Al set a fresh Manhattan down in front of him. Carmine stared at the faded blue anchor tattooed on Al's forearm. Al felt it and looked at him. He whipped a bar towel over his shoulder and leaned forward.

"He's all of five nothin', Carm. Leave him be. I mean it."

Carmine took his drink and smirked a scrunched-nosed face at Al. The little man nibbled the last bite of crust and pressed a wet finger onto the plate, gathering up leftover crumbs. When he'd collected them all, he put his finger in his mouth and ate them.

Carmine was on his third Manhattan. A half-hour had passed since Garbis left. The little man finally got up and stretched his legs. He twisted side-to-side and passed behind Carmine, heading to the back of the bar, toward the restrooms. Carmine saw Al was listening to the Mirabelli brothers' take on Vietnam. He got up and left his drink.

Sonny stirred the ice in his second highball, scanning the black faces that peppered the tables and walls of Back Alley Sally's Soul Food and Jazz Club. Near Washington Boulevard, Sally's was tucked in the alleyway behind the King Hotel. It was a rough area, and white patrons were few and far between, but those who entered were welcomed as lovers of both jazz and home-cooked cuisine, the way it was made in the real South. Sally Forster owned the place. She was a fifty-eight-year-old widow with a face that lost a fight with an ugly stick, but in the kitchen she was beautiful. Sally's recipes came from her girlhood home in Tuscumbia, Alabama, and her dishes made men cry, thinking of their own mothers' cooking. The music and food was so appealing that, despite the neighborhood, getting a seat there for lunch was no easy task.

Below a layer of smoke, a sinewy man blowing into a dented cornet stood alone on the small stage, playing a hybrid Nat Adderley/Chet Baker tune, free-styling his way around it until it dissipated into his own poem. A few whoops rose from the tables as he modulated his playing. The door opened and white light flooded in. Sonny straightened when he saw Gina Bertuzzi standing there, her silhouette freeze-framed in the sunlight before the door closed. Three men checked her out and one—the unofficial bouncer—nudged his pal, pointing at her with the tip of a longneck Stroh's, shouting, "Hot *dammm!*" Gina looked around, her purse clutched tightly to her ample chest. Wearing a blue sundress, with the light hitting her high cheekbones, she could have been Sophia Loren's twin.

Sonny took a deep breath and put on his best smile. He waved her over, and there was relief on her face upon seeing him.

"Did you have any trouble finding it?" Sonny asked, rising to come around the table and pull out her chair. She smiled and sat down; he nudged her chair in, taking the opportunity to look down over the top of her head.

"I missed the exit, but then I figured it out. So *tucked away*. Parking was tough. Kind of scary down here," Gina said. She adjusted a blue knit shawl over her bosom.

"Do you like jazz?" Sonny asked.

"What I know of it."

A large black man stood against a wall directly behind Sonny. He smiled at Gina with a mouthful of brown teeth, his eyes hidden by wraparound Ray Bans. She smiled nervously before averting her eyes. Sonny raised a hand and a waitress appeared. She had a strong face but looked too young to be working in a bar.

"Drink ma'am?" the waitress asked Gina. She winked at Sonny. "'Nuther beauty, huh, Rooster?"

Gina squinted at Sonny.

He laughed and whispered to her, *"Just a nickname, it's nothing."*

Gina bit her lip. "I'll have a Tom Collins, I guess. I don't drink this early ... "

"Right back," the waitress sniffed. She reappeared with Gina's drink and a fresh highball for Sonny. They clinked glasses.

"Wooo ... *strong*." Gina said, tasting it.

Sonny put his highball down. "Behold," he said.

His hands were out in front of him, his slender fingers, the nails manicured and buffed, presenting a maroon velvet ring-box. Gina smiled, her eyes sparkling and crinkling. He took in her milky skin, distracted by the way her chest rested on the tabletop.

"I want you to close your eyes."

"You're sure it's OK?" She glanced around. "In here I mean."

"This place is as safe as Switzerland."

"Oh, I can't wait!" she clapped. "I've been thinking about it since we talked."

"Wait no more. Behold, Gina," he said, opening the box. "OK, open."

She did, and immediately her hand went to her mouth. A gasp escaped her full painted lips. She looked from the ring to Sonny. He nodded yes, and she reached for it, her hand trembling as she removed it from the box. Holding it an inch above, the contrast was breathtaking. The center stone that Sonny had replaced her original with was far brighter, almost alive with light. The stone created a firestorm of imperceptible color, a brilliance of pale spectral beams that it harnessed from the available light in the room, holding it captive for its own dispersal.

"*Oh* Sonny, *oh* it's so ... " she couldn't say much more than that. She cried softly, her head shaking side-to-side, her eyes not leaving the stone.

"I told you it would be something. I reset the surrounding stones, too, but that bugger in the center, that's a rare one ... " He leaned in, "Just like the woman who wears it."

She looked up a moment. "Sonny, it's beautiful," then lowered her eyes. "How much more is this going to be than what Otto allowed me? Sonny, if I come back with a lot missing from the savings, he'll ... " Gina's thick brows pulled upward.

"Let me ask you; what kind of man would I be if I were to put you in such a position? It's my gift to you. You're a beautiful woman, Gina—majestic. And beauty like yours should be celebrated."

Sonny let the smile hang on his face long enough for the light to hit his gold cap. She stared at him, and he saw the gratitude, and he looked only at her face, using all of his countenance to not let his eyes drift to her chest. Not yet.

"That's so generous of you."

She put her hand on his. He looked at it like it was the hand of a queen, and took the ring from her grasp and slipped it on her finger. She admired it a moment and they said nothing, the sound of the cornet filling in the silence.

"Have you eaten? Stay awhile," he said, hoping she'd let the shawl unveil what lurked beneath. She smiled and reached for her drink.

"I wouldn't mind a little something, 'specially if I'm drinking." Then she fidgeted and asked him, "Is it hot in here?"

"Boiling," he replied.

She removed her shawl and there was no way to hide his happiness, so he didn't bother. She tilted her head and looked at him, lowering her face to see him directly.

"You OK, Sonny?"

His face picked up. That simple blue sundress, made of a modest, thin cotton, may as well have been a Bob Mackie original; she looked unbelievably sexy in it. Her dark, thick hair fell just to her shoulders, and her luminous alabaster skin glowed against the pale blue material. His hand dropped and he pressed down on his swelling erection and an image of her bouncing naked flashed in his addled brain.

"Huh? Yeah, I'm just … Gina, look around you. The men can't stop staring, all of 'em; white, the blacks—even *the broads* are looking. God broke the mold I tell you when He created you. Your Otto must worship the ground you walk on."

Gina flinched and her mouth shook up and down and her eyes shut. She only blinked twice before they squirted tears like a burst pipe.

"What's wrong Gina, what is it?"

She reached across and put her hand over Sonny's mouth, collecting herself before leaning forward. Without moving her face, she looked around then stared at the center of her ring, her hand still touching his lips. He was *that close* to heaven.

"Is there anywhere nearby, where we could go? Maybe just to, I don't know, be alone? Is there Sonny? Please tell me there is or I don't know … "

She kept her eyes on the ring, brushed aside her hair, before finally looking up, her wet eyelashes forming star points. And there it was.

Sonny's hand shot up. "I'll get the check," he said.

Inside the men's room at the Canary, Carmine saw the two empty urinals. Under the lone stall, a pair of little feet dangled—looking not unlike a schoolboy's—barely touching the floor, the pants draped over oxblood wingtips. He found a plunger from under the sink and shoved the wooden handle through the brass pull of the entry door. He lipped a Winston and sparked his lighter, putting the flame to the tip. The smell of the smoke and the fluid was strong. Looking at the clear lighter, he watched a pair of tiny red dice within the fluid sink slowly to the bottom, all the while listening to the little man grunting as he moved his bowels.

A couple of times, someone tried to enter, but Carmine ignored the sound of the door being pulled and the cussing that came from the other side of it.

The toilet flushed and the little man exited the stall whistling. He turned on the hot water at the sink and soaped up thoroughly, being fastidious with his fingernails before rinsing the suds off his little hands. As he turned, he saw Carmine leaning against the door.

"Everything come out all right?"

The little man jerked back.

"Please don't hurt me. I didn't mean to offend you," he said quietly. His leg started shaking and he tried to brace it with his damp hands.

His honesty caught Carmine off guard.

"*Easy.* I'm not gonna hurt you, friend. I been thinking though … why'd you call this a lumpy? This is a piece of ice like I never seen—and I know a little about ice."

Paper towels were stacked on the sink. Carmine handed the man a few. The little man dried off. He quickly went into his breast pocket, but Carmine grabbed his wrist.

"My loupe," he said, wincing.

"Right. The fucking loupe," Carmine nodded, relaxing his grip.

The little man took the loupe out and offered it. Carmine hesitated, then shoved it onto his right eye. He removed his pinky ring and gave it to the little man.

"Relax your eye. I'm going to place the stone underneath, and you tell me when it appears focused in, OK?" The little man steadied the ring under the loupe, and Carmine took the man's hand in his. He moved the man's little hand like a lazy trombone player, finally stopping it about an inch from the lens.

"OK, I can see crystals and stuff," Carmine said.

"Good. Now, the color on this stone is very nice, it's very pale, unusual for such a flawed piece."

Carmine peeked, frowning upon hearing the offending word.

"Sorry. The main part of a gem is the table. It's the largest area of the diamond and lets it produce the fire from inside out. If there's any inclusions, or flaws, on the table, the stone loses half its value right off the bat. A VVS quality stone usually is allowed a couple of small inclusions near the *cutlet* or the *girdle*—that's off to the sides—but *never directly on* the table. Now I'm embarrassed to tell you—what I mean is, *I'm sure* you can see it for yourself—but take a look; see that blackish line running through the table? Can't miss it, right? It should look like a piece of pencil lead … "

Carmine didn't need to study the area too hard. Literally, a piece of black charcoal, which magnified ten times looked like a train track crossing a snowy field, ran right across the area the little man described.

"I'll kill that no good Armenian son of a bitch … " Carmine said softly.

"That's why it's a *faux*—I mean, a *lumpy*. It's a tremendous one, too. There's enough colorless in it that it produces real fire, but it's best suited for more of a cocktail ring, something more playful—where it can hide. I'm very sorry to have even mentioned it. The average person would never know," the little man sighed. "Should've kept my big mouth shut."

"Sorry *my ass*. Come on." He returned the loupe to him.

Carmine wrested the plunger from the door handle. The door swung away and Cy Cirrico ran past.

"Dammit, Carm, ready to piss myself!" Cy blurted, shamelessly pulling his dick out as he ran. He corralled it and pointed at the sink. His mouth formed a look of ecstasy as he relieved himself there. Carmine barely snickered.

"He's peeing in the *sink*," the little man remarked.

Carmine walked him from the bathroom back to the bar.

Carmine leaned against the front door of the Canary, waiting for Garbis. He lit a cigarette. The day had stayed bright, but the wind had picked up. He looked down at the stone, watching the sun catch it. *That fucking Sonny,* he thought. A rainbow cast itself from the stone, shining onto the brick wall of the bar before clouds passed over, dulling its brilliance.

The stone looked like he remembered. It still sparkled just as much, didn't it? Now he wasn't sure. The news from the little man was akin to parking a new car at the store, and upon returning finding a scratch—a small ding on the door. The car still drives great; still looks beautiful; but you can't stop thinking about that little imperfection.

A couple of short honks took Carmine's attention away from the ring, and he saw his friend's Lincoln pull up to the curb. He took a long drag from his smoke and tossed it to the street.

"Hey-hey Carm, you ready?" Garbis asked, his eyes still on the traffic as Carmine settled his wide frame into the Lincoln's roomy front seat.

"Oh yeah," Carmine said. "I'm ready all right."

He didn't hold Garbis responsible for any of it, but he wasn't feeling very warm toward him either. Garbis pulled out into traffic. He immediately put a hand on Carmine's forearm as a squad car pulled alongside them. The cop glanced their way and stared. He was maybe thirty, clean-cut, blond and looked as out of place as a maggot in a bowl of black pearls.

"Stay cool a minute, Carm. I'm holding and I don't know him. Think he's new."

Garbis pulled ahead then swore, seeing the light cycle to red. He stopped and as the squad car came alongside him, the cop looked over. Garbis stared ahead, then casually glanced, grinning at the cop with just the right aplomb. Suddenly the flashers of the patrol car went on, and Garbis' heart skipped. Carmine on the other hand, did nothing but stare at his pinky, the beautiful lumpy twinkling in the partial sunlight.

As the cop sped off through the intersection, Garbis pounded the dash.

"Thought we were gonna get run. And me, holding my Beretta. I'd a been screwed, glued, and tat ... "

Then for the first time since Carmine had gotten in, Garbis looked at him. Carmine was still staring at his pinky, examining the ring. " ... Jesus, what is it, Carm?"

He removed the ring and held it out in the space between them. He never looked at Garbis, but now he didn't have to.

"Leopard don't change *its spots*. You take care of it. I see him, I may just fucking kill him." That was all Carmine said.

Garbis stared at the thick-knuckled fingers holding the ring. His eyes became black blades, and in his head, he cussed his brother's name over and over.

Room 23 of the King Hotel smelled of mothballs and Lysol. Sonny sat naked on the edge of the bed, wearing only his glasses and stretchy black, gold-toe stockings pulled just below the knee. He stared at the bathroom door. Behind him, a painting hung over the headboard—sweeping brushstrokes in crimson and gold—of a matador in a flowing red cape taunting a badly painted bull. Next to him in the space between the wall and the bed sat a radio under a desk light on the nightstand. He could hear the hum of traffic from nearby I-94, and he let his thoughts get lost in the drone of it. The doorknob clicked, and Gina emerged from the bathroom wearing Sonny's rose-colored, ill-fitting print silk shirt. She stood before him, a towering vision.

"Let me see 'em again Gina!" he said.

"Sonny, you're bad ... "

He opened the front of the shirt and exposed her breasts; so pale they looked as if they had never seen the light of day. Faint blue veins mapped just below the surface, and he reached for the pink thimbles in their centers. Gina let out a soft moan. Sonny hefted each one, and placed his head under them. Despite their size, they sagged only slightly from age and child rearing. He felt each one's weight as he let it drop, coming to rest on his head. Enveloping him to the neck, the pair swallowed him in a deep, crimson darkness.

Within the safety of her bosom, Sonny enjoyed the feeling of heat radiating from her, bathing his balding head like a hat made of sunshine. He moved his hands from them and grabbed the hammish cheeks of her bottom, massaging them and pressing himself against her. He felt things go turgid, and he thanked God for the ability to achieve his second erection of the afternoon so quickly.

He sat there like that a long time, and if someone had happened upon the scene, it would appear Gina's mountainous peaks were giving birth to the body of a headless, full-grown man who'd grown so tired by the birthing process, he'd decided to have a seat.

"Sonny this is *so* bad," Gina purred. Swaying ever so slightly, she reached down and helped him along.

"Oh baby, I'm feeling it now. I think I'm ready to go again, baby," his voice, though muffled from the flesh quilt he was buried under, rose in volume.

"Twice in one hour. Oh Sonny … "

He removed his head from beneath her and pulled her back with him. He lay backward on the pillows and she mounted him, the whole time her pendulous breasts swinging to and fro, hitting him in the face and smearing the lenses of his glasses with their oiliness. She rode him that way for a small time, her swinging chest inadvertently slapping his face, until his eyeglasses flew off from the force, causing both to giggle shamelessly. He heard the glasses hit the wall and slide down, landing next to the bed.

She leaned forward and pressed her palms over the headboard, against each side of the matador painting. Gina admired the beautiful new center diamond in her ring. She felt his hands find her bosom again, kneading each like a baker does stubborn dough, and it felt good for her to not be getting jarred from behind or thrown on her back, the way Otto had insisted on doing it since their kids had been born. It was as though she was nothing but warm, moist friction to him after providing him with his bloodline.

Otto treated her like shit. Their sex life had been reduced to him coming home late, tanked on *grappa*, knocking her around a little, then jamming himself into her. A minute later he would kiss the top of her head, slap her ass and fall asleep, turning into a snoring, hirsute gasbag.

In over twenty years, the only orgasm Otto Bertuzzi ever delivered to his wife came from a second-hand Whirlpool washing machine that needed balancing. He had it sent to the house on Mother's Day, a year after their youngest was born. Since their last child, Gina spent a lot of time on that washer, sitting just right, letting the wave of "Heavy Load" take her places Otto never could, closing her eyes and imagining handsome men, men who worshipped her—the way Otto once had—*making love* to her. But now, straddling Sonny, a real, live, breathing *man* who seemed interested in her pleasure, and who found her beautiful—saw her inner beauty, looking past what age had done to her body—this was the best thing she had felt since.

When they were done, Sonny breathed hard, feeling the weight of Gina's naked body on top of him. He looked up at her, squinting without his glasses, and from his point of view, she was an eight-foot tall ivory statue of some goddess, the bottoms of her breasts like bleached casks of honey shaded in a cool blue light.

"When the Lord passed out sweater meat, he must've let you come back for thirds, Gina. God you're beautiful," he said, unable to help himself from using the euphemism.

She laughed, and gently rolled off, leaning on her side to lie next to him. Gina kissed his forehead and rubbed his sweating temples. Sonny's black stockings were still pulled high, the gold toes pointing at the ceiling. Suddenly ashamed of his nakedness, he put his hands over his privates. She pretended not to notice and kissed him again.

"This was wonderful, but *so bad*. You satisfied me twice, Sonny." Her face grew wistful, and she traced a light circle around his nipple with a red fingernail.

"We can't do this ever again, Sonny. If Otto found out, he'd kill me. But you? You'd just wish he'd kill you. There's something I want you to know though; what you made me feel was better than what Otto ever could." She kissed him, and he nearly cried for her compliment. "I love my ring. The stone is so much sparklier. You have the soul of an artist, Sonny. A part of you will always be with me. Whenever I look at it I'm going to think of you."

"Ah, you deserve it baby. Perfection deserves perfection."

She smiled and rose up, standing at the edge of the bed. He sprang forward, grabbing her breasts one more time. She giggled, and allowed him to fondle them. He knelt there, intermittently regarding each one like a nursing child, and she let him continue for some time.

"So lovely … " he mumbled between nibbles.

She cradled his head. "I have to shower, but you take all the time you need, sweetheart." He stayed there for a full five minutes, suckling like a newborn piglet. When she finally freed herself from his wanting mouth, the centers looked like they'd spent the day soaking in mixing bowls of Hawaiian Punch. She peered down at them and laughed, giving him a mocking look of anger, and wagged a finger at him.

"So perfect," he shrugged, his face sheepish. "I could spend a *week* in there."

He leaned across the bed, his forehead hitting the wall as he searched blindly around the floor for his glasses. Gina watched his bony, white ass, his hairless scrotum hanging down like a pair of ping-pong balls. She sighed, and gathered her undergarments from the room's lone chair and then walked into the bathroom. She closed the door behind her but left it unlocked.

He spit on his glasses and used the bed sheets to wipe them. Sonny lay back down on the bed and smiled a satisfied smile. He heard the water of the shower trickle, then spray full on. Gina started singing in Italian, a folk song of a lover lost at sea. He whispered, "My Gina," hearing her voice, thinking how she must feel when a loveless thug like Otto was on top of her.

He felt sleepy. Sonny reached over and turned on the radio. He closed his eyes and remembered the image of her breasts, swaying above him, their weight and the fire they emitted. How safe that place felt. After a time, Sinatra crackled to life, one of his favorite songs, too. He hummed along, softly starting to sing with his eyes shut:

"I've got you under my skin...

I'd sacrifice anything come what might
For the sake of having you near
In spite of the warning voice that comes in the night
And repeats, repeats in my ear:
Don't you know, little fool, you never can win? ... "

"Oh man, Sonny, you fuck with your *socks on?*" Garbis said.

Sonny's eyes opened just in time to see his brother's fist. His glasses flew off and his neck snapped to the side as he tried to rise up from the bed. He felt nauseous. Garbis' thick eyebrows became one as he growled.

"You pin-dicked mother*fucker!* I should kill you right now!" Garbis spewed.

"Garbey—what are you doing here?" Sonny said, attempting to cover his nude body. He reached for his glasses, trying to shield his forehead, but Garbis wasn't done.

"You know why I'm here." Garbis continued slapping at Sonny's head with open-hand strikes. "Put your hands down so I can hit you!" Again and again Garbis slapped the top of Sonny's head. He couldn't stop, feeling detached now.

"Stop, Garbey! You're not even friendly with Otto," he said, trying to fend off his younger brother's attack. "Garbey—why are you doing this?"

Garbis was breathing hard, and spit came from his mouth like venom. He stepped back and stared at Sonny, aiming his eyes toward the bathroom door. He heard a woman singing. All of it seemed to crystallize then.

"*Minchia,* I should've known," Garbis said.

Sonny slumped against the headboard, covering his midsection with a sheet. He rubbed his forehead, a wounded look on his face, his black thin hair looking like a windblown comb-over. He pulled on his glasses, which had been bent in the attack, making his face appear lopsided.

"Gina *Bertuzzi?*"

"Ever see the tubes on that broad?" Sonny whispered, still trying to figure out why Garbis was spoiling what had been, up until that point, a blissful afternoon. "How did you get in here?"

"The Mick let me in. He knew better than to argue." His breathing evened out, and his face became less flushed.

"She's lonely. Gina's a beautiful woman, Garbey. I can't help myself sometimes. Why are you here? Is it because of her—are you sweet on her, too, Garb?" Sonny asked.

"You really don't know, do you?" Garbis asked.

Sonny shook his head like he was trying to interpret someone speaking in

Latin to him. Garbis reached into his pocket. He took out Carmine's ring and showed it to him.

Sonny looked at it nonplussed. "Why do you have Carm's ring? Don't he like it now? When you two picked it up he practically kissed me on the mouth," Sonny said, his face a portrait of virtue.

Garbis threw him a hard slap that bloodied his lip.

"Garbey!"

"I told you no funny business. *I fucking told you!*"

"Yeah? So what?" Sonny asked. He rubbed the lip, wincing at the blood on his fingertips.

"Put the real stone back," Garbis' voice rose up.

"What are you talking about, *the real stone?*" Sonny asked.

Garbis cuffed at his temple again, but Sonny caught his hand. "Please, Garbis."

Garbis relaxed. "You switched it with this lumpy. Don't tell me you didn't."

"Garbey I swear. I didn't switch nothing. That's the same stone you gave me."

"You're more full of shit than a Christmas turkey. Don't lie to me."

"I swear on our mother's grave," Sonny said. He stared at the bathroom door.

"What did you just say?" Garbis asked.

"I didn't switch it, I swear on Mother's grave."

All the color had been sucked from Sonny's face, leaving him looking as if he'd been born grey. Garbis stood up and leaned against the bathroom door.

"So you're telling me that if I open this door, and I pull that big-titted bitch from the shower, she's not going to be wearing a nearly flawless diamond that you stole from my friend—the man who calls me his *cugino*, his best *amico* in the whole world—that that cow-whore won't be wearing Carmine's stone on her finger?" Garbis said, his voice rising with each word.

Sonny cringed. "Please, *she'll hear!* Yeah, that's what I'm saying."

Garbis touched the doorknob and looked at him. Sonny didn't move. Garbis suddenly got stabbed with regret; he wanted to believe his brother so bad. "Last chance."

And even with the shower still running, Sonny didn't blink. Garbis gave a gentle nod, turning the doorknob with a metallic click.

"Oh, all right! I'll change it back, Garbey," Sonny hissed. He wore a culpable grin, his smile pasted on his face, and the light caught the gold cap. He smoothed his thin hair over the purple welt on the top of his pate. Garbis sighed and walked to the bed.

"On her grave. On Mother's grave. *Twice* you swore. And for what—to play with a pair of *fun bags*? Was she really worth it?"

Sonny lowered his eyes, shrugging with one shoulder.

"Can't help myself, Garb. You know how I am. The sweater meat on her ... "

Garbis frowned. He tried to touch Sonny's cheek, but he walked to the door instead, dragging his hand over his own wavy black hair. He felt like he had no saliva left.

"You switch that stone back. I'm coming by the store tomorrow morning at ten to pick it up, and it better look like the fucking Hope Diamond. And be glad I ain't bringing Carmine. Ten o'clock."

"Garbey, I promise I'll ... "

Garbis put his hand up. "Don't speak. Don't. After this, Son, we're done for a while. You understand? It's Carmine we're talking about. You're dead to me until I'm ready to resurrect your sorry ass."

"Garbey, don't say that. You don't mean that. Do you, Garb? Say you don't."

But Sonny could tell by the look his brother gave before leaving that he meant exactly that. The sound of the crackling radio was all that was left in the room.

Sonny looked at the pinky ring. It was the best lumpy he could find, actually a half-karat bigger than Carmine's diamond. *Why the hell didn't I just put the lumpy in Gina's ring? She'd a never known the difference,* he thought. But he knew the answer to the question.

He heard the water turn off. Five minutes later Gina stepped from the bathroom, the blue sundress open to the waist. She was attempting to put on an overbuilt, powder blue lace brassiere. The bra was half-obscured by the bottom curves of her resting breasts, their red-ringed centers still exposed. Sonny was transfixed, watching her adjust the custom-made device, ready to place her creamy missiles into the mixing bowl-sized cups. Seeing her again, she seemed fantastical and he noticed the true fullness of her beauty. Gina hadn't looked up at him yet, so busy was she with the task at hand.

"Were you talking to someone earlier?" she asked.

He leaned back and let his hand fall to the side of the bed. Bobby Darin was singing *Mack the Knife*.

"Must've been the radio."

"Last chance to see them this way. Then it'll have to just be in your mind," she said, her tone playful. "OK then." Gina reached behind herself and snapped the eight hooks closed. She felt pretty and was smiling.

He grinned diffidently at her and let Carmine's pinky ring drop at the side of the bed—onto the floor between the bed and the wall—out of her line of sight. Finally looking up, she caught him watching her. She focused on his bloody lip and the egg growing from the top of his head.

"What happened? Omigod, are you OK, Sonny?"

She bounded over, causing her chest to bounce. She touched his head.

"I stumbled getting up. I got up too quick. The blood drained from my head—you must've left me without any, I guess," he kidded. "I'm fine baby, don't you worry." Her bare chest was again inches from his face.

"You poor thing. Your lip's bleeding! Let me get you some ice," she said.

"No," he snapped. "I'll be fine, Gina. Don't worry yourself. Just a damn bump!"

Sonny clicked off the music. He reached over and grabbed his boxers. He pulled them on and stood all in one motion, suddenly wanting to be clothed and far away from her. He rolled his neck to the side and left her there, walking across the room to the bureau, where his wallet and keys were. Sonny never wore much jewelry himself, except for a scapula from Father Solanus' ministry and a modest, gold crucifix on a thin chain. He put both articles around his neck and fingered them before kissing the corpus.

He mussed his hair over the welt. Sonny took a long look at himself in the mirror, deep into his own eyes, as if trying to see if anyone was even home anymore. Gina was behind him, and she appeared as a blurry flesh-colored figure in his peripheral vision.

"You're a beautiful woman, Gina."

He frowned a little as she finally pulled her über-bra up and over her breasts, covering them for eternity. She adjusted the straps and then slipped the sundress on. She took the towel off her head, letting her black hair cascade along the sides of her face, framing her soft, high cheeks. She was truly the most beautiful woman he'd ever seen.

"The *ring* is breathtaking, Sonny. You really are an artist. Walk me to my car, will ya?" she asked. "Sonny, you OK?"

He watched her figure in the mirror and felt her approach behind him. She kissed his cheek and that was all it took to break the trance from everything that had transpired in the last few days. He bit his fattening lower lip and turned to face her.

"Gina, today was—what's *this?*" he said, staring at the ring. "Oh *no*. No, no ... "

"What's wrong?"

"I was afraid of that. Ahh, crap! Let me see a minute. Give me your hand, dear."

She offered it grudgingly. He glanced up at her, his gold cap glinting, but he couldn't quite meet her gaze. He examined her ring finger, closing his lips and pouting. She looked at his face, then the ring, a worried expression coming over her.

"What is it, Sonny?"

Carmine's nearly flawless, VVS1 diamond—a stone of near perfect symmetry—rested in the middle of a starburst of twenty small emerald-cut diamonds, giving the center gem the appearance of rays originating from a supernova.

"It's the master prong; the main one bracing that big bugger in the middle.

Today, on the way over here, I'd wondered, I said, 'Sonny, are you sure you heat-crimped it long enough?' and I guess in my haste to meet you, it's clear that I hadn't. See? Look, right here."

Sonny pointed to a prong that was fastened quite correctly. Gina studied it. He looked at her hair, and closed his eyes taking in the fragrance of powder and Aqua-Net.

"I don't see anything. Are you sure?"

"Unfortunately, yes. I need to take it back, dear. I'll give it a once-over, polish it up. Be good as new. You can pick it up in the morning. Actually, you know what? Why don't we say noon. How's that? Does noon work for you, Gina?"

She looked at him cautiously.

And then she looked down at her ring. "It's just that ... it looks fine."

He shook his head negatively, the wan smile trying to hold on.

"See, in my haste," he continued, as he touched her hand. She pulled it back.

"OK, noon, sure. I mean, you're the expert right?"

"That's me," Sonny laughed, trying his best to look her in the eyes. *"Guilty as charged!"* He smiled, feeling on the brink of overselling.

She returned a wary look. Finally capitulating, she slid the ring off her finger and reluctantly handed it to him.

"I'll see you at noon then, OK, Sonny?" she said, opening the door.

"Sure babe, noon," he smiled at her, never blinking.

"Think you could at least walk me to my car? It's kind of ... *dark* around here?"

"The *melanzana* won't bother you. They know you're with me."

She nodded, covering herself with her arms crossed over her breasts. She draped the shawl around her shoulders.

"It's a beautiful setting. You're an artist, Sonny. I really love it. Whenever I *look at it*, I'll think of you. Remember that. From *now on* Sonny. I swear it."

Sonny swallowed hard, and it felt like a dry tumor was trying to tunnel its way into the center of his soul. His eyes teared up.

"That's why I want to make sure there's not a snowball's chance in hell of it coming loose. Gina, today is a day that will live with me until the Lord calls me. That, I promise you."

She smiled, a close-lipped smile that appeared almost genuine.

"Me, too. I'll see you at noon then. To pick it up," she said. "Sonny? Can I just look at it one last time? I want to remember it."

He tried to look in her eyes, but his will was fading.

"Sure. Sure, Gina. Here you are," he said.

Gina studied the center stone, recording the depth of its beauty. She inhaled, and looking down at her bare ring finger, her face turned expressionless.

"Noon," she said.

She mouthed "bye Son," and walked out of room, making the long, lonely trek back to her car and back to her life as Otto's living blow-up doll.

Sonny stayed there for a long time. He stood in front of the mirror, seeing the reflection of the bed, rewinding for his mind's eye the antics that had taken place that afternoon. He saw the painting of the matador, getting lost in the thick brushstrokes.

He pulled the rosy silk shirt to his nose and inhaled her scent. He sniffed hard and closed his eyes. He dressed quickly, zipping the fly of his vermillion trousers. He put on his suit coat and fingered his puffy mouth. His eyes stung and his nose felt full with snot.

It'll still be beautiful to you, honey, he thought.

He knelt on the bed and reached between the space next to the wall, retrieving Carmine's ring from the floor. His head throbbed when he stood up. He put the two rings next to one another, comparing the stones. On their own, each gem sparkled with its own brilliance, but when placed side by side, the fire that emanated from the VVS1 diamond stolen from Janko Rosenvieg was like comparing the rays of a million-candle halogen lamp to the beam of a penlight.

However, these two stones would never again be seen side by side.

And Sonny knew diamonds.

And most of his customers, including Carmine and Garbis, did not.

"Aw, Gina! Why didya have to be so beautiful?" his voice echoed in the room.

With her trapped in his mind, Sonny took one last look around. He flicked off the wall switch of room 23, leaving it dark and hollow for the next sad sack or wayward soul to find respite in—away from whatever it was they, too, were running.

The Raccoon Killer

Frank's buzz was still with him, so he was a bit disoriented when he awoke. His scalp felt charged with static cling. Too much Chianti or whatever the hell that stuff was. It took him a second to remember he was at Roman's place, the hunting cabin on Starvation Lake. Frank grabbed the handrail. The carpeting pricked his bare feet as he descended, unsteadily navigating the stairs from his second-floor bedroom. It was around 11 a.m.

The view of the lake was spectacular from the first floor living room. Starvation Lake was three miles across and a mile wide, a glacial lake typical of Michigan's northern Lower Peninsula. The water was clear and deep through the middle— 120 feet in some spots. The lake's name seemed ill-conceived though, as the arrowhead-shaped body of water brimmed with perch, northern pike, and tiger musky, as well as lunker bass, all fattening up on the lake's plentiful baitfish. The surrounding state and federal land was rich with black bear, partridge, and woodcock, and the flyways over nearby Fletcher's Floodwaters drew flocks of waterfowl, making for easy shooting from Roman's dock. Throw into the mix the area's thriving population of white-tailed deer, and it wasn't hyperbole to call it an outdoorsman's dream.

Since Roman built the place in 1978, it seemed to be wearing well. The interior looked like it was put together with haste, as if another hunting season may find the inhabitants sleeping in a fleabag motel, or worse yet, tents. A honey stain on the tongue and groove poplar that looked applied with too heavy a brush showed drips when the light hit it. And though it would comfortably sleep twelve, it wasn't uncommon for another six guys to crash on cots or old couches.

Frank had hunted alone yesterday. Roman didn't hunt like he used to. Mainly, he was up there to spend time with his brothers and his son Nick, a hunter of legendary proportions. Frank had met Roman's kid only once. The upkeep of the cabin fell to Nick, and he made sure the place never got "too nice." He knew his father wanted no woman's touch to bastardize the patina of manliness that coated its walls. Looking around, Frank thought the kid was doing a hell of a job. The furniture was hodge-podge, garage-sale chic.

The carpeting, however, was brand-new.

Nothing pretty or lush, it was a striped pattern of greens, ochre, umber, and off-white. Commercial-grade and low nap, the stuff was perfect for the traffic of hunters. It was the color of peas, dryer lint, and baby shit, which is exactly what Roman wanted.

Presently, it was the fall of 1983. Frank thought Roman always looked at peace in his cabin, youthful, even when compared to army snapshots from thirty years earlier. The two became fast friends at Fort Bragg during basic training for the Korean War. After returning home to the terra firma of the Midwest—Frank to Cleveland, Roman to Detroit—they stayed in touch through Christmas cards and phone calls. Starting in '68, they started meeting once a year to hunt birds in northern Ohio cornfields and the game farms of southern Michigan cities like Jackson, Chelsea, and Coldwater.

Then two years after Roman built the cabin, he invited Frank up to Starvation Lake, some 400 miles north of Cleveland. This was Frank's third trip in a row to the "Sunrise Side" of Michigan. He loved the area and got along well with the few friends of Roman's he had met. They seemed to get a kick out of Frank's easy way and dry humor. And while Frank never knew what Roman and his pals did for work, he didn't ask—they seemed like solid men.

Dying embers in the fire still glowed, and he enjoyed its warmth. The cabin smelled of the forest and charred oak. Taxidermy done by Lombardi, a craftsman of mythic reputation amongst Detroit's East Side Dagos, hung all around; a drake mallard, three teal, and a lone, Giant Canada goose mounted between the windows of the peak in the cathedral ceiling. Trophy smallmouth stared from the wall next to the stairway. Frank could almost feel the ghosts of the animals.

Frank entered the dining area just off the kitchen, taking a seat at the large picnic-style table Roman had built. A condenser on one of the refrigerators kicked on. The men had left plates of lunch meat out. It looked like someone had robbed a deli. His brow creased from the dinger he had going, but the spread was too appetizing to deny, so he sat eating hard salami and chunked asiago cheese to take his mind off the throbbing. He decided he needed coffee before his head exploded.

He stood up woozily—his temples enduring drumbeats—and walked to the coffee pot at the long kitchen counter. Frank cracked the blinds at the window over the sink. Pushing aside empty beer cans, he slid the window up. A soft breeze entered, and it felt nice. The morning light and the hangover made him squint. Never did handle the effects of booze very well. The lake had circles on it from rising fish. He looked around the quiet cabin, still not sure where everyone was. An electric clock on the wall yet to be reset for daylight savings time hummed an uneven frequency until the noise hurt his ears.

"Roman? Vito?" he called out, his voice carrying.

He felt stupid speaking in an apparently empty cabin.

Unbeknownst to him, the men were grouse hunting, departing under the cover of predawn light. They left Frank in bed to sleep off the effects of Roman's homemade "Chianti," which was little more than brandy. No one dared tell him it was too strong to be considered wine. Besides, it tasted pretty good and gave one hell of a kick. But it would blister the heartiest of drinkers, and Frank wasn't one of those. He was, though, one hell of a card counter. He'd beaten them all at every game called the night before and imbibed a bit too much with four glasses. Now it felt like a squirrel was running around loose inside his head.

Frank removed the soggy coffee filter and the onrush of the burnt grounds didn't agree with him. He started to make a fresh pot when he heard a car engine. He went into the bathroom and looked out the window. Three men emerged from a black, late model Ford truck and looked around. He didn't recognize any of them, although the driver bore a resemblance to Vito Marsico, one of Roman's hunting buddies that Frank had just met the night before.

Behind an old recliner, next to the refrigerators, his uncased shotgun rested against the wall. Instinctively he grabbed it, returning to his seat at the table. He positioned the shotgun—a semi-automatic Remington 20-gauge—next to him so it was accessible to his right hand. He clicked the safety off and then ate another piece of the salami.

Frank stared at the corner of the back wall of the cabin, where whoever was about to walk through the door would be turning, and just to be on the safe side, he tested his ability to lift the gun from a sitting position. He stopped when he heard the screen door, leaning the gun against the wall beside him. He fussed with the placement of his hands, trying to act natural. Oddly, he felt like a thief, caught robbing the place. He willed himself to let go of a passing sense of presentiment, but was pricked by it when his wife's face mysteriously flashed in his head.

"Get up, Wops," a lyrical voice called out. "C'mon—chop, chop! Let's eat, greaseballs." The shout was accompanied by jackhammer laughter belonging to another man.

"Come on in," Frank called out with false aloofness.

The three came around the corner and did little to hide their shock at seeing Frank sitting all by himself at the big table.

"Who the hell are you?" the guy who resembled Vito asked him.

The other two straightened up. The guy who owned the laugh seemed wired on caffeine. He was stocky, with a head of hair that looked like a dandelion gone to seed; white tufts on a big head and round, pale blue eyes with white eyelashes that gave him a perpetually surprised look. He had pinkish skin and could have easily been mistaken for an albino. The biggest of the three, a dark, solid man, smiled at Frank. He wore an orange hunting vest. He had the thick shadow of a Sicilian and deep-set, dead, brown eyes. His skin was coppery, his features angular and lean.

"I'm Frank Candor. Roman's army bud from Ohio. How're you guys doing?" Frank threw it out there and it sounded like an actor giving a cue. They relaxed a little, though the dark man remained rigid.

"Better when I get some of that *capocolla*. Why the hell ain't you eating the *capocolla*?" the lead man asked.

"Got to eat the *capocolla*," the white-haired guy said.

"Roman told me not to eat it all," Frank replied.

"*Fuck* Roman," the man said. His eyes lit up at Frank's reaction. "Nero, look at his *face*—hey, I kid! Seriously, you're going to want to try the *capocolla* with these olives," the man said. In his nervousness, Frank hadn't noticed the large paper bag the white-haired man carried in. The dark man stood mute.

"I'm Gabe Marsico," the lead man said. "This is Casper, and that's Nero."

"Thought you favored Veets—I mean, Vito. You're brothers, right? He was here yesterday … I think they're at the store. Should be right back," Frank felt himself saying the words with an intonation that sounded scared, but it was too late to rephrase them. Nero finally relaxed. Gabe's face went slack, then returned to its gilded cheerfulness.

"You met Veets, huh? Well, I'm the *good-looking one*," Gabe said.

Casper laughed again. Nero regarded him and after a moment shook his head like a panther being pestered by flies. He sat directly across from Frank and stared at him.

"Gonna do some killing?" Nero said to Frank. His voice was throaty, hanging onto an accent in spots.

Frank stared at him for a second. Nero motioned with his eyes at the wall, and Frank didn't have to look to know he was talking about the shotgun resting to his right.

"You mean *hunting,* right?" Frank replied.

"If you like. That loaded?" Nero asked, his expression flat. "The safety's off. I can see that from here. I got really good eyes. Can't be too careful."

"No," Frank lied. "It's not loaded."

Casper plopped down. He spilled the final contents of the bag onto the table, and Gabe helped him spread it out. There were containers of olives in several varieties, marinated eggplant and roasted, oily red peppers with slivered garlic. Three huge wheels of cheese—bleu, port, and *fontinella*—rolled out along with a massive loaf of hard-crusted bread.

"That's some food! So, how do you all know Roman?" Frank asked them. Nero bristled, and for the first time he appeared less threatening than either of his two friends. Casper laughed. Nero looked sideways but Casper didn't catch it.

"The old neighborhood," Gabe said.

"Yeah," Nero said.

"I'm friends with these guys from Detroit," Casper added. "I know Roman through them. But I laid all the carpet in this place. Lotta carpet, I'll tell you."

"Did a real nice job," Frank said. "I've got to re-carpet my house."

"Casper'll go anywhere the money's at. Right, Casper?" Nero said, his rancor back. "Nice *color*, too. Like *merda*."

"Should've brought sandwich buns," Casper shrugged. "Sorry pal. Not going to Ohio."

Frank smiled and rolled up a piece of *capocolla*.

Nero started laughing—a building, resonating, out-of-place laugh holding all the warmth of a bucket of dead eels. He produced a wicked folding knife that extended to a foot in length. Upon further inspection, Frank noted it was actually a folding saw, the kind hunters use to cut small limbs that obscure their shooting lanes. Nero attacked the loaf of hard bread with the skill of a sushi chef, deftly sawing through half of it, resulting in hand-sized pieces, expertly cut through creating tops and bottoms, hinged at the sides like buns. The cuts were clean.

He moved to the dense *fontinella* and using the saw, carved off a cake slice-sized chunk. Nero smiled as he handled the saw, amused with it. He stabbed a big chunk of the cheese with the point and offered it to Frank, who was still staring at him.

"Don't be shy, friend. Best damn *fontinella* in the USA," Nero said.

Frank pulled the white chunk from the tip of Nero's saw.

Nero grinned, then said to Gabe and Casper, "Go on ladies*, mangi formaggio*."

They all dug in and the act of eating defused the situation, and so it seemed to Frank that Nero had settled into the idea that he was OK.

Frank had to agree with Nero, the taste of the cheese was pungent and its texture was excellent, very dense. The redolence of the food alternated between quelling and enhancing his hangover. The olives swam in a viscous, gold oil and a film of vinegars swirled on the surface. The feast sturdied his defenses, keeping at bay the headache Roman's fermented grapes had wrought.

"You get any birds yet?" Gabe asked.

"Four yesterday. Lucky shot, got a double on one."

"Wow. A double," Gabe's bottom lip jutted out. Frank felt Nero examining his face.

"Ever deer hunt?" Casper asked. He stacked layers of meat and cheese on the bread.

"I don't ever rifle hunt. Not really my kind of hunting. Don't care for it. I went once."

"Did you bag one?" Gabe asked.

Frank nodded between bites of the cheese. His tongue had gotten a filmy coating from it.

"Ten-point. I looked up and he was standing there. Broadside shot a hundred-fifty yards away. I gave it a whistle to get it running. Hit it in the lungs. I tracked him about fifty yards—"

"*You whistled?*" Gabe interrupted.

"Yeah. I whistled. I don't like shooting game that's not at least *moving*. Guess I'm funny that way," Frank offered.

"Why not?" Nero asked. He sat erect, suddenly interested in the conversation.

"I don't know," Frank replied. "Not sporting enough I guess."

Nero put both hands on the table and leaned in.

"Makes you feel like a killer. Am I right?" Nero said, the coldness back in his eyes, but this time accompanied by the slightest mirth. Frank looked at him, making himself steady. He felt the presence of the shotgun in his peripheral vision.

"Maybe. It's just not my way of hunting. Mind passing those peppers?" he asked Casper, never taking his eyes off Nero.

Casper happily passed the peppers. He grabbed a good share of olives and cheese first. Then he scooped up three fingers-worth of marinated eggplant, dripping oil on his flannel shirt.

"Look at him; guy eats like he has two assholes," Gabe mused.

"A hundred-fifty yards. *Pow!*" Casper said, russet oil dripping from the corner of his mouth and onto his shirt. "I need a beer. Beer'd be good now," Casper announced.

"The buck. That a lucky shot, too?" Nero asked.

"No. It wasn't." Frank said. "I can shoot a little ... so, what about you guys?"

"What do you mean—can we shoot?" Gabe asked between bites. "Casp, grab me a beer, too, will ya?" he asked. Casper put down his hastily made sandwich, and grudgingly jumped up and went to the refrigerator. He pulled out two beers.

"Anybody else need one?" he said, louder than he needed to. *"Anybody?"*

"No, thanks," Frank said, the thought of alcohol tickling his headache.

"Me either," said Nero, staring at Frank.

"You guys sure?" When no one replied, Casper handed Gabe a can of Pabst. He settled back into his seat and cracked open his own. Between chugging the beer, he ravaged his sandwich. Frank couldn't help but notice the powdery man's appetite.

"Know what? I am thirsty," Nero announced, still looking at Frank. Nero bit into a piece of bread, chewing it loudly with his mouth open. Frank watched, but saw Casper's face redden, framed by his white hair. Casper hesitated before slowly walking to the fridge that held the beer, which was easily within arm's reach of Nero. He placed the beer on the table. Nero looked up at him. Casper shrugged.

"*Minchia*, what am I, Harry Houdini?" Nero asked.

"Houdini ... Jesus," Casper muttered. He opened Nero's can and returned to his sandwich. Frank watched Nero smile and set the beer aside. A rush of wind came through, sending empties falling off the windowsill, clinking into the sink.

"We do a little deer hunting. Never *whistled*," Gabe laughed.

The tension left again, and though his gut boiled, Frank couldn't resist the plump strips of oily red pepper that resided on the chunk of bread in front of him.

"I like to bow hunt," Casper blurted out, his voice obfuscated by the food in his mouth. "I'm a good shot with the bow, ain't that right, Gabe?"

"Yeah. Gotta say, you are a dead-eye," Gabe answered.

"He is," Nero admitted, a harder edge to his voice now.

"Really? That takes skill. Have *you* gotten a buck lately?" Frank asked.

"No. I'll try the second season in December, after rifle season's over," Casper said, still eating as if he was in a huge hurry. He stopped and worked his tongue, trying to pry mushy bread from the roof of his mouth. Nero snapped the folding saw open and then closed it.

"Remember that time in '78 when we drove over to Gaylord? That monster swamp buck Joey the Rat kept talking about? Swamp buck went over two-fifty. Lived in that swamp behind the golf course," Casper said.

"The golf course," Nero's eyes crinkled.

"Rack three feet across," Gabe's eyes bugged as he told Frank of the buck's huge size.

Frank's interest was piqued. "Three feet? You shoot it?" he asked Casper.

"*Fuck no* he didn't! Guy can't shoot a gun to save his chalky *culo*," Nero barked, causing Frank to recoil.

Casper smacked his lips. "Yeah, but if raccoons were gold I'd be a rich man," he laughed his staccato laugh, continuing his death row-type meal, olive oil escaping his lips.

"Raccoons? They're nocturnal ... how many did you shoot?" Frank asked.

Casper put his sandwich down. He pondered the question as he rolled a pimento between his short fingers. When he had it squeezed into a tiny red ball he ate it.

"I dunno. Ten, twelve," Casper said. He examined his red fingertips.

"Don't know. *Thirteen,* you *mamaluke,*" Nero corrected.

"Two with one shot," Casper laughed, shaking his head. "Like you and the birds."

"*Thirteen?* With a *bow?* Holy shit, well that's some shooting," Frank said.

"Wiped out two families at least," Nero said. "He didn't *whistle* first, either."

"Stupid animals. Kept walking around while the others—" Casper couldn't finish from his laughing at the thought, eating and giggling, the spaces of his teeth packed with food.

"I left my blind to pick up Casper, right?" Gabe said to Frank, putting his sandwich down. "Looked like a voodoo ritual had taken place."

"How's that?" Frank asked. Casper's laughing increased at the sudden attention.

"Casp's up in his tree stand, laughing his ass off. Every tree within thirty yards has a raccoon stuck to it, speared right through the spine on most of 'em, stuck into the trunks while they were walking up. Mamas, daddies—"

"Babies, too," Casper bugged his big eyes and waved his arms, mimicking their distress.

"*Fuuuck ...* " Frank whispered at the image they painted.

"That's what *I* said," Gabe agreed. "I said, *fuck.* What the hell else *could* you say?"

"Right through the spine. *Pow!* Broke their little backs," Casper laughed.

"He's a killer, that Casper. Aren't you Casp? He's no *dicksmoker* though!" Nero said and laughed maniacally at the word. The laugh had a slant on it that seemed way too over the top. Nero said the word again. "Dicksmoker."

Casper gurgled, spitting out bits of meat.

Gabe stared at Nero.

"What's up with that? Whenever we talk about the raccoons! Dicksmoker. What's so funny about that?" Gabe shook his head making Nero laugh harder. Casper puckered his lips, stifling laughs, his reddening face shaking and his eyes clenched. Frank watched it all in detached amusement.

"*What?*" Gabe continued. "*Va fungool,* the both of you."

Casper turned to Frank. "Trucker was sweet for Nero. You had to be there," Casper said between laughing jags. "One punch. He didn't see that coming, the *fairy.*"

"Trucker was a *finocchio,*" Nero said, smiling at Frank.

Frank shrugged at the word.

"A *finoik, femminuccia,*" Nero explained. He chuckled and it elevated again.

"That's what I get for not going to the bar. I know—the *finoik* trucker, big deal—took the lot of you to kick his ass. News flash: It ain't *that* goddamn funny," Gabe said.

Nero's laughter was unsettling to all but Casper. Casper took a breath, staring teary-eyed at Frank. He wasn't ready to let his prowess with the bow fade, the memories of the raccoons apparently fresh in his mind. He looked up, his eyes glassy like blue marbles.

"Stupid things hung there, dangling in the air, waving their stupid little arms around until they died. I shoulda stopped at three, huh Nero?" Casper grumbled, at once turning sullen.

"What, your arm get tired?" Frank asked, trying to lighten the mood.

"Cost me three hundred bucks. DNR officer wrote me a ticket 'cuz I didn't have a license. Magistrate had a hard-on for raccoons," Casper complained.

Gabe continued, "Casper walks in to plead the ticket to this fat fag, guy looked like Mama Cass with a beard."

"Regina impetuosa," Nero said to Frank.

Frank looked to Gabe for translation. "Fiery queen," Gabe explained. "Anyway, this *finoik* is nuts for raccoons; raccoon post cards; raccoon dolls, you name it, fucking raccoons everywhere!" Gabe described the scene with a familiarity that bespoke he'd told the story before. Frank couldn't help but laugh at the image of raccoon tchotchkes surrounding the judge. Even Nero calmed down, his laughter playful for a moment.

Casper stared at his food.

"Said it was a display of poor sportsmanship. Damn good shooting, but poor sportsmanship," Nero said. "He liked your curls, though. Maybe there's something in the water up here," Nero looked at Frank. "Lot of *finoiks*."

"Chubby raccoon-loving queer," Casper groused. The pale man rose to his feet and picked up the empty plates.

"Fucking funny as *shit*, admit it," Nero said, but Casper ignored him.

The pall that had hung over the room left momentarily and Nero picked at a string of fat stuck between his perfect white teeth. Casper took his plate and lifted Nero's can of Pabst.

"You didn't drink your beer," Casper said, feeling its weight.

"Guess I wasn't that thirsty after all." Nero stood up and rolled his neck. "Drink it."

"No thanks," Casper said. He *harrumphed* and poured the beer down the drain. The only sounds were the foam bubbling in the sink and the hum of the clock. Gabe and Nero waited until Casper was done. Nero was staring at the shotgun.

Frank finally stood for the first time and almost pitched forward from the rush of blood to his head. He steadied himself on the table until it passed. The humming of the electric clock buzzed in his ear, and he wondered if anyone else could hear it.

"Nice meeting you guys," Frank said.

He held out his hand and Gabe and Casper shook it. Nero was the last one to do so, and he watched Frank's eyes closely as he did. Frank imagined Nero would squeeze his hand as hard as possible—so he got ready for it. Nero looked disappointed and held onto Frank's hand for what seemed like too long. Frank was surprised at the supple texture of the dark man's palm. Nero took a last look at Frank's idle Remington leaning against the wall behind Frank, his cold brown eyes holding onto their malevolence.

"Not just birds out there," Nero said. "Woods are full of dangerous animals, too. Got to be careful."

"I always am," said Frank.

Casper covertly stuffed three slices of *capocolla* in his mouth. "G'bye," he said.

Gabe waved. "Tell Roman we came by. And if you see that ugly-ass brother of mine, tell him he owes me dinner. Take care, pal," Gabe said, rounding the corner.

Nero tucked the folding saw into his vest pocket. "So long, Frank," he said.

Frank walked over to the window to make sure they were gone. He exhaled as the truck drove off. It was as if a poltergeist had been driven from the cabin. He felt a trickle, barely a drop but a drop nonetheless, of urine at the tip of his penis, which had turtled on him while the men were there. He took out a half-empty bottle of Canadian Club from a cupboard and poured two shots into a coffee cup, spilling some. He drank half of it and walked out the back.

Sitting outside, the soft fall wind stroked Frank's face. It had been a half-hour since they left. His headache pinged as he watched a flock of teal settle fifty yards from shore. *Had he gotten in the middle of some rift between those men and Roman?* he thought. He had no idea if his mention of Vito saved him or not. Flop-sweat soaked his armpits, and he could do nothing to stop it. He heard a vehicle and ran back inside. He held his shotgun, checking that the safety was still off.

The footsteps were more hurried now.

"Counting your winnings, you lucky piece of shit?" Roman yelled. "I'm so hungry I could eat the asshole out of a skunk ... "

Frank pointed the gun at the carpet, relieved to hear Roman's voice, the gravelly rasp in it calming him. The rest of the group rounded the corner to find Frank holding the Remington. Roman put his hands up.

"Officer, please, don't shoot," he said, his voice affecting mock concern. Along with Roman were Marco Calcaterra, Phil Barbierri, and Vito Marsico. Seeing

Vito, Frank realized how different he and Gabe actually looked. The brothers were similar in stature only and, despite Gabe's remark, Vito's features were finer. With his thin mustache and black pompadour, he resembled a European film star.

"You just missed your brother, says you owe him dinner," Frank said.

Vito smiled. "*Really?* Selective memory. Never told me he was coming up this weekend." Vito crossed his arms. "I'll run into him later, I'm sure. So what else did old Gabe have to say?"

"Probably a line of *merda*," Marco threw in.

"Guy's got a line of shit a mile long," Roman added.

"Thought I was going to have to go for my gun," Frank laughed with self-deprecation. "He dropped off all this stuff." He waved a hand over the cheeses and olives. "When I first saw him I thought he resembled you."

"I'm the good-looking one," Vito said.

"That ain't saying much—you look in a mirror lately, Veets?" Roman said.

Vito let the men's laughter fade before responding, "You're as funny as a fat broad in a miniskirt, Rome. Was Gabe by himself?"

Frank continued, "Couple guys with him. One was real pale—"

"Casper," Marco put a hand on each ear and flapped them, singing, "*Coo-coo, coo-coo.*"

"Yeah, kind of. The other guy was wound pretty tight, too," Frank continued.

Roman turned to him. "Who's that?" he asked.

"Dark guy, had a little accent ... "

Roman clicked his tongue and looked at Phil. "*Minchia,*" Roman muttered. "Nero."

"*Nero.* How did I forget a name like that?" Frank replied.

Roman disappeared to his bedroom. When he came back out, Frank noticed a .38 snub-nose tucked in his waistband.

"Were you wearing that all day?" Frank asked.

He examined himself and discovered the gun.

"Huh? Oh yeah. Waitress at the County Depot told me a bear's been getting into their garbage. Little too close to the cabins lately," he said without sincerity. "Veets. Thought Nero was staying close to Detroit these days."

"I thought he was 'vacationing' on the Boot again," Marco said.

"He's been hanging with Gabe. They got a deal with some union guys—Casper and his crew been re-carpeting all the UAW buildings. Big, *big* score. Felt like coming up north, I guess," Vito said. "Maybe Casper's knees needed to heal. Nero's still got the poor sap dead to rights."

"Well, that's true," Roman said, rubbing his chin. "Still. Didn't figure he'd be up—Frank! That Casper, he laid this carpet. Wears like iron," Roman said, admiring the baby shit-colored, ugly-as-hell carpeting.

"That's what he said. Like to find a guy like him in Cleveland. Just curious, Roman, how much did he charge you for all of this?"

The men looked at each other and Marco and Vito laughed. Roman rubbed his chin.

"Let me see ... seven hundred ... there's the premium pad ... another two hundo," Roman pantomimed doing a multiplication problem in the air. He continued mumbling, "Edges stitched on all runners, bathrooms ... carry the three, uh ... *zero!*"

Frank reddened hearing the group laugh as if they alone were listening to great stand-up.

"Forgive us, Frank. You're from Toledo, right?" Vito asked.

"Cleveland, actually, but yeah, Ohio—"

"Whatever. Anyway, Nero owed Gabe an old marker from the World Series that Nero let get too vigorish. And Gabe owed Roman on a bet those two made over Notre Dame-USC. So to square it all Casper had to lay Roman's carpet," Vito explained this to Frank as if he had just asked him did he know that two plus two equaled four.

"Hold on—how does *Nero* owing *Gabe* and *Gabe* owing *Roman* get *Casper* having to lay *Roman's* carpeting *for free?*"

"Casper lost his carpet business. Bad luck," Roman said.

"Mostly," Marco added.

"Well, that and because he didn't know when to quit betting football. He was into some New York boys for twelve Gs," Vito said.

Frank let out a whistle. "On football? That's a fortune," he said.

"No shit, Sherlock. So what does the Pillsbury Doughboy do to try to get right-side up? Make-Good Day: The Super Bowl. Genius bets the entire nut on the *over*—with two of the stingiest defenses in the league. Gabe even begged him to take the under, but Casp thought he could get off the snide playing the over. Shit-for-brains doubled himself right up."

"How's he still laying carpet?" Frank asked.

"Carpet's all he knows. He borrowed from Nero to pay the shylocks. He's on the hook to Nero for twenty-five large. He just switched lenders is all," Vito said.

"They must be good friends to lend him that much cash," Frank said.

"*The best*. And Nero wants to make sure Casper earns and stays healthy."

"Twenty-five thousand. From betting," Frank remarked. Then, setting aside his incredulity, "At least he didn't have to borrow from *a bank*. Interest would've been brutal—"

The men started laughing hysterically again. Vito put his hand up.

"Rome, this fuckin' guy! Where'd you find him? Oh man, my *stugots* ache!"

Marco was about to burst a vein in his neck from laughing, too.

Phil remained quiet.

"Never knew I was so funny," Frank said to the group.

"Casper couldn't get a loan at *a bank*—hell, they wouldn't let him park *his car* there! No one would back him. He begged Nero to pay them off. He had no choice. Know what he's charging him a month, just for the juice?" Vito asked.

Frank shrugged.

"The vig. The *shy*," Vito's hand went up. *"Interest!"* Vito accentuated his point by extending five slender fingers. "Just for the *juice!* Before he even touches the nut. Five hundo!" he said, showing everyone his fingers.

"That's fair. Still, a lot of carpet to lay," Roman added.

"But they're buddies, right?" Frank muttered, still trying to grasp the arrangement. Vito threw his hands up. As the chatter dwindled for a few moments, Frank realized that Phil hadn't spoken since walking in. He approached him.

"Get any partridge today?" he asked Phil, trying to coax him to talk.

"Uh, yeah. Got three," Phil said. "You got good instincts, Frank. I don't know what the hell Nero's doing up this way either. But I wouldn't piss on him if he were on fire."

Roman stared at Phil, the same as before.

"Nero still has a hard-on for Casper because of the raccoons—hey!" Vito snapped his fingers. "They say anything about shooting raccoons?" he laughed through the question.

"The raccoon killer," Marco said.

"Yeah, they mentioned it," Frank said. "Pretty wild."

"Nero fancies himself as Mr. Dead-Eye. About ten years ago, he stuck a raccoon when those three were bow hunting for deer. A few seasons later, had to be, what, '78?" Vito asked.

"Yeah," Roman said. "Five years ago."

Vito continued. "So now they're bow hunting again. Casper tells Gabe and Nero he saw 'a few' raccoons near his blind. Nero tells him he'll give him twenty bucks for every one he can kill, thinking he's seen Casper with a gun and *testa bianco* couldn't shoot a barn if you put him ten feet in front of it. He never figured him to go Sitting Bull on his ass! Thirteen at twenty a pop," Vito said.

Everyone but Phil and Roman were howling.

"They left that part out," Frank said.

"William Tell couldn't have done that!" Marco added.

"That prick. I don't like that guy," Phil turned his eyes from Frank to Roman.

"Hey Philly," Roman said. "We all heard you, OK?"

Phil went to the sink, leaning over it like he was tired. He let the water run, and cupped his hand under it, funneling it into his mouth. Roman watched his back. Despite Roman's subtlety, Frank observed the exchange.

"Those two kept talking about some trucker," Frank said. "I really don't want to know anything about it. I just come up to visit Roman, and hunt. That's all."

Frank watched Roman walk over to the picture window and stand there. He stared out at the lake. Standing there, under the high peak of the living room, Roman appeared small.

"Then later on at the bar, Nero starts a fight, he's still so pissed. Man, that poor trucker!" Vito said. He became animated, using his hands to talk. "Rome, Philly and me met up with Casper and Nero at a bar outside Gaylord. By then they're both just *u'pazza—crazy* drunk—already *hammered*. Casper is bragging to anyone who'll listen about all the raccoons. Nero was in a mood, too. I mean he's *seething*. Night goes on, he's giving the *malocchia*—the evil eye—to this big Polack trucker. Nero keeps saying, '*Look at that big* finoik—*I should kick that* finocchia's *ass*,' that kind of stuff."

"*Finoik*," Frank said, with an air of nonchalance. "Like a fag."

Vito pointed at him, his eyebrows up. "*Hey, very good!* Nero sees the trucker head to the john, he goes stumbling after him, knocking over beers. Well they came out of the toilet *swinging!* While he was pissing, Nero claimed the Polack grabbed his *martello*. The trucker accused Nero of the same thing. If you seen Nero's wife, *Maddon'* you know *that's* bullshit. So this Polack goes off, yelling, '*Dago dicksmoker! You wanna smoke something? Smoke this!*'"

Frank keyed in on the word.

Vito continued. "Nero, he's a gorilla! He got in some really good ones, but the Polack was too big. Threw Nero around like a rag doll, landing haymakers. Nero breaks a cue stick over this guy's coconut, and then it was really on. It just pissed the Polack off more."

Roman was back at the table. He cut Vito off.

"Before any of us can get to him, Casper spins the Polack around, drops him with one punch to the button. Folded like a goddamn umbrella. I was there and if I'm lying, I'm dying; dropped him stone cold. This guy was *huge*—I mean *troppo grande*. Made Sherman Armbrewster look like fucking Willie Shoemaker," Roman said, referring to Sherman, the huge contractor who had built his cabin. "We all kicked the guy around some while he was on the floor. Phil and I dragged him out, put him in his truck to sleep it off. Then we got out of there."

Phil was still at the sink, his back to them. He remained silent.

"They ever find that Polack? Didn't he go missing—remember that?" Marco said.

"See that picture of his old lady in the *Free Press?* I'd go missing, too," Vito joked.

"He turned up—" Roman emphasized. "Had a girlfriend in Georgian Bay. He expatriated. Lives up in Wawa with her. It was in the papers a while back."

Phil's head lifted, and he turned to look at Roman. Both men's expressions flattened out.

"Where the fuck's *Wawa?*" Marco asked. He started to arrange kindling in the corner fireplace. "*Wawa*. No shit. Must've missed that."

"Gabe told me Nero hopes Casper stays buried under that note forever. Especially because he nailed all those raccoons. Still pisses Nero off whenever it comes up. Shit. Casper will die owing him," Vito concluded.

Frank tapped Roman's forearm. "I know you're going to laugh, but I'm still confused. How the hell do you treat a friend that way? I mean, *they're friends,* right?"

"They are," Roman said. "Nero loves Casper. Seriously. But that's the way it works. He knows the rules. Casper's not a kid, he's a man."

Frank nodded at Roman. They sat there, at the table, and sitting among them was unnerving to him now. The clock buzzed like a hornet, the frequency hitting a weird pitch for a moment before returning to a dull hum. The men kept talking, but Frank didn't hear any of it.

After their partridge dinner that night, the men retired to the couches and chairs in the living room, drinking anisette and coffee by the fire. Frank waffled on leaving early and getting back to Cleveland, but after thinking about it, he decided he'd better spend the night as planned. The sun fell quick and the lake settled to a glassy calm. The lake breeze rattled the blinds on the picture window.

Phil slowly ascended the stairway without speaking. Roman watched him turn into a bedroom and saw the light go out at the top of the stairs.

"I'm gonna burn a cigar," Frank said, and started for the back deck.

"That sounds good, actually," Vito said. He and Marco started forward.

"I'll join you," Roman said. "You guys stay here, relax." The men listened to him dutifully.

Frank and Roman moved two wooden Adirondacks onto the grass in front of the deck, away from the house. Frank lit up and watched Roman get his cigar going. They watched the remnant sun, an enormous orange crescent, slicing through a strip of low purple clouds. The top of the sky was already blackish, and the first stars winked. A flock of geese called out from far off, and Frank let the breeze lick his face. The cigar had a nutty taste that mixed well with the anisette.

"Beautiful up here, Rome," Frank said. "Thanks for having me again."

"I apologize. I didn't think Nero would ever be back," Roman said. Then he gritted his teeth. "Shame on me."

Frank looked at him. "Forget it."

Roman took a long drag off the cigar. He looked at the lake. Frank could see something working at him, and he thought about Cleveland. Roman peeked toward the cabin. Vito and Marco were barely visible.

"The trucker," Roman said in a whisper.

"Roman, don't, *really*," Frank said, matching his tone.

"I only had this place a few months. Four a.m. that same night, Phil calls, says we got trouble. He's at a phone booth in Gaylord. He's crying while he's talking. A guy you know don't cry easy. I'm in my bed, just woke up, thinking, is it my wife in Detroit, one of my brothers, something bad with my Nicky, even. But no, Phil, he's *wailing*."

"*Phil?* The Phil in the cabin?" Frank asked.

"Yeah, I know," Roman replied.

Frank knew he was learning far more about his friend than he ever wanted to but saw no way out. Roman drew off the cigar. He looked at it and smiled.

"He starts going on about Severino. He's cussing holy hell, between the crying, he's cursing in Italian. Name didn't register. Just woke up."

"*Severino?*" Frank asked.

Roman exhaled.

"Nero's first name. Severino Nero Terrazzo. *Some* of those guys only know him as Nero. Not Philly and I. So Nero calls Phil. Tells him he needs some help with the *finoik* trucker."

"You said you and Phil put him in his cab ... " He saw Roman fix on a point across the lake, and his words fell away.

"We did put him in there. And he was alive when we did. Sure, he was a mess. The guy was a driver, no trailer, just a semi truck with that sleeping cab built into it, see? We even covered him up because we felt kind of sorry for him, figuring Nero probably started the whole thing anyway since he was so pissed about the fucking raccoons. I never told anyone this, Frank—not even Vito."

"Stays here," Frank said, feeling like he was on the priestly side of a confessional's screen. Even in the darkening light, he could see the uncertainty on Roman's face. And it seemed they both knew they were about to cross an untenable gap.

"Later, Nero made Phil take him back to the bar. Nero pointed at the truck. When Phil opened the cab, he puked himself."

Frank leaned toward Roman. "Why's that, Roman?"

"The Polack was sitting behind the wheel with something stuffed in his mouth ... " Roman stopped himself. "It was his joint, Frank. His own *martello*. Cut it off while the guy was still alive."

"*What?*"

"Phil said he knew because it was the only wound. Guy was bound with rope, bled to death. That cold son of a bitch tied him up while he slept, cut off his pecker and fed it to him."

"What? Come on," Frank said, suddenly tasting the cheese Nero offered him earlier that day. His stomach flipped and he choked back his cigar.

"I think Nero's the *finocchio*. No one knows except Phil. Nero ... queer as a three-dollar bill."

"*Nero?* Oh my God. *Oh my God,* Roman," Frank looked back at the window. His skin went clammy. "He sat on the *other side of the table* from me." When he caught his breath, Frank touched Roman's arm.

"My God, Roman. Why did Phil call you?" Frank asked.

Roman didn't answer. But he really didn't have to.

Shapes were harder to make out and any depth perception was gone. Frank didn't say anything. His mind replayed the image from earlier that day of Nero, sawing through the bread, the odd smile on the dark man's face as he cut into the wheel of *fontinella*.

"How the hell does someone get away with *that?*" Frank asked, surprised to find an ash two inches long at the end of his now-cold cigar.

"Ever look around while you're driving up north? There are ways. Without getting into it too much, they got rid of *everything*. Lots of places to lose stuff up here. Swamp behind a golf course in Gaylord. Hunt club out that way, got wild boars, bears, coyotes roaming around. It was a week before the Feds made it up there. The townies mentioned the fight, but so what? Deer hunting season. Guys get juiced up. Happens all the time. Nero was gone by then, 'vacationing' back home on the Island—his brother has a villa in Polizzi Generosa. Feds ain't stupid, though. Something didn't smell right. But ... no body, no Nero. No case, really."

A moth fluttered into the tip of Frank's cigar and it gave him a start.

"Casper? He involved?" Frank asked, but the question floated off.

Roman took a long drag off the cigar. He *tsked* the air.

Sitting next to him in the cooling night air, Frank felt claustrophobic.

"Gabe probably came by just to bullshit, bust my balls," Roman said as an aside.

Frank measured his thoughts, and in that time, he had a fleeting image from many years ago, of taking his two boys on a pontoon boat to catch bluegills with waxworms and bobbers. He shook it off like a rogue chill but it buzzed around in his brain and didn't leave.

"Roman. Why would you help that *animal?*" The whisper sounded loud in the darkness.

"Because that's the way it is. I told you; Nero's family ties go back to the Boot. Phil and me got put in a bad way. We did what we were told to do. I got a call from someone, from *somewhere*. Phil drew the short straw, had to clean it all up. Said Nero laughed the whole time. Philly still ain't right. That's the way it is, though. Get a call like that, you say, 'OK.' You're not the only one with kids, Frank."

Roman drew a deep lung full of smoke and blew it out. The light in the cabin went out and finally choked the dusk into total blackness.

"That trucker, he had a three-year-old daughter. Young wife. Ordinary schmuck from Battle Creek. Wife told the papers he was heading to Seney, to bring back a trailer of Christmas trees. Stopped in for a few beers in Gaylord. Had the bad luck of pissing next to Nero."

"Yeah, bad luck," Frank said, with a mouth dry as sand.

Roman spat on the grass and Frank wondered just how to make it all go away.

"Yeah," Roman sighed.

Everything was bathed in shades of blue and black. The two sat there saying nothing, and Frank felt like he was trying to breathe the remaining air a trapped miner does. The trickling streamlets that fed the lake, which on the past trips he found soothing, were now as loud as a dam. He scraped the ash off his cigar and relit it, the taste fouled by the remnant charring. The flame let him see Roman's face for a fleeting instant. The peepers' and crickets' songs became preternaturally loud in the enveloping blackness, drowning out everything until just offshore, a splash exploded in the inky water as something small was devoured by something large.

He could hear Roman's raspy breathing. Frank waited, looking for his out. It finally came.

"Did I tell you? My oldest son Lee and my daughter-in-law bought me an early birthday present. Next fall, he's taking me to Colorado with him on an elk hunt. Ever been there?"

"Colorado. No, never been," Roman replied.

"Me either," Frank said. "Never hunted elk. Looking forward to it."

Frank was relieved that neither man could see each other's eyes. In the blue shapelessness of the night, all Frank saw was the tip of Roman's cigar glowing and dimming as he inhaled and exhaled. He didn't know what to do except sit there, waiting for him to speak. And if Roman didn't say a word at all now, well maybe that would be OK, too.

In the space filled by the frog and insect sounds, Roman finally cleared his throat, then spoke. "I built this place to get away from things. In Detroit. You know, to be outdoors. Come up here with my brothers, my son."

Frank let it settle. He chewed the cigar, sucking hard. It had gone out again.

Roman's chair creaked.

"Elk hunting. That sounds nice. You're welcome up here anytime, Frank."

"Thanks, Rome."

"Sure. Tell you something, though. That Casper could really shoot that bow. Man, he was a dead-eye with that thing," Roman said.

Frank shivered.

He looked up at the dark cabin. Its color matched the thick woods surrounding them. The spaces in the trees were as black as he knew the cabin would be, later on, when he would eventually need to turn off the light in his room and finally drift off to sleep. There were plenty of spaces for a man to hide out there, if he were so inclined. And Frank grew fearful. It entered him like a poison, and it came on quicker than he could ever believe. It wasn't just the dark of the woods, or his waiting bedroom.

It was the knowing.

Lady Fatima

Albert Giardelli and his two brothers, Dom and Luigi—thirty-seven, thirty-five, and thirty-two respectively—were in and out of prison for extortion, armed robbery, and assault. Cumulatively, the three brothers had done more than fifteen years in Jackson Prison and until now, had never been free men for a stretch longer than six months. So it was by some miracle of God that in August of 1966, Fatima, their eighty-six-year-old widowed mother, found all of her boys out on parole at the same time. The three had just finished performing a thorough once-over of her home to see if anything was in need of repair.

Albert was married, and Dom and Luigi, both bachelors, shared a place two miles west near Chandler Park. The three brothers sat in the brick colonial, the house they grew up in, eating lunch at the dining room table. Fatima's home had three bedrooms on the second floor. The boys made sure the two deadbolts at the front and back still held. They installed hooks and eyes on all the windows to prevent anyone from sliding them open. They had a phone installed in Fatima's second floor bedroom. The neighborhood was turning, starting with an over-run of rundown homes and worse, drug users that did smash-and-grabs—addicts climbing through a broken window and gone like the wind after looting whatever they could stuff into a sack.

Before he went away for his last stint, Albert had painted the entire inside of the house, and aside from a few cracks, the plaster looked as fresh as the day it was applied. Photos of Fatima with their deceased father, Secundo, crowded the mantle of the fireplace—a loving, sepia-toned timeline of their married life from newlyweds until the year of Secundo's death.

Fatima didn't move very well, but still had the energy to prepare her boys a tasty lunch. Plates of olive oil and hard rolls sat in the middle of the table. She waddled over and set down a sizzling pan of roasted red and yellow peppers in front of Albert. The scent of garlic and lemon tickled the sizable noses of the brothers. Albert scooped up the lion's share before Luigi's fork could find them.

"I wanted that one!" Luigi scowled. "You little prick!"

"Not what your girlfriend says," Albert joked, popping it into his mouth. Luigi pointed a steak knife at him and stabbed the air.

Albert had opened up a garage on Hayes, and had convinced his younger brothers to join him, saying all three needed to keep their noses clean for the foreseeable future. Fatima's heart was failing, and although she was a feisty old woman, she probably wouldn't see ninety. She had begged them to go clean so she could spend her last days knowing her boys had come back to the church, even though none of them had been inside one since their father's funeral.

Secundo Giardelli, a reliable cement man, had died after falling from a bridge being constructed over the I-94 freeway. Secundo hung on for three days, his wife and sons keeping vigil at his bedside in North Detroit General Hospital. He made the boys swear they'd protect their mother to the death and live their days as law-abiding men. They had kept up half the bargain.

Fatima's sons were tough, prone to hitting someone before talking about things and pile-driving their stout bodies into anyone who gave them lip. Albert was the nastiest of the three, though Luigi and Dom weren't exactly pacifists. Some of the Mustache Petes in town offered them jobs collecting debts or heisting shipments from unknowing, out-of-state truckers. But as thieves, they weren't very good, so they did a lot of time. The boys had honor though, and were tight-lipped. Since they never ratted anyone out, they could always count on steady work after they got released.

Besides her pulmonary conditions, Fatima was deaf in one ear, so when the boys spoke to her they pretty much shouted everything.

"Mama, why won't you let us take you to Eden Glen? Italo Ciamataro's mother lives there. You remember Viola? She loves that Eden Glen," Albert said.

Fatima lifted a papery hand and crossed herself. She stood just under five feet and weighed less than ninety pounds. She had milky eyes and what little hair left on her head was white as salt. She gummed a hard roll with her slipping dentures.

"I'm not a leaving my house, Albert. I tolda' you boys; I *stay*," she said, her faltering voice refusing to let go of its Calabrese accent. "This is a *my* house."

"Mama. The *melanzana* are moving in, do you understand?" When he said the word, it came out *melonjohnny*. "They're animals. They'll knock you down and stick a knife in you just as soon as say hello. They're all juiceheads, Ma." Albert tried to scare her with his tone. "Right, Lu?"

Albert raised his eyebrows to Luigi.

"He's right, Mom. The eggplant are taking over," Luigi said. "You ain't safe no more in this house." He motioned to Albert, and the two watched Dom sucking up olives off the plate like a hairy anteater.

Dom smiled a little as he grabbed half a log of hard salami. He picked at the peppercorns and chewed them. Luigi and Albert looked at each other. They waited for Dom to say something. He finally spoke through his voracious eating.

"Olives are good for you," Dom said. He studied the food. "So's salami." He chomped the stump of lunch meat with such recklessness, he bit through the string netting that covered it. Pieces of string hung from his thick lips.

Albert shook his head. "Hey, *porcaccione*—ever hear of using a knife and fork?"

Luigi looked at Dom, his mouth curled in disgust. *"Minchia,"* he said.

"Boys, that talk!" Fatima said. "Luigi, you and Dommy, you can move back with me. Take you old rooms. You keep me safe." Fatima worked a black rosary with her fingers, weathered grey twigs that looked ready to snap at any time.

"Ma, maybe you could move in with Albert and Mariana? Mariana was talking about how much she loved having you as a mother-in-law. How's 'bout it, Al?" Luigi offered with a shit-eating grin.

Albert's smile faded. "You *mamaluke*," he whispered at his laughing brother. "At our next house, Ma," he continued. "Our little flat is pretty cramped."

Fatima's brow furrowed, and the friction caused by the speed in which she worked the beads of the rosary seemed capable of starting a fire.

"It'll be OK, though. We'll check on you every day. And look—I brought you a little something," Albert said.

He produced a souvenir Detroit Tigers bat. It was his only memento from the last game his father had taken him to before he died. Detroit had played the Yankees at what was then called Briggs Stadium. Fondling the bat, Albert smiled, flashing back to his father showing him the signatures of Schoolboy Rowe and Hank Greenberg at the souvenir stand. After Secundo died, Albert tucked it away in the corner of his bedroom. As a weapon of self-defense, it looked barely lethal enough to club a carp. Albert whacked his palm with it a couple of times. With each *thwap,* Fatima flinched.

"What the hell's she s'posed to do with that?" Luigi asked.

"Psychological you idiots!" Albert whispered, tapping his temple.

From the sunken living room floor, three steps up was a landing spacious enough for a desk and chair. An old Bible sat on the desk nestled in a wooden stand, and on days when the sun was right, Fatima tried to read it using an oversized magnifying glass, but the glaucoma was making that more difficult. Straight up from the landing at a ninety-degree angle were the second floor bedrooms.

"Ma, I'm gonna leave this here," Albert said, placing the little ball bat against the ledge of the stand. "You ever hear anyone inside the house, take the bat and lock yourself in the bedroom. Call one of us anytime, *capiece?*"

"Albert what am I gonna do? I can't a hit nobody," Fatima's mouth shook.

"Brilliant, bro," Luigi said, shaking his head at Albert. "Ma, you just call us if there's a problem, OK?"

"*Sangue mia*, you boys come home, stay with Mama?" Fatima pleaded to Dom and Luigi as she worked her rosary. "The devil, he scares me."

Albert picked the bat up from the Bible. "Ma, Pop bought me this when we went to the ballpark that time. You understand? The Tigers? *El Tigres!* The Yankees. Remember how proud Dad was to see DiMaggio?" Fatima's eyes perked up. "DiMaggio and Marius Russo, they said hello to us. Pop was so proud; he called them *Paisans in Pinstripes*."

That made Fatima smile. She studied the bat. "Secundo bought you this? He loved you boys," she said. Her eyes twinkled and her head nodded. She took the little bat from Albert and held it in her open palms. She put it to her breast and her three boys came together, tightly embracing their mother.

"Everything's going to be fine, Ma," Albert said.

In the next few weeks, two of the homes on Fatima's block were looted. Yet it seemed like hers would remain safe, until Ike Mackelroy, a cat burglar addicted to heroin, started to scope out her place. He had been watching Fatima's home closely since spying the old woman standing at her fireplace mantle late one night. For the three weeks he'd been around, he observed three brutish men randomly come and go. Fatima's street had gotten hot with patrol cars cruising the area, so Ike had to wait until the time was right before making his move on the easy mark.

From the corner of her front window, he'd peeked in and saw old clocks on the mantle and gold chains and Italian charms lying on the coffee table, stuff he knew he could fence on Woodward to score quick cash for his fix. All he needed was the least conspicuous point of entry. He found it on the side of the house: a window that was stationed at the foot of a small landing. He flattened himself against the wall and looked inside. At eye level was an old Bible sitting on a desk.

Finally on the night of a day Albert had visited, Fatima and Ike Mackelroy would both meet their devil face-to-face. At just past 11 p.m., Fatima turned out all the lights in her home. She prayed for safety and ascended the three steps from the main floor. Her fingers grazed the Bible before she started slowly up the other set of stairs. She was halfway to her bedroom door when she heard a rapping on the window.

"Jesus protect me from evil … Secundo, stay near me," she whispered.

Despite her sons' warning, she walked toward the noise instead of away from it. The sound of broken glass startled her as she stood on the steps, inches away from the chair. Her hand found the little baseball bat Albert had left for her.

Ambient light from a streetlamp illuminated a black-skinned hand that reached through the window. Slender fingers delicately plucked the jagged shards of glass that remained in the wooden pane. Fatima squinted, seeing a head poke through. The man's face was gaunt, her weak eyes managing to see some details as the light from the streetlamp hit his cheekbones. The whites of Ike Mackelroy's eyes looked fluorescent in the inky darkness. He wormed the top half of his sinewy body through the window, his palms on the floor of the landing, right below the Bible stand.

"Damn near cut my dick," Ike whispered, finally making his way inside. He turned on a flashlight and the top of his head burned. He fell to the floor in a heap.

"Hey now! What the hell—" his flashlight shined over the face of little Fatima.

"You dried up old bitch! Hit me on the coconut—" but before he could get the sentence finished she bopped him again. She had tapped him with all the force she could, but the effect seemed almost keystone in its delivery. When Ike tried to focus on his assailant, the old woman's face went blurry. He tried to break for the window. "Hey now! OK, OK! Just cut that shit out now!"

Ike's head rose one more time and he put his hand up. She gave him another three whacks, almost delicate in delivery but very well placed.

Nok … Nok … Nok …

Ike's eyes rolled back in his head, and before he went out cold, he saw Fatima looking down upon him, all of the ridges of her face highlighted by the streetlight.

When the boys arrived at her house, they practically knocked the door down charging inside. The home was still dark, with only the light of the streetlamp bathing the landing of the stairs. Frosty blue light painted Fatima's frail body. She was standing watch over Ike, the souvenir bat looking as big as a major league model clenched in her small hands. The weak beam of Ike's flashlight cut through the darkness, shining on his unconscious body. There was not a drop of blood on Ike's head. Just three lumps visible under his short nappy hair. He moved a little, and Albert hugged his mother, taking the baseball bat from her.

"*Maddon'!* Filthy *melanzana* … " Luigi said.

Albert touched her shoulder. "Ma, come on. Let's get you to the living room."

"I'm not moving from this house. I called *la polizia.*"

"Shit," Luigi said.

"That devil didn't see me standing here. Did I do good, Albert?" Fatima asked her oldest. He scooped up Fatima in his hirsute arms and whisked her down the three steps to the main floor. He walked her through the archway that led to the living room.

"You did great, Mama," Albert said.

"Yeah, you did. Listen, you let us handle this, OK?" Luigi said.

The two brothers watched Albert carry their mother like a sleeping child, seating her on the plastic-covered couch in the black living room. Albert turned toward the landing and then stopped. He clicked on the radio to full volume. The jarring Tarantella played as he made his way back to Ike and his waiting brothers, souvenir bat in hand.

Ike Mackelroy raised his head, but before he could open his eyes, Dom's size 9 EEE foot shattered the wafer-like bones of his septum. Mercifully, the thief was unconscious again as Albert lifted the little bat. He worked on Ike's side and broke five of his ribs and his left forearm. Luigi took fifty in cash from Ike's front pocket and for good measure, stepped on the fingers of his right hand. Dom removed a hunting knife from his own pocket, wiped it clean and placed it next to Ike's crushed fingers, as if Ike had dropped it. Dom looked at his two brothers. Both considered the planted weapon. Collectively shrugging their shoulders, the two nodded their approval.

"You wiped it down. Yeah," Albert remarked. "Let's try it on. I like it."

When the two squad cars pulled up, their red and blue lights danced across the dark room, highlighting the antiquated photos of young Fatima and Secundo. Albert caught a glimpse of his father's stoic face and silently apologized for what seemed like the millionth time since his deathbed request. He dropped the bat next to Ike's head.

Three cops came in with guns drawn. The lead cop, a big Irishman named Tanner who'd been on the force for fifteen years, pointed his revolver at Albert. He looked around the space of the dark house.

"Easy. We're her kids," Albert told Tanner. Tanner assessed the faces of the brothers and he had an idea about them. He holstered his gun.

"OK, greaseballs. Up against the wall. You've done this before, right?" His head turned toward the living room. "Turn down that God-awful noise."

One of the cops found the radio, scratchily playing Italian folk songs, and turned it off. He didn't notice Fatima sitting there.

"Hey, this *cocooza* tried to rob our mother. He attacked her," Luigi said. "This is her house. What'd you expect us to do?"

Tanner and one of the cops stepped up to the landing. "How about let us do our job? Jesus, what did you assholes do to him?" Tanner said, noticing the pool of blood around Ike's crushed face. "You guys aren't the ones who called this in."

"Maybe next time he won't rob an old woman," Dom said. "Look, he had a knife. See? Knife."

Tanner looked at the weapon next to Ike's ruined hand.

"Well gee whiz, you're *right! How* the hell did I *ever* miss that?" Tanner replied. "Let's make this easy on all of us," Tanner undid a pair of cuffs.

One of the other cops winced and gently nudged Ike. A paramedic hurried past and started surveying the man's injuries.

"It was me who hit him!" Fatima called out.

Tanner stood up. "Who said that?" he asked, looking for the voice.

"Mama, don't say nothing!" Albert yelled.

A light went on and the living room glowed. Fatima took her hand from the floor lamp next to the couch.

"Me. Fatima Giardelli. I hit that man. This is my house. And those are my boys."

The paramedic shook his head and mouthed, "no way" to Tanner.

"Ma'am, we know you love your sons, but you didn't do this. Let's go, you're all going in for assault. On probation?" He pointed at Albert. "You, I recognize."

"He's waking up," the paramedic called out.

Tanner leaned next to Ike. The man moaned like a dying cow.

"Old dried-up bitch hit a man without … "

"Watch your tongue, you lying *melanzana*," Albert said.

"Relax," Tanner told Albert and then turned his attention back to Ike. "We're bringing you to Detroit Receiving before we book you. Take a look, which one of these guys did this? Johnny, bring 'em over here," Tanner commanded. The other cop dutifully shoved the three brothers toward Ike. They stood at the bottom of the landing in a hastily made lineup. Tanner and the paramedic helped Ike get to a sitting position. The thief squinted at the three.

"Weren't none of them … " Ike mumbled.

"Say again?" Tanner asked.

"Watch your hands pal," Luigi told the officer grabbing his wrists. "What are you, a *finoik?*"

"Ahh, screw this," Albert said. "I did it, OK? Take me in, just get this thieving *melanzana* out of my mother's house and leave her be. It was *me*, OK?"

"Bullshit. I did it. I did it *all*," Luigi said.

"They're covering for me. I'm the guy. I did it," Dom chimed in.

Tanner looked at the men one by one and shook his head. "What is this, the Dago version of *Spartacus?* Get them away from me."

As the cops walked the boys toward the front door, Fatima suddenly appeared below at the first step of the landing. Ike saw her and his eyes bugged out.

"That's her! The devil!" Ike screamed.

"What?" Tanner asked.

"Get her away from me!" Ike howled. "Wasn't none of them mofos—it was her! That crazy old Dago bitch—right *there!* She's the motherfuckin' devil! She tried to kill me with that club!" The addict thrashed around, scooting against the wall. "Wouldn't let me out the house, crazy old Dago devil-bitch. Busted me up good."

Ike turned to the paramedic. "I needs me some morphine, doc! You gots to get me some morphine … gets me *something.* I think my ribs is busted, too. Don't let that old lady near me. She's a devil, I tell you!"

Albert eyed Luigi and Dom. They gave each other a shrug that said to run with Fatima's version. Ike Mackelroy had unknowingly opened an alibi door for the Giardelli brothers to walk right through and take residence in.

Tanner leaned down and shook Ike, whose words slurred like a warped LP.

"Look, boy! Don't tell me this little old woman—hey! Don't you pass out!"

Ike's eyes rolled back and closed shut, and his lights went out. The medic tried to put an IV into his arm while another packed gauze into Ike's nostrils.

"This guy's got massive trails. Can't find a good vein … " the medic said matter-of-factly. "We'll take him in. You going to meet us at Emergency?"

"I don't believe this … yeah, I guess I'll have to. Cuff these Guineas. We'll sort them out at the thirteenth. Let them sit awhile," Tanner said. "You three ain't getting away with a beating like this, hear me? No way. I don't give a shit *what* he did."

The other cops snapped the cuffs on.

"What are you taking us in for? You heard the *eggplant,*" Luigi protested.

"He was afraid of you three. What did you think he'd say? I wouldn't treat a fucking dog like that. Let's go. I'm sure I won't need to look too far to find you guys have violated at least one condition of your paroles," Tanner said.

"Albert! Dommy, Luigi! Please—don't go!" Fatima cried out softly. "Stay."

Tanner turned to Fatima. He was six feet two and had shoulders as wide as a door frame. Hearing the pain in her voice—her fear—his sharp blue eyes transformed from squinting daggers to open wounds as he took in the lines on the old woman's face. In his years on the force, Tanner had pulled so many shit calls that the bodies, the death, and decay—and all the bullshit alibis—had worn down the part of his soul that once held any sympathy for cons. And yet, the sight of the helpless always melted the hardened armor the job had forged over him.

The younger of the two cops held onto Luigi. "You want we should put them in the car?" he asked.

Tanner held his hand up. He walked Fatima back into the living room.

"One minute," Tanner said to the younger cops under his charge. "Mama, I know you made the call. You all alone here? Where's Papa at?" Tanner asked.

Fatima shook her head.

"Secundo been with the Lord, going to be eighteen years."

The big cop put his face next to hers. Fatima's eyes were unhealthy looking, the tear ducts raw and the lashes long gone from the lids. He could see she had been a beautiful woman once. He looked to the mantle, and in the soft light saw her as a fifteen-year-old girl, holding a basket of spring bouquets in front of a flower shop in Calabria. There was a photo from each of the boy's first communions, placed with reverence from oldest to youngest, all three wearing pious expressions. The photos were arranged outwardly, starting from the central wedding portrait.

"I hit him three good ones," she said, unblinking. "That's what did it."

Tanner smiled. Instincts told him a few things. One was that Ike, no matter how bad of a guy he was, didn't deserve the thrashing the Giardelli boys gave him. Not for a B&E. Two, was that *innocent men* don't just get their asses kicked for nothing, nor do they find themselves inside a house that's not their own. And finally, that these three Dagos would eventually get nabbed for something else. It didn't take a cop to see the old lady hadn't delivered this beating. But maybe, if he could just let himself take Ike's word on how things went down, maybe her boys could keep clean for a while, but only if he could swallow his cop's pride for this tiny old woman, who seemed to have little time left. Fatima didn't waver in the stare-down with Tanner.

"You did all that to the poor wretch over there? Really, Mama? C'mon."

"Mama, don't say another—" Albert interjected.

"I'm asking *her* the question. Now ... *Mama?* Tell me," Tanner continued.

"This is *my* house. Yes," Fatima replied, never flinching. "I hit him three good ones. Then I call my boys *after* I call *la polizia*."

"He's hurt real bad," Tanner said. "Broken nose, wrist. You're pretty tough."

"I'm all alone. All I have is my boys. They have no father for so long ... " Her voice deteriorated into a crying whimper. She finally looked away.

Tanner bit his lip. He looked at the photos on the mantle.

"OK then. You heard her, boys. Let 'em go," Tanner told the two cops.

The officers relaxed and closed their leather jackets tight. They took the cuffs off the brothers and walked out, muttering. Albert smiled at Luigi. The paramedics wheeled Ike out on the stretcher. Dom sneered down at the thief as they passed by, then seeing Ike's battered face, made a hasty sign of the cross.

Tanner started toward the three brothers, but not before Fatima grabbed his arm and slipped something into his hand. She closed his big palm around it.

"*La guerno!* This will keep you safe from evil, from the *malocchia*. Never let it go! You a good man officer. I don't want no *thing* to happen to you. *Il diavo-lo*—he visits us in many shapes. This is a shield for you, officer. Keep evil away—keep *il diavolo* away. Ward off the *malocchia!*"

"Mill-oik-yee-ah?" Tanner tried to sound the word out phonetically.

"*Malocchia!*" Fatima corrected him.

"The evil eye," Albert said from behind him.

Fatima looked at Tanner and pulled one of her eyelids closed. She moved forward and kissed him. Stiff whiskers tickled Officer Tanner's cheek, and he felt himself blush. He opened his hand and saw a gold Italian charm shaped like a slender horn—the *guerno*—believed by many to have the ability to ward off Satan. Tanner started to protest, but assessing Fatima's face, he thought better of it. He tipped his cap to her.

"The evil eye. Well, thank you, Mama. I've been a cop a long time. No one's ever done something like this for me. Not ever."

He patted her hand and walked toward the brothers. Tanner stood in front of Albert, staring at him the whole time as he addressed the three.

"I won't be hearing about the three of you, right? Despite my display of kindness here, I can be a mean sonofabitch when someone isn't appreciative of my generosity. I'm sure that if I were to look at someone's boots, I might find blood on them. And if I asked that poor black bastard they just wheeled out of here if that hunting knife was his, he *might* say it wasn't. That would get ugly for Mama. You know what I'm saying, right? About appreciating my generous ways? *Capiece?*"

"*Capiece,*" Dom mumbled.

Tanner was still locked in a stare-down with Albert, who stood mute.

"*Capiece,*" Luigi added.

Tanner moved a little closer to Albert, but Fatima's oldest boy didn't blink. When the bridge of his flat nose was even with the bottom of Tanner's, he sighed.

"Yeah, *capiece*," Albert finally said. "But she kicked his ass good, didn't she?"

Tanner stiffened but the feeling of the charm in his hand stopped him. He took a last look at Fatima before he walked out. The three brothers watched him leave, and it was a good minute before anyone spoke.

"*Minchia.* I'll be a son of a bitch," Luigi said.

"A cop who wasn't a certified prick. I seen it all now," Dom muttered.

Albert could only shake his head. He kissed Fatima, and she slapped his cheek lightly. He smiled and gave her a wink.

"Damn, you did good, Mama," Albert said. "Let's get you to bed. I'll stay the night." He put his arm around her.

"He had no right to come in my house, Albert. Your father, he did all the woodwork in this house. He made the mantle. That devil had a no right."

"I know, Mama," Albert agreed, as he kissed her forehead. "He had no right."

★ ★ ★

After Tanner had finished filing his report on the breaking and entering at Fatima's house, he left the thirteenth precinct in his Impala convertible. Most people didn't wear seatbelts in the '60s, and he was no exception. Yet for some reason he pulled his on that night. It was after 2 a.m., and as he traveled up Woodward, he glanced down to admire the 18-karat gold charm the tiny woman had given him. He smiled recalling Fatima's insistence about the *malocchia*. At that moment, a drunk driver doing eighty-five ran a red light, broadsiding Tanner's convertible. The *guerno* flew from his palm as the Impala skidded sideways across Woodward Avenue, slamming him into a utility pole. The pole snapped at the sidewalk and fell onto a storefront with Tanner's ragtop directly below it.

And while Tanner had never been the superstitious type, he became one in a real hurry. He had seen plenty of strange things happen in accidents when cars hit immovable objects. Once he had come upon a crash scene where a man's feet, still in their shoes, rested on the pedals, the rest of his body thrown fifty yards through the windshield, all from the effects of inertia.

When the drunk smashed into him, Tanner's car, along with the wooden pole, was pushed up against the brick façade of Leone Ophthalmology. The pole hit Dr. Leone's heavy box sign, loosening it from the building. Sparks rained down as the pole bounced off the sign, falling through the canvas top, finally coming to rest slightly above Tanner's right temple. The weight of the pole crumpled his car lengthwise. Tanner was dazed and pinned in his compressed seat. He looked above to see the cracked ophthalmology sign swinging, held to the wall by a single anchor bolt, and him right below it, unable to move. The sign creaked once and finally pulled away from the brick wall. It was aimed straight for his head, but as Tanner began making his peace with God, the sign crashed onto the crumpled hood instead. It settled in front of the spider-webbed windshield, tilted on an angle, the left half of it atop the wooden telephone pole just a foot in front of his face. He stared at it the whole hour he waited to be cut out. Dr. Leone's white sign was adorned with an unblinking, black eyeball.

Later, the firemen would tell Tanner the corner of the box sign had grazed the telephone pole first, redirecting its landing spot. It was the only reason it missed his head. Tanner walked away without a scratch. While inside the car, staring into the unyielding eyeball, Tanner had a lot of time to think. And when he remembered the *guerno*, he didn't have to look very far. It *stood* directly in front of him. The point of the gold horn was embedded in the vinyl dashboard—impossibly sticking straight up, as if it were balancing there on its own, between him and the sign.

Evil exists. It comes in many forms; black, white, or shades of grey. It can manifest itself as a drug that ruins your life, or in the body of a thief trying to rob you of your dignity, your security or your memories. It can reveal itself as armed resistance, using a weapon as benign as a souvenir bat or a cruel beating that doesn't fit the crime—administered by men with a collectively skewed moral compass. Sometimes it's a drunk wielding an 8,000-pound weapon on a darkened highway. But who can say what truly *repels* evil?

Officer Tanner filed for a leave of absence from the Detroit Police Department the next day. He retired three months later, taking a position in security with Ford Motor. Tanner had developed an odd taste in jewelry for an Irishman, considering he wore an Italian *guerno* around his neck for the rest of his life.

Even though he knew it was the combination of inertia and *chance*—some complicated physics formula—during the crash that had caused the *guerno* to fly from his hand and stick straight up from the spongy dashboard, Tanner took it for what it was. He realized that in his own way, Ike Mackelroy had rightly called Fatima a devil. Ike certainly had every right to feel that way, but really, he just happened to pick the wrong woman to steal from. Because that same night, Fatima Giardelli had seen her own devil coming through the window of her house. And she kicked its ass.

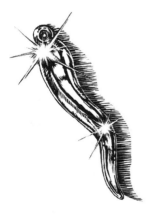

The Measure of a Man

Gino Boselli's athletically fit, forty-four-year-old body was so freezing cold that he had barely any feeling below the waist. He and Jim Perenetto, his best friend and hunting companion, had flown into Northern Labrador from Detroit—a fifteen-hour flight requiring three connections on puddle jumpers and prop planes—for the hunting trip of a lifetime. The predicament they were in was the last thing Gino would have expected.

After two weeks of temperatures that hovered in the teens, the men were greeted by a climate that had settled into a comfortable mid-thirty-degree range, perfect walking weather for the kind of hunting they would be doing, which required covering much of Labrador's hilly terrain by foot. Soaring out of low clouds, as the plane descended to land on the icy runway of Lake Boreal—the lake that Chilakoot Lodge looked out upon—the men could see ice fishing shanties dotting its white surface. Later that night, the two friends enjoyed a dinner of northern pike that Ray Wolfstalker, the owner of the lodge, had pulled through the holes that morning.

But that was yesterday, when after their meal the two vacationing firemen from Precinct 22 had savored their cognacs on leather couches, smoking fat, cheap cigars in front of an oaken fire in the great room surrounded by big game mounts.

Gino, a decorated, veteran Detroit fireman, was being groomed for promotion to lieutenant. He was fifteen years in and had survived every conceivable danger: collapsing walls, smoke inhalation, bullets from rioting residents, and of course, heat often approaching the core of the sun. At this moment, with winds gusting to fifty miles per hour, as he blindly trudged through snow two feet deep, and possessing the tacit knowledge of what it felt like to be burned alive, he found it cruelly ironic that he was going to freeze to death.

The Detroiters had arrived on the sheltered Canadian bay of Chilakoot two weeks before Thanksgiving of 1971 with lofty expectations. Jim was ten years Gino's senior and had broken him in as a rookie. He had three kids in high school and would retire a full captain at the end of the year. The two had set aside vacation days and a month's pay to make the trip a reality. Dying in the cold miles from home was not part of the plan.

Fate decided that the guide they had reserved for their trip a year in advance, a revered woodsman named Leslie Beauchamp, had to bail on them because of the recent passing of his wife's father. And so Leslie, who knew every fjord and valley in the region and the game that inhabited it, had handed off his duties to a fellow guide, Spencer Devereux. Wolfstalker assured them that their replacement guide was every bit as knowledgeable, and in fact it had been Spencer who taught Leslie everything he knew.

"I'm confident he'll help put trophies in your dens," Wolfstalker had waved a hand toward the great room as he spoke of Spencer.

The blizzard had caught everyone off guard. Spencer Devereux, a French-Canadian who was a quarter Indian and happened to be Leslie's cousin, had no explanation for the storm. Still, in hindsight, turning over duties to him for anything other than carrying gear was so reckless an act as to warrant legal action. But such a thing was unforeseeable to the Detroiters on holiday. The two were simply so excited to be that far north in prime big game country that they overlooked myriad red flags, accepting the ringing endorsement Wolfstalker had heaped on the replacement.

As a guide, Spencer's best days were behind him. He knew the terrain all right, but his preparatory skills had diminished severely, mostly because of a weakness for whiskey. Gino noticed him putting down the sour mash pretty good the night before, and worry had tugged at the edges of his conscience. He'd asked Spencer about maybe packing clothes warmer than the parkas and gloves they had, but was told it would only add unnecessary weight. Spencer didn't pack flares, and his emergency supplies were thin, limited to two moth-eaten blankets, some jerky, and a lantern. Instinctively, Gino slipped a flashlight into his own gear pocket before they turned in for bed. When he voiced his concerns about Spencer to Jim, his friend called him a "nervous Nellie."

"The guy's Leslie Beauchamp's cousin. How bad can he be? These Canuck Injuns are all alkies, Gino, you know that. When it comes time to get us to the game, he'll be fine. We'll both be bringing home trophy mounts. Relax—this is going to be the trip of our lives, Gino, the trip of our lives … "

Now, as they huddled in the open-air vault of frigidity they were entombed in, Jim could hardly meet Gino's gaze.

All three were not handling well the icy conditions that had dropped in as unexpected as a distant relative's surprise visit. As they prepared for their first night in the cedars, the lantern Spencer brought expired. He cussed as the last blue-tip match he found in his pockets refused to ignite. Had Gino not carried a lighter for his cigars, they wouldn't have gotten it lit at all, nor had any hope of starting a fire. Confirming his ineptitude, Spencer neglected to bring fuel. Hope and the dull flame faded in unison, and once the cotton mantle was out, that was that.

Chilakoot Lodge was thirty miles south. A brush plane had dropped them off in a field near the last valley before the hills on the landscape rose up into mountains. The plan was to hunt caribou for a day in the marshy, lowland areas of Churchill Falls then get picked up that afternoon. The next morning at first light, they would fly north, moving deeper, higher into the mountains of the Labrador Caribou Range to try their luck in the tree blinds Leslie had built them, this time for berry-fattened black bears. The trip would culminate with a leisurely two-day hunt for ptarmigan within the acreage surrounding Lake Boreal. The Indian cooks would ready some of their kill for a last supper of wild game.

As many accidents in the field are often birthed, the day started with beauty and anticipation. When they began hiking the morning temperature was thirty-one degrees Fahrenheit, and the ground was partially visible through a snowcap that had yet to completely claim its grip on the terrain. Under an evolving grey sky, the men had walked four miles tracking a small herd of caribou, concentrating on a pair of regal bulls, when heavy clouds moved in fast and a light freezing rain started. First masquerading as a breeze, the Arctic wind quit playing around, whipping up, soon changing the drizzle into a sluice of snow and sleet. Within three hours, four inches of snow blanketed the ground. The temperature fell to twelve degrees, suddenly making their parkas no warmer than windbreakers.

"Where'd this come from?" Spencer said. "S'posed to be mild, partly cloudy."

Jim was having an especially bad time keeping his footing. The snow came quicker than they could imagine, pouring out of a seemingly infinite supply. The quick descent of temperature caused moisture clinging to the trees to freeze, and the distant woods had the appearance of a crystal diorama; trees covered in powdered sugar. It was at once both beautiful and terrifying.

But the numbing cold that enshrouded them now made yesterday feel like an afternoon in Belize. A bad aura had settled over their tiny respite. While it was true they had survived the first night, Spencer, had developed a cough that had gotten worse. The hours in the deepening cold, huddled around the tenuous fire, hadn't done anything more than delay hypothermia. As the second nightfall approached, the guide's cough became harsh and phlegmy. He had somehow guided them into a small clutch of dead cedars—a pocket, really—in a frozen-over swamp that served as the only windbreak for two miles, but the wind shifted and swirled constantly, causing them to fight its chill from too many sides to feel anything approaching warmth.

They awoke that first morning to two feet of fresh snow covering the ground, and yet the storm actually felt stronger. Using a paring knife, Spencer scraped away the snow and weakly stuck it into the cold earth. An hour later, the tip of the bone handle was barely visible. The wind became so strong they had to shout to be heard over it.

"She don't want to stop. That opens up to 'bout eight centimeters. I checked the weather, eh, 'fore we went out ... " Spencer hacked up a wicked looking pea-green pellet. He looked at it and laughed. "Where she come from, this storm? Three centimeters in an hour, eh? I don't get it," he said, looking at the dove grey sky, as if by doing so the answer would appear printed across it.

The sharp wind tore at their parkas and through threadbare blankets that by the looks of them had provided nesting material for generations of Chilakoot field mice. The three buried their hands in their pockets, the gloves rendered insufficient. Gino looked at Jim, and he didn't like what he saw. His friend's eyes weren't right, and he caught him grimacing. For the last two hours, Jim's normally ruddy face was gone, and the look that healthy people have in their eyes was replaced with a grey pall. They sat on their packs trying to keep their rumps off the snowy ground, but the chill stayed.

"Jimmy, doing OK?" Gino asked.

Jim didn't answer right away. Then as if someone flicked a switch on, he snapped his head around.

"Feel funny. Think that pike we had yesterday is repeating on me." Jim licked sourly at his lips after he spoke. "Keep tasting it."

Spencer coughed hard, finally expelling a chunk of phlegm that settled onto the snow like a green and red marbled golf ball, right at the tip of Gino's boot.

"That can't be good, huh chief," the guide said matter-of-factly, as he studied the mass he'd just expelled from his lungs. "Hope it's only pneumonia."

The storm they were trapped in continued to pound Labrador's fjorded coast with uneven air masses, pelting it in swirling Arctic gales. The system was in a holding pattern, and the slow-moving storm produced massive amounts of precipitation inland and all across the region, south from Goose Bay and across, through Yellowknife, even as far north as Newfoundland.

Gino knew two things about their situation; they had to get into the open so they could be visible to a rescue plane, and if they didn't, they'd be dead very soon. The root of the conundrum was, in the open they were unprotected and probably wouldn't last long. Even knowing all that, he had no idea the fury above him would soon reduce any thought of visibility to anything but wishful thinking.

"We've got to get somewhere where they can spot us. Devereux, that field we just came through, that's wide enough for a plane to fly over. I'm just talking here, but maybe Jim and I can build a fire out there, where it's got a chance of being seen while you keep this one alive. Then we'll head back here for the night. *Well?*"

He looked at the two men, and they seemed about as willing to venture out into the white abyss as a vole would be crossing an open field lined with red-tailed hawks.

Spencer gazed at the flickering fire, fed stingily with what scant fallen branches they had found. He looked into the snowy sky, turning greyer with the approaching dusk, and closed his eyes, feeling the rushing wind seize his nostril hairs.

"That wind's a good thirty kilometers. Ain't gonna keep a fire in the open, not in that. We try walking in the dark, we'll die for sure." He hacked more phlegm at his feet. "Oh, I'm sorry about that, eh. That's disgustin', no doubt about that."

He covered his mouth and Gino noticed his hand shook uncontrollably.

"Whoa. What do you mean *die?*" Jim was suddenly anxious. He stood up and paced by the fire. "No, no, we're supposed to be *hunting*. We can't *die* out here! We have to get help—we can't die out here."

"We're not going to die, Jimmy. Now let's think."

"I say we go now. Let's just go. We'll make a big torch—grab an armful of wood. Get out in that field and maybe they can spot us," Jim urged the two men.

"Who's *they*, chief? Plane can't get up in this weather. If the storm breaks, morning will be the earliest they can start searching," Spencer said.

Gino considered his point. He looked to the edge of the stand of cedars they were penned in, and it became clear if they tried to go out into the unprotected field, they might not make it a hundred yards before losing their sense of direction. The wind blew stronger and the snow—its volume building—felt like road salt hitting their faces. The men looked like ghosts, the snow stuck to their coats and blankets, so each man's view of one another was seen through the static filter of the blizzard, a gauziness attached to it all.

"Devereux's right, Jimmy. Shit … have to wait out morning. We've got some jerky left. Melt some snow in our canteens." Gino looked at Spencer. "I can't believe there's not a camp or something, somewhere out—"

Spencer looked like he'd been shot. He tapped himself on the forehead.

"If smarts were a penny a pound, I'd be bankrupt. Little Wolf Lake. It's a few kilometers south over that field. Jackson Ozark, Indian friend from Hudson Bay, he keeps a hunting shack there, stays unlocked … courtesy system; leave a few bucks for supplies. It's set below the frost line into the side of a hill. Usually got hardtack, water, blankets even. Comes up in the spring for a couple months."

Gino stared at Spencer, dumbstruck.

And then Spencer sighed and blinked at the two Detroiters.

"Jesus, when were you gonna share *that* little tidbit with us?" Gino screamed through the howling wind. "God *dammit* you *fucking* stupid shit."

"It didn't occur to me 'cuz it was opposite of the herd—fellas, listen I'm sorry you got caught up in this. I know you don't know me from Adam. If Leslie were here he'd tell you; I swear I'm better than this. I used to be *better* than this … "

"*Save it!*" Jim snapped. "I don't feel right … this isn't right. No, this ain't right," he called out, stupefied, almost babbling. Gino looked at him and calmed him down.

"You OK?" he asked his friend.

"I think so," Jim replied.

Gino studied Jim's face. "He's right. Forget that for now, Devereux. Five kilometers, just how far is that from here?" he asked the guide.

"Three miles at best, more or less."

Gino winced hearing a distance that far away. "Can you guys make it?" he asked them, his focus back on Jim.

"Feel tired now, Gino. Can't explain it. Just … *tired*," Jim said. His head pivoted. "Think there'd be a fucking downed tree somewhere in here!" he suddenly screamed.

He was alert again, lively. He walked deeper into the cedars trying to knock down half-dead trees. A thick, low-hanging limb presented a possibility. It was about nine feet above the ground. Jim jumped at it.

"Dammit! Come on, you bastard!" he implored.

Gino rose from his small pack and fell forward, the circulation in his legs was that bad. Spencer helped him up.

"Thanks, Devereux. I'll remember to pack thicker socks next time," Gino said.

Gino vigorously rubbed his calves and thighs, trying to cajole his legs into a false sense of warmth. Spencer coughed again, trying to stifle it with his sleeve. He followed Gino, his head down as they plodded toward Jim. Gino jumped at the limb, and his feet tingled in pain when he launched. He landed awkwardly, almost turning his ankle.

"Hold up chief." Spencer got on all fours. "Now try."

Jim and Gino looked at each other.

"You're way lighter than me," Jim said.

Gino stepped on Spencer's back and felt only slight guilt at giving it a little extra as he did so. He easily reached the limb and snapped it off.

"Hah!" Jim's mood seemed to lift seeing the limb drop.

Spencer got up and rubbed the small of his back. Gino and Jim dragged the branch to the fire. They kicked at the heavy limb, managing to crack it in two. Spencer crisscrossed the limb atop the core of the fire, building a chute. "We'll feed it in as it burns," he said, referring to the excess length. "But we'll need more than this."

Night dropped in while they scoured the frozen swamp for fallen limbs. They were ten feet from the fire and could hardly see. Trees creaked as a rocket of icy wind sailed through the cedars and the fire disappeared, leaving them looking at glowing embers, the space immediately so black they lost each other. A flame flickered and that quick, the fire became alive. Gino's flashlight was dying so, re-membering a survival tactic he'd read, he took to stuffing the batteries under his armpits to try and save them.

"Let's go," he said.

They followed the weak beam in search of more wood.

Walking on his hands and knees—by this time, the flashlight was dead—Gino patted the snow in front of him. *How could the wind keep up this long?* he wondered. The thought that it would die down *sometime* brewed hollow in his cold brain. Twenty minutes later Gino was back at the fire with three pieces of wood. Spencer had good luck as well, finding a pile of brush and four limbs three feet in length.

"Where's Jim?" Gino searched the edge of the campfire's band of light. "Jim? *Jimmy!*" he screamed. He strained to hear through the hurricane-shriek of wind. He tilted an ear, then bolted toward what sounded like a soft scream. Gino glanced off a tree in the crisp darkness and stood alertly, trying to locate the sound.

"Jim!" Gino screamed again.

"Over here," Jim called out, barely audible. He located him, lying there no more than ten yards away. Gino knelt beside him. "Feels like Totie Fields is sit-ting on my chest," Jim said through chattering teeth.

His fireman training kicked in and he reached for the pulse on Jim's neck.

"Trying to lift that log. Felt something pull. Any idea what it might be?" Jim asked, already knowing the answer.

"Devereux," Gino shouted into the dark, trying to amplify his voice over the wind. *"Devereux where are you?"*

"Here chief." The guide was five feet behind them.

They carried Jim to the fire and spread the packs close to it, making a bed for him. Around them, the wind called and moaned, and distant trees cracked, sounding like a monster was snapping logs for kindling of its own. Gino shivered in spasms. He had put both blankets over Jim and periodically trickled water into his mouth. Spencer was shaking, too, spitting up chunks of phlegm. As long as there was fire, though, Gino felt they would all survive, at least until morning.

Sleep came stubbornly at first, then sucked the wakefulness from him with startling efficiency. He dreamt of his wife Elena and their children, highlighted by his youngest son Joey. He was running after him, trying to catch the boy, but he couldn't, and even in his sleep, Gino realized what the dream meant.

Hard snowflakes stung Gino's cheeks. He quickly snapped upright at sunrise, but that was inaptly named, as God swapped out an orange sky with an unending white palette. He stood up, his legs tingling, and was relieved to find both men breathing, though each was fitful in his sleep.

Gino walked to the edge of the solitary cedars and stared at the white before him. Looking into the swirling sky, he was beset by vertigo, the snow hypnotizing him with spinning patterns that played on his imagination. *You ever going to let it stop? You can make it stop. Please make it stop,* he shouted in his mind, not wanting to expose the others to his personal terror.

He crouched next to Spencer. Snow was still falling, but using Spencer's knife-estimate, it had slowed down. He roused him gently, the guide's eyes fluttering open. His lips were cracked, crusted with mucus.

"I'm going to try and make the cabin. You said this Ozark might've left flares?"

"Yeah. I can't get warm, chief," Spencer said in a ruined voice.

"You *have* to. Keep that fire going, can you do that?"

"I'll try."

Gino got very close to his face. He could smell the infection.

"Not *try*." He looked in Spencer's eyes, and he could see there was no way in hell that he would keep the fire going. Gino turned to Jim. "Think you could make it to that cabin? If I help you along?" Jim didn't answer. "Jimmy—"

Spencer tugged at Gino's sleeve.

"I wished you knew me when, what do they say, when I wore a younger man's clothes. Who you think taught Leslie? Wasn't such a fuckup back then." Spencer rocked forward. "Help me up. Let's give her a go chief," he said.

Gino started to say something, but held his tongue. He helped the guide stand.

"Jimmy, c'mon—we're going to that cabin."

Jim stirred, slowly managing to sit up.

"How? He said it's three miles. I can't make that," Jim said.

"We'll make it."

Jim looked at him and Gino knew what his friend was thinking.

"Devereux, take my gun. Leave the rest here." Spencer picked up Gino's rifle and slung it over his shoulder. The snow blew through them and a gust sheared off a branch somewhere behind the men. Gino dipped below Jim's waist, grabbed him under his arms and put him over his back, clutching his friend's legs.

"Taking the fireman's carry to a bit of an extreme, ain't you?" Jim remarked.

Gino smiled through the strain. Spencer followed them out of their tiny sanctuary and stood before the field. Without shelter from the wind, they had no bearing on which way was which. There was literally a white blanket of sky specked with intermittent grey strobes of a distant tree line.

Spencer pulled a tarnished compass from his plaid wool trousers. "Cabin's due south. Where'd this storm come from?" he asked, still puzzled. He held the compass in his palm. The arrow bounced, settling on north. He took his reading, stepped ahead, and aimed them south.

"This way, chief." Spencer kept his eyes focused on the arrow.

Gino concentrated only on each step, one at a time, trying to keep himself centered. The snow had been so steady it never formed a crust, making the walk more difficult than he imagined. Spencer started to yaw a little in his gait, and Gino watched him carefully. The guide continued expelling large amounts of mucus. His coughing jags grew so violent at times he had to stop and brace himself by squeezing his knees with both hands. Gino felt sorry for him, but *dammit,* he thought, *how does someone from "here" come afield so unprepared? Wolfstalker, too, that son of a bitch.* There was anger at himself, as well. He ignored that for the time being, along with Spencer's plight, and tried to take his mind off his immediate burden, namely the weight of his ailing friend.

They had walked a quarter-mile when Gino couldn't take another step.

"Gotta set you down, Jimmy. Get ready," he said, crouching to let Jim get his footing before freeing himself of the weight. Jim kept his hands on Gino's shoulders, and he stayed in his bent-over position, hands resting on his knees. Gino's thighs burned, feeling both cold and hot, as if being massaged with fiberglass.

Jim was breathing hard. He pushed off and straightened up, looking like a drunk trying to steady himself. He squinted and clenched his chest with both hands.

"Leave me here. I can't do this to you, Gino. It's too hard." Jim looked out at the vast space between them and the crest, barely visible, where the horizon fell downhill. "Maybe they'll send a plane while you two ... tell Sophie and the kids I love 'em."

"You tell them. Dammit, don't say shit like that," Gino said.

He looked up at the swirling snow.

"I'm not leaving you here. Devereux, you OK? We still heading south?"

Spencer looked at the compass and made a slight adjustment.

"Yeah. I checked … yeah—" his coughing returned before he could finish, so he pointed instead. Gino took a deep breath and bent over again.

"Get on," he said, waiting for Jim to lean over his shoulders. Gino sensed his friend's resignation as he allowed himself to be loaded. He followed Spencer's footprints.

The walking felt different. They had crested the hill, and then it was supposed to be maybe a mile. He had settled into a rhythm and had thought for some time the ground beneath felt firmer, though he had no way of knowing how far they had traveled, as the white surroundings were absent any landmarks against which to gauge distance.

"Shouldn't be much longer, right? I don't see shit except more snow," Gino yelled over the unrelenting wind. They'd walked and stopped seven times since leaving the isolated shelter of the cedar stand. *"Devereux,"* Gino yelled louder, ripping up his throat. In his hunchback posture, with Jim laying prone across his shoulders, he peeked around. The guide was nowhere to be seen. Gino pirouetted and saw Spencer doubled over ten feet behind him. Steam plumed from a slushy red stain in the snow the size of a silver dollar. Staggered breaths and foamy blood spewed from his mouth.

"Oh God, Jimmy, setting you down a minute," Gino yelled.

He dropped to his knees as gently as he could and laid his friend on the snow. He ran to Spencer and grabbed his face. The guide was blue and his eyes pitched back in his head. Gino yanked him up, got behind him, clasped his hands together under his sternum and lifted him. He bounced Spencer with what little strength he had left.

"C'mon Devereux! *Breathe*—cough it up now!"

Spencer's face contorted, transforming into a hideous mask. Finally on one inspired squeeze and a bounce off his thigh, Gino heard a Herculean cough followed by a sucking blast of air. He released his grasp and Spencer grabbed his sides, falling to his knees in a coughing jag. Thick ropes of crimson snot clung to his beard stubble like remoras. He pulled them off and threw them in horror. He finally stopped and studied what had just emerged from his lungs.

"Thanks for that chief, but no doubt, I think my Christmas just got cancelled," he said in a raw voice.

"*Your ass.* You Canucks owe us a hunting trip. Now where's this Godforsaken cabin? That Injun move the lake while you were sleeping?"

"It's here somewhere. We must've walked off the shoreline—"

The thick flakes made depth perception nil. In all the open space Gino was able to detect little but falling snow and the washed-out tree line. His eyes were strained from staring at only white for so long.

"What did you say?" Gino looked around at the expansive whiteness.

"We're *on* the lake, chief. Been for a while. I'm sorry. I was too weak—"

"Sorry. About *what?* What the hell could you possibly be *sorrier* about? No—don't say it. Don't you *fucking say it* you drunken Canadian hillbilly ... "

"I dropped the compass before we reached the top of the hill. Got no feeling in my fingers and ... it just ... *dropped*." His voice was in and out in the wind. "I thought I could figure it by memory, but there's no way to get a sight line." Spencer hung his head.

"The one thing you remembered to bring. That's fucking beautiful."

Gino thought at that moment he should just kill him. No one would know. But his own shame brought him back from the anger that was rising in him. He had felt privileged—superior even—that he was going to be pampered, and in the process he'd let his defenses down. His own instincts—shaped by sudden snow squalls experienced while deer hunting in upper Michigan—had taught him to prepare for surprise weather, and yet he had not. He was a *fireman*, for God's sake! The word *pride* kept reappearing in front of him, and he acknowledged it before addressing the guide.

"Devereux, concentrate. We *have* to find the cabin *now*. Look hard through the snow. Does anything about that tree line look familiar at all?"

Spencer squinted through the snowflakes. They were bigger now. Gino looked out, too, a clammy sweat coating his back as the first thought that he might freeze to death settled over him. The desire to lie down a moment and sleep popped into his mind.

"This way! I'm positive. We're across from it. Follow me."

Gino plodded back to Jim. He leaned over, pulling his friend's arm. He stopped.

"No," he whispered.

Jim's eyes were open, but he was clearly dead. His face was coated with a frosting of snow. It was his death mask and Gino quickly brushed the snow off.

"No. No, c'mon Jimmy, it's right over there—I mean it's right *there*," he pointed across the lake. He opened Jim's parka, pounding on his chest. He pressed his face against his heart, then pried open Jim's mouth.

"Let him go, chief. You did all you could do, more than any man would," Spencer said. Gino turned to him, his mouth agape, still prepared to blow one last fleeting prayer into his best friend's windpipe. "Got to save yourself now," said Spencer.

The guide's back was to him, his head turned, keeping an eye on the direction they needed to walk. Gino stared at his friend's ashen face. He looked skyward and clenched his eyes, and the faces of Jim's family flashed there, melding into the images of his own beloved children, his wife Elena, who deserved more from him. *Is this what goes through your mind before you die?* he thought. He opened his eyes and hefted Jim's rigid body to its feet. Gathering his resolve, he bent over, resuming the fireman's carry, draping Jim's body over his aching shoulders.

"Go," Gino said, waving a free hand to Spencer. "*Just fucking walk.*"

Spencer blinked and then slumped before trudging forward.

And as they walked, Gino cried freely, supporting the corpse of his best friend. James Perenetto, only minutes earlier a breathing husband, wonderful father, mentor and leader of men, had now become an encumbrance that was hastening his own demise.

Then he heard it. With each step, the sound of nothing crept into his ears.

The wind was dying. But the burning in his legs had gotten so bad he wasn't sure he would make the cabin. The faces of his kids returned, but the faces of others tagged along. He recalled the times he'd discovered a dead parent stretched out in a smoldering home, burned alive or, choked from the smoke, mere feet from an exit or their children's bedroom doors. They almost always died searching for their children. Those children's faces, upon learning their parents were dead, were the ones who taunted the call of death that he heard trying to seduce him to lay down and rest.

And it was why he had to stop, no matter how close to shelter they were.

"Hold on," he said. Gino leaned over and dropped Jim's body clumsily on its side. "They have to be able to find him," he said.

Spencer's breathing was asthmatic. "We're in the middle of the lake."

He searched the immediate area. Nothing but snow everywhere he looked. He walked circles around Jim's body, stopping at seven laps. He'd made it all the way down to the lake's frozen base, creating a kind of moat.

Gino rolled him over on his stomach, remembering something he'd heard about the survivor of a shipwreck on Lake Huron, who had turned the floating body of his father face down to keep seagulls from pecking away at his face. He didn't know if snow would cause damage to dead tissue or not. "I promise I'll bring you home to Detroit, Jim." He stayed kneeling. Spencer watched and coughed into his hand. "OK," Gino announced, and painfully got to his feet. The two forged ahead in the ongoing blizzard.

Spencer was listing again, and soon he fell forward in another coughing fit. They'd walked a quarter-mile from where Jim's body lay. Gino helped Spencer up, but he pushed his hand aside. His face contorted from simply trying to breathe.

"Chief, just keep walking straight. I'm warm enough. I can't walk no more though. Snow's letting up. But I'm tired."

Gino looked around and the snow-blindness gave everything a yellow cast. He wasn't feeling heroic, but he couldn't see how being alone was going to help reunite him with his family. He felt warm now, too; the soporific effects of hypothermia trying to lull him into sleep. He thought of his family.

"Come on," Gino said, helping Spencer to his feet. "Get on."

Spencer put his head down. The guilt painted his face like an unfortunate birthmark.

"I can't. You don't owe me that," Spencer said.

"We're wasting time, Spence."

The guide finally nodded and let his body go passive. Gino scooped him up. Spencer was much lighter than Jim. Gino recalled times blind-walking through burning houses, hunting for those trapped, screaming-for-help souls, and their cries helped take his mind from the pain as he put one foot in front of the other.

Now he knew; it was the ice underneath he had felt earlier. The outline of what looked like a woodpile next to a small structure was visible. Jackson Ozark's cabin at last felt within reach, 300 yards away, and through the snow—which had dissipated to a fine mist—the cabin looked painted in shades of grey.

He saw two sets of footprints; those made earlier by Spencer and him. Had he not been so close to breaking, he might have laughed at the sight. They had walked on the *shoreline*, within fifty yards of the woodpile, God knows how long ago, and hadn't even a clue it was there. The only thing that gave him solace was that in his heart, he knew it wouldn't have mattered in saving Jim's life.

Three mice ran from the center of the room as Gino pushed the door open. Snow flew in with them like diamond dust. He stumbled, falling to his knees onto the planked floor. Spencer slid off his back with a terrible thud.

"Sorry, Jimmy—what the hell am I saying—sorry, Spence."

He helped him to a sofa that had been eaten to its springs. The coils creaked, echoing in the musty air. They pulled off their wet gloves. Gino sat on a stool in front of the wood-burning stove, breathing into his hands. He massaged his legs and rocked back and forth, trying to get feeling into his toes and calves. A prickly sensation slowly crawled over his neck and shoulders as he fought off a dizzying headache.

He knelt next to Spencer, putting his hand on the man's shoulder. Spencer's face was windburned worse than his own, and adding to the wreckage of it, broken blood vessels caused by the coughing spells spread out across his visage like plant roots. The capillaries in the whites of his eyes had exploded, leaving the blue irises floating in circles of blood-red pools.

"Get a fire started, can you? Looks like your buddy left some dry oak."

"Least I can do, chief," Spencer said, the shakes returning to his body.

Gino helped him to his feet, and after a moment of steadying himself, Spencer plodded to the hearth. He kept an eye on him, watching Spencer pull matches from a mason jar on the mantle. He had to hand it to the guide; there was a resolve under the skin of the alkie, a definite resolve. Spencer fed bits of kindling into the belly of the stove. He dragged the white tip of a match against the fieldstones, but it didn't catch. Gino fought off the urge to help him and was relieved to see the match finally ignite.

Rejuvenated by an adrenaline reserve, Gino bounded to the water supply. A five-gallon oak barrel was tucked in the lowest corner of the cabin, a blanket wrapped around it for insulation. It had a brass spigot pierced into it. He rocked it side-to-side, happy to hear water sloshing inside.

While Spencer started the fire, he opened the sparse cupboards and took out two white Melmac coffee mugs. He blew dust out of each, then set one below the spigot and pulled the tap. Following a hiss of air, a hairy black spider plopped into the mug; it stretched itself from a hibernating ball across the white bottom. Mixing with the trickle of water, it looked not unlike an unfurling inkblot.

"*Eauggh! Spider!*" Gino said, dropping the mug. He smashed the insect over and over, more times than was necessary to kill it. He grabbed another mug from the cupboard and let the water run on the floor before filling them both.

Burning wood crackled and popped, soon replacing the cabin's dead air with the scent of oak, the fragrance filling him with hope, and finally a surer feeling that he might live.

"That smell … " Gino inhaled it. "Drink this slow." He offered a mug to Spencer. Both men's voices had been reduced to guttural whispers from screaming over the incessant wind.

"We get the fire going, then we'll warm your insides up. There's teabags in the cupboards. Need to find those flares though, or we'll be screwed royal."

Gino took a good look at Spencer, and the sight was an ugly one. It was as if now that they'd reached shelter, he could finally die honorably, like an ancient elephant returning to his birthplace.

"Check by that tall cupboard, the pantry next to the water. Dry-box. Might find blankets. I'm going to try and sleep, chief," Spencer said, laying his slack face against his own shoulder. "Thank you. I don't know what else to say."

Gino didn't reply to it.

"It'll be more comfortable on the couch." He scooped Spencer up and helped him to the sofa. The springs sang out but the guide was already asleep.

The cabin warmed up quick as Gino fed log after log of oak into the cavern of the stove. The pervading warmth finally raised his core temperature. A ladybug floated past his face and landed on his hand. It walked on his finger, up to the tip, and his chest hurt as the sight reminded him of his youngest son, how he explained to Joey how to make a wish before the beetle could fly away. He examined it, amused at seeing the spotted insect. Its wings alighted, and off it flew.

Then another appeared.

Then five. Ten, a dozen. Then a red cloud of hundreds of ladybugs materialized from every corner of the cabin, fluttering about the air with renewed spirit—the noise sounding like someone tossing fistfuls of sand against rice paper.

Spencer twitched his nose as the bugs landed. His eyes opened, and he lifted his head, looking around at the wave of insects. He swatted, while dodging hordes of flying beetles. Gino took in the sight and resigned himself to the wakefulness the heat spawned in the bugs, laughing heartily, though doing so hurt his throat. Spencer laughed, too, until his coughing got so violent he had to grip what was left of the sofa's arms.

Gino opened the door and began fanning the air, ushering as many of the beetles out of the cabin as he could. Scores had landed on him, and for a time he looked like a man wearing a moving, red jumpsuit. Upon flying into the freezing outside air, they sunk to the snow like red hailstones. He couldn't get all of them out, though, and after futilely trying, both men got used to the remaining ladybugs.

"Can't sleep now," Spencer said. "Did you find the flares?"

Inside the dry box Gino was pleased to see two Hudson's Bay blankets, four tins of sardines, a few cans of beans and a stash of beef jerky sealed in a hard can. He panicked a second until he uncovered seven flares across the bottom, looking like sticks of dynamite. He opened the tin of jerky and the odor of sweet hickory spices made his mouth water.

"Suck on this for a bit, then chew. Swallow a little at a time. Try to keep it down," he said, offering a good-sized piece to Spencer. The guide took it and sucked at the leathery strip of dried meat. He let the juices gather in his mouth and made a face as he swallowed.

"It burns, but Mary, does it taste good!" Spencer moaned.

Gino watched him. He was ravenous but wanted to make sure Spencer could stomach food before he himself ate. Watching the guide chew, he couldn't take it anymore, finally ripping off a piece. Nothing he remembered eating ever tasted so damned delicious. The two depleted the food supply—close to two pounds—eating everything up like they were going to the electric chair. The cabin was getting so warm that Gino felt the need to strip his parka and sweater off, finally walking around in only his damp thermal T-shirt. He put water to boil on top of the wood stove. Spencer started shivering again so he draped a blanket over him.

He walked to the small window and looked across the lake. A sliver of orange and blue at the horizon, an actual sunset, fought off the widespread grey that had cloaked the sky for so long. It looked fluorescent, painted on. He felt drunk seeing it. The snow let up to the point where he could make out the edges of clouds, and he heard himself whisper, "Thank you." His watch had stopped, frozen at 8 p.m. He knew it wouldn't be long before dark would creep across the sky.

Gino put his sweater and parka back on and grabbed the flares. Spencer's chills had subsided, and his rapid, shallow breathing produced a wheezing that sounded like a broken kazoo. The wind blew harmless gusts, nothing like the near-vertical shears they'd experienced over the past forty-eight hours, though he still heard it in his head.

Looking back, the solid blackness of the night sky was interrupted by the window of the cabin, glowing from the light of two kerosene lamps. He was 400 yards onto the ice of Little Wolf Lake, snow gathering at his knees with each step. Without warning, the ground glowed with a mauve glaze. He stopped dead, swearing he heard a buzz—something electric—in the atmosphere. There were stars, and the sky's inkiness melded into a swirling green haze. It was the curtain of the Aurora Borealis, seeming to fall from the top of a grand stage. It framed the perimeter of the far horizon, flashes of turquoise and violet giving way to a rosy pink wash that faded in and out at will. Gino stood there like a man who was about to meet God, which he indeed hoped to. Just not quite yet. And after a fair amount of idleness, he continued his walk in a state of awe.

He stood over the body. He snapped the top off the first flare and stared into the reddish-white flame until it hurt to look at it. He planted the flare into the snow. He repeated the step of igniting the other six, jamming each into the snow, thus forming a circle that from the air quite possibly looked like candles of a celebration. But this was no place for celebrating. The wilderness was unforgiving, and Gino knew that had it not been for the safe haven Jackson Ozark's cabin provided, he and Spencer would have taken their own frosty graves alongside Jim.

The howling of wolves carried over the landscape, but he wasn't frightened by it. He stood there a moment, quite still, looking at the pyre he'd constructed. *That was Jimmy,* he thought. *What the hell am I going to say to Sophie and the kids?*

Standing back at the entrance of the cabin, he turned to the openness of the lake. The Northern Lights danced around it and he felt as though it was God's face. And so Gino asked Him to grant at least one opportunity to see the sight again, with his family.

"And now we wait," he said out loud. His voice sounded hollow. He looked out one last time at the flares—a ring of pure fire—and entered the cabin.

Spencer was still breathing, though he sounded labored. Gino felt the rush of radiant heat touch his cheeks. A ladybug landed on his sleeve. He looked at it, letting it crawl onto his hand. He watched as it climbed up the tip of his ring finger. He was disappointed when it didn't fly away. It stayed perched on his fingertip as he collapsed in front of the stove. He slept dreamlessly until the next morning, when the pilot shook him awake.

Gino Boselli and Spencer Devereux were rescued after only one night in Jackson Ozark's cabin. Two search planes were finally able to make a broad run of the area the men were reported to be hunting in, and on a whim—knowing of a solitary cabin—one of the pilots decided to try a flyover across Little Wolf Lake. Appearing as black specks, he saw two eagles claiming Jim Perenetto's body as they fended off five ravens. The moat Gino had walked around his friend—blackened by the spent flares—caught the pilot's attention. From the air it had looked like a letter O with a line in the center. The pilot set the plane down on the ice, causing the scavengers to fly off. Jim Perenetto's corpse was treated with dignity, flown to Detroit to his waiting family.

Gino's gaunt, bearded face and black, disheveled hair graced the front pages of both *The Detroit News* and *Detroit Free Press.* Each paper featured the same photo of him debarking a plane at Detroit Metro Airport, kneeling as he greeted his joyous family. Both stories outlined his heroic part in the adventure of survival. They mentioned that because he had the presence of mind to roll Captain James Perenetto's body over, his face had been preserved from predators, allowing an open casket for the funeral.

On an appropriately snowy November morning, Gino attended Jim's funeral dressed in full uniform, and though he couldn't muster up the strength to do a eulogy, he had enough left to help carry his best friend one last time, acting as a pallbearer. The procession to Mt. Olivet Cemetery was two miles long, and the streets were lined with fire trucks and men representing houses as far away as New York City. Sophie requested that Gino and Elena ride in the limousine with her and her children. From inside the warm vehicle Gino saluted the men on the side of the road; a snake of blue overcoats standing in a snowfall of large flakes. It was a beautiful sight.

Only two weeks had passed when, against the advice of his doctors—he was still recovering from frostbitten digits—Gino visited a holiday bazaar at St. Jude's, the Catholic grade school his children attended. His face seemed different as he looked vacantly at the priests, nuns, teachers, and parents who sought him out to shake his hand, slap his back, and embrace him—to tell him they had prayed for his rescue. He thanked them, smiling well enough, still managing to be cordial with everyone. The heat was working overtime in the school, but he kept his coat on the whole time.

The brass were stunned when he turned down the promotion to lieutenant, choosing instead to stay close to the business of fighting fires. And after getting settled back into the routine of that work and his life at home, he grew disinterested in things he previously had held too loftily as priorities. Weightlifting gave way to coaching his son's hockey team. Hobbies like bocce, betting the horses; extracurricular activities like the Usher's Club, his euchre night and other time grabbers, which now felt so wasteful and mundane, were left for men who weren't blessed to discover how little time there is on this Earth.

He ate well, too, letting himself enjoy a fine meal, and took to smoking the most expensive cigars available, even cigarettes if he felt like it. Elena impressed upon him her love of good wines, and soon beer took a back seat. Gino gained fifteen pounds, not concerned so much anymore with maintaining his physique at all costs and keeping his waist size at a trim 32. And after happily giving all the time his kids demanded of him, he took to staying in the house with his wife for long mornings in their bedroom. They kept the door locked often, even when the two youngest came knocking, asking their parents what they were doing in there.

You're damn right Ray Wolfstalker footed the bill. The caribou Gino shot while staying at Chilakoot Lodge was killed three miles from Jackson Ozark's cabin. The bull recorded a Boone and Crockett score of 433, a trophy that today hangs in the den of Gino's youngest son, Joe. The bull was shot in November of 1972, with none other than the sober and limping—he had lost three toes to frostbite—Spencer Devereux, along with his cousin Leslie Beauchamp, acting as guides. Gino Boselli was, if anything, a man who believed in getting right back on the horse.

Twin Pines Savior

Bruno Montenegro had left Italo Ciamataro's block party with his whole family in tow. Italo's bash had been a big, no-holds-barred blow-out, replete with roasted pig on a spit, three half-barrels of Stroh's— he even had "strollers," two guys with violins and a chesty brunette playing an accordion, walking around performing old Dago tunes. It was September, still warm enough for water balloon fights. Italo paid a neighbor boy who was an amateur magician ten bucks to do sleight of hand. With all the distractions, he figured a craps game in his basement would go unnoticed by the wives.

He was almost right. Big mouth Zena Vitterelli spoiled it when she came traipsing down the stairs looking for her nervous husband, Marty, and that broke the game up. Bruno was happy, though. He left the table two hundred ahead—at Italo's expense no less—so who the hell was that hurting? Bruno said his good-byes and summoned his wife Tina. They had to get on the kids to gather their stuff for the ride home, their son Anthony especially.

"Anthony! Put your shoes on right now or I'll stick needles in your feet," Bruno warned. That was all the prompting the boy needed.

The ride back to their Detroit home was loud. Bruno looked at the big St. Clair Shores homes as he drove south on Jefferson Avenue, which later would turn into Lakeshore Drive as it passed through Grosse Pointe alongside Lake

St. Clair. After that it would become Jefferson again, once you got past the mansions. He would make a right turn at Moross and head west to Detroit.

His two older daughters, Mary and Josephine, took care of the baby, Ava, while his Anthony made his oldest sister's life miserable by placing his finger an inch from her face and taunting, "I'm not touching you, I'm not touching you, I'm not touching you …" Bruno's chin lifted.

"Anthony. Knock it off or we're both going to the hospital—me to get my foot out of your ass, *capiece?*"

Bruno stared into the rearview mirror, and Anthony knew it was no time to test his father.

Bruno snorted. "That smug *Calabrese mamaluke*. Mr. Deep Pockets living in St. Clair Shores. I used to lend him lunch money," he whispered, his eyes narrowing. Tina looked over at him and put a hand on his knee. He regarded it and looked at her. She smiled, and damn it if she couldn't always disarm his darkest moods with that face. Then he thought about taking two Benjis from Italo and he felt good again.

Mary scrunched her nose at Anthony as she tickled the baby, strapped safely into the bench seat. Ava was nearly two years old, and her siblings doted on her. Tina looked over her shoulder and smiled. The girls had a motherly instinct that warmed her heart. She reached and touched Ava's face.

"Are we going to stop?" Tina asked. "Go on. You tell them."

The memory of making his point three rolls in a row flooded over Bruno, and the two new hundos from Italo rubber-banded on top of the already thick wad in his pocket was comforting. But being with the family on such a beautiful day, there was no price he could put on that. He winked at Tina.

"Hey, you kids, listen up!" Bruno shouted, affecting a scolding tone.

The girls obediently straightened and Anthony's mouth opened, ready to plead his case that he was innocent of any wrongdoing.

"What, Dad?" Mary asked.

He turned around and in an instant, he smiled. "Lemon ice or frozen custard?"

"Yay! Dad is great! Dad is great!" the girls sang in a chorus so happy that Anthony even joined in. "Frozen custard! Frozen custard!"

"Captain Nemo's, here we come." The store was a half-mile ahead.

The three oldest kids tumbled out of the car at Captain Nemo's. Bruno gave Mary a ten spot and told her to get everyone whatever they wanted. "Mary, bring the baby a kiddy cone with a face on it, too," he told her. Bruno looked back at little Ava, reached behind and pinched her cheek.

"Ice keeem," Ava babbled.

"Right, ice keem," Bruno repeated.

Tina watched him with their youngest.

"Sure you want her to be the last one?" she asked.

"What choice do we have?"

"I'm willing to risk it."

"I'm not. We've been blessed with four healthy children and you've gotten through all of it in one piece. Let's not tempt fate," Bruno said.

Tina sighed and watched Mary making the order. The kids were getting so big, and Mary was such a mother to her younger siblings.

"Want to eat here?" Tina asked.

Lake St. Clair was barely visible, but Bruno looked out and was still able to pick up a distant flock of ducks on the low horizon. Goldeneyes, he guessed. The sky was as blue as he'd ever seen, with a few late clouds. The air was lake-induced with a coolness that he loved.

"Why the hell not. I'll get the baby. Grab that table over there."

As usual, the kids' eyes were bigger than their stomachs, so Bruno licked the end of the vanilla custard before getting to what was left of Josephine's cone. Tina finished off what Ava couldn't. They loaded up and headed for home, just a few miles southwest. It would be nice to drive along the lake, past the mansions of the rich, watching the sailboats and freighters adrift on the huge lake.

Driving south on Lakeshore, the lake was on Bruno's left separated only by a grass median and northbound traffic. There were a fair amount of cars on the road, and the beautiful people of the Pointes did what they do on lazy Sundays. On Tina's side of the road, fit blonde girls in tennis skirts walked whippets and poodles along sidewalks that bordered palatial mansions, rising like monuments above hilly acres of landscaping.

Autumnal colors invaded the lush green canopies of sugar maples and towering oaks. Anthony was seated behind Tina, and he crowded against Mary, Ava, and Josephine to get a glimpse of Lake St. Clair, its greenish-blue water twinkling with sunlight, glittering like a billion stars that all decided to explode at once. Yachts and smaller boats dotted the water, and two miles offshore, smoke plumed from a freighter that was coasting for nearby Canadian waters.

Bruno looked above a thin veil of pinkish clouds and spotted a quadrant of mute swans. Tina tuned in the radio, delighted to find Bobby Darin, her favorite crooner. She hummed along with his silky voice. The kids frowned at the selection of the oldies station. Bruno tapped the wheel and sang along quietly with his wife,

> "Somewhere beyond the sea, somewhere waitin' for me,
> My lover stands on golden sands
> And watches the ships that go sailin' … "

He stopped at a red light. A married couple out for a stroll with their Pomeranian crossed in front of him. The man looked at Bruno and immediately averted his eyes. Bruno knew the look. Most Italians knew *the look*. *We're just a notch above the* melanzanas *to these folks,* he thought. Just passing through? No problem. Keep going. Just keep driving to Detroit and there's no problem.

He stared at the guy, seeing if he dared look sideways at him again.

As he waited for the light to cycle green, the man's expression changed. *You don't want any of me,* Bruno thought. The guy, a flabby, pink-skinned, Waspy type, grew agitated, pointing past him, and just as Bruno was about to tell him to shove it up his Anglo ass, Old Flabby's wife shrieked,

"Look out!"

Bruno instinctively glanced in his side-view mirror to see a black car bearing down on him. The car, a monstrous Coupe de Ville, was swerving from left to right in a yawning, serpentine path. Bruno turned and straddled the curb.

"Tina, kids, hold on—" Bruno kicked it and kept going.

The kids shrieked as Bruno swung the big Lincoln to the right, farther up the grass and over the sidewalk. Josephine giggled while Mary held her close.

"Why did we drive on the sidewalk, Dad?" Anthony asked.

"Bruno!" Tina yelled.

The Caddy locked up its brakes and screeched to a halt halfway through the red light, past the same spot where the Lincoln had been seconds earlier. Bruno looked into the passenger-side window, but it was tinted. That didn't stop him from screaming at the unseen driver.

"You *mamaluke!* What the hell's wrong with you?" Bruno's voice cracked. He was heading out the door when Tina grabbed his arm. He glared at it.

"Bruno, please. The kids," she pleaded with him to stay put.

He took a deep breath in an attempt to quell his anger. Old Flabby and his wife were huddled together on the sidewalk, visibly shaken, their yapping dog's leash lassoed around their legs.

"Dad, the light's green," Anthony said.

Bruno looked in the rearview mirror and his eyes softened upon seeing his son's, a matched set of his own. He wanted Anthony to be better than him.

"It's OK, kids. Just a little excitement. Everything's gonna be OK." He patted Tina's knee and drove off the curb, putting a little distance between him and the black Caddy, whose driver had decided to stay put at the green light. A couple of cars had stacked up by now and honked at the car, but when it became apparent the driver was unresponsive, they drove around him. Bruno kept an eye on his rearview mirror before finally glancing at Tina. He shook his head and laughed facetiously.

"That was so *close,*" she said.

"You ain't shitting," he whispered. "Sonofabitch would've killed us. My God. I mean, lights out—the whole family." He looked at his kids. The incident was already forgotten, except in the eyes of his oldest. Mary met his gaze, and his head lifted, seeing the concerned look of his almond-eyed daughter.

"Taking care of things back there, hon?" he asked her, as if they were the only two in the car. Mary smiled back, and in so doing, offered him a glimpse of his wife's beautiful face, the face he fell in love with twenty years earlier.

He was still looking at Mary when the Lincoln jerked suddenly forward, causing all of the kids to startle, their heads tapping against the back of the front seats. Mary had Ava braced with her arm to prevent her from whiplashing her neck. Tina's palms were against the dashboard. The impact caused the disc in Bruno's lower back to tingle.

"You *mother*—" he cut himself short, thinking of the kids.

In the rearview mirror, the late day sun hit the black Caddy's chrome windshield trim. The glare shielded the face of the driver, but Bruno swore he saw a smile on the sonofabitch. This time the kids really screamed.

"Bruno, what's happening?" Tina asked.

"It's OK, hold tight. Kids, seatbelts on! Mary, hold onto the baby."

"I will, Dad," Mary said, snuggling Ava.

Bruno sped ahead, getting farther from the nose of the Cadillac. Lakeshore wound lazily and the opportunity to turn off didn't present itself. There were people walking, jogging, riding bikes. He was peripherally aware of them backing away as the Caddy gave chase. He pulled to the right to let the guy pass, but it was no use; the bastard got behind him, almost jumping the curb in the process. People threw themselves off the sidewalk.

The Caddy's bumper tapped Bruno's rear end, and again the kids shrieked. Tina held fast to the dashboard, her eyes closed.

"Lord, send your guardian angels to keep us safe. Stop this evil man from entering our life, Lord … " Tina rambled an eloquent, albeit nervous, prayer.

"Pray with your, mother kids," Bruno shouted.

Bruno glanced at the lake one last time. He needed distance fast. He was approaching seventy on a road intended for half that, and for the first time in his life, he wished there was a cop around. Seeing none, he decided to bring the game to this sonofabitch himself.

"Hold on kids. Tina, be ready."

"Hail Mary, full of grace … " the kids joined Tina.

"Anthony, Josephine, scooch to the middle, away from the door. Everyone get behind your mother. Do it!"

Anthony held tight to the door. "Dad, I'm scared—"

"Don't you worry," he said, trying to sound calm.

The three bunched up, clustered together as a shield around Ava, who was starting to fuss. Ava began crying, her shrieks winding into a hyper kind of rhythm. Mary stroked her cheek, and Bruno felt the anger rising. He watched in the rearview mirror. He slowed down, reeling the guy in. He let the guy's front bumper get close, slowing to forty-five, then forty.

The Caddy was suddenly five feet away.

Bruno could finally see him. The driver was a grey-haired, fifty-ish swinger type with dark sunglasses. And now Bruno confirmed it; the bastard was definitely *smiling*.

Bruno veered right, using as much of the narrow road as he could, and at the last minute, cut the wheel hard left. The kids screamed during the half-doughnut, leaving Bruno's side of the car exposed, perpendicular to the lake. His Lincoln blocked both lanes of southbound traffic. The Caddy overcompensated by steering too far left. The car went airborne as it jumped the curb of the median, heading straight toward northbound traffic. Smoke billowed from a blown front tire, and a piece of plastic trim dragged noisily. Bruno braked before hitting the curb himself and watched the boat-like Coupe deVille bottom out on the grassy island.

"Gotcha, you sonofabitch," Bruno whispered. He looked in the backseat. "Everyone OK?"

He did a cursory check of his wife and kids. He reached below his seat and felt the carpeted floor mat. The anger traveled now from the coldness of his heart to the tips of his fingers. It matched the feeling of the steel crowbar he kept under his seat, a trick he learned from his brother for just such an occasion. Tina reached for him, but the rage flashing in his eyes repelled her.

"Bruno, the kids—" she begged.

He laughed sarcastically and was out of the car like a cougar, at the door of the Cadillac in ten steps. People had migrated and stopped on the grassy hill above the shore of the lake. Crowds formed on the sidewalks as well.

Smoke poured from the hood of the Caddy, and the driver locked his doors. Bruno didn't hesitate, smashing the driver's window with the crowbar. He unlocked the door, but not before hitting the guy flush in the jaw with a hard left.

He practically ripped the door off and extricated the guy from his leather seat. Two brass buttons sprang from the man's navy blazer. Empty beer cans and glass spilled out with him, along with a silver flask that he had in his lap. Bruno could smell a mix of beer and bourbon as he pulled him from the car.

"Hey, hold on now," the drunk protested.

Bruno dragged him to the front bumper of the Caddy, holding the crowbar in his right hand. He stretched the guy out and gave him two quick knees to the kidneys. The guy doubled over, groaning. Bruno grabbed a handful of his silk shirt.

"You drunken motherfucker. You coulda killed us!"

"Jus' playin' around. Come on, don't hurt me. My wife, she left me today, come on ... have a heart," the drunk cried, reaching for Bruno's face with small, flailing hands.

"Smart lady," Bruno said.

He felt it now; the uncontrollable anger, the bile—a poisonous rage a man feels when his family is threatened. The cries of Tina begging him to come back were ambient noise. It all became static as he felt his hand gripping the steel rod and raising it. He kicked the guy's legs out, forcing him into a kneeling position. He stared at a pink spot on top of the man's head. And he felt his hand rise up in a graceful arc, holding the crowbar high at the apex. He looked at the lake and saw a flock of ducks cupping their wings to land. Maybe the same ones he had seen flying earlier. Bobby Darin's voice played on a radio in his mind,

"Somewhere beyond the sea, she's there watchin' for me,
If I could fly like birds on high, then straight to her arms I'd go sailin' ... "

And still the rage wouldn't abate, even over the sobbing of the drunk and Tina's pleas. Bruno's arm flexed. He felt his weight shift, ready to release the poison.

"Mister, don't hit him with that crowbar. You'll kill him."

The voice cut through the air, calm, devoid of malice or interference, but it stopped Bruno, as if the invisible hand of God had reached down to grab his wrist. He turned his head to the voice, his eyes bugged out.

A Twin Pines Dairy truck was parked next to his Lincoln. The driver was standing ten feet away. Barely older looking than a teenager, the milkman was thin with a wholesome, fair complexion. The kid was dressed in a white short-sleeved shirt and a green hat. He looked slightly more intimidating than a census taker. Bruno blinked at him, then regarded the drunk, shaking him by his collar.

"This sonofabitch almost killed my family! My *children* ... " he screamed, spitting the words out rabidly. The drunk clutched at Bruno's hands, trying to break free from this maniacal beast hellbent on exacting justice.

"Please, c'mon I was playing was all. Look, you tore my shirt and made me go flat ... oh, Lordy, I think I'm going to piss myself," the drunk wailed mournfully. "Uh—too late."

"Shut the fuck up," Bruno snapped.

The milkman left the side of his Twin Pines truck and edged closer, drifting seamlessly through the gathering crowd. Bruno's hand was shaking. The milkman grinned. A shock of radiant auburn hair was softened by a splash of freckles that looked sprayed across the bridge of his nose. His eyes were startling in their blueness, set off by pure white sclera. There was something in those eyes that compelled Bruno to wait, to hear what the kid had to say. This was out of character. Bruno was prone to act first and second, then *maybe* think third.

"You don't want to do that to your family. Do something like *that* in front of them, in front of your wife? With your little girls and your son watching? You'll just end up going to jail, and for what? Throw it all away for *him?* He's not worth all that. Let the police handle it."

"*Fuck* the police, what the hell do they know?" The crowbar was still raised and he *so* wanted to crack the guy's head like a coconut.

The milkman pursed his small mouth and shrugged, his russet eyebrows arching as he removed his hat. He rubbed the inside of the brim with one hand as he let the hat settle at his waist.

"They need you. Don't do it. Please?" the milkman asked, his face angelic, almost cheerful, as if he were watching a tee-ball game with his family.

Bruno felt the energy leave his hand. He relaxed his grip. The crowbar dropped to his side.

"Praise Jesus!" Tina called out.

Bruno shoved the drunk down against the hood of the Caddy and walked around it, his eyes locked on the milkman the whole time. He ignored the open driver's door, instead reaching through the smashed window, kicking aside the beer cans and trash. He took the keys from the ignition. He stared at the milkman and searched those eyes once more for falsity but found none. He took two steps toward Lake St. Clair, some thirty-five yards away, and hurled the drunk's keys into its green water.

The drunk squinted into the sun and was able to follow the flight of his keys, jingling and glittering like fool's gold as they soared through the blue sky. They settled ten feet offshore, sinking eight feet to the lake bottom, spooking a trio of feeding carp.

"Awww, now how'm I gonna get home?" the drunk lamented.

Bruno raised his hand, waving at the guy in disgust. He spit at the pink spot on his head. The act elicited a groan from the onlookers. A couple of kids sitting on bikes said, "Gross!" Bruno looked at the milkman one last time. He raised his hands and nodded at the boyish face in a subtle, unspoken gesture of gratitude. The milkman nodded, and put his hat on. Bruno got into his Lincoln and drove home.

The kids were getting ready for bed when two of Grosse Pointe's finest rang Bruno's doorbell at a little after 8:30 p.m. Bruno told Tina to wait inside.

He stepped onto the porch to talk to the two policemen. He wasn't familiar with Grosse Pointe cops. One was a ruddy six-footer with a black crew cut, no more than twenty, some twenty-five years younger than Bruno. He noted the cop's name, McPherson. *Great, another Mick pig who hates Dagos*, he thought. The other one was a no-nonsense-looking veteran, a sergeant whose red hair was tipped grey. His nose was mapped with rosacea. Bruno looked studiously at the man. The sergeant blinked oddly when his eyes met Bruno's, and he looked away momentarily. Bruno never forgot a face, and this guy looked *too* familiar. His nameplate read "Jones," a surname that struck Bruno more benignly than the Irishman's.

"That your Continental?" Sergeant Jones pointed with his thumb to the Lincoln parked in the driveway.

"Yeah," Bruno answered. "What about it?"

"Watch your tone, Monty *Negro*," McPherson said.

Bruno stared at the pink-skinned cop, knowing in another setting he'd eat him alive. Sergeant Jones looked at McPherson, and whatever was in it made the bigger cop shrink like a fourteen-year-old caught skinning it to his father's *Playboys*.

"Can I see your license, please? For verification," Sergeant Jones asked.

"Here," Bruno said, surrendering his wallet.

"Thank you." The sergeant inspected the license, comparing it against Bruno's face. "Shaved your mustache," Sergeant Jones commented.

"Gives some people the wrong idea." Bruno replied. Sergeant Jones smiled.

"You were involved in a traffic altercation today, on Lakeshore?" Sergeant Jones asked, a smile trying to form on his round face.

"Who said that?" Bruno asked.

"We don't divulge that, not yet. We have witnesses. Said you hit a guy."

"These *witnesses* tell you what that drunk bastard tried to do to my family?"

"He was drunk—so what? We took him in," McPherson said, edging closer.

"*Drunk?*" Bruno said. "What'd he blow? Tell me it's under a two-five and you're a goddamn liar."

"Remember who you're talking to," McPherson said.

The sergeant smiled at McPherson, and the big officer quieted down.

"Yeah, he was pickled good," Sergeant Jones said. "Point two-eight. Nearly three times over. But that doesn't give you the right to hit the man. See, if you hadn't hit him, we'd probably be OK here. But I ran your Lincoln through, and you have a bit of a record. Been quiet for a while, which could mean you've stayed clean or you're just hiding it well. Now, Mr. Montenegro, if I search your vehicle, am I going to find any guns or knives in there? Maybe a piece of pipe. You know, like a crowbar?"

"Chrissakes, you even have a search warrant?" Bruno asked.

"Yeah. Right here." McPherson tapped the silver shield on his chest.

"Actually, we have cause, so ... do you own any guns?" asked Sergeant Jones.

Bruno stared at the sergeant, but was keenly aware of McPherson, who was now smiling and waving at him. Finally, Bruno leaned forward to meet his mocking gaze.

"Hey—what the *fuck* are *you* lookin' at?" Bruno asked through gritted teeth.

McPherson face went flat. He pointed behind Bruno.

Bruno turned and sighed. "*Maddon'*... "

In the window off the porch, his three oldest kids pressed their faces against the screen. Sergeant Jones waved and smiled at them, their foreheads creating circular *moire'* patterns on the mesh. The kids waved back.

"Tina—" Bruno said. The kids sprang away from the screen like frightened quail. Tina appeared behind the children. The officers tipped their caps at her.

"Good evening," said Sergeant Jones.

"Put them to bed, please," Bruno demanded. Tina lowered her eyes and shuttled the kids toward their bedrooms.

"G'night, Daddy," Anthony called out.

"'Night, son." Bruno ran his tongue on a cavity he felt coming on.

"No, I don't have any guns. Not anymore," Bruno lied. "Look, I got out of all that shit a long time ago. My brothers and I ... we were street kids, OK? In the old neighborhood. I pay my taxes. I don't even have a parking ticket."

"You hit the guy and threatened him. That's assault," McPherson said, a little smile curling up on his smug, pink face. Bruno could smell his Hai Karate cologne and wanted to drive his hands deep into the cop's ruddy cheeks and strip them from his skull.

"Crowbar can be considered a deadly weapon," Sergeant Jones added, shaking his head at McPherson, who was getting more amped by the moment.

"If I wanted to kill him, he'd be dead. That Twin Pincs driver, he tell you this?" The cops looked at one another. "Milkman. Redheaded kid," Bruno added.

Sergeant Jones flinched. "We don't know anything about any *milkman*. We caught the call on the radio and ran the plate. A little kid on a bike scribbled your license number down in the dirt. There were plenty of witnesses saying that you both were swerving around Lakeshore, and the guy had tried to pass, but you cut him off. He hit a curb and you, well you went—" Sergeant Jones stared into Bruno's eyes.

"The milkman, he'd tell you. You didn't talk to a milkman?" Bruno asked.

"People said you went goddamn *ape shit*," McPherson said.

"For lack of a more useful term, yeah, you went ape shit," Sergeant Jones agreed.

Bruno studied the sergeant. He was probably a few years from retirement. Through his life in Detroit, dealing with all kinds of cops—crooked, by the book, and every kind in between—Bruno could tell this guy would see right through any kind of bullshit. McPherson unsnapped a pair of handcuffs from his belt, and Jones' eyes moved at the sound. Bruno stepped back and slumped his shoulders. He closed his eyes a moment and tried to imagine what effect being cuffed here would have on his kids. Especially Anthony.

"Can I just say something first?"

Sergeant Jones nodded.

"I had just gotten the kids ice cream, frozen custard. It was a beautiful day. Nice family day, you know? Then this drunk mother ... this *mamaluke,* he almost *rear-ends* me at a red light. I tried to get some distance between us, but he don't stop. He bumps me, *on purpose!* Then he chases me all the way down Lakeshore, in and out of traffic. He wouldn't let me get away from him. I had no other choice but to block the road with my side of the car. Luckily, he hit the curb first and blew his tire. He would've killed me at least, hell, all of us. So when I pulled the sonofabitch out, yeah, I was a little *hot.* And if it weren't for that milkman, I'm pretty sure I would have murdered him. But I didn't."

Bruno looked across the street and noticed several neighbors standing on their porches. He kept his head up, never blinking at the men.

"There. I'm admitting it. So can't you maybe give me a break?" He lowered his voice. "So my kids don't have to see this. Just let me be, to get back to my life. At least let me follow you to the station?"

Sergeant Jones glanced at McPherson. He turned to Bruno and held up a finger.

"Stay right here."

He put his hand on the much taller McPherson and walked him to the squad car parked at the curb. Bruno watched warily as Sergeant Jones counseled McPherson with soft tones, gesturing with his hand toward the porch. McPherson put his hands on his hips. Sergeant Jones crossed his arms and pointed at the squad car. Finally, McPherson slumped and entered the vehicle, shutting the door behind him.

Sergeant Jones walked slowly back to the porch. He had a slight paunch. He stood below Bruno. That face, its link to him was floating inside Bruno's head. The sergeant held out his hand with Bruno's fat wallet in it.

"I'm breaking him in. He's actually a pretty good kid, real by the book, you know? Anyway, you're all set. I'm letting you go with a warning."

Bruno blinked. He took his wallet and glanced inside it. He looked at the sergeant. "You're shitting me. C'mon."

"No, for real. Watch your temper. *That's* the warning," Sergeant Jones said. "Take care of those kids." Bruno watched him walk away.

When he had reached the squad car, Bruno called out, "The drunk. Who was he?"

Sergeant Jones stopped. "I don't want to have to come back here again. Let it go."

"Guy a judge or something? He was, wasn't he?" Bruno said, pressing the point.

The sergeant tilted his head. "Maybe. Maybe not. Maybe he was just … a *drunk*." Sergeant Jones walked back toward Bruno and again stood below the porch. He glanced once at McPherson, still seated in the patrol car. "Just let it go at, maybe today's the day you won the *lottery*, OK? You understand that? I'm not talking about the kind of lottery you used to run with those brothers of yours, either. Today, you won the *cop* lottery."

Bruno leaned back. "*Cop* lottery?"

The sergeant shrugged. "Theodore Jeffrey Jones, born this day in 1952. Would've been twenty-eight. We called him TJ. He was just riding home from his paper route, broad daylight. I was working the jail that day. Kid was excited because the Tigers were on fire—it was '68, you see. Kid loved Mickey Stanley. We were going to the game that night … " The sergeant's voice stopped and his eyes were fixed on the window screen, still dented by the heads of Bruno's children. "There was this guy, had a fight with his wife. Went bowling, downed a six-pack, added a couple of snorts of hooch for good measure. Gets this idea that he should just go kill his old lady. Decides to take a shortcut through my neighborhood so he can get to her right away—still has the rental shoes on—walked out of the bowling alley wearing those ugly god-damn shoes. Who'd have thought … middle of the day a guy would get so tanked. Sixteen-year-old kid, riding his bike. On the sidewalk even."

Bruno listened. The sergeant took a moment.

"Guy jumped the curb, knocked over a fire hydrant. Dragged him all the way to Jefferson—half a mile … before TJ's body finally …" Sergeant Jones caught himself. "Broad daylight. Kid's on the sidewalk."

"Lord," Bruno said quietly. "Oh, Lord."

The sergeant swallowed. "His brother-in-law was a big-shot lawyer. Found a technicality … diabetic medication, some such bullshit. He did a year then walked."

Bruno tried to say something but nothing came out.

"Yeah, I know, a year, do that lying down. After what *he did*, you imagine that? But. Sometimes justice is delayed. That drunk you ran into today? He'll get his." He squinted at Bruno. "They always do." Sergeant Jones straightened a little, his mouth returning to the curious smile he wore earlier. "My TJ. My beautiful boy."

"I'm very sorry," Bruno said, his voice hardly audible. "Really."

"I believe you. I am, too," Sergeant Jones said.

He adjusted his cap and walked away.

Officer McPherson stood outside the driver's side door, his forearms crossed on the roof. He smirked at Bruno as the sergeant got into the patrol car. Bruno stood there a long time after they drove off. One of his neighbors, a widow from the old country, remained on the porch across the street—the others had all retreated to their homes. She stared at him, then went inside her bungalow.

Bruno closed his eyes again, studying faces in his mind like leafing through holographic mug shot books full of every prick cop who ever hassled him and his brothers, every jamoke he ever scrapped with, trying to place Sergeant Jones' non-distinctive, yet so familiar face. But that visage was missing features, an empty pink oval with characteristics yet to be sketched in. It was like a game his kids played and similarly, in his mind, Bruno was left to use a virtual magnet to push around metal shavings, creating different hairdos and mustaches on the pink oval until he created a face he liked.

It was in the middle of the night, a week after Italo Ciamataro's block party, that the features of Sergeant Jones' face were finally filled in. Bruno sprung from the bed in a cold sweat. He saw the moonlit profile of his Tina lying there, smiling, as was her habit when she slept. He put his watch to the window, a lumpy Piaget he bought from Lenny Allessandro. Its glow-in-the-dark hands were already losing their luster, but it looked genuine in the daylight. It was 5 a.m. and his heart was pounding.

As he entered the girls' room, he passed Mary and Josephine, their faces worry-free in their dream state. He stood over little Ava—old enough for a day bed, yet still looking so small lying there. He gently kissed each girl's cheek, soaking in their smell, inhaling it into his memory.

From the doorway of Anthony's room, he watched as his only son slept crazily across the sheets, his body writhing in fits of some feral nightmare. Bruno waited a moment and then could take it no longer. He lay next to him and wrapped an arm around the boy. At first Anthony tightened. Then, as if sensing the strength and the protective heart of his father, he relaxed. His body loosened and he moaned, surrendering to the embrace. Bruno stroked his hair and kissed the boy's cheek repeatedly. His eyes moistened, but he stood up. When he was sure Anthony was still, he left the room.

Standing in the black living room, he dialed the number by memory. It was three hours earlier in Nevada, but he didn't care. After what seemed like ten rings, the phone picked up.

"This better be important or I'll track you down, motherfucka," a whiskey-ravaged voice croaked into the receiver.

"It is, Bags. It is. It's me, Bruno—"

"Don't say your name, you East Side *mamaluke*. Call you back. Two minutes," Bags said.

Bruno listened to the dead line and hung up. A protracted five minutes later, the phone rang. He lifted it midway into the first ring.

"What's so important that you call me at two in the fucking morning? I was right in the wiggly toe part of my sleep. One of your brothers in trouble?"

"No, they're fine, Bags. It's something else. 'Bout ten years ago, you flew in for some work."

There was a pause. "I came in to do a piece of work for a guy … I might have painted a few houses while I was in town. *That?*"

"Yeah! When you were painting," Bruno said, picking up on Bags' coded message. "I drove for you, when you went to pick up the paint. When we were at the train station, this guy stopped us. He told me to park near some pallets that were stacked up. You made me wait in the car, but I got a good look at him. You got out and talked to him. Right after I parked, you remember? Redheaded guy."

"What guy?"

"His nose had a skin thing. Red, like a drunk's nose. He handed you something."

"Bruno, you were paid five hundred bones to drive me from the airport to the train station. So I talked to *a guy*. You need a reference for a goddamn limo license? What the fuck you bringing up ancient history for—what's this about?"

"I just need to know, I won't even ask you the guy's name who paid you—"

"You know I can't tell you that anyway," Bags said.

"Right. Just answer me this; was *he* the guy who wanted the work done? Did you paint a house for him?"

"Look, kid … " Bruno could hear the man breathing.

"Bags, I know, but this is *eating me alive*. If it was for him, just hang up. You don't even have to say another word. I just need to *know*, because this guy I met the other day, he had a familiar face is all—"

The phone went dead, the tone echoing in his ear like a ghost's wail.

Bruno looked at the receiver and replaced the handset on the cradle. He stood there for a full five minutes in the dark. A breeze came through the window screen at the front of the house. He walked out of the dark living room and nestled himself in a spooning position next to Tina, who smiled even wider feeling Bruno's embrace.

Eight Dogs Named Jack

Naming all eight German shorthairs Jack made sense to Mike Materra. That way there was no confusing any of them with a member of the family. It also reduced the temptation for his kids to treat them like pets. Mike hated the idea of a hunting dog being kept as a pet and was fond of saying, *"You want a pet? Buy a poodle."* Arguably, the most disturbing habit he enforced with the dogs was a rule that upset most of his hunting buddies—hell, even guides at the northern game farms they visited questioned him on it: his insistence that all dogs ride in the trunk.

Didn't matter if someone had a Gremlin or a Caddy, dogs traveled in the trunk. Never, ever *inside* the vehicle. That's where people belonged.

The trunk of Mike's old Continental suited the Jacks—as far as he could tell anyway—just fine.

The sound eight dogs can generate (well, seven actually; Mike had left one behind in the woods—it kept chasing birds after the flush) barking all at once can be deafening. But stuff that many shorthairs into the trunk of a car? That's an orchestra of noise rivaled only by a flock of ravens in a broom closet.

Aside from his four brothers, Mike's favorite guy to be in the field with was Tom Marshall. Tom had married Mike's sister-in-law, Marina, two years after Mike and Julia had gotten hitched. And though Tom wasn't Sicilian, or even

Italian (as any Sicilian will tell you, there *is* a difference), he was still a guy's guy. He was tight-lipped about any of the shit he saw Mike and his brothers get into back when they were younger, and he was a great shot to boot.

While it was true Tom was a more than capable outdoorsman, at times he was just not able to rise to the level of Mike's effortless ways. In the field or on water, he sometimes fell a bird or fish short. Whether it was handling a gun, angling for bass or filling a vest with game, Mike almost always ended up on top. And now it seemed that the same held true in Tom's choice of dogs, present in the form of Duke.

"A Lab? Why the hell didn't you buy a shorthair like I told you?" Mike said to Tom when he looked at the huge chocolate Labrador retriever for the first time in Tom's driveway. The Lab was incredibly strong and unusually large—as a one-year-old, its paws were already clumsily oversized—making it hard for Mike to believe it could possibly get any bigger. Duke's coat was root beer brown and its head was shaped perfectly. Still, Mike doubted the animal's purported lineage. He knew his dogs.

"This is a mutt, gotta be."

"I got the papers on it, says he's pure, sired from Satan's Scud in Kalamazoo. Vendor in Midland gave him to me for awarding him a wiper motor project—no bid, if you know what I mean. Guy's father-in-law's a breeder. Told me Duke's worth over five hundred." Tom's voice dripped with pride at trading a $3 million manufacturing contract for a dog that was worth half a G-note.

"*Five bills?* Let me look at him."

Mike massaged Duke's neck. The whole time the animal's tongue lapped, panting crazily as if drinking water from an invisible bowl. Duke was all energy, constantly moving. And he seemed smitten with Mike.

"Nice animal, huh? Think he likes you," Tom said.

Mike grumbled at that, looking sideways at Tom. He glanced side-to-side, studying the animal's lively caramel brown eyes.

"Duke, huh?" Mike asked.

"Yeah, Duke,"

"Like John Wayne."

"Ellington," Tom said.

Mike made a sour face. "Named him after a *melanzana*? What are you, a Democrat all of a sudden?"

"What if I am?" Tom laughed. "Ellington is the man. Maybe if he was a *golden* Lab I'd have named him after Wayne." Tom patted Duke's drum-tight belly. "Problem is, he runs ahead of me too much."

"What's wrong with Jack? *Jacks* know their place. Jacks *listen*," Mike said.

"Jesus, don't you think eight dogs named Jack is enough for one family?"

Mike looked at Tom as if he'd just asked him to explain an advanced trig formula.

"Put him in the trunk, we'll take him up to Caseville, run him ragged. Farm up there I have exclusive permission to hunt on. I'll fix his ass. And by the way, there's only seven Jacks now," Mike said with little regret.

"Oh right. Forgot."

Tom reluctantly placed Duke in the trunk of Mike's car. The dog whined a low howl. He hesitated before closing the lid on his beloved pet.

"Hey Mike—"

"Trunk," Mike said, cutting Tom off before he could ask the question.

"Yeah. Trunk. Well at least you got the whole space to yourself. Sorry, Duke," Tom said, his face a sad look of compliance as he carefully closed the hatch on the energetic dog. Duke's bark faded to a low whine.

It had stormed for three days straight, and the farming community in Michigan's Thumb was thankful for it. When Mike and Tom got to the farmer's field around 4 p.m., the sky was ridding itself of the last grey clouds, and a robin's egg blue was all that remained. Pulling into the first field of the rural acreage, they startled a trio of does drinking from the meandering Pigeon Creek—part of the Pigeon River—a tributary that fed into Lakes Huron and St. Clair. Throughout most of the property the creek was only a trickle, no more than a couple of feet across, although in the neighboring woods Mike heard it spread to widths of ten feet or more. In those wider stretches there were supposedly deep holes, as much as seven feet, and tales of fisherman wrestling huge channel catfish up to five feet in length ran through the county.

Mike had never entered those woods.

Art Chesney, the old farmer whose land he was on, told him the piece was off-limits, owned by a "sum-bitch liberal" who hated hunters and all they stood for. *Fuck him*, Mike had thought when the farmer first told him of the landowner. But truly appreciating Chesney's generosity, and wanting to respect the old man's wishes, Mike kept off the hunter-hating neighbor's land, never venturing more than a cursory look.

For the two years he'd been running his dogs on the property—1972 through 1974—Mike had obeyed Art's request. He and his brothers had hunted in the Thumb for years, but he'd found Chesney's place on his own. He had never even brought his brother Sam there, preferring to hunt and train the Jacks in solitude. There he could lose himself in the beauty of the animals and their singular joy of performing for him the tasks he trained them for. One of his favorite things to do was to light a cigarette while one of the Jacks held point. He'd watch the anticipation of the shorthair grow as he smoked a whole Chesterfield, finally saying, "Hup!" as the heat hit his fingers. He reveled in the fact that his dogs were *that* disciplined. Teaching that kind of discipline was lost on his brothers.

"This place is a score, Mike," Tom said, surveying the habitat.

"No shit. The cornfield's loaded with ring-necks, even some partridge. Hell, all of Caseville used to have nice grouse numbers. Partridge are down throughout the county now."

"What, from foxes?"

"Maybe. Probably more because my nephew, Roman's Nick, cleaned 'em out last year, goddamn *conservationist* that he is. Why take two when you can take ten?"

Tom scanned the forbidden woods on the right and then turned his attention to the left of the trail. There, through the twigs of aspen growth, he marveled at the sea of dead gold stalks, dappling against the vertical grey aspen trunks like sunlight on water.

"Is that all corn? Look at it all. What do we do first?" Tom asked.

"Could start by letting Duke out of the fucking trunk," Mike replied.

"Shit, you're *right!*" Tom ran to the back of the car.

Mike tossed him the keys then lit a cigarette. Duke sprang from the trunk like he was jumping from a burning building, leaping right into Tom's chest before he could react, dog and owner going ass-over-teakettle. He and the barking, tongue-lapping dog rolled around like two Russian acrobats.

"Who's my big boy? Who's my *big boy?* Dukey is, that's who," Tom egged on Duke with baby talk. Mike took a drag of the smoke and laughed with a disgusted slant. He glowered at his brother-in-law.

"Man, stop that shit before I puke. First things first: It's an animal. You act like that's your kid. Don't baby him. This is about work, not fun. *We* have the fun. *They* do the work. That's what they're bred for."

Tom nodded and got up off the ground.

Both men wore orange canvas hunting vests with loose pouches on their backs to hold killed game. Mike took out his Remington semi-auto. He loaded it with five bird loads and chambered the first shell. He made sure the safety was on. Tom got his Winchester pump and loaded it as well.

"Let's watch him work that bramble there. See how he does with rabbits," Mike said, pointing to a brush pile that he always worked at least once before getting lost in the gold of the cornfields where the pheasants hid.

"Give him a command," Mike said.

Tom readied his gun.

"Go get him Duke—go get that rabbit," Tom encouraged the animal. Duke just stared at him, his head tilted impishly to the side.

Tom looked at Mike.

"Again," Mike nodded, smoke swirling above his head.

"Get that rabbit, Duke—go on now! Duke. *Duke,*" Tom prodded with a forceful bite in his voice. Nothing. He slumped his shoulders toward Mike.

"Watch, and learn." Mike took one last drag and stamped out his smoke. He walked over to the animal. Leaning close, he put his hand on Duke's shoulder and pointed toward the bramble.

"Duke! *Rabbit!*" But when Mike said it, there was nothing approaching warmth in his command, only the cold tone of a drill sergeant. And sure as shit, the dog bolted for the brush. It took off in loping strides, and Mike and Tom had to hurry to keep close behind. Mike felt his knee give a little, the lingering effects of a ball bat to the kneecap taken during a brawl he and his brothers had gotten into. He was nineteen then, the altercation precipitated by a rival group trying to move in on their thing. The knee had never been looked at it until two years ago, and his doctor recommended having it replaced. It was pretty much bone on bone. He ignored the pain and pushed forward after Duke.

"Look at him. That's great, Mike." Tom was absolutely jubilant.

Duke got into the brush pile and nosed around. Tom got on one side of the thicket, Mike on the other. Duke stopped on point and Mike shouldered his gun. "So far, not bad," he whispered. He clicked off the safety, and as he did a big cottontail shot out to his left. Mike let it get about fifteen yards away, leading it a few feet before plugging it in the nose. The shot nearly decapitated the rabbit, sending it tumbling to the grass like a flat tire, kicking once before coming to rest.

"Minchia—" Mike yelled, seeing Duke's huge frame pass through the end of his smoking barrel. "*Lucky* dog, Tom! *Lucky ass* dog ... " He lowered the shotgun and exhaled in relief.

"Dammit to hell, Duke!" Tom snapped, running toward his dog.

Duke sniffed the dead rabbit and circled it. Then he sprinted toward the car in a zigzag, big paws pumping like pistons.

"See what I mean? No interest, and too much damn energy. He's worse with birds. God, I thought he was a goner there," Tom said.

Mike lifted the rabbit by its rear legs and stuck it in the pouch of his game vest.

"Me, too. Let's take him out there, past that small stand of popples," Mike pointed to the entryway that opened up to acres of corn and the early growth aspen, prime bird cover. As the aspen thinned out, the corn became more visible. It broke off left from there, into a clearing that buffered the field from the off-limit woods on the right. The cornfield glowed yellow with papery stalks long since harvested, but still standing six feet high.

To the right of the trail, the woods quickly thickened up with tall pines and oaks, and the property was far more rolling. The creek wandered through the valleys there. Knowing it had to be loaded with game took every ounce of restraint Mike possessed to honor the farmer's request to keep out. The birds spent most of the time deep in the aspen and corn anyway, eating the nutrient-rich buds of the saplings and cobs of corn that Art Chesney's machines and the feeding whitetails left behind. But Mike had seen so many startled and pursued birds and rabbits seek respite in the sanctuary of those woods that he was well aware how prime the acreage was. It beckoned him, but he'd resisted.

"Duke!" Tom yelled.

The dog ran up to him at breakneck speed, all legs and paws. He stopped five feet short of Tom, lowered his big head, and then took off again just as fast.

Mike raised his gun and fired over Duke's head. The dog stopped in his tracks.

"*Duke!*" Mike commanded. He walked toward the jumpy animal.

"Jeezus, Mike," Tom said quietly, padding after him.

They got to the dog and walked him to Mike's Continental. Mike opened the trunk and moved a bunch of crap around, searching for something. Tom watched as Mike shuffled through debris: a tire iron, three wooden clubs, a pouch of screwdrivers and, most notably, a metal "Slim Jim" blade. Tom arched an eyebrow at the Slim Jim.

"Every contractor carries one. Sometimes a window sticks. Mind your business," Mike said, shoving all of it to the side. "Ah … there you are." He uncovered a huge, seven-foot, rusty steel chain made of thick links. There was a snap hook at one end. "Duke—c'mere boy," Mike barked. The dog bounded over to him, bobbing his head.

"What are you gonna do with that?" Tom said, his voice steeped in concern at the sight of the heavy chain. Mike took one end of it and draped the chain around Duke's neck and looped it once, then fastened it on itself with the snap hook. Duke kept panting away. Mike got up and grabbed his gun, pointing it past the aspen toward the cornfield.

"Let's see him run *now*. We'll take him out there and if he starts to run, the chain will slow his ass down. It's about twenty pounds. He'll get the idea quick, but we'll reinforce it with verbal commands," Mike said.

Tom looked warily at the length of oxidized chain around Duke's neck, not unlike a hangman's noose.

"I don't know, Mike … seems like too much of a strain for him."

Mike picked up the chain's slack, almost using it like a leash.

"Trust me. You hunt first. We'll switch off. When he starts to run, I'll drop the chain. Every time he wants to run ahead, we drop it. It works. Let's go."

They had walked hard, Tom with his shotgun at his side, Mike carrying his in his left hand, gripping the chain with his right. Mike's knee pulsed, but he grinded through the throbbing pain.

Duke trotted slightly, nowhere near as fast as before, but still at a decent pace. As they neared the aspen saplings, the cornfield still a good 400 yards past the split, the lush rolling woods started forming to the right. Mike glanced at them, and then looked away, but Duke pulled hard toward the woods, barking, as if being called there. Mike had the chain and kept him at bay, yanking him back.

And then suddenly Duke ran. A flat-out dead running sprint.

Mike was pulled forward and threw the chain down. Instantly Duke looked like he'd been zapped with a ray gun that forced him to run in slow motion.

"Son of a bitch will you look at that," Tom watched, damn near awestruck.

Duke ran ten feet but it looked like he was running under water. He panted hard and then promptly sat.

"Told you it works," Mike smiled in satisfaction. "The question is, why the hell did he even run at all?"

"I don't know if he just smells game or what," Tom replied.

They approached Duke, and Mike picked up the chain, again using it like a leash. They continued on when something within the rows of corn caused the stalks to sway. Gracefully, two deer bounded out. They were button bucks, healthy and moving fast, crashing and crunching through the dried corn. Mike whistled as the deer crossed from left to right, 100 yards in front of them. The two bucks stopped, their large ears pointed up, their heads erect, motionless.

"Must be twins," Tom said. "How come shit like this doesn't happen to us during rifle season?"

Mike smiled mischievously. "If you're in the mood for venison ... "

Before Tom could answer, Duke bolted for the deer, as if he wanted to see if they would play. He barked incessantly. Mike took two steps after him, and then dropped the chain hard. It clanked in the grass, but this time Duke never slowed down. The chain bounced along, sounding like cans being dragged from a wedding limo.

"What the hell?" Mike said, stunned that the dog was able to keep running. "That's one strong-ass dog. He'll slow down though, you watch."

The two ran after him, Mike limping it out, but Duke broke when the deer broke to the right, into the thicker, neighboring woods and its hilly terrain. The deer stood motionless for a second, then leapt as if charged with electricity. They crashed over a stand of six-foot pines up a hill and disappeared over a ridge. Duke followed in pursuit, some thirty yards behind the bucks, and like that—he was gone, his barking fading in the cool, fall air.

"What the—how the *hell* does he keep on running?" Mike said, impressed with the dog's strength, albeit dismayed that his training method wasn't working worth a shit anymore. Tom ran ten steps ahead, concern washing over his face.

They could barely hear Duke breaking through the brush. He barked several times, but the sound faded fast.

"What's over that way?" Tom said, his heart racing.

"Other than trees, don't know. I never hunt there. I only run the Jacks in the cornfields for rabbits and birds. The farmer told me to stay out of the woods because his neighbor's a certified bleeding-heart prick." Mike was wheezing now, trying to keep up with Tom.

The narrow deer run was littered with sticks and branches. They negotiated the huge trunk of a red pine that had blown across it. The leaves were mostly gone from the small portion of gnarled oaks that made up the hardwoods in the coniferous-heavy tree mix, the towering pines and spruce choking off most of the oak growth.

"How the hell was he able to get up this hill with that chain?" Tom said, barely able to get the words out from exertion. Mike felt his knee giving out. He clenched onto it, willing it to work, trying to keep pace as gravity worked against him. They were near the top when the barking started again.

"You hear him?" Mike asked.

Tom rested just before the crest of the hill. He tipped his ear toward the barking, and as he did, there was a half bark-howl that abruptly clipped dead. Now there was just the silence of the woods save for the occasional bird chirping and red squirrel chattering.

Tom looked confused. Mike finally caught up, standing next to him, panting heavily. He listened, too, but there was no sound. The two searched around through the tops of the trees as they scanned the woods below for any sign of Duke.

"Duke! *Duke!*" Tom cupped his hands over his mouth, shouting into the green-black void. He paced the hilltop and looked in an arc from left to right, his eyes narrowing to focus through the branches, trying to find his beloved dog. Mike squinted, then stepped ahead of Tom.

"This way, the trail picks up here," Mike said, pointing to matted-down grass. It was worn bare from the deer that traveled back and forth, making trips from the bedding areas to the cornfield where the animals fed. Mike walked carefully down the hill, traversing the steep decline, wincing each time he put weight on the knee. They got to the bottom and looked both ways. A dragline was visible through the leaves there. He looked up, his mouth opening to form an O.

"Shit, hear that?" Mike suddenly found a reserve of energy. He shuffled quickly and ran hard past Tom, straight ahead on the land as it leveled out in front of them.

"What's that noise?" Tom said, running step for step just a couple of yards behind.

"Water," Mike yelled. Tom's stomach turned.

They saw it twenty yards ahead through the end of the tunnel-like deer run. Pigeon Creek passed directly in front of them, swollen with water from the recent rainfall and moving in a lazy roil, the distance between the banks a good twelve feet across.

"Oh no. Duke, no," Tom said.

At the edge of the creek bank they saw a gurgling burst of bubbles. Mike noticed movement on the other side of the bank. The two button bucks, their tails up, bobbed their heads up and down like ostriches in a mating dance. Tom's neck grew cool with sweat and he ran up and down the creek bank, frantically looking back and forth, alternating with peeks into the tannic water.

"Can't believe that chain didn't slow him down. Shit, that's a real pisser. He might've made a decent duck dog," Mike said. "Course, he wasn't much of a swimmer." Mike's flippant comment hung in the air between them.

Tom looked at him and his eyes flared.

"It's not funny, Mike. That poor thing … oh God. *Oh God, Duke.* Duke, I'm sorry, pal. The hell was I thinking? A chain! My poor Duke," Tom leaned against a tree, not wanting Mike to see his face.

Mike looked down at his boots, letting Tom get through it. He picked up a rock and tossed it into the river. He watched it disappear in the slow-moving creek. He grabbed a fallen branch that was nearly seven feet in length. Tom peeked up from the tree he was leaning on. Mike reached out and poked the water. It bottomed out at three feet.

"The deer probably leapt over the creek off these rocks. Here … hold this."

Tom took Mike's gun and rested it on the ground. Mike waded into the creek, the whole time poking in front of him with the long stick, testing the depth and the bottom. His testicles sucked into his body, and he lost his breath for a moment as the icy water made itself at home in his boots and field pants.

"Maddon' fa freddo!" he gasped as it passed his crotch.

He reached and poked once more, his mouth puckering like he was working a stubborn chive from between his teeth. The water was at his hips now. He snapped his head down, and reached into the water all the way to his shoulder. The stick he'd used floated to the surface and drifted with the current away from them.

"Be careful," Tom cautioned. "What are you doing?"

Mike's right cheek touched the cold surface of the water and he squinted. And then his eyes flickered open. He grunted once and pulled straight up, his hand around Duke's collar, the other underneath, cradling the huge Lab's soaked body.

"What?" was all Tom said. He started toward Mike. "You're lying! You are fucking *lying!*" Tom howled, seeing Duke's wet corpse.

Mike splashed up the creek bank with the drenched, lifeless dog, all seven feet of chain still draped around Duke like shackles on a buried treasure. Tom dropped the guns and crashed into the water, both men now soaked from the waist down.

"Take him, Tom! He's too heavy," Mike said, his face straining under the weight of the chain and the dead animal. Tom took Duke's body just as Mike's knee popped, buckling for good. He dropped into the creek, hitting the wounded knee on a submersed boulder. "Sonofabitchin' rock!" he wailed. The pain seared, coursing through his body like battery acid and collecting in the knee.

Tom gently laid Duke on the grass. He removed the chain from Duke's neck and threw it to the ground. He just looked at his dead dog for a second, then started shaking him vigorously, trying to will the life back into him.

"Duke!" he yelled. "What do we do, Mike? What do we do to save him? We have to do something." Tom was wild-eyed and Mike looked at him like he'd just sprouted a third head.

"What the hell dya' mean 'what do *we* do?' *We* leave him. He's history. The raccoons and turkey buzzards will eat him. Get my chain and help me back to the car ... " Mike stared at Tom, holding his hand out for help. Tom couldn't accept it, any of it. He shook his head and felt the neck of the animal. His face lit up.

"I think I feel a pulse! He's still alive. Mike, we can save him, maybe give him CPR or somethin' ... I don't know ... " Tom pleaded, the pitch of his voice quavering.

Mike stared at him then laughed, despite the immense pain he was feeling.

"You been smoking hippy hair with the boys on the assembly line? You gonna put your *mouth* on that dog's? You're high, boy. Mouth-to-mouth on a dog." Mike shook his head and grabbed his knee. Tom started pounding on the dog's chest. Nothing happened. "Forget it. It's done," Mike said.

"I'm going for help," Tom said.

He was up the hill quickly. Mike tried to get up, but the knee said stay.

"Tom! Get your Frog-Irish ass back here you stupid shit! My knee—Tom ... *Goddammit Tom!*" he yelled. Tom was up the hill with an insane fury and he could see trying to stop him now was useless.

"For a mutt ... God *damn* my knee!"

He rocked back and forth and stared at the top of the hill, as if concentrating on the spot where Tom disappeared would make him appear from thin air. He looked at Duke's wet body. He watched his eyes and saw nothing alive there. They were half open, like two yawning clams, each holding a dull gold pearl in their cold flesh.

He dragged himself closer to Duke, and the pain that shot through his knee made him cry out loud. He bit down hard and knelt near the dog.

"Stupid son of a bitch ... you wouldn't have run this don't happen. How the hell were you able to run with that chain? You were a strong son of a bitch, weren't you?"

He put his hand on the dog's neck. Keeping it there, he strained his eyes, concentrating on his fingertip, as if trying to feel the tumblers on a combination lock.

"Warm … that's strange. Can't be. How strong are you?"

Mike put his ear to Duke's wet chest. He placed his hand on the dog's broad ribcage and pressed hard. Nothing happened. When he pressed down again, he could've swore he saw Duke's eyes open, but figured it was just nerves. He looked closely at the dog's mouth. The tongue was rolled out like a freed conch, as it had looked when he had been running so alive and full of energy minutes earlier. Mike put his mouth close to Duke, and made a face, smelling a meaty odor.

"I can't believe I'm even—" his ear was next to Duke's snout. Mike's eyes opened wide. "Omigod, Duke!" He massaged the animal's ribs, its chest, all to no effect. He slapped hard at Duke's face, but the dog's nose just moved side to side with each swipe of his palm. Mike looked upward, as if waiting for God to shout down proper instructions to him for reanimation. He blinked once. Hard.

And then his head dropped forward, as if he heard the answer from Him, one that he disagreed with but grudgingly had to accept.

"You gotta be shittin' me. You are *shitting* me. That's crazy!" he yelled, sounding like the babbling, lone survivor of a shipwreck.

He looked to the top of the hill where Tom had disappeared. He stared at Duke's still frame. He opened Duke's considerable mouth and peered inside. The black and pink gums of the animal gave him pause; the large canine teeth striking him as primitive. He pulled on Duke's rubbery tongue, checking his airway for obstructions. From his windpipe, Mike fished out creek muck; rotting oak leaves and twig stems. He gently grabbed the animal from behind its large head and brought Duke's snout skyward, pinching it. He took some deep breaths and a last look into the alley of Duke's mouth.

"Fuckin' ay," he said.

Mike breathed in a huge lung full of air, then put his mouth against the dog's and breathed his breath deep into the animal's lungs. He brought his mouth away and wiped it with his shirtsleeve, choking back the urge to vomit. A little water escaped Duke's slack mouth, but still no sign of life.

Then he remembered: *dead space.*

The two words seemed to almost float past his eyes, like type beamed into the air in front of him. He remembered that most of a dog's breathing happens in the nose—it was one of many stupid facts he'd read years ago in a training manual about dogs and animal first aid. The term caught his eye and must've stuck because here it was now, in front of him like the lingering effect of a past LSD trip; *dead space.* If you ever wanted to perform CPR on a dog, you had to put air into their *nose.* Not their mouth. It had to do with how a canine breathes a column of dead space air in their trachea during the exchange that happens when they pant.

Or something like that.

He clamped Duke's big mouth shut and felt his tongue scrape the rough, moist surface of the dog's wet nose. The muzzle was so big it felt like he was trying to swallow an uncanned cylinder of cranberry jelly covered in fur.

He took another deep breath, and with his lips forming an airtight seal around Duke's nostrils, expelled his air into the dog's snout. This time he almost passed out, his head going dizzy, and for a moment, God help him, he swore he saw his mother Maria's face there, long dead from this world.

Mike opened his eyes, blinking out of the darkening expanse, and was met face-to-face with Duke's large, golden brown eyeballs—wide open and staring a whisper away from Mike's own. He pulled his mouth away just as a sea of creek water back-splashed from Duke's mouth into his, causing him to puke up the last bit of linguine with clam sauce he'd eaten from the refrigerator as a pre-hunt snack.

"Duke!" Mike spat, his throat raw with vomit.

Duke coughed loud, harshly, like a toddler with croup, and then rolled over twice before springing to his feet, his head tilted in puzzlement at Mike.

Mike's eyes watered from the acidic snot that flooded his esophagus and the inside of his nose. He thought he was seeing things and felt something otherworldly gripping his trachea, preventing him from speaking out. Duke looked back and forth, like a visitor from a foreign world might. He tilted his perfect head again at Mike and barked hard, as if trying to chase away the last remnants of death. More creek water sprayed forward, hitting Mike in the face. He finally found his voice.

"You crazy mutt! I don't believe it ... you're *alive* you crazy-ass dog!"

Mike was rambling like a tongue-speaker, not really believing the Lazarus-like animal was resurrected before him, shaking his chocolate brown coat dry. Water droplets peppered Mike's cheeks, stinging him. And although he couldn't believe it himself, he felt his eyes water, knowing it wasn't just from the residual dry heaves. Duke's head popped up and he broke right back toward the creek. Mike grabbed his collar just in time. The force of the dog pulled him a good three feet toward the water.

"Duke you stupid son of a bitch! You didn't learn shit!"

Duke barked and then Mike saw the cause of the dog's irritation. The two button bucks were still on the other side of the creek bank, motionless, gazing as if amazed at what they'd just witnessed. Mike looked at them and could only stare, watching their faces mimic cement lawn ornaments. Then, as if a spell had been broken, the bucks bolted deeper into the woods, disappearing into the dark tangle of trees. Mike heard a rustle of leaves.

"Oh my God! *Duke!*" Tom screamed from the top of the hill.

Mike's stomach dropped when he heard Tom's voice, and saw him step from between the opening of an oak tree with twin trunks. Tom sprinted down the hill. Halfway down he dropped to one leg, sliding the rest of the way like a ten-year-old boy playing army.

"How fuckin' long you been standing up there?" Mike asked.

Mike was still breathing hard. He wiped vomit from his mouth with his shirtsleeve and eyed Tom suspiciously. Before he could reply, Duke broke from Mike's grip and bolted into Tom's arms, overtaking him in a barrel roll. The two rolled around like lost friends and Mike watched, genuinely amused.

"I just got back."

Mike fixed a closer look on him.

"I *did!* I was running to get help and then I thought, by the time I got to the farmer's house, called a vet or a fireman or, well shit … it was too late anyway." He stared at the dog, still in disbelief. "My God I can't believe it. Duke's *alive—you're alive!*" Tom let Duke lick his face and he patted his wet head and scratched Duke's snout. Mike studied Tom's expression. He'd known Tom a long time. "My Duke … How Mike? What happened here?"

"What the hell do you mean? *Minchia*, I'm sitting here in pain—no thanks to you leaving me—and this crazy mutt of yours just jumped up and started running after the deer again. I couldn't believe it either. Dog was born under a lucky star, I guess. Should've named him Luciano," Mike said.

Tom looked at Mike and nodded his head back and forth.

Mike went to light a cigarette, but his matches wouldn't catch, and the cigarette was soaked through. "Fucking *fuck!*" He threw them into the creek, his cussing lapsing into Sicilian. Tom walked over and put an arm around him. He helped him up, sitting him on an aspen trunk. Mike settled onto it and flinched at the pain.

"I'm going take the guns to the car, and I'll come back and we'll get you home, OK?" Tom said to him. He took a freshly opened pack of Chesterfield's from his vest pocket, which caused Mike's face to glow like a kid on Christmas morning. Tom handed him the cigarettes, a dry pack of matches tucked in the cellophane wrapping.

"God bless you," Mike said, taking one to his mouth and striking a crisp, dry match to the end of it. The smell of the match made him happy.

Tom gathered the guns. He started leading Duke up the hill, but the dog pulled from his hand to stay with Mike. Tom looked at his brother-in-law, but Mike wasn't paying attention, squeezing his swollen knee instead.

"I'll leave Duke with you," he said.

Mike looked at Duke, who settled by his side like an obedient son.

"Suit yourself," Mike replied.

Tom watched Duke's protection act with Mike and did what he could to hide a smile. "Almost forgot your chain," Tom said, reaching for it.

"Leave it. All rusty anyway. Rusted to shit." Mike smoked his cigarette.

"Sure. Be right back."

Tom took off up the hill and Mike winced with every step he saw him take, anticipating the climb awaiting him. He looked at Duke's sloppy tongue and the dog's golden eyes staring at him. He shook his head and let out a hearty, unbridled peal of laughter.

"Crazy mutt. Unbelievable."

Duke moved his snout close to Mike's left hand and kept it there. Mike pushed it away, but Duke was determined. His tail pulsed, furiously beating up and down like a jackhammer. He put his nose back under Mike's hand again, this time nudging it. Mike stared at him, and looking up the hill—seeing that Tom was nowhere in sight—scratched Duke's snout a little. Duke purred a low, pleasurable growl. Finally, Mike stroked Duke's fur with vigor and patted his ribs, scratching the sides of the dog. He mouthed the cigarette and rubbed Duke's ribs with both hands. He held the dog's face with one hand and pointed to Duke with the other, talking while clenching the smoke in his teeth.

"Just you and me, Duke. Tell anybody about this, I'll kick your ass, you hear me, boy? If I'm lying I'm dying," Mike said. He looked up and thought he saw movement behind the large twin oak at the hilltop.

It was twenty minutes before Tom returned with a rake handle he'd found on the trail near the car. He brought Duke's leash and made his way down the hill to Mike and his dog. Upon seeing Tom, Duke looked at Mike as if awaiting permission to leave his post. Mike said, "Hup!" and Duke broke for Tom, meeting him halfway up the steep, leaf-covered hill.

Tom gave the rake handle to Mike, who regarded it dubiously.

"Hey Duke, look who's back; Florence-fucking-Nightingale," Mike said, grabbing the rake handle like a shepherd. Tom put the leash around Duke's collar. He put his arm around Mike, helping him straighten up. Mike used the rake as a crutch for one step before casting it aside.

"Screw that." He bit his tongue and with each step, his grip on Tom grew a little tighter. Duke walked in cadence with them.

Tom opened the trunk of the Lincoln. He looked at Mike, who rested against the car breathing heavily, his face mapped with pain. Tom went to the trunk and grabbed a duffel bag Mike had "found" in one of the houses he was working on. He reached in and unfurled three luxurious white bath towels, *The Whittier Hotel~Detroit*, embroidered in red script across the bottoms.

Tom opened up the rear driver's side door and helped Mike stand in front of it, his back facing the interior. He rolled the towels up and placed them on the rear bench seat.

"Back in this way. Lean your back up against the passenger door and prop your leg on these. Stretch that leg out," Tom said.

Mike scooted himself into the Lincoln's roomy backseat, squirming backward until he felt his spine resting against the rear passenger door.

Tom gingerly picked up Mike's leg and placed it on the rolled-up towels, elevating it.

Mike grinned. "Feels pretty good, up like that," he said. "Thanks, Tom."

"Sure." Tom hesitated a second. "C'mon, Duke. Duke!" he commanded.

Duke ran over dutifully at Tom's voice and sat frozen at his feet.

"The hell did you do, put a spell on him? He's like a new dog. Look at him. C'mon Duke, get in the trunk." Tom led Duke to the trunk. Mike's head spun around. He knocked on the rear window. Tom leaned over and looked at Mike. "What?" he said.

Mike motioned for him.

Tom walked over and poked his head in the driver's side window.

"Maybe we let him ride shotgun. Just this once, though," Mike said.

Tom looked back at the open trunk. He didn't need to be told twice. He walked back, slammed the trunk and scratched Duke's head, leading him by the collar to the front passenger side door.

"Go on, boy, hop in," Tom urged Duke, patting the passenger seat. Mike leaned his head back against the glass and closed his eyes. Duke jumped into the car and rested his chin on the back of the big bench seat, staring at Mike. Mike opened one eye and closed it again, a Cheshire grin forming on his face. He lowered the brim of his hunting hat over his eyes.

"I'm gonna try and grab a few winks, Tom. When we get to Ubly, stop at Macy's—the bakery—can't miss it. Do me a favor and pick up some cinnamon rolls for the kids. Kraut baker does a pretty good job with them."

"Right," Tom said. He closed the front passenger door and got behind the wheel. He reached back, offering an open silver flask. "Want some? Homemade blackberry brandy from my Yugo neighbor, old man Kurowicz. It'll really knock your ball bag around," Tom said, handing it to him.

"Oh yeahhh. *Salute,*" Mike said. He took a long swallow from the flask. He grimaced and breathed out a basso whoop. Duke howled wolfishly in response. He tilted his big head at Mike and shook, settling against Tom's thigh.

"Whoa! That's some shit, there. Hot damn," Mike said.

He gave the flask back to Tom. Tom took a small snort and snapped his head like he was about to sneeze.

They had driven a few miles when Duke startled awake and barked a couple of times; nothing more than quiet, soft yaps. Then he rested his head down next to Tom's thigh. Tom looked at the Lab, still not believing his dog was sitting there—*breathing*—right next to him. He started to say Mike's name, then stopped himself, instead stroking the dog's brown fur, massaging its big jaw. He mumbled a barely audible prayer of thanks which if Mike heard, he didn't acknowledge. After a silent five minutes, Mike cleared his throat. Tom peered into the rearview mirror.

"Tom," Mike said, his voice low and even.

He saw Mike tilt his head up and stare at him from under the pulled-down brim of his hat. "What's that, Mike?" Tom asked.

"You ever tell my brothers, or Dominic Frabetta, or *especially* that prick Frank Stefani—or anyone else for that matter—that this mangy, smelly mutt rode inside my car, in *my front seat*, no less … I'll not only kick your *ass*, I'll cut your arms off and beat you to death with them. You hear me? If I'm lying I'm dying. I'll kill ya' … *capiece?*"

Mike looked at him once. Tom grinned at him.

"*Capiece,* brother-in-law. Wouldn't want anyone to think you cared for some stupid hunting dog. What would all the Jacks think?"

"Go to hell. Now goodnight," Mike said, pulling the brim of his hat down farther. Tom saw a little grin spread over Mike's face.

They were about a mile out of Ubly when Tom looked down to find Duke was sound asleep. He peeked in the backseat and saw that Mike was, too.

Tom parked the Lincoln in front of Macy's Bakery and scratched Duke's big head. The dog's tongue splashed about his mouth like a pink trout. Tom walked into the bakery, which smelled of bread and fried dough. The proprietor, Othell Macy, wiped his hands. Tom ordered two dozen of the enormous, glazed cinnamon rolls and had them wrapped in separate boxes, deciding to bring a dozen home for his own kids.

He paid Othell and accepted his change. He was at the door when he stopped and turned to the baker, a roundly fat immigrant who still held onto his accent. Othell looked back with tired, blue eyes. Tom started to talk, then stopped to peek out the window. He had his hand on the door handle, but something tugged at him. Tom turned back to Othell, his face scrunched up, as if pressurized.

"Can I tell you something? Because I've got to tell someone. Please?" Tom practically begged. Othell looked at Tom and squinted, shrugging his round back and nodded.

Tom pointed out the window of the store. "That guy sleeping in the car out there, in the backseat. See him? And that dog riding shotgun?" Othell looked at him. "Dog's in the passenger seat."

Othell looked out. He saw Duke sitting upright in the passenger seat and behind him, the back of Mike's head leaning against the window. Othell nodded yes, that he saw.

"That's my brother-in-law, Mike. The dog's mine. His name's Duke."

Othell's face relaxed. "Like the great Wayne?"

"*Exactly* … like John Wayne."

Othell smiled and looked closer at Mike's Continental. "Been here before. Nice man. What of this?" he asked.

Tom breathed out a lung full of air. "I don't even know you. An absolute miracle."

Othell's blank face grew even blanker. Tom started to talk, more excited, the way Americans get trying to communicate in English while visiting foreign countries.

"Today, I shit you not, I watched him do it! Do you understand what I'm telling you? That's *Mike Materra!* That it worked, but that *he* would even *try*. Mike Materra! With *his* mouth—into Duke's smelly ass dog-mouth and by God he saved my Duke, and shit, I don't think I'll ever see anything as beautiful as that in my life ever again."

Othell stared closely at Tom, saying nothing.

Tom sighed, frustrated. "Man, you don't get it. A *dog* is sitting in Mike's front seat—*Mike Materra!*"

They stood there a second.

Othell picked at a stray ear hair. Feeling compelled to finally speak, the baker mumbled, "So front seat? What's this big deal about the front seat?"

"Because … " Tom shrugged and stopped talking. He shook his head in lieu of pursuing it any further.

"Bitch of it is, I can't tell anyone I know about what I saw. Any of it."

Othell stared at him, letting him continue.

"But man, I just had to tell *somebody*, you know? To hear myself say the words out loud I guess. Just to hear it spoken. Because this really happened. It did."

Tom took a breath and stood there, remembering every piece, replaying it in his mind; the incredible sights he witnessed earlier, covertly spying from between a twin oak that grew from a single trunk, high above the forbidden woods below him.

Othell nodded, unsure of what to do or say next. He looked at some bread dough that he'd probably have to throw away. Tom said goodbye to the befuddled man. With a bounce in his step, like someone who's just been told the tumor is benign, he set the bell on the door chiming, a white box of Macy's famous cinnamon rolls in each hand. He left Othell standing inside his modest bakery to scratch his unnaturally large, round head at the exchange that just occurred.

Hearing the car start, Othell walked to the door. He took a cautionary look outside and watched Mike's tan, riveted-together Continental pull away from the curb, driving off into the explosion of purpled dusk. He turned away, grumbling *harrumphs,* still unclear at the meaning of the nonsense he just heard.

Fetishes of the Heartless

Supposedly at any moment, they would encounter the "barking-chasing dog." They had run out of roads. As the Bonneville bounced in the rutted two-track, they searched for the last farmhouse, the last landmark before the cabin. The two friends started in Marquette, using the bar napkin like a treasure map. Marc studied the hastily scrawled directions the chubby bartender from The Plugged Nickel had given them. All that was left to do was to find the trapper's cabin in the coming darkness, wangle the fur hats, and head downstate the next morning.

Marc Scettico and Julian Protetto were up from the Lower Peninsula—both grew up on Detroit's East Side, in Copper Corner—visiting a friend at Northern Michigan University. NMU, *the school* as the locals refer to it, was the main employer for the region, at least since the mining business took its latest shit a half-century earlier.

Marc's entrepreneurial nature was the catalyst that sent them to find "Trapper Dan." It was 1987, and a trendy resurgence in animal skin hats, specifically coonskin caps, had emerged as a funky, urban fashion statement around the Detroit club scene. Marc thought he might even like one for himself, but this side trip was about making money. That's why they were searching the backcountry of the western Upper Peninsula, instead of getting hammered on cheap beer in Marquette.

It was late March and the snow was slower to melt than usual. High brown and white marbled slush piles were stacked willy-nilly, wherever the plows could find a place to push the stuff. Most of the back roads were covered with a base that had melted and refroze into a pad of sand and ice, a cycle that would continue for weeks, until begrudgingly—usually late May—an actual semblance of spring would appear. The heart of the winter had been the typical Upper Peninsula variety; a languid white chunk off the calendar that took its time. But the false endings in the later months toyed with its citizens' collective psyche, playing weather tricks that tested their patience and mettle. Cabin fever cloaked the Yoopers—the name the residents proudly cop to—with its usual symptoms; short-fused fights, road rage fender-benders, and in the most extreme cases, random shooting deaths of wife-beating husbands disguised as hunting accidents.

"There, that's the farmhouse. Now turn here and look for that barking-chasing dog," Marc said. Julian looked at him funny. "Hey, *she* said it, I didn't."

Julian let his look linger and then stared straight ahead.

"Barking-chasing dog. I could've gotten laid. Instead I'm looking for Grizzly Adams and the roving Hound of Death."

"Don't tell me you're bummed you didn't get to dip your wick in someone from *that* place? Let me guess ... " Marc sarcastically batted his eyes at his friend. "Was it Large Marge, that broad who kept throwing you the goo-goo eyes?"

Julian grunted in reply.

Marc stared at Julian until he *tsked*. "That's what I thought. Just keep an eye out for the barking-chasing dog,"

Julian fluttered his lips. "Barking-chasing. This is bullshit."

And a minute later, a dog *did* bark. Quietly at first, then loud enough to be heard over The Doors' *The End*. The spiraling dirge groaned from the cassette player, the bass set too high. Hearing the timely bark, Julian laughed nervously. Upon seeing the dog *chasing* his car, sweat formed on the small of his back. He felt it drip into his ass crack.

"Holy shit, roll up the windows," Julian cranked the knob. "Stop fucking around, roll it up."

Marc looked out the open passenger window. The big dog loped toward them as the Bonneville turned, barking away. When the high beams hit the animal's eyes, they could see the glowing retinas and the color of its fur. It was a mutt of some kind, a mix of shepherd and malamute, brackish colored with a red tinge across its coat. It was a large beast, all of the grace bred from the thing, as if any evolved characteristics its lineage may have possessed had been genetically removed, making it appear more menacing than either man imagined.

"Damn. He should let up at the end of the block," Marc said. "Least that's what Shiva said. Let's hope she's right."

"Just roll up your window. Please?" Julian asked.

"Chill yourself. Man," Marc said as he watched Julian rub the carving. It was small as a bead and reddish in color, laced through a licorice whip-like strand of brown leather that hung from his neck.

Before Marc could roll up the window, the barking quieted. The dog stopped and stood watch. "Hmm. Look at that," Marc said.

"All I wanted to do was get a little drunk, play some pool, maybe screw a Yooper girl and go home tomorrow," Julian said. "So damn money-hungry that we're here on a snipe hunt from the mouth of a fat Indian chick bartender at that shit-hole of a bar. This is fucked up like Chinese music."

"Drive," Marc said.

He's right about the bar, Marc thought. The Plugged Nickel was nothing more than a biker's pub that allowed occasionally brave college students to hang and drink beers with the underbelly of the Upper Peninsula. Chris Orlando, the friend they were staying with, had taken them to the Nickel for last call the night before as a goof after leaving The Alibi, the best pick-up joint in town. The Nickel did a good business and the students could brag how they partied with members of the Marquette Jokers or the Negaunee Highwaymen, most of the time without getting their ass kicked (although Marquette's finest did get called to the Nickel thrice weekly). The three friends had a good time at the bar, but this Saturday night it was just the two of them. Chris had begged off to study for a Monday morning science exam—he was majoring in Conservation—that gauged the impact of predators, namely wolves and coyotes, on the local livestock population. So Marc and Julian ended up at The Plugged Nickel without him.

They didn't serve food at The Plugged Nickel. Just packaged snacks and free, stale popcorn from an old popper nestled in the corner. All the beer was draft, thus cutting down on the temptation to crack the neck off a Leinenkugel during the inevitable fights, though it seemed a jagged bar glass had to be extracted from the forearm of some drunken student bi-monthly at Marquette General's ER.

No one would ever accuse the Nickel of being the cleanest drinking establishment north of the Mackinac Bridge either, but you had to give it four stars for atmosphere. It wasn't unusual to see a professor hitting on a local girl or smoking a joint with a biker chick. Sometimes soldiers from K.I. Sawyer Air Force Base, just thirty miles south in Gwinn, ventured to the bar, trying to stir up some trouble. Most would take one look at the bikers, turn around and walk out.

Returning to the Nickel without their friend's familiar face, the place seemed bereft of the charm it possessed the night before. The crowd gave the two Detroiters hard looks. It wasn't until Marc bought a round for three nearby tables that everyone got nice and friendly. The beers were ridiculously cheap—sixty-five cents a shell—and the three pitchers only set him back eight bucks and change. Their present bartender hadn't worked the night before; at least, neither of them remembered her. It was odd seeing a girl with a dot on her forehead that far north. When Marc first ordered beers from Shiva Mankiller, the chubby Indian-*Indian* barkeep—her father was Huron, her mother had roots in Calcutta—blew into the glasses, stirring up dust motes that had settled inside. She filled two shells from a tapper.

"Ever think of stacking the glasses bottoms *up?*" Marc asked her.

"Yeah," Julian squinted as he spoke. "That's kind of gross."

Shiva turned back to the two, the sparest of smiles revealing tiny teeth, looking like two rows of beige corn kernels.

"No. My mouth's clean," Shiva said.

She slammed the beers down. A timid head of foam rose on the pale liquid.

"Buck-thirty. Want peanuts?" she asked, presenting the beers.

"Why the hell not?" Marc said, feeling the bikers' eyes on him.

Shiva pulled two foil bags of beer nuts from a rack.

"Buck-ninety," She said, tossing the bags next to the beers.

The plump woman looked at Marc. Her eyes were dark, small like charred beetles. Coupled with the black *tika* on her forehead, her face assumed the pattern of a triangle made up of little black circles. Her skin was a smooth ochre complexion.

"Think I can swing that." Marc shook his head and handed her three singles. Heading to the register, she paused when she noticed the third dollar.

"Keep that extra buck for yourself," Marc said.

Her eyes actually got a little bigger. She smiled again, showing her little teeth, and then rang a cowbell above the register, a signal that a big tipper was in the Nickel. A little cheer rose up from the patrons, and someone threw handfuls of popcorn at them.

"Well, aren't *you* the Sultan of Brunei?" Julian said quietly, swallowing half the beer before grimacing. "What is *this* shit, *Hamms?* Tastes like piss water."

"Quit your bitching. It's cold, right?" Marc said.

A local girl with an enormous ass smiled at Julian. Pretty in a Britt Eklund way—ice blue eyes and natural, platinum hair—the Nordic girl had marked him from the moment they entered. It was as if she was formed from two women; small-shouldered, with tiny hands and a modest bust, set atop a wasp-narrow waist with ample hips and that *gigantic* rear-end following her around.

Marc watched the two potential lovebirds with the morbid fascination one gets from seeing a zit popped. "Julesy, two words: *snow cow*," he whispered. Julian looked away from the girl as if he been caught picking his nose. "That's what Chris calls them. Winter keeps a lot of girls up here pretty sedentary."

"*What?*" Julian asked.

"*Sedentary*. Unmoving. They're kind of like veal. She's pretty enough, if you could get past that ass. But I don't know, man … *that's* an ass!"

"They're all the same size when they're laying down." Julian smiled at her, trying to look seductive as he choked down the nasty ale.

Marc looked behind the bar and noticed a fur tail draped over a coat rack. Upon closer inspection, he saw a full coonskin cap with the arms tied up behind the animal's skinned-out face.

"Honey, is that *yours?*" Marc asked Shiva.

She turned to see what he was looking at. After a moment, she turned back.

"Uh-huh. Dan Jokopi made it. Trapper Dan."

"That thing's *kicking*. What did you pay for it? I'll buy it off ya."

Shiva smiled kittenishly. "I didn't. It was a *special gift*. But you don't want one of those." Shiva's expression flattened out. "Seriously, you don't."

Julian stared at the black dot on the center of her forehead. "What's that thing for?" he asked, pointing at it with the rim of his glass.

"It repels the evil eye," she said, pushing her silky black hair behind her ears, affording him a clearer view of the *tika*. Julian was mesmerized by it.

"Back to the cap—*hell yes, I do*. How do I find this trapper guy?" Marc asked.

Shiva paused, keeping her gaze on Julian before she finally addressed Marc. Her eyes turned smaller, and she leaned over the bar.

"I don't think you two should go out there." She peeked back at Julian again. "It's in the middle of nowhere. And you're not from around here. You don't want any of that. 'Specially not at night."

"You let me be the judge. I could sell the *shit* out of those in Detroit. Julesy, can you imagine what the *brothers* would pay for one? Where's Trapper Dan live?"

That was the question that led Shiva to give them the directions.

They had drunk way too many beers getting her to come clean. Shiva said she thought Dan sold them for maybe "a hundred dollars or so." Downstate at flea markets, Marc had seen coonskin caps selling for twice that. And those were only the tail—not the skinned-out face—nowhere near as well-made as Shiva's. He knew black guys at dance clubs that were into something different— even a coonskin hat. They would wear one to complement a $400 adidas sweat suit. He figured if he could make a deal with this trapper, the clubbers in Detroit would easily pay $300-plus for hats of such quality, especially ones with the faces left on. It was all about creating a buzz.

Now at a little after 9 p.m., they were outside of Negaunee, halfway to Ishpeming. Leaving well-marked U.S. 41 South, they had driven all the back roads through the deserted mining communities that Shiva described in her map, crudely scribbled on a bar napkin. She drew the dog with tiny horns.

Marc laughed when she showed it to him, and Shiva seemed offended.

"It's a barking-*chasing* dog," she'd said. She asked if Marc was as superstitious "as your friend," and he'd assured her no, he was not. Again as she spoke, she stared at Julian in a sort of telepathic communion, drawing harder on the bar napkin until the force of her pen stroke caused the ballpoint to rip through.

Shiva insisted the dog would scare Julian.

The dog was wild, without an owner. Some of the elders in her tribe believed it was the reincarnated spirit of a long-dead member who had been running liquor during Prohibition, was shot outside a sugar beet farm, and then dumped in the woods behind what is now Trapper Dan's home. Left for dead, the man had called aimlessly for help. A roving pack of wild dogs answered his cries instead and devoured his heart. Because his remains were buried without it, he was bound to the Earth, roaming the parameters of his killing fields in search of a suitable replacement.

"Do you believe that?" Julian asked her.

She only smiled in answer.

The story had freaked Julian out, and Shiva made it worse by continuing to stare at him after she told it. It made him wonder if she actually knew what his fears were. Before they left, she would confirm his suspicions by bestowing him with the carving. Marc just shook his head while she placed it around Julian's neck.

Shiva said because of it, the dog would stop barking and chasing once they got past the farmhouse at the corner, and it *had*, as if withheld by an invisible fence, three blocks from Dan's quaint home. Trapper Dan's cabin was to the right of the neighboring set of snow-covered beet fields the dog had disappeared into. A tidy, tar-papered cottage with a rusty tin roof, it was situated outside the wire fence-rows separating the fields. It looked dinky amongst all the white acreage. A Wisconsin paper company owned the surrounding woods bordering the fields. After strafing the forest, the company left the obligatory perimeter of "show pines" to hide the clear-cut destruction. Isolated from the last neighboring farmhouse, there was loneliness apparent in the cabin's sparse architecture. Smoke blew out of a metal pipe jutting from the roof, and its two windows glowed like square amber eyes.

Snow crunched underneath the tires as Julian turned the car into the driveway. He looked at the dark front porch ahead on his left. Marc opened his door as Julian fiddled with the radio, coaxing clearer reception. Finding none, he revisited The Doors cassette.

"C'mon, let's make this quick," Marc said, his breath visible in the night.

"I'll wait here. Freaking cold out there. I'll keep her running," Julian replied.

Marc stood next to the car and looked down the road. The huge dog had reappeared. It was standing at attention seventy-five yards away. He could almost smell the thing in the frosty air.

"It's not going to come and attack you. Look. It's just standing there. And if I remember correctly, *hero boy*, Mrs. Marinelli practically wanted to bang you afterwards."

Julian's memory flashed to the attractive Italian neighbor lady in her tight housedress, but the erotic image was quickly replaced by the redolence of urine and the distant memory of a German shepherd. The porch light went on before he could offer a retort.

"She was beautiful," Julian said.

"God, you're such a pussy," Marc said.

Julian held up the bone carving for Marc to inspect. "Least I'll be safe."

"A *superstitious* pussy at that," Marc added.

Suddenly the dog barked again, the sound reverberating like a gunshot across the fields. Marc turned his head to the sound of the dog and flinched but kept walking to the porch. He saw the dog disappear into the fields. Marc rapped on the screen door. The sky had turned a deep blue-grey, and the moon hung like a white communion host in the crystallized air, looming with startling detail. The door opened, and Marc saw him. His feet slid underneath him and his head ached. The silhouette of a giant was backlit from an overhead jelly jar fixture in the hallway. Marc—himself a true six-three—looked up at the massive body that blacked out the doorframe. Only when the man pressed his face against the screen did the trapper's features become clear. Russet tufts of beard hair, coarse as wire, poked through the mesh. It was a great beard, and if he stopped shaving right then, Marc knew he couldn't grow anything like it if he lived to be 106. The trapper held a coyote pelt in his large paws.

"Hi there," Marc said.

"Car trouble, eh?" the man asked. Not threatening, but more like he was answering the phone, and in a clear tenor, belying the behemoth the voice belonged to. Marc glanced over his shoulder at Julian, then turned to face the huge man.

"Uh, no. We came from Marquette. I'm looking for Trapper Dan."

"Well ... *I'm* Danny," he said, not connecting the dots at all. His face bore down on Marc, who noticed how the stiff beard grew to just below the sockets of the man's creased, brown eyes. Under the red flannel shirt was an enormous chest, and on each side of his size 10 head were shoulders resembling bowling balls.

"Any chance you might happen to be a *trapper,* too?"

The man looked at Marc and then his eyes opened slightly wider. He hefted the pelt in his hands. "Yeah, I am," Dan replied. "What can I do for you?"

Marc laughed, relaxing a little, but Dan still appeared clueless as to the nickname.

"Shiva, from the Nickel, she showed me a hat you made. Coonskin. Never seen one like it. I was interested in maybe buying some—if you have any more to sell, that is."

Dan opened the door a crack.

"Oh *yeah!* Shiva does call me that sometimes, now that you mention it. Come on in." He looked past Marc. "I make nothing but full skin hats. Very strict, traditional." Dan looked past him. "What about your friend? He want to come in out of the cold?"

Marc waved at Julian to join him, but he was returning dismissive waves.

"He's tired and a little buzzed. Said he'll listen to the radio."

Dan stared at Julian and seemed lost for a moment, staring deeper into the car, focusing on something. Marc examined him. He could see red hair growing on the bridge of Dan's nose.

Marc felt his feet slide under him on the slippery porch, and he grabbed the railing. It snapped Dan out of his trance. He shrugged and let the screen door shut, lumbering down a short hallway. He spoke without turning back. "Coming in or what, friend?"

Marc's head throbbed. He looked once at Julian and walked through the door.

The heat from a wood stove radiated and the aroma of burning maple was heavenly, but inside Marc felt as cold as if he were still on the porch. He inhaled and looked down at the dirty linoleum floor. The crackling fire's smell dissipated, overwhelmed by the odors of boiling meat mixing with those of brine and alcohol. The scent of wet fur was pervasive. He looked at the tent of red flannel across Dan's broad back. The sound of boiling water grew louder as they entered the kitchen. A white porcelain gas stove, its four burners occupied with dented pots, took up residence against one wall. A crust formed on the edge of the pots as grey foam gurgled over, running down the sides. The foam hissed as it hit the coils of the burners and the hot porcelain stovetop. The partially fleshed-out skull of a six-point buck poked from the bubbling surface of the largest pot. Marc detected the musk of urine and other gamey scents as he studied the fragile skulls, the muscle, bone, and fats stripped clean from the skin of their owners. Small and white, they bobbed like something found in the cauldron of a shaman's brew.

Dan placed the coyote pelt on a countertop and checked the pots, ladling brownish scum off the top of the water from each and pouring it into a fluffy pile on the floor. There was a hiss as some water occasionally splashed onto the burners. The trapper was so big, the place looked like a cheap Mystery Spot attraction, built small to accentuate the height of its visitors.

"Nice buck. Used a muzzleloader," Dan said. "Coons in this one. Others are a mix of fox, skunk, mink. Skunk ain't as bad as people think, dontcha know?"

The aged kitchen wallpaper was smoke damaged, a golden base covered by a design of squirrels gathering acorns on a red gingham field. Random shapes of picture frames and plaques in a brighter version of the pattern were visible, as if the items that had been there forever were recently removed.

Around the room, drying animal pelts were pinned to the soffits, stretched tight, tacked to the wall through their skinned-out little limbs. Luxurious coats of ermine, fisher, and fox mingled with skunk, coyote, beaver, and raccoon. Dozens of them were strewn around the kitchen like a border on the den of some furrier from a hundred years ago or the cave wall of a primordial hunter-gatherer. The eyeholes in the pelts seemed to stare vacantly down at Marc.

"Fuckin' *ayyyyy* … " he said upon seeing Dan's inventory. The trapper moved bloody knives and heavy-duty scissors to the side, the blades caked with tendons and bone shards. He poured coffee into a stained white plastic Shopko mug.

"It's a little rank," Dan said, offering the pot. In his hands it looked like a play teakettle. Marc saw the utensils of his trade, watery rivulets of blood left in their wake.

"You know what, I think I'm good. But thanks."

At the end of the sink and to the left of the stove was a cellar door made of rough planks painted mint green. It was secured with a brass deadbolt and Marc wondered why, then the thought disappeared, as he got lost in the richness of other pelts stacked in piles on the sink countertop. His body still could not seem to warm up.

"What kind of hat are you looking for?" Dan asked. "You seem like a fox."

"I thought raccoon, but now that I'm here, hell, I'm thinking coyote. Or maybe a skunk. Skunk'd go over big time in Detroit. How much are they?"

Dan rubbed the hair under his lower lip and Marc saw his teeth for the first time. He had incisors that grew crooked out of the top gum, giving his mouth a slight canine look. The two teeth stuck out a little more forward than the rest.

"Coon's one-fifty, coyote's two-hundred, skunk's the same. Goes up from there … " Marc was waving his arms dismissively. "Something wrong, eh?" Dan asked.

"Well, yeah. Bit pricier than what Shiva quoted me."

Dan's face reddened. "Shiva and me have a *special arrangement*. Special price 'count of special *circumstances*, eh?"

Marc was about to say something, and then a light went on and he got it.

"OK, well, how about if I bought a bunch? Like a bulk rate?"

"How many is a *bulk?*"

Marc tried to keep his face screwed on straight.

"Let's say I were to buy, I don't know, *twenty?* Maybe ten of the coon and five each of the skunk and coyote. What kind of price break could you give me?"

Dan stroked the pelts. He walked to the stove and ladled off another heap of foam. He used the ladle to lift the skulls halfway from the boiling water, inspecting the eyeholes for remnants of flesh and tendons.

Marc looked into the black eye sockets waiting for Dan's reply.

"I like the way they get when all the meat's gone from 'em," Dan said, staring at the skulls. "What are you planning on doin' with them? Sell 'em at some Dee-troit flea market I suppose, eh?" he asked.

"Well, yeah. I could probably get a decent mark-up on them downstate."

"Make yourself a bunch of *money*, huh? Can't believe any Troll would be caught dead wearing such outdoorsy stuff."

Marc looked at Dan, his face plied into confusion. "Troll?"

"Downstaters. People that live *below* the bridge. You know, *Trolls*?"

"Yeah, I get it."

Dan stared down at him. One of his eyebrows went askance.

"Guy come up here last year. Met him at a flea market in Newberry. He liked my caps, too—big talker from Flint. Said he thought he'd be able to make us both rich. Made a deal with him on a handshake—left with thirty hats. Never seen him again. Troll."

Dan made a face and lowered the flames on the burners. Marc noticed that he didn't have to bend over too far to do so, which struck him as odd given his height. Then he saw the cinder blocks that the stove rested on.

Before he could assuage Dan's fears of his intent, a feral scratching noise came from behind the mint green door. Marc reacted to it, but the big trapper calmly stirred froth off the smaller pot and put the ladle down, the water popping and hissing on the stovetop.

Dan sighed and walked the couple of steps to the door and fingered the deadbolt. He slid back the bar on the lock and put his hand on the door pull. He blocked the door with his girth, partially opening it, creating a rush of colder air.

"I have to go do something *right now*. You stay here. Close this door and lock it behind me, you hear?"

Marc's skin went goose-pimply.

"Why—what's behind there?"

"My dog." Dan replied. "I need to deal with him. He has some real issues."

Marc looked at the bloody knives on the counter.

"OK, I guess. How long will you be?"

Dan stuck his head through the door as he was closing it, his hair scraping the header.

"Long as it takes. I'll knock when I'm done. Stay inside," Dan said, shutting the door. "Go on, slide the deadbolt." His voice sounded muffled behind the mint-green door.

Marc imagined what kind of dog *clawed* like that. It sounded big. He slid the deadbolt shut and stepped away, staring at the boiling skulls.

★　★　★

Julian wished Marc would just shit or get off the pot. He could've been getting his nut off with the blonde from the Nickel, *snow cow* that she was, instead of watching his friend try to take this Yooper for a ride.

The tiny carving—a crude likeness of a wolf—hung from the single leather licorice whip around his neck. Shiva had given it to him before he and Marc left the Nickel. It was deep red, slightly translucent. She told him it would protect him. It was a *fetish*—that's what Shiva called it—carved from the fossilized bone of a long-dead wolf. Native American artisans carved the bone chips—they were plentiful throughout the Upper Peninsula—and polished the figures to a high luster. A fetish supposedly contained the spirits of the animals they were derived from. Julian fingered the pendant.

His fear of dogs was borne from an attack that occurred when he was in the seventh grade at St. Jude's Elementary School in Copper Corner. That winter had been exceptionally frigid, and the ground was slick—two feet of snow that had fallen over the past week. Parents bundled their children in parkas and snowpants. Julian was walking the Marinelli twins home from school. The twin girls, two years younger than him, lived down his block.

A vicious German shepherd was roaming the area. The dog had gotten loose from the yard of its careless owner, a contractor who'd been ticketed before for the unlicensed canine, an animal he abused and left unfed. The principal of St. Jude's had made an announcement that the children should be self-aware, sending a note home with the students when sightings of the shepherd were reported near the school.

Wayne County Animal Control had been looking for the dog for a week. It had killed two cats, a poodle, and mauled the leg of a little boy. Julian told Mrs. Marinelli not to worry; he would walk the girls home until the rogue animal was captured. She was his first real crush, and perhaps his pre-teen lust had fed his bravado in offering to protect them.

"You're a brave young man, Julian Protetto," she had said in her stilted English. And then Mrs. Marinelli brushed aside her thick, raven hair and kissed him on his hairless cheek. He could smell the scent of her, the whole time feeling her breasts press against his beating heart. *"Thank you for watching over my angels, Julian."*

Walking home one day, Julian's head patrolled like a periscope, scanning the front yards as the twins shuffled five steps ahead of him. Turning the corner at the cross streets of Lappin and Rex, the dog seemed to appear from thin air. He literally hadn't time to catch his breath when Laura Marinelli shrieked, in turn setting off her sister, Anna. Julian froze as the two screaming sisters turned and ran toward him, triggering the dog's predatory instinct. The shepherd loped past Julian, and before he could react, grabbed the lagging Anna by her upper thigh. She cried out and her body vibrated with fear. Laura came to her sister's aid, punching the dog in the snout, but the animal only shook Anna's leg harder. Julian sensed that the fabric of Anna's snow-pants would soon give way and her flesh would be ripped from the bone. He dropped his books and grabbed a statue from the nearest Virgin Mary shrine. He lunged at the dog and swiped it across the skull with the plaster statue, causing it to release Anna. Laura dragged her sister away.

The twins clutched each other, huddled behind Julian. The shepherd came at him, swaying its head, snapping its jaws. White froth spilled from its gums. Blood appeared on the short fur of its forehead, turning the tips burgundy and soaking into the nap. Julian could smell the dog's breath, and steam escaped with each low growl and bark. He flailed at it with the statue before he realized he'd smashed the dog's skull twice more.

He had saved the two girls from being mauled, but was left a shaking, terrified hero. A neighbor called the police. When one of the animal control officers tried to calm him down—as the other officer body-bagged the dead shepherd—Julian caught the man staring at his waist. The officer quickly looked away, but Julian picked up on something barely concealed in the older man's expression. He looked down at his tan corduroys and saw a yellow stain soaking his crotch. He felt the coolness of the air as it hit the warmth of his own urine, the pungent odor entering his nostrils. The officer mouthed something to his partner, and he stopped bagging the dog to see Julian's wet crotch give off steam. From that day forward, whenever Julian saw *any* dog, he heard the men's stifled giggles.

Presently, the fetish felt cool in his fingers. He removed it from his neck for a closer look. Julian held it up to the rearview mirror, trying to study the details. It must have been carved with something like dental tools, he thought. It had the stylized flavor of an Inuit sculpture, and yet the amulet's lupine features were clearly recognizable. A light went on at the back of the house, cutting into the dark farmland separating the woods behind it. Straight ahead of him, on the dark side of the house, he saw a tornado shelter door open from the ground. Something leapt out of the light emanating from below. Four-legged with a loping gait, it disappeared into the dark, a blur that again brought the urge to urinate into Julian's groin. His heartbeat quickened, and he felt as though he were breathing inside a paper bag. He returned the fetish around his neck and banged the car door locks down. His eyes went to the porch. He looked at Marc. It took every ounce of courage to roll down his window.

"Hurry! What're you doing?" His voice didn't sound like his own in the night, and he quickly rolled the window back up. And then it was fogged over, and that's when he heard his own screams drown out Jim Morrison's voice.

Trapper Dan hadn't been gone two minutes when Marc got a bad case of the skeeves. He was ready to run out the front door when he heard a knock. His heart raced as he imagined being pulled through the door and getting corn-holed by the carrot-topped ogre.

"Dan?" Marc called out. "Is that you?"

"*What?* Yeah, it's me. C'mon open up." It *sounded* like Dan.

Marc slid open the deadbolt and stepped away.

The door opened and the cold air intensified his already chilled body. Dan ducked his head, closing the mint green door behind him. The sound of the boiling water was deafening, made more disturbing by the hissing from the spitting foam. Dan slid the bolt back. His face was pale, and his long hair looked different—wetter and pushed straight back in a kind of mane. He smelled like damp earth.

"Sorry—thought I finally had it figured out. Well, you make up your mind?"

Marc was eager to do business and get out. A dozen freshly prepared drying skulls—they looked like ivory carvings—were laid out on the dining room table, including the six-point buck that had been boiling on the stove. Marc hadn't remembered seeing any skulls there when he walked in. He looked at the stove and the pots were gone, washed and stacked neatly at the sink. Dan caressed the skull of a beaver, looking like a fragile egg in his long, pink fingers. Bundled next to the skulls lay twenty caps. The fur caps were separated by species; ten raccoon, five coyote, and five of the skunk.

"What do you suppose these would pull in Marquette?" Marc asked him.

Dan squinted with one eye and his lips appeared to do the math silently. He seemed pained as his thick fingers did the carry-overs.

"Couple thousand, eh, I guess, give or take," Dan said. "Course, that's if you can find anyone's got money to spend. Most people up here spend it on beer or food."

Marc knew he could move the fur. All he had to do was show up at a dance club sporting one, and the brothers would beg to be hooked up with an animal cap like the white boy. Probably sell the whole lot in one night. None of that seemed important now.

"When you wear a fur, you honor the life of the animal that died," Dan said.

"I can see that." Marc felt claustrophobic and colder.

Dan continued. "Still, there are times when I feel brutish. A trap doesn't set right and I have to put an animal out of its misery. Last week I had to destroy a beaver I found trying to suck air from below the surface—foot was stuck. Poor thing gnawed off two of its own legs. Freed itself but it was still attached by the ligaments." Dan picked up a limbless beaver pelt and stroked the fur. "This was him."

Marc swallowed as he listened. His head still ached, and he heard a dog growling. The pungency of wet fur mixed with the other smells of the cabin. He could taste it.

"I removed his heart and buried it in the stream bank. It was difficult. Ground was still frozen." Dan looked down at him, the beaver skull in one hand, the pelt in the other.

"I have to leave. I'll give you two grand for the lot. Thousand now, another grand after I sell the rest. Send you a money order for the balance. What do you think?"

Dan was staring at Marc, but the trapper's face appeared cloudy, as if separated by mesh. Marc looked away, directly into the eyeholes of the beaver skull.

"Let me think about it," Dan said.

"OK. I'm leaving tomorrow morning, though. Will you be around?"

"All day." Dan's expression was flat now.

"If you don't like the deal, I'll at least come back and buy one for myself."

"Sure you will," Dan said. "Just like the big talker from Flint."

Marc held out his hand. They shook and his nerves tingled in the trapper's grip.

"Tomorrow," Marc said. Then the porch light went out.

Stepping off the porch, Marc waved to Julian. He didn't respond. *Stupid shit fell asleep*, Marc thought. The cold air tweaked his headache to a higher intensity. Near the car, he heard the fan belt whirring, and the snow was silver, electrified by the light cast from the moon. He saw a circle of tracks start at the driver's door. He followed them around the passenger side, the tracks plainly visible in the sparkly snow. Julian was as Marc had left him when he'd entered Dan's house, sitting behind the steering wheel. He opened the passenger door and sat down. The odor of wet fur stunk up the car.

"That smell ... hey, Julesy, wake up. No deal. Let's get back to Chris' place."

Julian didn't respond. He was frozen, staring straight ahead, still holding the fetish. The cassette had stopped, white scratchy noise prattled over the speakers, filling the car with crackling fissures of a migraine-producing sound.

"What the hell's wrong with you—" Marc asked.

He felt an excruciating jolt in his brain and there was a constricting feeling, like a noose was tightening around his skull. Then everything went white.

The radio was in and out, and George Jones' mournful voice stirred him. He was aware of the scent of a wet animal again. The car was bouncing down the rutted two-track. Marc finally opened his eyes, feeling ready to vomit. "Fuckin' slow down, Andretti," he said.

"Thank God," Julian said. Marc turned and saw him, his face whiter than Sparky Anderson's hair. "Fuck ... are you all right?"

"Yeah." Marc squinted. "Bit of a dinger going. Dude, I had the weirdest *dream*. When I tried to talk to you in the car, you were just *staring*, and you wouldn't answer me, wouldn't move! Like a statue. You think the tap lines were moldy at the Nickel?"

"Are you serious?" Julian asked.

"Hell yeah. It happens. Mold gets in there and the beer ferments. Makes you hallucinate. You even said it tasted like piss. I drank this dark beer once at a party—"

"Not that! You don't remember? Maybe we should get you to Marquette General. Man, you fell on his porch. I had to go and pick you up, but it wasn't easy. That little shit. He kept trying to get me to bring you inside the cabin … "

Marc rubbed his head and squinted. "That's funny," he laughed.

"What is?" Julian asked.

"Little shit. One of those oxymorons … *Slightly* pregnant. *Sober* Irishman. No, that's not right—fuck, you know what I mean."

Julian looked at him. "Marc, the guy was a *runt*."

Marc felt the back of his head, surprised to find a lump there. It pained him to the touch. They were traveling on the road that led back to U.S. 41 when Julian finally took a breath and slowed down a little.

"Julesy, what the *hell* are you talking about?"

"OK, but let me finish. God, it all happened so fast. You had been standing there after Trapper Dan shut the door. I thought I saw something leap from the storm shelter on the side of his house. It looked like a big dog—"

" … Said he kept a dog. Behind the green door … like a minty-green," Marc spoke in a lazy drawl, staring straight ahead.

"Now what the hell are *you* talking about?" Julian asked.

Marc turned to him. "Just finish your story."

"This is going to sound like bullshit, but I'm telling you, that *barking-chasing* dog, its face was on *my window* after the trapper shut the screen door on you, came out of nowhere. I never took my eye off that storm shelter door—it must've circled the car. It looked bigger up close, huge. And I freaked! Before I knew it, I took this thing Shiva gave me … " He held up the fetish and the features of the wolf were readable like rosary beads in his fingertips. "I jammed it right against the window—its breath steamed it all up—and when I did it, the thing howled and ran right at you, toward the porch."

"*What?* You're full of shit!"

"No. That's when you slipped and hit your head. I almost pissed myself because that thing was coming for you. I ran to the porch, but I was too late. The weird thing is, the dog stopped dead. Just did a Walter Payton and turned on a dime. Then it bounded around the side of the house, yelping like it was in pain. And then that trapper, he opened the door and tried to convince me to bring you inside the cabin—"

"Get the hell out of here. That's nuts. I was *talking* to Dan, and I remember leaving the kitchen and getting in the car. I *walked out* and got in the car on my own, and that's—"

"What do you mean *leaving the kitchen?*" Julian grabbed his arm.

Marc stared at his friend. "Dan had pelts pinned up. I looked at all his skins, and then after he went into the basement and came back, we talked about me buying some different caps. All kinds; fox, skunk, raccoons. I *left* the kitchen. I told him we'd come back tomorrow before we went home."

Julian stared at him open-mouthed. *"Now what?"* Marc implored.

"You're *really* scaring me, Marc. You *never* went in the house. You *wouldn't*. It looked like the guy invited you, but you wouldn't budge."

Marc blinked once. He sniffed and grabbed Julian's forearm.

"OK, you're full of shit. Turn around right now—turn the *fucking car* around and we'll go back and settle this." Marc's eyes were wild. "Turn the fuck around!"

Julian looked away from the road for a moment and stopped. The Bonneville idled in the middle of the two-lane highway. He turned off the radio and it was quiet.

"You never went into the cabin. You talked to Dan through the *screen door*. You stood on the porch. Kept looking back at me. But you *never* were inside."

"But, I *was!* He went through the green door. I stood in his kitchen ... the skulls, the pelts—it's not possible. And he was *huge* ... "

Julian shook his head. "You slipped on the porch and hit your head. I swear, Marc." He never blinked. "And that guy wasn't a hair over five-seven."

"That's not possible. We shook hands." Marc stared at his own large hand. "I'm supposed to go back—" he gripped his neck and stopped. "What the? Are you screwing with my head—how did you do it?" Marc's fingers trembled on the leather licorice whip, smooth and supple. He showed it to Julian. "How did this get on me?"

Julian turned, and what he saw made his blood sizzle and his mind's nose smell urine. His hand went to his sweating throat, just to make sure Marc hadn't tricked him. But he hadn't. Julian touched the reddish bone carving, a twin of the very one Marc was holding, a perfect match to the one Shiva had somehow slipped around Marc's neck.

"Trapper Dan was *small?*" Marc asked, his eyes fitful.

Julian didn't answer. He hit the gas and the car lurched forward, the road feeling narrower as they sped off under the still enormous moon.

"What do we tell Chris? He's expecting us tonight," Marc said.

"Let me think about that," Julian said, studying himself in the rearview mirror. "Let's just keep driving for now."

The two didn't say anything for hours. They drove silently past Marquette, forging onward through all the little Upper Peninsula towns that led to the Mackinac Bridge, the whole time watching the headlights throw strange markings against the snow-covered highway, shape-shifting beams playing at their eyes, pointing them south toward Detroit.

Bow Season

Aldo Vendetti had no children of his own. He was, however, the oldest uncle to thirteen nieces and ten nephews from two brothers and three sisters, all of whom he loved with equal measure. Inevitably, though, when a man is blessed with that much fortune, favorites tend to pull away from the rest of the pack. And in Aldo's case, at least as far as the nephews were concerned, it was clear that Nino, Don, and Mauro were the ones he revered most. The three were first cousins. Nino, Don's younger brother, was twenty-six. Mauro was an only child. He and Don were both twenty-eight that October. And as they had since they were old enough to know better, the three boys showed their uncle nothing but the utmost respect. His nephews were good kids, certainly not perfect, but in Aldo Vendetti's eyes, their flaws were non-existent. He would stand in front of a train for them.

It happened the opening weekend of bow season in 1998. Mauro's father couldn't make it up north for the fall hunt. Don and Nino's father had passed away six years earlier, and since his death Aldo had become something of a surrogate father to them, a position he accepted with sad pride, albeit great commitment. Mauro and Don were excited to squeeze in a weekend of deer hunting at Aldo's cabin on Island Lake, while Nino planned on spending his time fishing.

★ ★ ★

Off the eastern tip of northern lower Michigan—the rougher side of the mitten—nestled a few miles inland from Lake Huron was Island Lake. The lake was 200 acres of clear water, loaded with bass, pike, walleye, and jumbo perch. Aldo's cabin was the only material thing he loved, and he took care of it with the seriousness of a mother bear protecting a lone cub. He'd owned it for twenty years, using it in the fall and summer, but after Valentina's death in '95, the cabin became his year-round residence, causing him to forego the winter-time condominium growing cobwebs in Naples. Valentina never cared for the cabin, preferring the hot climes of Florida, and there was still too much of her in that condo for him to go back just yet, maybe ever.

At present, Aldo stood on the deck, surveying the lake. He rotated his thick left arm, wincing at the stiffness. Every year he received a wood-harvesting permit from the DNR, allowing him access to the nearby Huron National Forest where he could legally cut firewood from blown-down and still-standing dead hardwoods. He prided himself that, as a seventy-three-year-old man, he could enter the forest alone with his chainsaw and by day's end return with nearly a full cord. It kept his body strong and his mind from dwelling too long. Valentina's death was an agonizingly slow ordeal. At times, he still heard her weak voice, begging him to hasten the end of her suffering:

"My Aldo, the pillow. I love you husband ... but the pain is too great—I beg you—the pillow, Aldo!"

The few times he had come close to honoring her requests, he could only stop short and shake his head. Because each time he would touch the edge of her pillow, he couldn't get past the enchanting blue-grey eyes, still possessing the spirit of the eighteen-year-old stunner he'd met one summer night in a Greektown bar, in 1949. It was she who saved him from the memories of war in Italy. And so in the hospital bed, with tubes feeding her like so many artificial veins, Valentina would nod back at him—her face swollen by steroids—with a silent acceptance of knowing that after she was gone, he would have to go on living, and she indeed understood; this was one sin Aldo wouldn't be able to add onto the many he'd already notched in his long life.

He'd enlisted as a nineteen-year-old, first-generation American, and as bad luck would have it, was sent to the Boot to fight against his father's country-men. During his service as a ground soldier over there, he killed seventeen Italians—in Persamo, eight came in hand-to-hand combat. There he delivered death with the intimacy of a bayonet or combat knife. He won two Purple Hearts and a Bronze Star, a fact revealed only after one of his war buddies spilled the beans about his heroism to his family. On the rare occasions Aldo would talk about his war experiences, it was always the same:

"It's different killing a man with your bare hands," Aldo would say. "You use a gun, you don't get to see his eyes roll wild and hear him scream, begging you for his life. When it's him and you and you hear the last breath leave his body, and you know you were the one who took it? Killing someone's husband, their brother. Maybe their son—that's just ... *different*. I don't fear death. I seen it. It don't scare me. I just hope Our Lord gives me a chance to tell Him that I did what I had to do, so I could live another day. Not getting the chance to explain my side of things to Him *face-to-face*, that's what I fear."

And everyone believed him when he said it.

Mauro and Don drove the dirt road leading to Aldo's house with the excitement of another bow season fresh in front of them. Mauro, a chiropractor, had bought into a thriving practice. He was the darker of the two, and though his hair was thinning, his arms and chest were covered with thick black hair. Don always teased him, telling Mauro he was "three DNA strands away from being a Yeti."

Don was fair, with smooth skin and blue eyes, looking more Danish than Sicilian. He was partnered in with an orthodontist in a suburb of Detroit. Their fathers were younger brothers to Aldo, and the two were as close as first cousins could be—*brothers,* for all intents and purposes. Both were deadly with a bow, though Mauro had the edge because of his acute vision. His eyesight was better than 15-20 and he could see detail at great distances.

As Mauro eased his black Jeep Cherokee into the driveway, they were greeted by the image of their Uncle Aldo standing on his porch, a steaming mug of coffee in his thick hands. He wore a wool cap and orange down vest, his chainsaw at his feet in a battered, red plastic case. He was solid as stone and had a square face with deep-set eyes that while warm, possessed a kind of hawkish quality. Wavy silver hair, combed straight back, gave him a dignified persona, but he still looked like he could kick almost anyone's ass. His chest was unnaturally large for a man of his years, and even this late in life, there were athletes who would have envied his biceps. He swiveled his thick neck like a falcon and proudly gazed at the two boys.

They could barely get the doors open fast enough to greet him. Mauro hurried over and hugged him, following up with a traditional kiss on the cheek. Don did the same, his embrace a little tighter, longer. Mauro followed up with another hug.

"There's my boys," Aldo said, his familiar clipped voice comforting to them.

"More firewood, huh, Unc?" Mauro said, pointing at the saw case. There were two woodpiles of split oak to the side of the cabin that could heat three houses for four winters without putting a dent in either. "Save some wood for the animals to hide in."

"The hell with them animals. Love getting that oak. I've got my stove burning hotter than a hooker's ass on Eight Mile Road. Like a sauna in there." He looked at the empty Cherokee. "Thought Nino was coming ... "

"Had paperwork at the hospital to clean up. Be here later on," Don said.

"All my nephews did so well; doctors, lawyers, tradesmen—all professionals. If them prick cops from the thirteenth could only see my brothers and me now, the way they harassed us, them bastards. Especially that spud-eating motorcycle cop, O'Brien. That Mick bastard, he hated us Vendetti boys."

Mauro and Don eyed each other. Don nodded at Mauro as if he'd just lost a bet.

"So, Unc, we all set with your farmer pal?" Mauro asked.

Aldo's face became serious. He looked around as if he were about to let them in on a tip about a hot horse.

"You're in, Killer. Now you boys listen. My friend, Ed Troyer—I told you about Farmer Troyer, remember? Man's a prince. Salt of the Earth. You won't believe the woods he has—crawling with deer! If it weren't for his Esther this woulda been a regular thing. He finally convinced her though, because the damn deer are eating his crops to shit!"

"We'll do our share to help him with that," Mauro laughed.

"You just mind yourself! People up here, takes years to get them to trust you. Mennonite, he is. Little easier to get to know than the Amish, but not too much. Mennonites are honest, but they're skeptical of us downstaters. He's been good to me, though, so you boys are all set. Got the *whole place* to yourselves. Ed's a good man. Get some rest. He's expecting you there tomorrow at five."

"He'll be up that early?" Mauro asked.

"Hell yeah, he'll be up. He's a fucking farmer, ain't he?" Aldo chuckled a little at his nephew. "I know you'll be respectful now, you wouldn't embarrass your uncle, right? He gives me fresh green beans—and the corn? *Maddon'!* I bring him split oak and if I'm lucky enough to catch me a mess of perch, I pop over with some fillets. Esther cooks us up a nice fish dinner." Mauro tried to interject but Aldo wasn't done. "Don't screw off out there now, you hear? Good man, Ed Troyer, and I gave him my word you two were good kids."

They waited out his endless diatribe. He had always repeated himself, and though it had gotten worse recently, they put up with it because it was what it was.

"C'mon, Unc, *Maddon'* yourself, we promise," Mauro said.

"OK then. Be careful and have fun." Aldo held a hard look on his nephews, then tipped his cap with a little smile. "Look out oaks!"

They watched him walk stiffly to his brown Chevy truck. He threw the chainsaw into the bed as easily as one tosses a Frisbee. He honked twice as he drove the dirt road toward the waiting forest.

"Can you believe the shape he's in? Trade bodies with him in a heartbeat," Mauro said. "I'm ready to slay. We gonna nail a couple this weekend or what?"

"Depends on how this farmer's place sets up. We'll have to see the property," Don said. "Unc exaggerates, but Nino said he was on the phone with him, told him this Troyer built tree stands for us."

"No shit? He really *is* the salt of the Earth," Mauro said. "So, when the hell's *Doctor* Nino getting up?"

"Should be here soon. Pediatrics is stressing his ass out. You know how he is with kids. He's anxious to get on the water. Maybe we'll have walleye for dinner tomorrow. Right now I'm so hungry I'm farting dust. Let's grub."

They unpacked the Cherokee and carried their stuff into the cabin.

Aldo's brown truck was parked on the shoulder of M–72. He was two miles into his allotted section of the Huron National Forest, using old fire trails and abandoned deer runs to get there. Yellow light filtered through rows of tall trees, remnants of diligent work performed by the Civilian Conservation Corps sixty years earlier. But that was red pine, and he had no use for soft woods. Aldo wanted oak, so he headed in further, away from the main road, deep in. It worried his family that he always went so far off the highway, but it was what he had to do.

He worked the saw into a felled white oak four feet in diameter. Shredded wood chips flew past his face and he let the sour smell burn his nostrils, inhaling the scent into his lungs. The oak was stuck under the trunk of an aspen that had been blown across it by a vertical wind shear that came through that past summer. The chain bore down deep as he tried to free it from the aspen. The blade chugged and gnawed. He braced himself for leverage against the half-circle of earth that still held onto the shallow roots of the dead aspen. The oak started pinching the chain and the engine labored.

"Come on you dirty little *puttana*," he cursed at the saw.

Finally the blade went through, but the chain jumped off the track as the collapsing pieces of oak clamped down on it.

"*Minchia!*" Aldo said, killing the engine. "You *puttana!*"

"Can't call her a whore and expect her to love you," said a voice from behind.

Aldo turned and gave a little laugh at the sight of Nino.

"You want I should talk nice to her, huh?" Aldo said, a grin blossoming.

At six feet two, Nino Vendetti was the tallest of Aldo's nephews, and his love of family matched his size. Everyone adored Nino, especially the younger cousins. He was a big, lovable kid whose favorite thing to do was play Santa each year at the family's huge Christmas party. Nino loped up to Aldo and picked him up in a tight bear hug. He delivered a loud smack on both cheeks of his uncle's square jaw.

"Nino, *my man!* How you doing? You gonna catch some fish for us tonight or what? I mean, you been stone blanked the last two times you been up here," Aldo joked.

"I sure hope so, Uncle. Ain't been able to catch a cold lately. Mauro and Don get up OK?" he asked. Aldo took in the whole sight of Nino and smiled.

"Oh yeah, they're primed. I got 'em set up at Ed Troyer's place. He's a good man, good friend of mine. I ever tell you about Ed? Man's salt of the Earth—"

"Unc, last week—remember? We talked for half an hour on the phone."

Aldo nodded, finally recollecting their conversation. "Goddamn CRS disease is kicking in on me," he mumbled. Nino squinted at the mention of the word *disease*. Aldo waved him off.

"Don't worry, *Doctor*. CRS: *Can't Remember Shit.* Little joke old people tell. Your Aunt Val always laughed at that one," Aldo smiled.

"Oh, OK. Had me worried. Let me help you with that chain."

They put the chain back on its track using the open tailgate on Aldo's truck as a workbench. Nino's Taurus was parked behind. Aldo poured bar chain oil into the saw's housing. Nino held the saw steady and watched his uncle's trembling hand spill the amber oil onto the handle. He said nothing of it, trying instead to move the porthole under the shifting stream to catch it cleanly. Aldo cursed, upset that his body was betraying him. He adjusted the tension of the chain with an Allen wrench before hastily wiping the housing down with a rag.

"OK, I'm good here, thanks. Now go catch some fish, nephew."

"Don't suppose you'll let me help you load that wood first?"

"Ha! Don't you worry about me; I'll outwork any of you boys and you know it. I'll take care of that wood and I still got more to cut. You just take care of the walleye. There's a lot of perch hitting, too. Catch a bunch, because I'd like to take some to Ed Troyer. There's three dozen wax worms in the fridge next to some leftover eggplant."

"Perch, carp; I'd be glad to catch *anything.*"

"Don't you kids eat all that *melanzana* either!"

"Yeah, yeah. Thanks for getting the wax worms. Be careful out here, OK?"

Aldo shrugged off his concern. As his uncle trudged back into the forest, Nino watched him walk, and before long the old man disappeared. Nino got into his car and headed toward Island Lake.

It had been two months since he'd had a chance to do any fishing, and when he saw the lake reflecting the orange treetops, the anticipation to get out on the water made him anxious. But in the quiet, he stood and stared across the lake, taking in the sight.

Nino opened the cabin door and watched them, not saying a word as his brother and Mauro feasted on heavy sandwiches made of thick-crusted Italian bread. The aroma of burning oak greeted him, and seeing them made him smile. Interning at

Henry Ford Hospital in Detroit was awful. The rounds on the pediatric unit had challenged Nino's resolve, eroding his cheerful disposition. Most of his patients were either being treated for burns or were the innocent victims of car accidents and drive-by shootings.

"Is this the homo cafe? I got a delivery of ring bologna I can slice in half," Nino announced.

"Don't you mean cocktail wienie?" Mauro said, without looking up.

Then they dropped their food, rising in mid-bite to greet him.

Don and Nino shared a long hug. Mauro watched covetously as the two brothers embraced before he gave Nino a hug and a grazing peck on the cheek. He returned to his meal while the two siblings talked with each other, getting reacquainted.

"How're the rounds going?" Mauro asked.

Nino's face softened, only briefly losing his smile. "Good. It's kinda ... you know. It's OK. Hey, I'm so hungry, shit sandwiches are sounding good."

"Sit your big Dago ass down and eat. The olives are awesome," Don said.

Nino plopped down and cut two large pieces of Italian bread. He heaped on five pieces of hard salami, two *mortadella* and three slices of the *prosciutto* that he loved so much. He added two slices of provolone and a thick onion, piling onto the burgeoning sandwich. There were roasted peppers in oil, rich olive medleys loaded with jumbo greens, and wine-soaked *calamata*. Crushed cloves of garlic peeked out from the holes of some of the jumbo greens, the scent of which made his mouth water.

He took a ladle of oil from the olive medley and spread it across the meat, letting it ooze over the hard crust of the bottom piece. Don watched with amusement as Nino stacked roasted red peppers onto the heap of lunch meat.

"Mauro, watch your fingers; he might confuse them with some garnish," Don said. "Eats like he's going to the chair." The remark prompted a comedic glance from Nino.

"I don't think you got enough olive oil on that," Mauro said to him.

They laughed watching him continue his creation. He took a big bite of the sandwich, oil dripping down each corner of his mouth like blood on Nosferatu. He made a face as if deciding whether it was to his liking, then he looked studiously at Mauro.

"Know what, cuz? I think you're right," he said, dipping the whole thing into the olives before taking another horse bite, his fingers now coated with oil.

Mauro and Don threw their heads back, laughing, the whole time Nino chewed the sandwich, oil dribbling from his mouth. "Now it's not so dry," he said with perfect comic timing, finally letting himself laugh with them.

Mauro wiped his eyes and broke off a chunk of stinky *fontinella*. "Look, you're gonna get us some walleye tonight, right? Tired of hearing your five-that-got-away bullshit stories," Mauro said.

"I'll try. Man, these weekends go by so fast and my stomach always hurts from laughing. Let me ask *you*; you two going to get me some venison?" Nino asked.

"If they're out there we'll stick 'em," Mauro said. "Supposed to be a lot of big-ass bucks. I may nab two or three. Screw that farmer's PETA-loving wife. Lombardi the taxidermist has to eat, too. Am I right? Should be fun, huh Donny?"

Don studied Mauro's face and recognized the look his cousin got when they were getting ready to go head-to-head on a quest for any kind of game, be it fur, fins, or fowl.

"Definitely. Let's just take it easy, though," Don said.

Nino looked at his brother. "Farmer's supposed to be a pretty good guy, huh?"

"You're kidding, right? That's the understatement of the fuckin' century. You obviously haven't heard the 'salt-of-the-Earth' speech yet?" Mauro asked Nino rhetorically.

"Guy's a prince, I give him oak, he gives me corn ... " Nino mimicked Aldo spot on, nodding with a chuckle. Then he thought of Aldo forgetting their phone conversation and he grew somber. Not wanting to kill the mood, he decided against bringing up his suspicions. They returned to their meal, eating the way young guys with flat bellies tend to, as if immune to the effects of carbohydrates and caloric intake.

Mauro watched the brothers eat. It had been five years since he had killed a big buck with a bow, and he never felt more hopeful for a successful hunt than he did now. He was stoked. The prospect of having forty acres just for the two of them was too much to ask for, but somehow his uncle had delivered.

Nino didn't hunt anymore, not since working with the small kids at the hospital. He'd seen too much death. He stood up, stretched and scratched his stomach, puffing it out to simulate a beer belly.

"I may have to bust a grumpy before I get in the boat. Starting to grow a tail ... " Nino said, disappearing into the bathroom. Making no effort to close the door, the sound of the seat clanking against the porcelain bowl echoed from the bathroom.

"At least put the fan on," Don called out.

"You ladies have a good hunt if I don't see you tonight," he yelled between mock grunting and straining noises.

Wisps of rim-lit clouds settled on the horizon. The air was perfect, and the light breeze felt wonderful. Nino trolled the five-horse Johnson with the patience of a model ship builder. Setting the choke just so to keep the motor from stalling, he circled around the west side of the small island that the lake was named after and headed for a point off its far shoreline. The island was centered within the lake, and the deepest hole was beyond the drop-off he was searching for. Tall cabbage weeds peeking just below the surface were dissipating, indicating he was near. He'd brought along the wax worms in case the walleye and bass weren't hitting. He pulled a fat night crawler from the cool, moist dirt in the bait box and threaded it onto the snelled hooks of the crawler harness. He checked his drag once more and cast to the left of the boat.

He slowed the engine down to its lowest speed. Holding his rod parallel with the water, he let out twenty yards of line. He looked into the island's interior, wondering if there really were deer on it as Aldo had told him. Nino had been coming up since he was six and the only wildlife he'd seen there was the resident osprey that perched on the tall dead pine at the island's eastern side.

Just then his rod bent in half, forming an upside-down U.

"Whoaaa, *Momma!*"

He set the hook hard and pulled straight up. Feeling the tension, he knew it was a good one. The rod bucked once, and he kept with it. His heart started to pound harder, growing quicker as he felt for the net. His frantic search came up empty. Sweat formed on the back of his neck as he saw Aldo's cabin, small across the lake.

"Oh, that's perfect. You stupid *mamaluke* ... "

In his haste to get out before nightfall, he'd left the net on the dock.

The fish went on a long run, and Nino kept the rod tip up as he'd been taught. Finally he started gaining on the fish, bringing it to the surface with steady cranks of the reel handle. Slowly, the shape of the fish became clearer, and the bronze walleye looked enormous—magnified by the water—in the fading light. Seeing the boat, it ran again, but the fish was spent.

"*Minchia*, look at you," he whispered.

Nino used body English to coax the fish next to the boat.

He pulled high and steady on the rod with his right arm and lifted the fish out of the water; he gilled it with his left hand, trying to avoid the walleye's razor-sharp back teeth. It flapped its tail when the air hit it, and its unblinking, milky eye looked as big as a pearl from a cocktail ring. As Nino hoisted it up to eye level, a cloud of perch fry flew from the walleye's mouth, hitting his cheek like a spray of tiny silver arrows. He laughed out loud, reveling in the kind of moments sportsmen are sometimes blessed with.

He threaded the point of a nylon stringer through the gill, made a loop and held the walleye in front of him. It swung, thrashing side-to-side. The scales glowed an iridescent gold. The fish's lungs were engorged with air after being lifted from such depths, and Nino always wondered what was going through a fish's nut-sized brain when it realized it had been caught. *Did it know such things? Did it feel foolish or something akin to panic or regret?* The thoughts left him and he felt silly for thinking them. He admired the fish once more and tied the stringer to an oarlock, returning it to the safety of the water. It slapped its tail and settled below the surface.

Uncle Aldo sat near the shore. He scanned the lake and squinted at the sun—a pale orange ball—starting its dip behind the tree line on the opposite shore. He chuckled upon seeing the landing net, and regarded the flavor of the Cuban cigar he smoked, a gift from a friend in Tampa who'd mailed him a box. Orange leaves on sugar maples and the yellowing leaves of oaks looked afire as sweet light bathed their full canopies, radiating with golden warmth. He caught sight of his fishing boat bobbing on the lake, studying Nino's profile as his nephew anchored. Aldo's eyes were still good for distance, and he saw the kid waving. He didn't know how many more years the good Lord had left for him on this Earth, but he took the opportunity to drink in the sight of his nephew and record the memory of it. He waved and then looked to the sky.

"Thank you for giving me this cabin, and gracing me with these nephews to share it with. I know I don't deserve this happiness. Keep my Val company until you call me home."

He heard a loud squawk and delighted in watching a pair of great blue herons coasting toward the island. The pair looked prehistoric, especially with the low-key light that silhouetted their large bodies. Their wing beats were in unison, and he knew they were mated for life. That thought gave him hope. Aldo put the cigar down and reclined farther into the old Adirondack, letting sleep pull him away from the image.

The dreams always started the same, especially since her death. He was on the shore of the Mediterranean, looking into the face of the dying Italian soldier, the dream so real he could smell the gunpowder. All of this filtered into geometric patterns, suddenly turning into the comely face of his Valentina, the beautiful young bride she was. She stood before him, his hands raising her white cotton gown to reveal her breasts, finally allowing him to see and touch them naked for the first time. They were ravenous in their lovemaking, and he felt—even in his dream state—frustration knowing the reunion was unrequited, that he had no control over when God would deem they be together again. And though his dream-self fought the best it could, he was pulled awake and Valentina's features faded away.

"Unc—wake up. It's ten o'clock."

Nino's voice gained volume, and Aldo didn't know where he was for a moment. He looked up to see Nino standing over him with an outstretched hand. His stringer had five walleye on it. It was dark out and the lamp from the porch cast an amber light on the slippery fish and Nino's large frame.

"Sweet Jesus, those are beautiful, Nino!" Aldo practically shouted.

"You like these? Look at their cousins."

Nino kicked over a five-gallon pail. More than three-dozen perch—many as big as his hand—flopped in the grass.

"You hit the mother lode!" Aldo said. "They love them wax worms. I'll have enough to send to Ed Troyer now. He loves perch, Farmer Troyer does."

"So you've said. Want to help me fillet 'em?" Nino asked.

"Hell yes, I do. *Minchia*, how you kids *still* butcher them fillets. Let Uncle Aldo show you how to do it—*again,*" he gently teased Nino.

Nino smiled, enjoying the ball busting.

"That'd be great, Unc. I'm a little rusty."

Nino gathered up the perch and walked with his stringer and the pail into the garage.

Aldo looked to the heavens, now dotted with a billion stars, and held his arms up in a quiet acknowledgment of the grace he felt bestowed upon him.

A gibbous moon illuminated hazy ground fog as they drove along M-72 West, looking for the landmark that would lead them to the two-track into Ed Troyer's farm. It was only ten miles to the Mennonite's property, but the trip was chock full of sideways roads and bendy trails. Mauro drove cautiously as Don navigated through Aldo's handwritten directions.

"So Unc says I don't have the upper lip for a mustache. 'Killer, your lip's not *flat* enough. The hair don't lie down,' he says. What the hell's that mean?" Mauro lamented, glancing at Don.

"Watch the fucking road, please," Don replied. "Unc's just busting your balls. There's porn stars don't have mustaches as good as yours."

Mauro sniffed, "Really? Hey, thanks."

Driving with caution, he squinted at the odd shapes the headlight beams created. Don nudged and pointed the way through false turns and wrong bends.

"Look for a pair of wagon wheels, and then it's right at the second fork. See, Unc drew a little fork?" Don said, pointing at the crude map.

"That's a *fork?* Shit, they all look like forks! Why couldn't we just take the highway?" Mauro said, trying to decipher and drive simultaneously. His headlights shone twenty yards ahead. Thicker fog seemed to ooze from the deepening woods, as if it were a living entity. "Remember the Angel of Death in the Ten Commandments—"

Don braced the dash. "Look out!"

Mauro locked up the brakes. The car skidded on wet oak leaves and stopped five feet from the biggest buck either of them had ever seen. Behind the deer sat a pair of overgrown wagon wheels, just as the map indicated.

"Hol*eeee* shittt ... " Mauro's voice was *sotto voce* as they stared at the buck, whose presence seemed apparitional. It couldn't have inspired more awe had it been made entirely of gold. "Look at that fucking rack! It's gotta be—"

"Eighteen points?" Don whispered. "Mauro, it's not even moving."

The deer stood there in all its majestic height, 250-plus pounds worth. It was as if it was saying to them, *"You want me? You think you can? Well come and get me, motherfuckers."* Steam puffed from its black muzzle.

Its coat was a silvery-brown, greying like an aging Indian chief. The animal turned once, raised its head and then with an effortless leap, seemed to evaporate as quickly as it had appeared.

"Was that *real?*" Don asked in utter shock.

Mauro had already crawled over the back seat into the cargo area of the Cherokee. "Let's go get him," he said, simultaneously starting to uncase his bow.

"He's gone. C'mon. Let's get into the stands. He ran into the forty we'll be hunting from. We'll have a better chance of getting a look at him in there than if we track him now. He's spooked. Besides, look," Don pointed to the rusted wagon wheels. Mauro glumly acknowledged the antiques. "It's only a half-mile from here to the guy's house," Don said. Indeed, in the distance was a modest, white farmhouse. Its kitchen lights were on, glowing squares in the dark.

Mauro peered into the stand of trees the monster had crashed through.

"Man he was *beautiful*. I've got to ... " Mauro stopped himself. He got back behind the wheel. Still shaking from the near-collision, he drove past the wagon wheels toward the farmhouse.

The sky was navy and because of the absolute purity and crispness of the fall air, revealed the faint outline of the moon's dark side. It looked as though God had cleaned the remnants of silver pigment from a paintbrush against an infinite bolt of blue fabric, the Milky Way practically lost amongst infinite stars.

Don knocked on the window of the wood door, louder than he'd wanted. He looked back sheepishly at Mauro.

"Smooth move, Ex-Lax," Mauro whispered.

Clad in full camouflage, both had their faces made up like Mayan warriors, bold green and black markings drawn on. The door opened, and Ed Troyer's lean body filled the frame.

"Good morning. Aldo's nephews, eh? Welcome," Troyer said.

His long, heart-shaped face sat underneath thick white hair, combed neatly, giving him the appearance of an accountant, spoiled only by a Lincoln-esque beard. His tan Carhartt overalls were worn pale. He had enormous hands that engulfed theirs. They entered the house. The spring in his step seemed unattainable at such an early hour.

A fat, caramel-colored tabby sat on a red and white quilt draped over a lounge chair. Mauro reached down and petted the animal's striped fur, and it purred.

"Coffee. Just brewed." When he spoke, even statements sounded like a question.

"No thanks. I'll have to piss too much if I do," Mauro said. "Sorry—I meant, uh, *urinate.*"

"Plenty of trees out there," Troyer said, "for *pissin'* and such."

The cousins looked at each other as Troyer sipped his coffee.

"Pretty cat," Mauro said, looking down at the large feline.

"Butternut rules the roost, eh," he said. He leaned against the counter and stirred cream into his coffee, staring at the cat. "If you fellas walk back three hundred yards due south, you'll cross that same road you came in on. Cut in from there. That's the forty. Put two tree seats in there. You won't miss the trees, 'count of I flagged them, eh. One's in a big scrub oak, other in a dead maple, only a hundred yards from each other. Hordes of deer in there. Rats with horns. Need to keep my bean fields intact, so I'm counting on ya. There's deer in there. Shoot ten all I care."

"We just saw an absolute—" Don started to speak before Mauro stopped him with a glare. Don felt his armpits moisten for spilling such sacred information. The farmer snickered.

"You saw him. Huge, ain't he?" Troyer asked. He took a long drink of his coffee and licked his lips. "Had a trespasser a year ago went after him. Man got nasty with me," he stopped in the act of recollection, fingering the mug. "So, I had to get nasty with him." He stared directly at Mauro, and it made him self-aware. "Anyways ... my Esther calls him the 'Grey Ghost,' 'count of his coat. She thinks he's *beautiful.* Well, kill him, too. Thing's been rutting them does and ruining my beans, my corn. All he's doing is passing on that size to his heirs. Rats with horns. That's what they are, rats with horns." The farmer drank the rest of his coffee in one gulp.

"We'll do whatever it takes," Mauro said.

"Don't get me wrong; love animals. Don't like seeing suffering. Not against hunting, eh. Just that Esther, she—"

Mauro looked at Don, and suddenly Troyer's face turned shy, and he looked away, as if he'd just admitted some great foible. He started to rinse his coffee mug.

"Have to get to my barn, burning daylight yapping away, nothing personal, see. If you're gonna kill any deer, make sure you got a good shot first, all I ask, 'count of Esther. Got to get to my barn."

"Mauro's a killer, a real dead-eye. You don't have to worry about him," Don said.

Mauro's chin rose up. Troyer placed his mug in the dryer rack.

"Esther's down south of Bay City, shopping for my grandkids at one of them *malls*. Spoils those kids, she does. When you finish up, don't worry 'bout coming by, not necessary. Now that you're situated, tomorrow morning you can head straight to the woods." He pulled his beard hair. "Maybe Aldo can send over some steaks if you bag one. Esther ain't much for hunting, but the woman can eat two pounds of venison in one sitting."

"If we're so lucky, you bet. We really appreciate this, Mr. Troyer," Don said.

"Yeah, this is really generous of you," Mauro added.

The farmer *tsked* them and shook their hands once again.

"Do anything for Aldo. He gave me his word on you two. He's a good man, eh. Good *friend*. Welcome back anytime."

They followed him out and watched as he strode to the barn, his quick steps equal to two of theirs. Mauro opened the hatch and grabbed his compound bow. Don unzipped his case, removing the powerful weapon. They were graceful, wooden-handled killing machines, made contemporary by titanium wheels with steel cables on top and bottom that aided the archer to draw the forceful string back with little effort.

Each bow had a quiver of eight arrows attached to it.

"Pretty folksy. Son of a bitch was tall, huh?" Mauro said.

"See the hands on that guy? Gotta have a dick as long as my arm," Don said.

Their flashlights created darting beams in the fog as they headed to the blinds. The darkness was lifting slightly. A great horned owl flew undetected over their heads, causing them to seek the source of the drumbeat its wings made. Crunching leaves prompted both to stop.

"Squirrel. Come on. We have to get in the stands before dawn," Mauro said, pointing at the thick woods they were about to enter.

The oak was easy to find. Mauro had dropped Don off, making sure he was safely in the maple before walking to his own hunting spot. He loved his cousin, but there were times when he felt like he had to carry him with the nuances that made for a successful hunt.

He had walked what he estimated to be exactly 100 yards when his flashlight beam touched the orange flag. Viewing the woods around him, he noticed large buck rubs on several trees. His nose picked up a malodorous scent, and he shined his flashlight at it. A pair of skunks feasted languidly on a steaming pile of deer scat, which looked like a mound of moist Milk Duds. He grimaced at their voracity.

Mauro put his bow down and pulled out a mayonnaise jar, urinating into it. He had read too many stories of hunters who literally pissed away their best chance at a monster buck from their scent being detected. He twisted the lid back on tight, still unable to shake off the image of the huge, silver-tipped stag. He set the jar down.

He reached into his carry-on pack and grabbed a screw-in foothold. He was starting to twist one in when he noticed a ladder, set with care against the side of the tree.

"Damn," he whispered.

He picked up the bow and checked the quiver snapped to it; eight arrows, their orange and white plastic vanes nestled in two rows of four. He strapped the bow over his back and started his ascent. He saw the small seat nailed in place.

This can't get *any better,* he thought.

The platform built into the crotch of the towering oak was three-by-three feet and solid enough for him to eschew the use of a safety harness. Pinkish light crept into the sky, and the air turned a bit warmer as he felt the blow of a south wind over his face. He nocked an arrow and waited. His eyes adjusted to the oncoming light of sunrise, and shapes became more discernible. He closed his eyes and listened to the space.

An hour passed and the sun had made a small dent on the pre-dawn light, but then clouds moved in, causing everything to look soft-edged and muted in color. There was a rustling, and Don was instantly aware that he'd fallen asleep after Mauro had walked out of earshot. His breathing quickened. He felt for his bow, relieved it hadn't fallen. He looked down at two deer fifteen yards away. The big maple had no leaves, but its numerous limbs broke up his outline. One snorted, and he strained to see if they were does or bucks. He guessed they were does and was correct. They were huge, healthy females, and he could only surmise what the rest of the herd must look like. He drew his bow but stopped, the mirage of that massively racked giant teasing him.

The deer run along which they were positioned led to and from Troyer's bean and cornfields, as well as a stand of some remaining apple trees that stubbornly refused to give way to the harsh, northern Michigan winters. There didn't seem to be a better place anywhere in the world if you wanted to kill a trophy buck.

And that's what Don really wanted. Though he always claimed it was more about the meat, if he was honest with himself, it had to do with killing a deer bigger than Mauro's.

He relaxed the string. He decided to wait for a good one, nothing less than a six-point. Unless, of course, it was getting late and if he wasn't offered anything substantial to shoot, then all bets were off. He'd kill Bambi if that's what walked by. He wanted to get Aldo some venison. Don knew Mauro was the better hunter, but he also knew he had a temper and the potential to get anxious. There had been healthy competition between them since boyhood. Lately, it seemed it

206 | *Eight Dogs Named Jack*

was for Aldo's affection. Don craved it in the worst way, and knowing his uncle respected Mauro as an outdoorsman, he felt bagging that monster would even the playing field. But winning at all costs wasn't in Don. And he knew it.

The sun was high, though the clouds had covered it all morning. Mauro couldn't believe he'd seen mostly does, two of which had trotted into his area from Don's direction. Ignoring Troyer's pleas, he wanted to wait for a shot at that silver giant they'd seen earlier. Mauro's head lifted at the quiet sound of something like drumsticks being smacked together. He listened to the clacking compete with the chattering of a red squirrel.

His head swung, searching. It was antlers rattling, which to a deer hunter was as lovely as classical music to a socialite.

And it was getting closer.

A loud snort preceded three big does, exploding through the aspens bordering the field leading to Troyer's home. They ran like gazelles, hopping and leaping with no rhyme or reason, tails raised high like white flags. A large eight-point trailed, chasing ten yards behind them, but the buck moved too fast, scared even, a wash of blood between its eyes. And though Mauro could have taken a chance, he paused, visualizing a nasty gut shot—Troyer's words resonating in his head.

His legs shook as he waited for what he hoped would be chasing the eight-point. It had to be the monster—the "Grey Ghost" Troyer had called it. He heard a thunderous snort fifty yards away, and his mouth went dry. The eight-point had been thick in the neck with that blood spot the size of a half-dollar on its forehead. Experience from killing many bucks in his young life told him a much larger deer had inflicted that damage, and he was counting on it being the Ghost. Then bleating snorts trumpeted. He looked deep into the tangle of trees and swore he saw the monochromatic body of their giant.

His giant.

Soft, rustling leaves countered the snorts. But it seemed too quiet for such a titanic animal. *Sometimes the biggest deer walk quietly amongst their domain*, he remembered reading. He pulled the string halfway back. The weapon quavered, shaking. *Settle down*, he thought. He steadied the bow, fighting off the buck fever. Mauro pinpointed the sound with his ears. But instead of the heavy-beamed, basket rack emerging from the aspens, this was something else.

Are you kidding me? he thought.

A lean, black cat sauntered toward him from the aspens. The cat was relatively small compared to the Jabba-the-Hutt-sized Butternut belonging to Troyer. Other than wild dogs, feral cats were among the worst thing for a hunter to happen upon. They made game run scared, and the squirrels and other rodents they chased had a disquieting effect on the woods around them. Deer were skittish and wary enough. And big deer grew *big* because they were survivors, wise to warning sounds. The last thing he wanted was some wild cat messing up their chance at that trophy.

A selfish thought overtook him; he hoped it would be him or *nobody* to bag the Ghost. He loved Don like the brother he never had, but the competition in his family was too fierce for Mauro to live with if anyone but him brought the head of that deer to Lombardi, the taxidermist. That giant would cement Mauro's legacy as the superior hunter in their huge family. Why this farmer allowed them a crack at such a trophy was really of no importance to him. It was just happenstance relevant to what fueled him: to be better than any of them, no matter what it took.

Some acorns lay scattered at his feet. Against his better judgment, he picked one up and chucked it at the cat. Instead of bolting, the thing kept walking toward him. Looking like a miniature panther, it approached twenty-five yards from his tree and showed no sign of leaving. The cat stopped to lick its paws.

Shit, he thought, *careful here, don't want to make things worse.*

He looked at the quiver on his bow handle. His arrows were carbon fiber, the shafts thirty-two inches in length and finished in a flat, olive camo with three plastic vanes—two orange and a single white—at the ends. The one nocked on his bowstring had a razor-tipped broadhead screwed into the end. He removed the deadly looking arrow, returning it into the empty slot in the quiver in exchange for the single smooth, tapered target-point. He always carried one if he felt like trying for a squirrel or a meandering grouse. Mauro nocked the new arrow, and pulled back slowly, the white vane horizontal from the taut string. He held the release point at the corner of his mouth as he'd done thousands of times while honing his skill.

Maybe I'll just scare him, he thought.

The Ghost flashed in his mind, its head and huge antlers mounted on his den wall.

"Yeah, fuck that," he whispered, making the slightest adjustment, zeroing in on the cat's heart.

Something on the animal sparkled—metallic, perhaps—but it was too late to stop. The arrow flew, springing off his bowstring like a cheetah being freed from a cage. At the sound of the string's *twang*, the cat jumped slightly, and the arrow, which was set to pass right through the kill zone, instead entered the cat's hindquarters, slicing into the muscle of its haunches. It leapt straight in the air and did a complete flip. Mauro was stunned to see his arrow sticking through its rear end.

"Oh, *son of a bitch!*" he said, startled at the sound of his voice.

The wounded cat ran in circles, as if trying to run the pain from its shattered hip, looking as if it had been trained to imitate Curly of the Three Stooges. It snapped at the air and meowed in pain. Mauro adroitly descended the tree like a gibbon and got on his knees. He crawled, a Buck knife in his right hand. Finding sudden resolve, the wounded animal dragged its broken body from the spot where it had been shot. Mauro tried to be quiet and kept stalking, crouched down now, the heavy blade of the knife at the ready. The cat disappeared through the aspens, practically shape shifting to become a part of the trees in a way only animals seem to be able to do.

"You bastard ... where'd you go?" he hissed.

He tracked drops of blood for fifty yards when he became aware of a presence.

"What are we hunting, Hadji?" Don said, making a reference to Jonny Quest's sidekick.

Mauro turned to see Don squatting next to him, knife in hand, also at the ready.

He dropped his head, laughing softly. "*Cat,*" he said.

Don let it sink in a second. "A cat. A bobcat?"

"A *cat*-cat. Wild cat. Tried scaring it, stinkin' thing wouldn't go away. So I shot it, but it moved. Hit it in the ass."

They continued stalking.

"*Chrissakes,* Mauro." Don's voice took a sudden edge. "For Christ *sakes.*"

They were just entering the edge of the aspen saplings when the solitude of the woods was shattered by a mournful cry. A scream of agony pierced the crisp fall air, primal, filled with implanted memories; thousands of years of its descendants dying at the hands of larger predators. The cat's scream made the considerable hair on the back of Mauro's neck stand up, because he knew the cause of its pain.

"It pulled the arrow out. Dammit to hell," Mauro said.

Don rose to his feet and stretched his knee joints. "Well, guess that's that," he said, starting back toward the maple. Mauro looked after him.

"Where you going?"

"Back to my stand."

Mauro shook him off. "Gotta finish it. Put it out of its misery."

"It's feral. Said so yourself. You heard it. Thing's dead."

"No. It's not. That's from pulling the arrow out. I'm telling you we *need* to go kill it. It'll scare the deer. And besides ... " Mauro thought better of mentioning the sparkle. He kept walking out of the woods, the farmer's house a white speck across the fields.

"Go ahead. I'm waiting for that Grey Ghost," Don replied.

The words latched onto him like ticks. Watching Don walk away, a bitter memory visited Mauro. It was the year before his Aunt Valentina died. Uncle Aldo fished with him and Don that day. Don had limited out on bass. Mauro saw the way his uncle had looked at Don. *"He's knocking you off your perch,*

Killer!" Aldo had said. That day in the boat, Don couldn't miss. Mauro did nothing but net fish for his cousin all day long.

Mauro slid his knife into its sheath. "You're right, Donny. Probably dead by now," he said. "I'll come get you at dark."

Don walked away, smiling. He could see Mauro's mind working.

Taking a last look at the fields, Mauro headed back to his spot. Sitting again in the crotch of the oak, he eyed his quiver; seven arrows and one empty hole. The black hole filled him with dread, looming in his gut like an undigested meal. Something about that cat nagged at him.

The drive back to Aldo's was quiet. Don kicked himself that he'd passed on a fork horn he'd seen at the edge of dusk. Mauro showed up at his tree stand ten minutes later. That surprised Don. Usually, he had to drag his cousin from the woods in pitch black.

"Other than a few spikes and the one eight-point, nothing but does. *Huge* does, but fucking does just the same," Mauro fumed.

As Mauro drove, Don watched the sun sink below the horizon, the trees creating a flickering effect. Mauro tilted his head side-to-side, still pissed about the cat. He couldn't believe he missed it. The idea of its suffering didn't bother him at first. Now though, he could hear the awful scream. It was like the sound inside your head two days after a rock concert; you know you're not hearing it at that moment, but make no mistake, you *are* hearing it.

The cat *was* feral, he rationalized. In addition to the threat to the small game population, they often grew rabid. He wasn't superstitious, but a black cat still made him uneasy, and something about it bothered him. That glint of light as it jumped. He couldn't be sure. He tried not to think about it. Maybe tomorrow he would still have a chance at the Grey Ghost.

When they walked in from the back steps of the cabin, Nino was at the table.

"Bro, you should've seen the buck we saw! Like twenty points on it—"

The strange look on Nino's face cut Don short. He recognized it as his brother's poker face, the one he made when he was trying to bluff a shit hand. Mauro picked up on it, too. Nino shook his head at them and pursed his lips.

"*Meeeoowww ...* " he imitated a sad purr.

Mauro looked at him, nonplussed. He turned to Don who could only shrug. Aldo had the phone on his ear, his bulldog jaw set and his eyes bugged out, dark and serious.

"Well, I don't know nothing about that—hey, they just got in. I'll call you back. Yeah. I'll ask them." He looked at the phone a moment and nodded once. As he hung up, Aldo turned to them, staring hard at his nephews.

Then he redirected his gaze, settling on Mauro.

"Which one of you shot that farmer's cat?" he asked.

Don stiffened.

Mauro didn't hesitate.

"Wasn't us, Uncle," he said. Had Mauro gone all-in on a pair of deuces wearing the same stoic face, an opponent holding a royal flush would've felt compelled to muck it.

Don didn't do as well. His inclination was to just fess up. But he felt Mauro there.

"Not me, Unc," he added, bobbing slightly under Aldo's gaze.

Aldo held his stare on Don then flashed his bulging eyes back at Mauro.

"Well then. That's an amazing *fucking* coincidence, isn't it? Because Ed Troyer just came in from the fields and found his cat on the porch, bleeding like a virgin on her goddamn honeymoon," Aldo roared.

"*His* cat?" Mauro asked, surprised. "What color was it?"

"What's that got to do with anything?" Aldo asked, a vein growing in his neck the size of a garter snake. "Black. Had what looked like an *arrow* wound. Tell me now; what are the chances of that? You two bow-hunting motherfuckers, and this cat—who's minding its own goddamn business on *his owner's* property—gets shot from a bow and arrow? Now, if it was an accident, Ed, he'd understand. Man's a prince. So tell me right now; did you shoot that farmer's cat? *Did you?*"

"His cat was like a, caramely color," Don said, latching on to Mauro's logic.

"Yeah, caramel-colored, like butterscotch pudding ... Butterscotch-ish-like," Mauro added. "Thing was so fat it looked like a stuffed animal, Unc—hardly moved. No, his cat was definitely not black. You're right, Don ... *Butternut!* That was its name."

Aldo's eyes looked as though they might explode right from their sockets.

"*Butterscotch, Butternut! Minchia!* He's a *fucking farmer!* You think he's only got one cat? Farmer's got shitloads of cats you dumb *mamalukes!* You shot that fucking cat, didn't you? Mauro, tell me! Didn't you? It was you," Aldo pointed at Mauro.

Mauro didn't react.

"Uncle, it wasn't us. Could've been anyone," he said. "Hell, I saw a guy walking around the edge of the woods when I was in my tree. He was all camoed up—"

Don snapped his head toward Mauro.

"Guy was carrying a bow. I didn't think nothing of it at the time ... "

The phone rang, quelling the tension a moment. There was a stare down between uncle and nephew as the ringing reverberated throughout the toasty cabin.

"Another guy? OK. You give me your word, and that's all I need to hear—no bullshit. It wasn't you?"

Nino looked at his brother, then at Mauro. He wasn't sure now if he'd been wrong or if, as he suspected, he and Aldo were being played.

"Got my word, I swear. Wasn't us," Mauro said, never blinking.

Aldo finally answered on the fourth ring.

"Hello ... hey Ed ... ah, you're kidding? Damn, really ... well, they said it wasn't them, so—yeah, I know how it looks, but if they said it wasn't them, I believe 'em. Listen, my nephew Mauro mentioned seeing another guy on your property—whoa, I'm just telling you what he told *me* and—I'm sorry to hear that, that's a real kick in the teeth ... I hope he pulls through ... "

Mauro glanced at Don, whose contempt for his cousin was growing.

Aldo raised his hand. "Say again, Ed ... "

The three boys looked at each other. Aldo's gaze never left Mauro, but his anger seemed directed elsewhere now. He listened intently, his mouth drawn tight into a sneering mask.

"Are you growing wacky-tobacky on that farm, Eddy? *Four hundred dollars?* You could buy a hundred cats ... I know Ed, but come on; it's a *fucking cat!* Pardon my French, but it's not like it's a person. She'll have to get over it. Yeah, it *looks* suspicious, but it coulda been a hawk or an owl went after him ... damn straight I've seen it happen. And like Mauro said, this other guy—"

Nino searched the faces of his brother and cousin. He felt a tinge guilty for not giving them the benefit of the doubt.

Aldo listened to Troyer's protestations, his eyes seeming to test the anatomical limits of his orbital bones. Then he relaxed.

"Oh," he said, sounding quite deflated. "You found an arrow."

Mauro felt his balls sweat but resisted the impulse to look away, feeling like Lot must have, waiting for his wife to catch up as he sprinted from the wrath of God.

Aldo and Mauro locked stares as Aldo spoke. "Well, they didn't do it. No, I'm not going to check the arrows, I'm sorry—no, I wouldn't do that to them—*I won't* do it!"

Don looked at Mauro, but Mauro stared straight ahead. Don focused on the head of a merganser featured on a Hautman print that hung above the couch, sure that if he looked anywhere else he'd start singing like a canary, buckling under Aldo's interrogation. He wanted it to stop. It was a mistake, not worth getting his uncle this upset.

"I understand. Goodbye then ... I'm sorry you feel that way."

Aldo looked at the phone as if it were a *New York Times* crossword. Then he quietly hung up. He twisted his neck at Mauro.

"You shot that farmer's cat, didn't you? Didn't you, Mauro? Come clean."

"Uncle, it wasn't me. It *wasn't*. Why would I shoot a cat, let alone *his* cat? The guy set up tree stands for us!" Mauro protested. "He was a prince, I mean, he's your friend!"

"Not anymore. Cat needs emergency surgery. Four hundred dollars. That's crazy," Aldo chewed the inside of his cheek. "You shot that fucking cat, didn't you? Orange and white vanes, he said. You shot it," he accused him again; more livid than before. "My boy, Killer. Had to shoot it, didn't you?"

Mauro's face grew ashen. He stared at Don but didn't say anything in response to the accusation. Instead, he bolted from the cabin. They heard his Cherokee's hatch open.

"I'll go after him, Unc." Don started for the door.

"Don't you move, nephew," Aldo chided. He approached Don, his eyes narrowing and torched with heat. He looked quickly at the back door. "It was him, wasn't it? Tell me Donny. He hates cats and I know he loves killing shit. That's something Mauro would do. Tell me now. It's OK." Aldo's tone was insistent.

"Uncle, it wasn't us. There's state land nearby ... could've been anyone—"

"But it wasn't anyone, was it?" Aldo snapped.

"Mauro saw some guy," Don said, evidently having learned something from Mauro, because now Nino was buying in to their innocence, even in the face of such damning evidence.

Aldo studied him. Don's throat tightened, and he felt faint. The door swung open, and Mauro stormed back in. He placed both bows on the table, their two quivers full of arrows. The shafts were both green camo, but one set had red and yellow vanes, the other were trimmed with green and blue.

"The red and yellow ones are Don's, and mine are the green and blue. I don't know what else I have to do to prove it to you. All the arrows are accounted for, all eight of them in each quiver. Go on, count 'em, Unc." Mauro's face was absolutely beatific, and he spoke with the sincerity of a cleric.

Upon seeing the green and blue fletched arrows, Don momentarily found even himself somehow believing his cousin. Nino couldn't be sure of anything now. Aldo fingered the arrows, regarding the evidence and he slumped, looking his age for the first time any of them could recall. Mostly, he looked relieved.

"Thank you nephew," Aldo said, his voice a whisper. "I'm sorry I accused you, but you can see how it looked. I'm glad I can try to mend fences with Ed now, with a clean conscience." Aldo stared at the phone. "There's some state land you kids can hunt on. I'll draw you a map. I want you three to go into Spruce Township for me and pick up a lawnmower being fixed, anyway. Mennonite kid there is a whiz at that shit. It'll take you right by the state land." He rubbed his temples. "I'll call Ed tomorrow, try straightening things ... I'm gonna turn in now. 'Night, my nephews," Aldo said.

He waited with open arms for the three. Each dutifully kissed his cheek. First Nino, then Don. Don fought off a sick feeling in his stomach as Aldo patted his back. Mauro waited an uncomfortable half-minute as Aldo wrenched himself from Don's embrace.

When Mauro hugged him, Aldo held on tight, gripping him by the shoulders for what seemed like an eternity. He finally pulled away and looked into Mauro's large brown eyes. He smiled at his nephew, making him uncomfortable.

"You look like your father. I love your daddy, you know that. You're a lot like him. He never lied either, because he was terrible at it. But only a *tremendous* liar could've lied after the way I came at you. I *had* to do it, Mauro, you know that, right?"

Mauro nodded.

"Thank you for telling me the truth. You're a good kid."

He kissed Mauro again and walked toward his bedroom, looking defeated. Mauro's heart raced. The three stood there a minute, the bows still on the table.

Mauro opened the refrigerator and poured a large glass of milk. Nino said nothing, just watched him. Mauro held up the milk in an offertory gesture to them.

"Yeah, OK," Don said. Nino shook his head, no.

Mauro poured another glass and sat down with the two brothers. There was a plate of biscotti Nino had brought up from Alinosi's in Detroit. He grabbed one and dunked it, letting it soak until it was soggy.

"So Mauro, you shot the cat, right?" Nino asked, testing the waters one last time.

Mauro looked right through him—unwavering—then at Don, and he could tell that his cousin was ready to back him up even though Nino was his brother. He took a bite of the mushy cookie and chewed it once, feeling the texture on his tongue.

And then he looked straight into Nino's eyes.

"No, wasn't us." He kept looking at him and continued chewing.

Nino shrugged, then walked to the refrigerator. Mauro looked at Don and placed his finger to his lips. Don squinted dismissively.

Nino returned displaying a platter heaping with white walleye fillets and surrounded by a border of perch.

Don let out a long wolf whistle. "Damn, Neen, those are beauties," he said.

"Nice. How big were the walleye?" Mauro asked, the cat incident evaporating.

"Biggest was near five pounds. Hog practically straightened my hook. Be eating good tomorrow night. Unc was going to drop some of the perch off to the farmer, but I don't know now. It'd be more like a peace offering. Sounds like he's convinced one of you guys tried to snuff his pussy," Nino said.

Don laughed, "Good one, Neen."

Nino turned to his brother. "Donny, take a breath—it wasn't that funny."

Mauro tightened his forearms, sitting coiled tensely as Nino returned the platter.

"Hey—let's get that mower early tomorrow. Leave around seven," Mauro said.

Nino shrugged. "OK. I'll sit with you, Don, bring my Nikon with me."

"Sounds good. We'll hunt the state land there and on the way back. Guys wake me up," Mauro said. He drank slowly from the glass of milk.

"Will do," Nino said. "'Night, guys."

"'Night, bro," Don said.

Nino hunched near the hallway, his face suddenly filling with great exertion. He blew them a sarcastic kiss, lifted his leg and farted magnificently, breaking Don and Mauro up. He walked into his bedroom, satisfied to end the evening on such a low note.

They waited several minutes until they were sure Nino was asleep. Don tiptoed to the bedroom they shared, down the back hallway of the cabin. He cracked open the door. Before he could shut it, snoring rang out, so loud it sounded like a hydraulic pump had run amok. Don returned to the kitchen. They both released nervous peals of suppressed laughter.

"You son of a *bitch!* Why didn't you just admit it? You know I'm a terrible liar," Don said, his voice low. Mauro looked toward the hallway leading to the bedrooms.

"Did pretty fucking good if you ask me," Mauro said, his voice also hushed.

"How the hell did you pull the color trick with the vanes?"

"Trust me," Mauro said. "Tell you later."

Don just looked past him. He stared at Aldo's chair, fixating on the worn fabric of the armrests. Aldo, his beloved uncle, a man who saw things as black or white; absolutes—the man had never so much as told him a harmless fib. That was *his* chair.

Mauro ran his fingers through his prematurely thinning hair, seeing the fleeting look of contempt on Don's face. He knew it was for the shame of being pulled into Mauro's lie. The shooting may have been Mauro's *act*, but now the lie was just as much Don's.

"OK, *what?* Spit it out, cuz." Mauro said.

"I just wish you would've told him. If you would've told him, he'd have understood," Don said, glancing away as he spoke. "*We* should've told him. Making up that other guy ... it's not right. If we told the truth, he'd understand."

"*If.* Well to quote both our fathers, *'If my aunt had balls, she'd be my uncle.'* Just let it go. It's over. We'll skate through unscathed," Mauro said.

★   ★   ★

The smell of fish assaulted him, competing for air space with gasoline and fresh split oak. Mauro felt for the switch on the wall and was relieved to get his hand on it. He scanned the rafters for a place to stash the arrows. Uncle Aldo was a notorious pack rat, and Mauro considered rows of odd boxes, cargo crates, suitcases, and myriad containers that could serve as his Pandora's Box.

He found what he was looking for in the form of a weathered, olive green crate, stacked high, directly over the top of the workbench. A blanket of dust made the green paint look mossy. It probably hadn't been moved since he was a teen. He passed the card table Nino and Aldo had cleaned the fish on. The garbage cans wobbled, and he about pissed himself when a raccoon the size of a Volkswagen scampered by, the discarded offal of the big walleye Nino caught—namely its heart—dangling from its bearish mouth.

Mauro exhaled and stood atop the bench. Using an old rag, he carefully pulled the crate down, surprised at its weight. With great effort, he set it onto the bench. Stenciled in black letters on the sides and top were the words, DETROIT EDISON-CABLE TIES. The top was covered with tunneled spider webs and littered with mouse droppings. Breathing hard, Mauro lifted the lid and removed wads of yellowed, balled up newspaper. Underneath he found the tie-downs, neatly stacked in rows.

Where's he find this crap? Mauro thought.

The suitcase-size box weighed a good forty-five pounds. He examined the first layer of tie-downs—galvanized steel, baseball-size nut and bolt sets—and laid the seven arrows over the top of them. Then he covered them with the newspaper. He inspected his work, and finding the arrows undetectable, got that greedy feeling one does when they're about to get away with something untoward.

Mauro slid the top back on. He returned the crate exactly as he found it. He dropped to the floor of the garage and cased the area like a cat burglar. Satisfied, he turned off the light and walked out into the crisp night air.

In the morning, Mauro, already dressed, walked down the hallway toward the kitchen. He knocked on the bathroom door, and Nino opened it, almost getting clonked on the forehead by Mauro's fist.

"It's all yours," Nino said, extending his arm.

Mauro passed him as he entered the bathroom. Nino giggled softly.

"*Eaughhh*, my *God!* Did someone open up a can of smashed assholes in here?" Mauro yelled, covering his nose.

"That would be like spraying Glade after he craps," Don piled on.

"Oh, because you shit roses, right bro?" Nino said, in mock indignation.

"What in God's name did you eat?" Mauro asked. He pissed hard into the iron stained toilet, wincing as he emptied his bladder.

"Burning tires and cabbage," Nino deadpanned.

Mauro walked out of the john, his eyes squinting. He shook his head sharply.

"That was brutal. Where's Unc?" he asked.

"Went to dump a bunch of stuff at the Rescue Auction," Nino replied.

"Thought they do those in the summer," Mauro said. "We could've given him a hand."

"Nah, Jack LaLanne already had his truck loaded by the time we woke up," Don said. "They're doing a special auction now. *Arrgh!* Captain Hook needs help making the rent," Don held up his arm, imitating a pirate.

Nino tilted his head at his brother. "Oh, that's real fuckin' nice. *Sheesh.*"

Mauro looked at both of them, confused.

Don finished his thought. "Some young farmer lost his arm in a thresher accident, so they're trying to raise money for him. It's over at the Mennonite Hall in Fairview. C'mon, let's grab that mower and see if we can't bag some deer." Don slugged Mauro in the arm. They headed out the back door to the lake.

The sun brought all the saturation of fall's color to greet them, a sharp contrast to the dreariness of yesterday's grey afternoon. Standing on the deck, they watched for a minute as the osprey circled high above, near what appeared to be the ceiling of the clouds. With incredible speed, as if jettisoned from an invisible cannon pointed at the water, the raptor's sleek body plummeted, for a second looking like it was made of feathery mercury. The water exploded as the fish hawk pierced the glassy surface, somehow reemerging just as quickly as it entered, a three-pound pike firmly in its talons. It was the most wondrous thing they had ever witnessed in the outdoors, and Mauro couldn't conceive how the bird was wired with the fearlessness to perform such a feat, let alone possess the body to survive it.

This place Uncle Aldo had shared with him, his father and cousins, had given back so much, so many warm memories. Mauro looked toward the garage.

Aldo drove along M-72 West toward Fairview. He passed dairy farms and looked out at the landscape. He'd heard about the young farmer who might lose his arm and felt a kinship to him. Aldo had been shot twice in World War II, both times through the left arm. The first time he went right back to fighting a week later. The second time was so bad that they finally sent him home to Detroit. He went begrudgingly, well aware he'd left a part of his soul in Italy.

When the bullet ripped through him in the fall of 1944 on the Mediterranean coast, only five minutes earlier he had driven his combat knife deep into the heart of the last man he would kill in hand-to-hand combat, a man who could've easily been his relative. He'd returned fire from his carbine with one arm until a soldier in his unit covered him, allowing him to flee to safety.

Aldo was fond of saying, *"There are no accidents."* It became his mantra.

God had put him in Italy for a reason. He felt no worse that it was Italian men he was trying to kill, than it was Italians who were trying to kill him. Both were there to defend *their* country. He was born in Detroit, and he knew had it not been for a yearning that burned within his father's heart to come to the United States, it could've easily been Aldo dying at the hands of an American.

The enemy he killed was his own age, not even twenty. The man had reached out, tightly holding onto Aldo's face as he kept pressure on the knife that caused the life to drain from the Italian. For some reason, he felt a need to allow the dying enemy to keep his hand there—clutching his face—thinking maybe the human contact, in some strange way, would trick the man into thinking it was all a bad dream; that surely this American with the knife—this *straniero* who was now displaying compassion—wasn't really taking away his young life at that moment.

As the light started to leave the man's eyes, he stammered, whispering to Aldo in his native tongue, as if speaking to an angel, or to God himself:

"Forgive me. I did what I had to do. I don't hate. I was just doing my job. I was a cook. A cook."

Aldo instinctively answered him in Italian.

"We're all just doing what we have to do. He knows that."

And in the moment of dying, seeing the look in the Italian's eyes—inches from his own—Aldo swore he saw comfort there, because the man knew that this *straniero* was able to understand his last prayer. Moments later the bullet hit.

There are no accidents.

The road sign marking the Rescue Auction in Fairview was adorned with a large wooden auctioneer's gavel, carved from laminated oak. It was as long as a dinner table, suspended from two heavy chains. Aldo liked the look of it, and when his travels brought him to the small town he always stopped to admire it. He marveled at what artistic men could create when given the chance.

Pulling away from the loading dock, he watched in his rearview mirror as the kids sorted the items he had dropped off. Aldo felt sorrow, hearing the news from the elder who accepted his donations, that the reattachment didn't take and that the man had lost the arm after infection set in. He made a mental note to light a candle for the young farmer and his family at Sunday's mass.

He pulled to the end of the driveway and stopped next to the oversized gavel. The carving, sculpted by simple men with skillful hands, lifted his mood. He looked at the farm across the road, and as he did a horse and buggy driven by a young Amish man passed by. The clack of the hooves on pavement was a sound he'd heard in Detroit as a young boy, riding a horse-drawn trailer with his father as he delivered bread and bootleg whiskey. The teen-ager tipped his straw hat at Aldo. He waved back. When the buggy passed, he was left looking at the farm, focusing on the white colonial; a plain structure in the middle of the open, dying fields. Aldo clucked his tongue and turned onto the highway to head back to Island Lake.

Don sipped on a bottle of OJ as he drove Mauro's Cherokee. Mauro sat in the middle and Nino rode shotgun. They each ate pepperoni sticks Mauro bought from the IGA owned by the bearded woman. Mauro was the only one of the three who could look her in the eyes and not stare at the pronounced shadow on her face. The lady was homelier than any woman Goya could've conjured up, and she seemed to truly appreciate Mauro's efforts.

"She must have a weird hormone imbalance," Don said.

"After menopause, a lot of women grow hair in unlikely places because they have a surge of testosterone," Nino said. "Sometimes it's treatable."

"I wonder if she has a lot of hair on her nuts, too," Mauro said.

Don blew the orange juice out of his nose. They all laughed hard for the first time that morning.

"*Fucker,*" Don said, wiping at the spittle on the windshield.

"So where did you get the big walleye? Off the point?" Mauro asked Nino.

"A great fisherman doesn't give away his secrets," Nino replied.

Don leaned over, "We know, but he asked *you.*"

Nino flipped him the bird. "Yeah, it was the point," he sighed. He chewed on the pepperoni. "Hey, either of you guys ever see any deer on the island?"

"Unc said he's seen a line of does cross the ice from the west shore onto the island. Never seen any there, though. Probably bullshitting," Mauro said.

"If he said it, I believe it," Don snapped. Mauro glanced at him.

They drove for a few miles, Don taking the gentle bends of the highway, flanked on each side by flame orange maples and yellow oaks—standing like sentries—laid out specifically for their travel. Pulling into Spruce they came to the only traffic light on the highway. A farmer pulled a trailer stacked high with sugar beets hitched to a slow-moving tractor. Don brought the Cherokee to a halt, idling behind it.

Mauro focused on the traffic light's red ball in the sudden silence.

"So Mauro, why did you shoot that farmer's cat?" Nino asked.

He turned and looked at Mauro. Mauro met his stare with total seriousness, but this time the façade wasn't right or quick enough. His face cracked and he started laughing, a wheezing-through-the-nose laugh that gave way to all-out, high-pitched giggles.

Don felt the weight of guilt unshackle itself and he laughed, too. Nino just shook his head and chuckled.

"*How* did I know?" Nino asked.

Tears ran down Mauro's face. He wiped at his eyes.

"Oh Nino, oh shit, Neen! Who the hell knew the guy'd have more than one cat?" Mauro said.

"Mauro, let me help you with this: The guy's a farmer. Farmers have cat*s*. That's cats with an *s*, cuz. *Plural.* Farms attract *mice*, ergo *farmers* keep *cats*. What the hell were you thinking?" Nino asked.

"Shit, I didn't want any cat spoiling my hunt. That monster was out there, we told you, he was huge! Wish I never would've seen the thing now," Mauro said. "I feel terrible about lying to Unc. I just froze up, I couldn't cop to it."

Don interrupted, "What I want to know is, how the hell did you manage to change all your vanes from orange and white? How do you even know *how* to?"

"Who do I look like, Fred Bear? *I don't.* I hunt with carbon shafts, but I always bring a set of aluminum, too. If it's really windy or raining, I'll use them because they're heavier. The shafts are identical, so I had the vanes made up with green and blue. That way, I don't accidentally grab the wrong ones." There was smugness in his voice.

Don looked at him, a mixture of respect and loathing. "What happened to the rest of the orange and white ones?" he asked.

"They're history. I *wanted* to tell Unc, but then Troyer called about the operation, and even he seemed to be getting pissed about it ... I feel really bad—I do. Farmer Troyer was a nice guy. Sure as shit wasn't going to pay four hundo to save a fucking *cat*. That was my cat, the thing'd be pushing up a pine tree," Mauro said.

"People are a little different up here than they are in the three-one-three," Don said, referring to Detroit's notorious area code. "Thing wasn't hurting anything. All this shit now."

He suddenly hated that Mauro's shoulder was touching his.

Ed Troyer drove his huge work truck away from the auction site. He'd found a fair price on a cedar chest crafted by Josef Stearns as well as some other tools and sundries. There was a comforter made by the Fairview Ladies Quilting Circle. It took Esther's mind off things, and she was more than content acquiring a box of thirty-six mason jars and lids.

Esther Troyer sat in the passenger seat next to him. She was the Hardy to his Laurel, round with a moon-shaped face. Esther hadn't been able to sleep since her return from Bay City, having to rush immediately to the vet fifty-five miles north in Alpena to be with her Lightning. The cat died twice on the table and miraculously had been revived each time. The vet kidded that Lightning now had only seven lives left.

"I still can't believe poor lil' Lightning was able to pull that arrow out all by himself. Doctor Cooley said that if a human tried to do that, why he would've passed out from the pain. Poor thing." She shook her head dismissively, and her thin lips quivered.

Troyer pursed his mouth but said nothing. She waited before testing him.

"Edward? May I ask you something?"

He took a moment, studying the asphalt highway.

"I'm your husband of thirty-nine years, eh? Ask," he said.

"Do you believe Aldo's boys weren't the ones?"

Troyer let the question simmer a while. He noted the fencerow on Grace Johansson's farm. The widow's white staggered gateposts looked like fractured limbs, the cables pulling away from them.

"Aldo loves his nephews, Esther. Lord, would you look at that gate? Can't stand looking at that fence any more. Family is family. Especially to those people."

"City folk, you mean? The downstaters," she said.

"Sure, them too. I meant the Eye-tallians. Thick as thieves, they are," he said, his creased face looking resolute. "But Aldo is a good man, and if he gives me his word, I've got to take him at it. He told me on the phone that one saw a trespasser. All just seems a little too ... *neat*. Some folks don't change. I don't think Aldo would lie to me." He groused under his breath, unintelligible rambling that Esther let continue.

He drove on, the load in the back of the truck bouncing up and down. He glanced once more in his rearview mirror.

"Can't stand looking at that fence no more, that's a fact," he said.

It was late afternoon when he made his way to mend fences. Beside him was a decorative platter. He drove the two-track carefully, watching the platter hop lazily with each bump. He preferred taking the back way in lieu of the main roads. He loved seeing the woods viewed differently than from what the highways provided.

Maneuvering through an exceptionally large rut, the platter bounced high, causing him reflexively to turn his head toward it. He placed his right hand on the levitating dish. Before he could return his hand to the steering wheel, shards of glass sprayed at him, the noise like coins falling on a church floor. A powerful whiteness burst forth, concussing against his face. Then his mind went dark.

When he awoke, the airbag in his truck was deflated on him like a bed sheet. The front end of the vehicle's driver-side was crumpled. Aldo looked around trying to remember where he was, and for a second he thought we was on foreign soil, fighting for his life again.

Or maybe he was dead.

Until he saw the perch fillets stuck to the inside of the passenger's side windshield, looking like pale stickers some child had randomly affixed there. And then he remembered where he had been heading.

A shooting pain hit his knee. He forced his door open, stumbled out and looked at his truck. He couldn't understand what he had hit. He was on the two-track, trees on each side of him; there was nothing *to* hit. *Did I hit a tree?* he wondered.

He examined the front bumper and saw a swatch of blood and tufts of coarse, silver hair sticking to the driver's side headlight.

Then he heard it; behind him, a gentle bleating; a call not unlike a lost lamb's.

He looked past the rear of the truck. Twenty yards beyond, the monster buck lay on its side. The deer's back was broken and its legs grotesquely, impossibly positioned around it, like a chair whose legs had been collapsed, smashed flat by the hand of an ogre.

"Oh no, Lord! I didn't see you, where did you come from? I was looking down," Aldo tried to reconnect the dots prior to the collision. "You must've come out of nowhere. You magnificent creature."

He lurched toward the dying buck. Aggravated by the force of the crash, his left arm hung down limply, the old war injury coming back to haunt him one more time. He knelt down, painfully, next to the broken animal. He stroked its fur and felt its lungs expand. The beams on its antlers were as thick as Aldo's formidable wrists, and some of the tines were five inches high. Its silver coat glistened in the sunlight. It was the most incredible animal Aldo had ever seen, and he'd hunted deer his entire life.

He looked into the buck's emotionless eyes and felt in his grip a familiar texture; knurled, checkered. He pulled up his right hand and there was the knife he wore on his waist, instinctively held combat style. Aldo stumbled to his feet, putting his injured left forearm under the swollen neck of the deer. He straddled it and pressed his weight down, mindful of the sharp antlers. It bleated.

The deer's head was on its side, its large brown eye looking up at the blue sky for the last time. It snapped feebly at Aldo's passing hand with what waning strength remained. He lifted the buck's huge head.

"My God, you're magnificent. Look at you," Aldo said through gritted teeth.

The buck's mouth clamped around the flannel of his injured forearm, yet Aldo accepted the pain. He felt the edge of the knife slice into the muscle of the great buck's neck. Blood gurgled out of its throat and the worn teeth of the ancient animal's bite stopped at the fabric of his thermal shirt, ceasing short of breaking Aldo's skin. A fountain of blood sprayed a thick, red stripe across the deathbed of leaves on which the big deer lay. He felt the Grey Ghost's body spasm as he rode out the animal's last breath.

Aldo stood, alone in the woods. He regarded the bloody knife in his hand.

It looked like he had immersed his arm in red paint all the way to the elbow; his pant legs were crimson, also soaked through. As his adrenaline settled back down he started to shake, the whole time looking at the knife in his hands, and suddenly Italy felt like it was right where he stood. He pushed the thought away and prayed for forgiveness for not watching the road.

Aldo heard the approach of a distant engine. He smiled wanly seeing Troyer rounding the fork, sitting atop an old John Deere tiller. When the farmer saw Aldo, he leapt from the seat in one movement and trotted toward him, the tractor crawling to a stop against a big oak.

"Are you OK? My God, you killed him, eh? Holy balls will you look at the size of that devil?" Troyer stood over the deer and marveled at it. "I was setting on paying you a visit myself ... Lord, what happened to you? Bolted in front of your path no doubt," he asked, his eyes still drawn to the animal's girth. "How bad are you hurt?"

"Knee feels tight. My arm's sprained—don't think it's broke, a stinger maybe. I'm OK, Ed. Little dizzy. I was bringing some perch over, but hell ... " Aldo grimaced as he twisted his body. "Ruined now." He listed and Troyer grabbed his arm. "Oh Ed, that was a beautiful animal. What did I do?"

"Yes. Yes he was. We'll get you some tea now. I got a chain, we'll drag him to the barn. Meat's still edible. You tenderized him, good Aldo, you did!" Troyer tried to lighten the situation, and Aldo accepted it, remembering now about the cat.

"Look at his antlers ... Hey—you want 'em?" Aldo asked.

Troyer reacted sourly, "What the heck would I want with them?"

"I don't know ... maybe I'll give it to my nephew, Mauro. He wanted that bastard so bad he could taste it. By hook or by crook, I guess he'll finally get him on his wall."

Troyer took the remark in and let it ruminate in a quiet, darker space of his mind.

"*Mauro*, you say? He'd be the dark-haired one?" Troyer asked.

"Yeah, that's right," Aldo said, gripping the farmer's arm to remain upright.

Troyer stood still, just a moment, before trotting back to the tiller. He attached a heavy chain to the deer's antlers, securing it with latching hooks.

"He would like them, wouldn't he? We'll see about that, eh ... uh, you and me will split the meat," Troyer said, though it came out more of a command.

"You take it, Ed," Aldo spoke through gritted teeth. "I'm really sorry about Esther's cat, but my nephews didn't shoot it," Aldo said with conviction. "He even showed me the colors of the vanes on his arrows. They were different colors than you said; blue and green, Ed. Blue and green."

Troyer raised his chin and his brow tightened.

"That right? Showed 'em to you, did he?" His tone grew terse.

"Yeah. He did. Just wish you and me could get past this."

Troyer looked at Aldo and started to speak out, but changed course.

"You really love those boys, don't you?" Troyer asked.

Aldo *tsked*. "The sons I never had."

"Yes. As you've said."

They clasped hands like old friends and he helped Aldo onto the tiller. The farmer looked at the truck's windshield.

"Glass isn't even broken on that side. I'll wash them fillets up and no one'll be the wiser." He walked over to the vehicle and peeled the perch off the glass. "Don't like letting food go to waste, 'specially your Island Lake perch," Troyer called out.

Aldo looked around and felt dizzy. He leaned back and rested his arm. Something pricked him.

"Minchia puttana!" he looked at the source of his pain.

Troyer approached the tractor and noticed Aldo staring down.

"Aldo. Let's talk about this," he said, walking fast toward him.

"Did you buy this *today?* I dropped it off at the auction!" Aldo said, looking at the green crate as if it was a lost key.

Having seen it once in the only movie he ever watched—a comedy with Abbott & Costello—Ed Troyer actually felt himself do a double-take.

"*You did?* You took it to auction?" he asked, almost yelling.

"Yeah, why?" Aldo asked.

Troyer's face softened, like he remembered something.

"Not your nephews, eh? *You* brought it yourself? It's heavy, Aldo—"

"They were in Spruce all day, hunting state land." Aldo grew indignant. "Think I can't lift it? *You* did, didn't you? Cleared out a bunch of stuff from my garage. Every now and then, gotta rid yourself of old stuff."

"I'd been looking for some fasteners, tie-downs, eh. I had dangling cables by them apple trees I wanted to take care of. I used the rest to fix a gate and fence-row by the highway. They's handy. Used them all up. Every one of 'em."

"Hope you didn't pay too much. Hell, those have been in my rafters for years. Wished I knew you needed them. Would've saved you the money," Aldo said, regret and pain splitting time in his voice. His coloring had turned grey.

Troyer looked at the crate.

"So you never bothered to look inside? Did you look inside—*just now* I mean."

"Why would I? I know what's in it. I stole it off an Edison truck in Warren thirty-some years ago," Aldo said, making a hasty sign of the cross. "Did you use them all?"

Troyer smiled, remembering the newspapers with headlines from 1967 about the race riots in Detroit.

"Yes. I just told you that. So you don't ... " Troyer's voice trailed off. "*I knew it,*" the farmer snorted.

"What's funny?" Aldo asked.

"Nothing. Nothing at all. Money well spent, Aldo. Solved all my problems."

He looked at Aldo for a long moment, his heart suddenly torn at what he pieced together—had literally uncovered. He waited for a sign; directions on what to say next.

And a voice whispered into his ears.

Aldo stared at Troyer, the effects of shock clinging to his expression now.

"Can I tell you something?" Troyer asked. "This is heavy on my heart. Will you promise you'll do me a favor? You know my religion abhors a lie."

"Sure, Ed," Aldo replied. "Name it."

"Your nephew got me thinking. I believe I know who really shot Lightning. I feel bad about the way things played out. I want to make sure your nephews know I'm serious about this. So I'm asking for a favor, I guess. Will you give them a message for me?" Troyer asked, casually covering the box with his coat. Aldo looked humbled.

"Anything, Ed. Thank you. Sure, you name it. What do you got in mind?"

"Let's get you tended to first," Troyer said. "I want Esther to hear this."

The hunt had produced zero activity. Only a few does came within range and there were no bucks. After returning with Aldo's lawnmower, the boys were setting up the table for dinner when Nino looked out the window over the sink.

"Holy shit!" he yelled, throwing the front door of the cabin open. Mauro and Don knew he wasn't joking when the dishes hit the floor. Aldo emerged from a DNR vehicle, his left arm wrapped in a sling. Reynolds Gauthier, a local conservation officer, wore a green uniform and a blond crew cut. A pink roll of fat on his neck spilled over his collar. It labored him to breathe as he walked Aldo toward the porch. Mauro's stomach dipped at the sight of the officer. Then he noticed his uncle's condition.

"What happened? You OK, Unc?" Mauro cried.

They were fast upon him; all three took turns embracing, patting, and kissing him.

"Yeah," Aldo said. "Couple bumps."

"I'll have the garage bring your rental car over tomorrow, Aldo. Boys gonna be up here for a while?" Reynolds asked.

"Supposed to leave after our fish dinner tonight, but *minchia*, look at your arm, Unc. We aren't going anywhere—" Nino said.

Before Aldo could protest, Mauro cut him off.

"I'll stay, guys. You two drive back home together in Nino's car. I'll make sure his rental gets here, that he's OK. My week's clear. It's cool, really. Guys, please? Let me stay?" Mauro was adamant. Don and Nino looked at each other.

"I don't want you kids missing work on my account. I'll be fine," Aldo said.

Reynolds looked at the boys and gave them a positive nod.

"You sure, Mauro? A med student owes me a favor," Nino tried.

"I'd hate to see him fall," Reynolds continued, in loud, perfectly annunciated words. "Stubborn man wouldn't go to the hospital. Are you sure you don't want me to take you to Alpena General? The clinic at least?"

"Hey—I didn't smash my eardrums. No, I'm fine. Thank you, Reynolds, but I'll be fine. Don't need no one to wipe my ass just yet," Aldo scoffed.

Officer Gauthier blinked and fluttered his lips in exasperation. Aldo shook his hand and thanked him. The boys patted his walrus-like back and saw him off. The three took their uncle into the cabin.

Mauro carried two thick towels as they walked toward the bathroom. "So tell us; what the hell happened?" he asked. Don and Nino helped Aldo along.

"Reynolds said the Ghost maybe thought my truck was a bigger deer," Aldo said.

He closed his eyes for a moment in recall, and recounted to the boys how he was trying to make amends with Troyer, and that he didn't remember anything about the crash. He took them through waking up and seeing he'd hit the Grey Ghost, and how he ended the animal's suffering with his bare hands.

Mauro's face dropped as he heard the replay of the accident, forming an image of the beautiful animal splattered across the two-track, a broken bag of bones that once contained the pure muscle of a kingly whitetail. More than anything, though, what made Mauro ill was knowing that his uncle had gotten into an accident trying to mend fences because of something he believed Mauro was innocent of.

Don tested the hot water in the bathtub. They helped Aldo into the tub, averting their eyes from his nude body, and lowered him into an Epsom bath.

"*Yeaahh! Minchia*, my *stugots* are burning ... ahhhh, that's better ... Nino, put that fish on, sauté it will you—whip up some lemon *amogue*. And don't over-cook it," Aldo ordered.

"Sure, Unc," Nino answered. Don stared at Mauro, but he didn't catch it.

The three nephews sat at the dinner table, glumly picking at their fish. Aldo ate heartily, the way a man does when he's trying to mend. His left arm was cocked in the sling as he shoveled in forkfuls of walleye and flaky perch. He eyed the boys indignantly.

"What the hell's wrong with you kids? Nino caught us a hell of a meal. Eat! *Mangia pesce adesso! Andiamo!*"

"Just not hungry, Unc, seeing you like that," Nino said.

Aldo scoffed at them.

"What? You see me feeling sorry for myself? Hell no. I got a bump or two, big fucking deal. Now eat this fish dammit, or it's *your* arms that are gonna look like this!"

The three solemnly poked their forks into the tender fillets and started to sample the white, delicious meat. Aldo watched them closely, not returning to his own meal until he was satisfied that they were truly eating.

Nino and Don hugged their uncle tenderly and made sure he was comfortable, more for their own peace of mind.

"Good seeing you boys. Sorry you didn't get your deer, Donny," Aldo said, scowling as a tug of pain radiated down the length of his left arm.

"That's OK. Not why I came, Unc," Don said. "We'll call later to see how you're holding up. Keep you in my prayers."

"Love you, Unc," Nino said.

"Me, too," Don added. "I love you, Uncle Aldo." Letting go was hard.

They kissed him once more and patted his broad shoulders. He took each of their hands with his good one and laughed his easy laugh.

"*Maddon'* the love from you boys," Aldo said. "I'm thrice blessed."

"I'll walk out with you guys. Be right back, Unc," Mauro said.

Nino opened the driver's door. Don was already near the passenger side, distancing himself from Mauro. Mauro kissed Nino and gave him a big hug before walking around the car. He grabbed Don's shoulder.

"Sorry, cuz. It all went south after that thing with the cat."

Don gave an indifferent shrug, but there was a silence that had started to grow, building between them now. Nino did his best to break it up.

"Mauro, don't blame yourself. Shit like this happens. You drive these roads enough, sooner or later you're going to hit a deer. Unc just happened to pick the fucking Shaquille O'Neal of 'em all." The two laughed at Nino's incomparable way with words.

"Still—well, you're right, can't cry over spilt milk I guess," Mauro said.

"Let's get going, Neen. Take care of him, OK?" Don said. He got in the car.

Mauro leaned on the window. "You know it," he replied.

He watched the two brothers drive into the approaching dusk. Don's head turned back at him. And while he couldn't make out his expression, he was sure the "f-bombs" were flying. His stomach churned. The rafters in the garage called him, and he started that way, until the loud squawk of the mated herons echoed above, and he stopped and watched them a moment instead.

He walked around to the lake side and looked across at the island. For a moment, he swore he saw the silhouette of a huge buck with a high set of antlers walking through the dense trees there. He squinted and, convinced his excellent vision had betrayed him, Mauro blinked. He walked back inside the cabin.

It was after 9 p.m. when Mauro got Aldo into bed, making sure he was comfortable, propping his injured arm with a pillow. He gave him one of the codeine tablets Nino had left, placing a glass of water on the nightstand.

"I'll be across the hall if you need anything," Mauro said.

"I'm fine. Thanks for staying, Mauro. You're a good kid. Always were. Oh, I meant to tell you; Ed said everything's forgiven. Wants you to come back next year. Says the missus will be calmed down by then. Man's a prince, I tell you. Took care of me today ... made sure I was OK. Oh and you won't believe it—can't believe I almost forgot to tell you—"

"Wait. He said all that? *Really?* What else is there?" Mauro asked.

"Wants you to stop by before you leave. Says you might be right about that hunter you saw. Guy he never gave permission to, chased him from his woods—last year, he said. Thinks it was him getting even," Aldo said, sleep starting to pull him into its grasp. "You remember how to get there? I can tell you again if you forgot ... " His voice trailed out and his eyes closed. Mauro didn't like seeing him so still.

He put the covers over Aldo and turned the light off. He stood in the dark for a while before leaving, hearing Aldo's shallow breathing.

Standing beside his uncle's chair, Mauro stroked the bald armrest, listening to the crackle of dried oak, the residual moisture trapped inside snapping and popping like a cap gun going off. The smell was redolent of so many nights up there, and he nursed three fingers of Jack Daniels recalling times he and Don would sneak off with a bottle of the stuff, fishing for new moon bass and catching a buzz, returning drunk under the cover of darkness to the warmed cabin.

Why does Farmer Troyer want me to come see him? Mauro thought.

It pecked at his conscience as he sipped the whiskey. Did Troyer *really* believe him? The idea of pinning the blame on another hunter wasn't original, but it folded into his lie neatly and efficiently—and from the farmer's mouth, too. Yet his stomach still felt queasy, and the thought of the cat pulling the arrow out of itself, a vision he was only able to imagine, haunted him since the moment he heard the wounded animal shrieking in the distance.

But if the farmer was willing to give him a second chance, he'd take it. He felt guilty wondering what his real motivation was for wanting to visit the farmer so badly. Was it truly the chance to put the incident behind him, or was it the prospect of a shot at another huge buck next year?

Or, he thought—*better yet; maybe Troyer will give me the head and antlers? God, stop it,* he told himself. He tried to suppress the thoughts, but found he just could not make them go away.

Even with the chance at bagging the Grey Ghost forever gone, genetics had a way of passing along certain traits, and there had to be other monsters lurking out there. Mauro chased away the selfish visions like a swarm of black flies. Either way, he'd go see Troyer on his way out of town, back to Detroit.

He figured he owed his uncle that much.

Mauro pulled on his jeans and smelled the aroma of percolated coffee. He saw Aldo, still walking stiffly, settle in at the dining room table. It was as though he'd willed himself to heal, his coloring much rosier than the day before. He had already cooked up a half-dozen eggs and some perch. Mauro saw two steaming plates.

"Who's up, and cooking, too? Look at all of this! How're you feeling?" Mauro asked, pouring himself a cup of coffee.

"Been better; been a hell of a lot worse, too, nephew. Got out of bed before your young ass, didn't I? Heh, heh ... " Aldo groaned reaching for a butter knife.

Mauro quickly grabbed it for him. He handed him the knife and looked at his uncle's hands, the skin hairless and getting papery. So many times he had watched those hands grab tools, pound in stakes, split wood, or twist a wounded pheasant's neck.

Mauro rubbed the hood of the Oldsmobile the drivers had left his uncle and went back into the cabin.

"Truck will be ready next Thursday. You think you'll be OK here while I'm gone? I can stay another day, long as you like," Mauro said.

Aldo peeked out the window of the cabin door. He *tsked.*

"They gave me an old man car. Can't put much oak in that trunk ... no, I'll be fine, Mauro. Thanks for staying. Maybe next year you'll bag one over at Ed's. That giant has sons. Such a shame to waste a beautiful animal like I did. I'm getting old I guess, not paying attention like I should."

Mauro tried to shoot back a snappy rejoinder, but his brain couldn't come up with one. He smiled at his uncle instead.

"Well. Better hit the road."

"See Ed Troyer. He's a good man. Nothing to worry about with him. I gave him my word, nephew. Told him that you'd stop by. He may even let you have the rack."

Aldo ate a piece of toast. Mauro watched him chew. It seemed like time stopped; he was unable to speak. Finally, he felt his voice, but it didn't sound like him speaking.

"Uncle. I've got something I need to tell you ... "

Aldo looked at him, oblivious to anything but his breakfast.

Mauro met his eyes and felt the weight of his deception grow heavier somehow. This *something* that had started out as an error in judgment—like a pinprick—had grown into a festering boil, but it was all his doing. He wanted to release the pressure of it, but looking into his uncle's trusting, aged face, it remained buried.

"Spit it out. Cat got your tongue?" Aldo said.

The choice of words made Mauro falter.

"No. I wanted to tell you, that I really love coming up here. I just wanted you to know it's been some of my best memories as a kid, *ever*, being up here with you," he said.

Aldo smiled, visibly moved by Mauro's admission. A rush of warmth surged inside him.

"Those aren't easy words for people to say sometimes. But you have no idea how much it means to hear them. Thank you, nephew," Aldo said.

Mauro bent down to hug him and kiss his cheek. He tried to get up, but Mauro placed a hand against his broad chest, urging him to stay seated, which Aldo gladly did.

Driving to Troyer's property, the weight of the lie would leave Mauro momentarily, only to rush back like a fever into his stomach. He passed gas that was so pungent he had to roll down the windows. He watched the turns and forks go by and saw the rusty pair of wagon wheels. He looked upon the scene where Aldo had crashed into the Ghost. Debris from the truck was pushed in a small pile to the side of the two-track. He tried to ignore it and kept driving. He saw the farmhouse ahead, and there was Troyer at his truck. Mauro pulled up beside him.

"How's it going?" Mauro said as he got out of his vehicle, his voice masking the discomfort of the meeting.

Troyer walked over and extended his right hand, the huge fingers grappling Mauro's own like some sea creature intent on devouring it.

"Where's your hunting partner?" Troyer asked, looking past Mauro.

"Went back home to Detroit."

"Oh. Well then. You I really wanted to see, eh? Just wanted to make sure you *both* knew I was a man of my word," Troyer said, his face absent of anything but sincerity. Mauro's throat went dry but he swallowed hard and nodded through it.

"Please, it's you who should get the thanks. We appreciate how you took care of my uncle, and well, your consideration with the … *misunderstanding* of things. How's your cat doing anyway? What's her name?"

"Lightning. And it's a *he. Esther's* Lightning. Turned out to be one tough customer. He's going to pull through it looks like, eh. Probably have stiff legs the rest of his days. That's the life of an animal, I guess. I still need to get the police involved with that rapscallion who shot him. Just can't believe he wasn't man enough to talk to me face-to-face."

"The police. Oh. Well, I'm glad he's going to recover," Mauro said, and the farmer looked at him hard.

"I'm sure you are. Come to the barn … want you to see something."

Mauro hesitated and watched Troyer walk, feeling as though his own feet were stuck in a bog. A wave of panic and bizarre thoughts swirled around him, and an image of the farmer sticking him in the heart with a pitchfork flickered there. He dismissed all of it as foolishness and guilt and followed him inside.

Troyer slid open the large wood doors and Mauro stood at the entrance, his face breaking into a look of wonderment. It smelled of hay. Inside, a single shaft of buttery sunlight shone through a high loft window, cutting through the dull atmosphere. Specks of dust swam lazily as the light pointed to a startling image; the regal, silver stag, slowly twisting in the air. It was dressed out, a wooden stake spreading apart the grotto of its formidable chest, which was now gutted and raw.

The buck was headless, which seemed somehow inappropriate, a violation. The carcass hung above them from a large beam, impaled on a meat hook that was stuck high through its spine. The body cavity was big enough for a ten-year-old child to hide within. Wavy heat from a standing woodstove made Mauro's face feel sunburned.

"He was a big-un. Maybe next year you'll get a shot at one just like him, eh?" Troyer said, standing close behind him.

"He's incredible. A trophy—where's the—I mean, what'd you do with the head? The antlers?" Mauro asked.

Troyer moved next to Mauro. He rubbed his equine face and fixed a pained look on it.

"Well, that's a funny story, eh? Some conservation fellow came snoopin' 'round, wanting to take measurements when word got out 'bout what happened with Aldo. I told him my suspicions, but all he cared about was the antlers. Told me the Ghost was probably a state record in the—what'd he call it now—the *typical* category. Then he said something about some books, Boone and Pope and what's that name—like old pioneer names?" Troyer's lips closed as he reached for the correct titles.

"Crockett. Boone and Crockett and Pope and Young," Mauro said, the color draining from his face.

"Yes! Crockett. Reminded me of Daniel Boone and Davy Crockett. That all mean something to you—those names, I mean, besides the pioneer part?"

Mauro stared impassively at the man's ignorance about the magnitude of what he'd just reported. Guilt and the thoughts of what could have been chewed at his conscience.

"Yeah," Mauro said. "That was a perfect matched set of antlers—that's called *typical*. Holy ... that rack is the state record, maybe the world, bigger than the Hanson buck. Pope and Young sanctions bow hunting records. A buck registered in both is ... " Troyer listened with amused interest. Mauro let the explanation fade out. "That would be worth a lot to a collector. To have the state record alone, that's *priceless*."

He scanned the barn trying to locate the deer's giant head.

"I told you; rats with horns, that's all they are to me. Nothing more. Tasty rats they are. I love venison, but I got no use for the rest of them, eh? So I ground up those horns, fed 'em to my hogs," Troyer said.

Mauro's face went slack and the thought of such a trophy being destroyed in so reckless a manner made him physically ill. The farmer's thin mouth popped open and he unleashed a hearty guffaw.

"You should see your face! I'm just funning. Oh, that's grand," the farmer beamed, trying to withhold giggles from his mouth with his long fingers.

Mauro's face reanimated and the color returned. His ears glowed red, and he laughed in spite of himself, along with the gangly Troyer.

"Oh, you are *cruel*. Man, I was going to say that was too beautiful a rack to do something like that to. You had me going," Mauro said.

The farmer chuckled some more, and Mauro let him go on as he tried to formulate a subtle way to ask the farmer the question he'd been wanting to all along.

"I'm not sure if you'd be interested, but if you really don't want them, I'd love to have the head and antlers. I'd have it mounted, he was just so memorable. You know ... beautiful?" Mauro delivered the line with the perfect amount of nonchalance. He felt like he'd just sold a Frigidaire to an Inuit family. "I'll gladly pay you for them."

The farmer's face screwed up like he'd just swallowed a jar of pickle juice.

"I wish I'd known. I ended up putting it up for sale at the Rescue Auction in Fairview. I heard a guy bought the antlers for sixty bucks. Some fellow, he collects all sorts of antlers, makes fancy furniture, lamps and such out of them. Well, he thought he hit the lottery, can you imagine that? For some horns?"

"Sixty dollars," Mauro said.

"Hard to believe an animal can live that long and grow horns that big and only be worth sixty bucks in the end, eh?" Troyer said, biting his lip hard. "*Hmmph!*"

Mauro's stomach cramped up and he felt vomit and the runs trying to decide which would go first. He clenched his buttocks tight and tasted bile on the back of his tongue.

The farmer shook his head again and seemed truly disheartened.

"Wish I would've called Aldo beforehand, eh? Dang it to blazes. What can you do though; we were still so ... *distraught*, with Esther's Lightning and all. People probably think I'm crazy, paying over four hundred dollars to save a farm cat, eh? Four hundred ... lot of money. I'll get it back though, don't look so concerned. That trespasser will pay, don't you worry."

Mauro couldn't really say anything. He kind of nodded his head, his eyes fixed on the cleanly severed neck of the biggest deer he'd ever seen, now hanging from a hook.

"I just don't like to see animals suffer. I'm going to have this monster butchered up and make sure Aldo gets plenty of the meat. Some was ruined in the accident, but a lot was salvageable. Give some to that young farmer who lost his arm."

Ed Troyer patted the haunch that wasn't hit by Aldo's truck. The huge carcass yawed in a slow, swaying circle, its front legs bent. Mauro watched it, remembering how it looked when it ran off, silver-haired, yet so powerful and alive.

"Well, I should get going. Thanks again for taking care of my uncle. Don't know what would've happened to him if you hadn't been there." Mauro started to leave the barn with the farmer in tow. He saw a squat, chubby woman he assumed was Esther Troyer standing near his Cherokee. He watched her stealthily shuffle back to the porch of the farmhouse.

"That your wife?" Mauro asked, pointing ahead.

The farmer acted as if he didn't hear the question. Just stared at Mauro with a kind of loathing. "Your uncle really loves his nephews, that's for sure, eh?" Troyer said.

"We love him very much. He's like a second father to most of us," Mauro said.

Seeing the expression on the farmer's face, Mauro felt the skeeves, so he walked quickly to the Cherokee. Esther Troyer stood on the porch, a serious look on her doughy face. Her lips curled into a little grin and her double chins heaved as she watched them approach. Mauro stared at her.

"Hello, Mrs. Troyer," he said. "How are you?"

"Now aren't I some kind of host? This is my Esther. Esther, this here's Aldo's nephew, *Mauro*. I told you about him." She held a look on her husband before acknowledging Mauro.

"Of course. I'm fine young man. Edward, I did as you asked. Now I got my canning to do if you'll excuse me. Be needing your help Ed, so hurry on. Good day young man." She was rushing now and her hand went to her mouth, abruptly, "*Oh!* I'm sorry—" She opened the door and shut it behind her before Mauro had a chance to say goodbye. He looked at the farmer. Troyer bit his lip and shrugged.

Esther let out a loud belly laugh, then cut it short, as if stifling a sneeze. Mauro looked at Troyer, who again seemed as if his mind was in another place, and he also seemed to be holding something back.

"Don't mind her, she's still sore about Lightning. Have to be honest with you," Troyer got really close to Mauro as he opened the driver's side door. "She's sure it was you who shot him. Between you and me, I could give two shits who shot that goddamn mangy cat." Mauro flinched at the man's sudden use of profanity. Troyer caught himself. "Forgive my language. Esther, her cats mean the world to her. But I told her it wasn't you or your cousin, because you gave your *word* to your uncle. And your uncle, he gave me *his* word. Aldo gave me his word on all that, see?"

Mauro looked at Troyer's eyes, trying to read what the hell was happening. The man's demeanor hadn't changed much since he met him that first morning with Don, and he couldn't be sure if it was just his guilty conscience pricking at him or if this was a test, maybe a last chance. They stared at each other a moment.

"I appreciate that," Mauro said.

He held out his hand. The farmer studied it, and then he took it, shaking it just as solidly as he had before, with just a little more on it. Mauro didn't let on how much his fingers ached. Troyer finally let go, and Mauro got into his Cherokee.

"Aldo is special. It's like he's lived up here his entire life. Go to the mat for anyone. I've seen him help folks up here, never say two words about it, you see? He ain't *typical* of most city folks move up this way; all brash talkers, putting themselves on folks, forcing their opinions. You understand what I'm telling you?"

"I do. He's special. Like I said, we love him, too."

"Maybe next year, you and your cousin can come back, try and bag the Ghost's kin if you like. Nothing but rats with horns ... "

"Right; rats, you've mentioned that. Thanks again," Mauro said.

The farmer snapped his fingers, startling Mauro. He walked over, leaning his lanky frame against the window ledge. Mauro's face was a foot away from Troyer's, so close he could see the pores on his cheeks and his eyelashes. His breath reeked of coffee.

"I collected a bushel of apples for you. That grove of mine still manages to produce some nice Granny Smiths. Had Esther load them up in your trunk while we was yapping away in the barn. You *like* apples, son?"

Mauro looked at the door on the porch. He swore he saw Esther Troyer's face looking at him from behind the lace curtains.

"Huh? Uh, sure, yeah. Thanks," Mauro said. "Goodbye, Mr. Troyer."

Mauro looked at him one last time. Troyer backed away, and stood there. Mauro started down the driveway and turned, speeding away from the farm. In his side mirror he saw the farmer waving, so he threw his hand out the window in return.

Ed Troyer heard tapping on the window. Esther's plump hands held Lightning under his armpits, his black face peeking through the parted curtains. Her stubby fingers held the cat's front paw, tapping it against the windowpane.

The paw was stained blue. She dragged it downward, leaving an indigo streak of ink on the glass. She waved at Troyer, using Lightning's paw like a puppet's. She was giggling.

"Meowww. Hello, Master of the House. I'm mending fine," Esther said in a whispery mix of baby talk and purring. Troyer shook his head and walked to the barn.

Troyer stood staring at the wavy effects of the woodstove's intense heat. He walked over to a large cabinet and opened it. Inside, hanging from a rope by its heavy antlers, was the head of the Grey Ghost, the huge eyes of the buck glazed over, a film of dust on their surface making them look like dirty gelatin. He didn't know what he would do with it, who he might give the trophy to, but he knew who *wouldn't* be getting it. He considered selling it to pay for the cat's operation. Maybe he would. He shut the cabinet doors knowing he would revisit the head many times before deciding.

He walked over to a pile of boxes stacked against hay bales. The top one was open. Troyer reached inside it, humming a Mennonite hymn as he gathered what needed to be destroyed. *Someone, on a day far from now*, he thought, *might shatter Aldo's belief in the boy, but it won't be me.*

Troyer opened the potbelly stove. The rumbling draft pulled the whitish flame upward, the fire crackling with energy. He threw the seven arrows, their vanes of orange and white, deep into the fire. He stoked them around—sure they had started to melt—using the tip of a remaining arrow as a poker.

It was one arrow he decided to save.

There was a target point attached to its end ... the arrow Lightning pulled from himself. This Troyer felt compelled to keep. He looked up at the twisting carcass of the Grey Ghost, the sheer brutality of the image giving him a chill, even with the baking warmth of the fire blazing next to him.

"I pray that was *your* voice I heard, whispering in my ear, oh Lord," Troyer said.

"Fucking stupid country-ass son-of-a-whore-bitch! Sixty bucks! Hillbilly whore-bitch cocksucker hick asshole dumb shit, cornbread-eating mother*fucker!*"

If someone had been sitting next to Mauro, they would've thought he'd been cursed with the worst case of Tourette's ever diagnosed. His speedometer approached seventy-five, and he knew he had better let up on the rural highway or surely the local cops would nab him. But now he couldn't get home fast enough.

He sped by a green highway sign reading, GLENNIE 22 MILES/I-75 55 MILES. His brain ached like a boxer was using it for a speed bag. It was a good four-hour drive back to Detroit, and he feared he might puke or shit at any minute. The eggs he ate with Aldo were repeating on him, and as he saw the blurry fence posts of a neighboring farm give way to guardrails, the strobing effect made his gut ache worse.

Mauro replayed the weekend in his mind over and over, but each time that split-second moment where he decided to shoot the cat knocked at the walls of his conscience.

"Could've just shot at its feet, but no, " he said out loud.

Driving for ten miles on I-75 South, his gut still didn't feel right. After putting some seventy miles between him and Troyer, his stomach groaned and knotted. The earlier nausea had given way to a hollow feeling in his gut. He kept watch for an exit where he could grab something light to eat and fill his gas tank at the same time. A Coke sounded good, too. The odor of apples overcame him, and in his rearview mirror he noticed a red and white quilt covering the bushel basket of apples in the cargo space of the Cherokee. He saw a sign for a Marathon Food Mart in Pinconning ten miles south. He hammered the gas and got it up to ninety. *Cops be damned,* he thought.

As his car was parked in the bay, filling up with unleaded, he walked stiff-legged to the back of the food mart and found a line of one at the door of the men's room. An old man stood in front of him, and Mauro tightened his pelvic muscles to control his piss-swollen member. He clenched his ass cheeks to hold off his brewing stomach. The short man smiled, his liver-spotted head shaking from some kind of palsy, causing the few wispy hairs he had to wave.

"One or two?" the old man asked, an odd smile tipped on his face.

Mauro looked at him. "I'm sorry?"

The man exhaled, rolling his eyes, clearly frustrated. "In this land of fun and sun, we do not flush for number one ... " the man took a breath, " ... but, if you do a number two, a flush is what we ask of you," he finished reciting.

And then he dipped his head and asked Mauro again, "So. One or two?"

"Uh, just one, I think."

The old man nodded, accepting his answer.

The door opened and a father and his toddler son scooted out. The old man shuffled inside and closed the door. From within the bathroom, Mauro could hear the toilet seat drop and the man emit explosive gas. Loud, grunting noises were accompanied by unabashed laughter and "Oh, yessir thank you for *that!*"

"Great," Mauro whispered.

Ten minutes later, the door opened. The old man emerged, his short-sleeved shirt riding out of his pants, pulled high on his hips. He grinned at Mauro, completely brazen.

"Beets and broccoli never agree with me," he said as he waddled past. "Number twos don't come around so easy these days." He added, "Not flushing good, by the way."

Mauro walked in and was overcome by old-man smell mixing with a strong odor of toxic stool that had run through the geezer's abdominal tract. He unzipped and pissed without looking down, trying to get it all out before needing to take another fast breath. He inadvertently peeked down after the initial rush and saw a chunky, dark smear on the toilet seat. He gagged once and short-breathed it, not inhaling again while he tried to finish. Cutting it short, he dribbled urine on his pant leg and hastily zipped up.

Fleeing the food mart, trying not to shit himself, he ran bowlegged. Still, he flew past the old man who was dawdling toward his Grand Marquis, parked in a handicapped spot, making it only another five steps before retching all over a pallet stacked with gallons of windshield fluid.

A female attendant changing plastic numbers on the gas prices saw him vomit. He was still on all fours when she finally got to him.

"Hey, you OK buddy?" she asked, leaning over.

"No. I'm so sorry. Oh, what a mess," Mauro said. "That men's room—it's really gross, better have someone clean it. The smell ... I'm really sorry about this," he said.

"Don't sweat it. I'll just spray it off. Make sure the locals don't buy it, but no one else'll know the difference."

He picked at his tongue as he walked to his Cherokee. He went back into the station and paid for the gas, returning with a bottle of warm Coke. He pulled out and nursed the pop as he drove. It burned his throat going down.

Mauro's very empty stomach rolled a couple of times. He was outside of Frankenmuth—maybe thirty-five miles—when he felt true hunger grip him. Whatever poison had invaded his system was finally gone, and he was thankful for that. He was tempted to eat, thinking he might have a chance to keep something down, but the idea of having to exit again wasn't appealing. Then he thought of the bushel of apples. An apple actually sounded good to him, if for nothing else than to get something in his gut. He'd order a pizza when he got home.

He pulled over to the side of the highway and got out, keeping a wide berth from the drivers speeding by, rushing home to the insane pace of their hurried lives downstate. They pulled trailers with jet skis, winterized boats of every length and kind, and off-road vehicles; all the things the people "up north" rued about those who lived "downstate."

He opened the hatch and pulled down the lift gate. He saw the red and white quilt draped over the bushel basket. It seemed strange to him that Esther would use such a lovely wrap for so modest a gift. He lifted it and was hit with the rush of a strong, sour scent the blanket had sealed in. A black swarm of fruit flies lifted with the blanket like a burst of pepper, and he swatted at them aggressively, a horrified look taking over his features. The odor of cider was overpowering.

What he saw made his face turn pale, as if God had decided at that very moment that Mauro should now live his life as an albino.

The apples weren't in a bushel basket.

"Oh shit. Oh shit. Oh no, no ... oh fuck no ... "

The green Detroit Edison crate was tucked next to his duffel bags, brimming with rotten fruit. Fright gripped him hard, like he'd just discovered a tumor while showering. The apples were mushy, mealy, covered with black spots and worm-filled. White gall wasp larvae crawled over them.

He grabbed the sides of the crate, pulled it toward him and rested it on the folded-down lift gate. There was a note on top of the mess. Mauro reached for it, and though made only of paper, it required every ounce of his quickly fading strength to lift it to his face. Humming sounds of traffic—mere white noise—sizzled in his head like a swarm. The note shook as he read it.

> *"Mauro,*
> *Aldo loves you boys, but I guess I don't.*
> *You and that chickenshit cousin of yours better never step anywhere*
> *near my farm again. This is one lie Esther and I can live with.*
> *Next year, if he asks you why you don't want to hunt my land,*
> *I'm sure you'll come up with an excuse that's believable.*
> *Now, how do you like them apples?*
> *Sincerely,*
> *Edward and Esther Troyer"*

A little paw print, pressed in blue ink, was set next to the couple's properly cursive signatures.

Mauro dropped the note and sat on the lift gate of his Cherokee.

He looked at the green crate. He slumped to the ground—the back of his head hitting the lift gate on the way down hard enough to make him dizzy, and his head rested against the rear bumper underneath it. Shadowed under the ceiling of the lift gate, he finally gave in to heaving sobs, all the guilt he'd held back since the moment he lied to Uncle Aldo bursting forth. Mauro ignored the pain in the back of his head. He sat on the road gravel, crying harder, his body racking convulsively as he let it all go.

Then Mauro backed out, rising urgently to his feet, sprinting to the side of the highway. He bent over, his hands on his knees, and as a series of dry heaves overtook him, he felt the pungent taste of bile on the back of his tongue as he retched. Remnants of fish and eggs came up strong and he spat out what was left in his cramping stomach. He straightened up when it was over and returned weak-kneed to his Cherokee.

He took the crate and hefted it, trying to avoid the rotting scent that invaded the cargo space. He ran along the roadside with it, and using the motion of throwing out a bucket of mop water, heaved it into the scrubby bushes that buffered the vast pine forests creeping beyond the highway. The crate lay half-hidden in the roadside ravine. Mauro stood above it, breathing hard, sweating, staring at it like a serial killer revisiting the crime scene of his latest victim.

After a time, he returned to the vehicle and took his bow, still secured in its case. He went back to the shoulder, intent on throwing it away as well, but held back at the last moment. He thought of the pain Uncle Aldo was in right now, knowing he was the one who caused it. He thought of what his lie had set into motion. Shame cloaked his soul and he let it envelop him.

He remembered when his father and Aldo had taught him to shoot. He was just thirteen years old. They had encouraged him, patiently coaching him when he would miss the target completely. He thought of his uncle's resolve, standing by him because he was his nephew, his blood. Even in the sure appearance of his guilt, he hadn't wavered.

Because Mauro had given Aldo his word that he was innocent.

And he saw Uncle Aldo's face, clearly recognizing for the first time that an old man, at the dusk of his life, is what he had become.

A portent voice whispered to Mauro that Uncle Aldo needed to believe in his integrity; to keep a fire burning inside, to help him stay strong for however long he had left on this Earth. And Mauro somehow knew that the green crate was Troyer's promise that Aldo would be able to do that, most assuredly. Because to the farmer, Mauro meant absolutely nothing, but Aldo Vendetti, who had integrated himself into the moral fabric of a community that didn't give out free passes, well, he meant everything.

Mauro held the bow case with crossed arms, his body becoming submissive to his guilt, as if in a futile attempt to hug himself. He stood like that for a while before the wind and noise from passing vehicles woke him from his torpor. He placed the bow case back inside and quietly closed the lift gate and hatch.

He leaned against the Cherokee, watching the vehicles zip past, towing the toys the downstaters use to get away from it all. He went to the driver's door and leaned in, opening all the windows. He *wished* the fresh air through the Cherokee, hoping the circulating, rushing wind would erase the odious stench of the rotting apples, but he knew it would remain, locked forever in its fabric.

Mauro finally settled behind the wheel. He leaned out the window. When it was clear, he pulled out onto the interstate, determined to leave everything that happened—all of it—behind him in those bushes on the side of the highway. Once on the road, he floored it, fleeing the beauty of up north, quickly making his way to the city, back to the life that waited for him in Detroit, where guys like him belonged.

Flight of the Hopper

The lights were out in the parking lot at Naji's Party Store & Wireless, so at first all you could see was the kid's white tank top bouncing up and down, glowing from the light of a street lamp on the corner. Al Fortuna was parked on a side street, watching from inside his Cadillac. His doors were locked. When he'd driven to Naji's, he'd wondered if the kid would be there. But he knew he would be, because the kid was *always there,* no matter what time of day or month. He seemed to be a part of the landscape. And though Al didn't venture to this part of town too often, somehow at midnight, here he sat. When he watched the kid on the bike, Al filled in the blanks of the boy's life, but no one really knew those kinds of things. He didn't know anything about the kid except what he could extract from him at the bike shop. Al sighed after secretly watching for a while, amazed at the things the boy could make that old bike do.

Hopper stood on the pedals. That's how it always started. He had owned the bike for three years and was now too big for it. That he knew. He worked the concrete parking blocks—hopping them one at a time—as he'd done every day since he first got it. He turned seventeen years old last week and what the hell was ahead? School? That was a joke. *This* was his school. He had become great on a trick bike. Beyond great—the best around—maybe anywhere. When he was hopping, it felt like *floating*.

The cars on Whittier raced by. Dusk was an hour ago—nights were best because the lot was empty—and he had to make the circuit once more before heading home. The yellow lines marking the parking spaces were faded on the pocked blacktop.

Fifteen concrete parking blocks bordered Naji's lot. The shape of the lot suited him—a tilted rectangle with enough grab in the asphalt's texture for the bike to do its thing.

Naji's lot was a safe place for him to exist, to be free and easy. Working those concrete blocks—hopping atop them, between them or wheeling around bits of glass, rusted metal, and ragged sawn pipe poking through the asphalt surface—had become everything. And even with his eyes closed he knew every nuance of its shape. Like a lover, he was familiar with its imperfections and bumps, moss that hugged the damp depressions, the potholes; it was a part of him, a connective limb, so much that he knew how many rotations his sprockets took to roam its perimeter. Like "gould" in a game of tag, Naji's lot was his safe place where nothing bad was allowed to touch him, and being there kept him aware—aware of the dangers that lurked everywhere other than *right here*.

He put in five hours a day, ten or more on weekends. The drunks would watch him sometimes. They'd sip on hooch from brown bags, and he smelled body odor mixed with the alcohol in their sweat. Their hollow eyes would track him, but he never paid them any mind. Not while he was hopping blocks. Too much concentration. Just kept concentrating on *the spot*.

Hopper.

That's what they called him. The only black kid anyone ever saw working a trick bike. The white bikers received him but tired of him quickly when it was apparent he'd never stop long enough to hang and smoke a joint or drink a beer.

"Why you always be hoppin', dawg?" they'd ask, affecting street talk—a *blaccent*, the brothers called it. He didn't crave their acceptance. Just needed to hop.

He stood on the pedals, the back tire of the bike high in the air on a forty-five-degree angle, all his weight balanced on the bike's knobby front tire. It was an older Diamondback. He loved the feel of it. For 500 chips he could get himself a new one; the Joker. Secretly, that's what he had his eye on. The Joker had a twenty-six-inch frame. Wouldn't look like a man-child riding a kiddy trike any more.

But his mom had bought him this bike. Got it off a user who knocked some white kid from it. The guy was a horse-head, fixing really bad, and she was at the right place at the right time. She waved fifty-five bucks past him, and he could taste it.

Hopper knew how long she had to work to make fifty-five bills. When he saw her wheel it into the garage, it pissed off her boyfriend, Suggs, to no end, but Hopper was her Sweet Potato Pie, *"So don't you pay him* no *mind,"* she had told Hopper while gifting him with the bike.

"Jesus made you to do great things, Levan. I know it."

He was christened Levan Chatman but born Hopper the first day he rode the bike up to the corner of Whittier and Chandler Park Drive, when he went on a milk run to Naji's. He didn't even know how he could do it. Never had any *intention* of doing it—just happy to have a bike to ride.

Hopper realized how hard his mom worked, sewing seat bucks on the afternoon shift at the Lear plant for cars she could never afford, taking all the overtime they would give her. It was a good job until she got laid off. Since then she worked as a dishwasher at Red Lobster, feet always swollen from standing the whole night, scouring pots and pans and dumping grease.

"Can't get the smell out, Sweet Potato. Smell like shrimp all the time."

The bike was scuffed up and he saw the spots where she'd carefully brushed baby blue to hide the bare metal wearing through the sparkly navy paint. He never said anything about that. Just said it was the best bike he ever saw and he loved her.

When he rode up to Naji's, the white boys in the parking lot laughed when they saw his bike. He'd seen them before, when he used to *walk* there for the milk. They were rich kids from the Grosse Pointes, probably got anything they wanted. Essentially, Hopper's bike was the same type as theirs. But theirs had names like *Trek, Specialized.* And one guy's—his had to be the Cadillac of bikes— was called a *Cannondale*. It was slick as snot and rode as fast as a scalded dog. A kid with a dark mop haircut sat on it. Levan drove by their snickering faces, watching them do wheelies and spinning their handlebars.

He parked in front of Naji's and wrapped his chain through the frame and around the pole of a No Standing sign. There was no Naji anymore. Naji Rashid had been killed in 2001 during a hold-up that went bad. His sons, George and Samir, owned the place now, although it was George, the younger son, who ran it. George was there all the time. The wireless was his idea. Since his father died, he kept the display case stacked with the latest cell phones, Bluetooth headsets, and PDAs, all set under glass cases. The dealers and bangers loved that stuff. Street guys would look, never buy, and George's car had been jacked in the alley twice. He refused to install bulletproof glass, though.

For he prayed that his father's killer might decide to return one day.

Samir Rashid was hardly ever there. He came in once a month to grab bottles of the good vodka or the latest model phone. He'd usually relieve the register of a few hundred, too. Once, Hopper was there on his milk run. He waited to pay at the front counter and could hear George and Samir screaming at each other in Assyrian, all the way from inside the beer cooler at the back of the store. He hadn't seen Samir much since.

Hopper walked in and heard jingly Middle Eastern music. Behind the long front counter, George watched Jerry Springer on a black-and-white TV. He was squatty with blue-black hair and a heavy face. His head looked like a tan pumpkin in a wig. He talked into a wireless gadget, a cigarette dangling from his lips. He barely looked up at Hopper.

Reams of scratch-off lottery tickets hung down from above the counter. The surface was cluttered with jars of pepperoni sticks, torch lighters, and laser pointers. Dream interpretation books were stacked next to imported chocolate and tins of Altoids. Hopper nodded to George and turned right, walking down an aisle stacked with wines that led to the dairy cooler.

He slid open the door, and the cold air hit his face. He grabbed a gallon of whole white and a half-gallon of chocolate. Suggs loved chocolate milk and groused holy hell if he caught Hopper drinking any of it. If his mom didn't occasionally drink from Suggs' glass, Hopper would've pissed in the chocolate every chance he got. Looking up, he saw George watching him in the curved mirror above the cooler, but he wasn't bothered by it. Hopper walked, swinging the milk by the handles. He set it down on the counter.

"Hey, Mr. Rashid," he said. George didn't say anything, just stared at the set.

He rang it up. "That's six-eighty-five, boss … " and then it was like he switched tones. "Believe me when I tell you, it's *expensive* being Samir's brother!"

Hopper was confused until George pointed to the Bluetooth on his ear.

From his angle, Hopper could see the partially obscured, checkered handle of a shotgun behind George. It looked expensive; etched game birds and hunting dogs with gold filigrees winked at him in the fluorescent lights. He sensed George knew he'd seen it, felt it probably gave him comfort; one more *abeed*—that's what the Chaldeans called the blacks—who knew he was packing. George grinned and adjusted a flattened-out Kool carton as a sort of shield over the gun. If Hopper hadn't seen the weapon, it would've just looked like an old piece of box to him.

He dug into his pocket and pulled out single after single, unrolling green balls until they became wrinkled dollar bills. George exhaled a stream of smoke from his nostrils watching the kid try to iron out the ones. Hopper patiently worked through his change, counting out seventy-eight cents. He saw a little yellow dish with a Skoal logo on it. *"Have a penny, leave a penny. Need a penny, take a penny. Don't abuse it!"* was handwritten on a note taped in front of it.

"I'm short," he said, as he reached and grabbed the last pennies from it.

"You're good." George bagged the milk, tossing the coins back in the Skoal dish. "See you around, boss."

Hopper went outside and put the bag down. As he unlocked his bike, he watched one of the kids trying to hop on his front tire from one skinny parking block to the next. The boy's red bike gleamed, looking more like a sculpture. The kid made two blocks before falling ass-over-teakettle onto the third one. His three pals busted his balls and laughed at him. The kid winced, rubbing the cheek of his ass. He picked himself up and kicked the red bike. Hopper wondered what the tires alone for it cost.

"Dawg, you suck. Watch *moi*," the mop-haired kid on the Cannondale said. He seemed the strongest of the four. Hopper pedaled up and stopped by the other three. They didn't say anything to him, just nodded. He stood there holding the bag. It was getting late, and he knew Suggs would get angry if his milk came home warm.

"Bet Zack gets six," one said. Red Bike rocked back and snorted.

Hopper watched the angle Zack held the bike at, studying the way he braced his arms, how he started his motion, the way he hopped—three hops per block. He did the first two easily. He balanced, then jumped the third and quickly did the fourth. He seemed to hover there before vaulting to the fifth block. Two of his buddies whooped and then groaned when he landed on both tires next to the sixth block. He pumped his fist and walked the bike back to them—front tire to back tire—in a skipping stone motion, never leaving the seat.

Hopper found himself smiling, a mouthful of contrasting white teeth. Zack stopped next to him and looked over his scarred blue ride.

"'Sup man? How many can you do?" Zack asked. Hopper looked at him like he didn't understand the question.

"None. I never tried," he answered.

"*What?* Give it a shot, homes," Red Bike challenged him.

Hopper didn't like any of them. Maybe it was because of their being white and trying to sound black, or because they gave off a bad vibe. He had an innate feel for the hearts of people, and these guys ... well, they seemed like punks to him. But he couldn't just drive off, not now.

"Can you keep an eye on the milk?" he asked.

The four friends traded smirks. Zack nodded and took the bag from him. "I'll bet each of you dickwads a candy blunt my man here can do two."

The three looked at each other. Hopper saw it on their faces: It would be the easiest bet they ever made. He pedaled to the front edge of the first block. Each block was staked into the asphalt with rusted rebar. He studied the width, height and length of it: less than seven inches wide, six inches high, and six feet long. There were fifteen total. Nine to the corner and another six down the side street that veered off Whittier, forming an L design. There was a foot between each block, but because it took about three hops to do one, jumping *one* looked challenging enough.

An Indian man slowed down to watch. His son sat in the passenger seat of the Jaguar. When the young boy's dark eyes met Hopper's, the kid slumped down so he couldn't be seen, but Hopper looked past the top of his head into the stare of the father.

Hopper made a forward move and got up on the front tire. It was easier than he thought. He hopped on it a second before falling off. The three white kids raised their eyes; they didn't think he'd get that far. Hopper got back on his bike. He looked at Zack. The kid's dark hair was messy, as if he woke up and that's the way it stayed all day.

"You can do at least *two,* man. Robitussin and weed—mmm, *dee-lishus!*" Zack said, referring to the marijuana-laced cigars dipped in cough syrup he'd wagered.

Hopper positioned himself again and got back on the front tire. This time he concentrated on one spot just over the edge of the knobby, black rubber—a floating area the size of a dime—that he could lose himself in. He jerked the back tire up; keeping his bike at the same angle he'd seen Zack hold his at, like being on a big pogo stick. It was fun actually. He never would've thought to use the bike for anything more than getting from point A to point B, but this felt so different, like flying must feel. He took the first three blocks effortlessly. Didn't even acknowledge the white boys howling at him. Just looked at that floating dime and kept hopping. He jumped four to five to six to seven.

Seven—*hop, hop, hop*—to eight.

Eight—*hop, hop, hop*—to nine. Number nine made him pause. He balanced there like a Wallenda, scheming out how to make the turn down the side street. He realized he'd done nearly five times what was expected of him, and if this was some kind of initiation, he'd easily survived.

"Never tried it *my ass!*" Red Bike yelled.

Hopper attacked the next six blocks and did them no problem. He landed, absolutely exhilarated.

"My man *Hopper!* That was some shit, motherfucker!" Zack said. The white kids rode over, patted his back. Even Red Bike tapped him five. It embarrassed him—a little.

That was three years ago when the bike still fit. He had *become* Hopper. The punks and drug dealers, loitering meth addicts, bums hauling smelly bags of returnable bottles and cans to Naji's—they'd walk by and be all, "Hopper man, you still doing *that?*" But he could do other tricks, too, many that the white kids had never seen. Because he made them up on the fly. Weird twists and jumps, moves that would give Dominique Dawes trouble. Truth was, he still loved hopping the most.

Hopper was the only biker left, anyway. George had chased off the rest, and barely tolerated him. The white kids stopped coming around. The neighbor-hood got darker and the rich boys stood out, easy marks for anyone who needed a quick shakedown to fix on their drug of choice. Then there were those who just liked "rolling a whitey" for shits and grins.

Hopper did see Zack once more. It was on a Saturday night. He was jump-ing the blocks when a black Mercedes pulled into the parking lot. A sticker on the window read, *Lochmoor CC-Member.* Hopper didn't recognize Zack at first; he'd shorn the messy hair and now looked like an Abercrombie & Fitch model.

"Still riding that old Diamondback?" Zack said as he got out.

Hopper stared at him, then nodded. He studied the car's black paint and it looked ten inches deep. A blonde girl got out from the passenger side. When she did, her sweater rode up a little and he saw a black silk thong strap form a whale tail across the alabaster skin of her hips. She had dents in the small of her back and a tattoo of some tribal design, and he wondered why the hell she'd want to mess up that perfection. She was beautiful in a way he'd never seen close up. Her face looked like it was lit from within, and her eyes were clear green, with whites that seemed made of china. He suddenly felt very small and wished he could shrink into the seat of his bike or meld into its worn frame.

"Bike still works so, you know how I roll … 'sup? You all right?" he asked.

"Chillin' like Bob Dylan. This is Elise," Zack said. The girl grinned at him showing no teeth. She flipped her hair, letting it fan across her cheeks. She seemed bored.

Zack puffed his chest and put his hand on her waist, letting it ride under the thong over the bare skin of her ass. Hopper imagined what kinds of things Zack made her do. He nodded hello to her.

"My man Hopper's the best trickster in the three-one-three, El," Zack said.

Elise said nothing, but now showed her teeth. They were perfect; straight and white as sticks of chalk. Zack shook his head at him.

"Thought you'd be famous by now, Hops."

Hopper turned his jaw like trying to check his chin in the mirror. His face was hot.

"Famous. Famous for what?" he asked, genuinely wondering the answer.

"C'mon … the *bike,* homes," Zack said. Hopper stared at the car's enormity.

"Ain't seen you riding in a whole long time."

Zack *tsked* at him. "Gave it up; on to better things." He pulled Elise closer. "Hey man, we better jet, see if George will sell me a pint of schnapps. Great see-ing you, Hops," he held his fist out. Hopper tapped it.

Zack shook his head, "Famous for what … *shiiiitttt.*"

Hopper watched them walk into Naji's. He saw something in the car; his reflection—fish-eyed in the bowed fender—looking fat and aged. He lurched up, pedaling away as fast as his legs would pump, thankful Zack hadn't asked him to do any tricks for Elise. He crossed the street and rode, hopping from side-to-side, alternating in a pogo-stick motion between the front and back tires. He hopped ten sidewalk squares in a row.

Then his tire went flat.

Al Fortuna stopped taking credit cards. Cash only. No checks either. Bloom-Fortuna Bikes 'n' More had been his since he bought the shop from Sherman Bloom in 1983. He got the building and all the equipment—machinery for fixing tires and derailleurs, air pressure tanks, and tools—all for about what he paid for his first house. He carried all the big brands, even Cannondale. Business was flat, but he'd been burned one too many times by check kiters and folks with lousy credit, so he said screw it. Cash is king. With the building paid off, he didn't care if he was busy or not. He had one foot in his condo in Naples. He was seventy-two, and any day was ready to flip the place to either Starbucks or Caribou, whoever made him the best offer. He could practically *smell* the ocean.

He watched Hopper wheeling his bike on the sidewalk. He always liked the kid. The kid was polite. Not one of those smart-mouths. Never used bad language. Nothing but "Hello, Mr. Fortuna," or "Thank you, Mr. Fortuna." Al liked that sort of thing. The boy looked like he stuck to himself most of the time, because Al never saw him with any friends. Not even a girlfriend. But everybody knew him. You could always find him at Naji's parking lot hopping around on that old bike of his.

He saw Hopper's eyes between the spokes of the new Cannondales, staring through the front window. The kid's face was interesting. His eyes slanted up a little and were large, inviting. He wore his hair in a tangle of short, stubby dread-locks, and his skin was as brown as a Hershey's label. The kid was looking at the bike he always looked at, a Cannondale—the Chase 2—the best bike he sold. Al got them for a G-note and was able to mark them up to $2,100. Two thousand, for a *bike!* He'd sold two since January, both to an Indian surgeon from U of M who bought a pair of red ones for his twin daughters. Al tried to talk him into mountain bikes—some Treks—but the girls wanted the Cannondales. Who was Al to tell the doctor it was too much bike for his little princesses? He guessed the girls would soon graduate to matching Ferraris, anyway.

The bells chimed at the door, and Hopper wheeled his bike into the store. Al waited for him at the counter, hearing the *thwop, thwop, thwop* of the blown front tube.

"Hey, Mr. Fortuna. Lost me a tire."

"Levan, I wonder how." He smiled at the kid. "Let's look … "

They wheeled the bike around the counter and put it up on the rack. Al tightened the brace onto the main frame. He ran his fingers over the bumpy paint where Hopper's mom had touched it up. The tires were balding, and he could see cloth threads on the sidewalls where the rubber was cracking. The kid had come in the last two years for spoke replacement and tightening. Al liked seeing him.

"Don't see any nails … no glass … you've rubbed these down to the radials."

Hopper put his hands in his back pockets. He licked at his lip and ran his tongue over his upper teeth.

"Guess I ran out of time. Can you throw a fix on it?"

It was nine bucks to fix a flat. Rears cost fifteen dollars because of all the monkeying you had to do with the derailleur. New tires were as much as fifty-five each, but that included mounting.

"You're not thinking I can patch this, are you?"

"Well, actually, yeah. I think it could hold. Do you?"

Al watched him, the way his eyes drifted toward that Cannondale, as if it were a siren calling out to him. Al's friends had warned him about letting the "colored" kids get too familiar with his store, casing the joint for alarms or distracting him so they could leave a window open, but he didn't believe any of that crap. They hadn't met *this* kid.

Al snapped his fingers. "Hey, had a guy dump an order on me last week—supposed to pick up a set of tires for his kid—same as these. SOB stuck me, believe that?"

"I can't really afford a new tire Mr. Fortuna … "

"Two tires."

"Can't afford one, two'd be twice as unaffordable."

That made Al laugh pretty good. Hopper thought he said something wrong, but when he saw the store owner's eyes were crinkled, he knew it was cool.

"Can't send them back either … tell you what. I'll put two new skins on for what I would have charged you for fixing the flat. How does that sound?"

Hopper swallowed. He looked around the store with its stacks of tires, many the same as his. He shifted his feet, staring at his shoes a moment.

"That's really nice Mr. Fortuna, but … well, why you wanna go and do that for me?"

Al put his hands down. "Because I do, OK? Sometimes, you have to let people who *want* to do something for you … just *do it*." He smiled, "Take about fifteen minutes. Look around a bit. Go 'head. Maybe you'll see a bike you like, one more your size?"

Hopper rubbed at his eyes, wondering if the old man was messing with him. He glanced toward the front of the store, at the Cannondales.

"OK. Thanks, Mr. Fortuna. Guess I will." He never understood how some white people could be so nice to him whereas others looked away or ignored his presence completely. Mr. Fortuna always treated him like any other kid that came in the store. He wondered if he was a widower, or if he had any children.

Hopper loved being in the bike shop. He inhaled, letting the aroma of new rubber and lubricants settle in. The floor felt gritty beneath his shoes and he slid a little with each step. It was old clay tile, just like in his grade school—dark brown with flecks of blue, yellow, and pink. He missed that school. Back then, he still liked going.

The Chase 2 was so sweet he could barely look at it. The difference between his Diamondback and this one would be apparent even to his grandmother, if she were still around. The main bar had an aerodynamic slope to it and the weld seams were invisible. It was jet black and it looked like a weapon more than anything else. He looked behind at the counter before letting himself touch any part of it. It smelled of new rubber. The sidewalls were the color of putty and the little nubs stuck out from the tires like blades of black grass. Running his hand over them, he smiled as they tickled his fingertips. He saw himself on it, straddling the frame at the top of a ramp, competing in the X Games. Maybe he'd have to travel to cities like San Diego or Miami, somewhere that was always warm.

"You're Hopper. All you *ever* gonna be is just Hopper," he heard himself say quietly, and it tingled his scalp. He tensed as he felt Mr. Fortuna behind him.

"She's ready for you," Al said, wheeling up Hopper's old bike. "Nice piece of equipment isn't she?" Hopper relaxed; relieved the man hadn't heard him talking to himself.

"Yessir," he gazed at the shiny black bike, "she's one bad wammer jammer."

Al chuckled, rubbing his neck with a bandanna then wiped at his forehead.

"Take a look," Al said. Levan touched his tires and smiled. He ran his fingers across the little nubs. "Let's call it an even nine bucks."

Hopper shrugged, acceptingly. He took out his wallet, an orange nylon job he'd won from a claw machine at Meijer. In it were three wilted fives and several ones. He knew an incredible deal had just dropped from the sky and felt guilty counting out the nine bucks, but Mr. Fortuna didn't seem to mind. Al looked away until the kid was ready before taking it from him.

"Thanks, Mr. Fortuna. Almost look like a brand-new bike, don't it?"

"Sure does. C'mon, let's get you a receipt."

At the counter, Al carefully inscribed the receipt with an ink pen, noting the model numbers on the tires, going so far as to look them up in a catalog. Hopper glanced up at the rafters, intoxicated by the huge inventory; bikes hanging from their back rims on metal hooks. He tried to estimate what they were all worth.

"Ever think about upgrading?" Al asked, taking his time with the receipt.

Hopper's eyebrows arched, as if pulled upward by fishing line.

"Huh? Oh, I don't know. Thinking if I can save me some money, I'd maybe try to get me another D-Back in a year or so. Saw a picture of one … the Joker, it's called."

Al stuck his lower lip out and sniffed.

"Joker. Good bike, *nice* bike. I can get it … not really the best choice for a guy your size. What about that one you were looking at? By the front window. Bike like that last you a lifetime … that black one?"

Hopper laughed, "Oh man, I can't even think about the *Chase*. That's a Cannondale. For rich people, Mr. Fortuna."

Al looked at the kid. His store was twelve blocks from Naji's Detroit location, but it may as well have been in Sweden for as different as the residents were. The corner that separated Whittier from Torrey Lake Road—the street Al's store resided on in the City of Grosse Pointe—was the dividing line where thugs from Detroit didn't cross. It wasn't coincidence that Naji's sold phones, gadgets—and cashed checks, too. George knew his clientele very well. The parking lot was a great place for narcs to stake out and make easy collars on drug buys. This kid was different, though. Al felt it.

"Can I ask you something?" Al asked. Hopper nodded. "Don't take this the wrong way now, but why do you hang out at that party store? There's nothing but trouble for you there."

Hopper thought about how many times he'd hopped those parking blocks to meditate, to work out the anger or hurt, feeling it dissipate into the air like a spring shower. Or to celebrate fleeting happiness when he occasionally dared to dream big.

"They got them parking blocks there. I hop on them."

Al put the pen down and sighed. He kept the top copy of the receipt and handed Hopper the pink and yellow carbon. He removed his Ben Franklin reading glasses.

"You planning on going to college at all?"

"Nah, I ain't really feeling that, Mr. Fortuna."

Al tipped his head down.

"How are you going to live? Levan, you can't just *hop* your way through life." He saw the hurt in the kid's face and felt bad, immediately knowing he overstepped his bounds trying to counsel the boy. "What I mean is, you have to do *something*. For work. What is it that you like to do?"

Hopper swallowed and held the air in his lungs. Part of him wanted to grab Mr. Fortuna by the shirt and shake him, ask him, *What the hell you know about what I got to or not got to do?* But he knew the old man was trying, reaching out.

"I like being on wheels. I'm really good at it. I'm the best I ever seen and that's not me glossin' myself, that's the truth Mr. Fortuna … I just like hopping."

Al grimaced like a frog and shrugged, throwing up one hand.

"Thanks for the tires. Was real nice of you." Hopper started to wheel his bike out the door, staring at the brown tile, wondering how so much dust could get on a floor so quickly.

"Hey," Al walked briskly around the counter and past the helmets and weird recumbent bikes to hold the door open for him. Hopper wheeled it out and jumped on as easily as sitting in a chair. "Almost ashamed to admit it, I get those Cannondales for a lot less than you'd believe. You like the black one, don't you?" Hopper lowered his eyes. "C'mon, you know how much Windex I went through this year from you sticking your nose on my window? When you're ready, come see me."

He looked at the man. Why was he messing with him like this? He just told him he didn't even have enough money to buy two tires, let alone a Joker, so how the hell was he going to afford that sleek, black rocket—discount or not?

"Man, Mr. Fortuna, I ain't ever gonna get that kind of coin … "

"Don't sell yourself short. What do I know? Maybe anyone who can do the kind of things I seen you do on a bicycle … " Hopper looked at him and turned bashful. "What, you think I never drive by that way? I lock my doors if my travels take me through that neighborhood, but I've seen you. Watched you hopping in that lot, seen you riding those wheelies and spinning those handlebars like a gyroscope. Used to be kids rode a bicycle on *two* wheels. My father told me, when I was a kid, he said, '*Alan, the secret is to find a job you love. That way, work will become your passion, not your job.*' We'll figure something out, maybe like a payment plan. When you're ready."

Hopper swallowed down the pit of hope growing in his belly. It tasted like a tablet of bile scraping his throat muscles, trying to cut its way out from the inside.

He stood on the pedals. "Thanks for the tires, Mr. Fortuna. You're all right."

"Sure." Al watched the kid balance there a second, then Hopper jerked the back end off the ground, stopping the rear tire at a comfortable angle; watched as he tested the cushion of new rubber. He hopped away from the storefront. Al saw him allow himself a last look at the Chase 2 before walking his old blue bike—front tire to back—zigzagging all over the sidewalk like a drunken spider crab. *Maybe I should've been more forceful with the offer*, he thought. He went back into the store and stared at the Cannondale.

Hopper pulled up to the house and saw his mother standing on the porch. He was excited to show her the new rubber. The home was looking tired. Maybe he'd throw some paint on the trim. It wasn't as bad as the others on his block. Those houses, bungalows mostly, were overrun with weeds and drab siding that streaked the brick foundations white, looking as if pigeons with diarrhea had crapped on them. He said "yo Mama" to his mother. Fiona Chatman stood still, staring down the road with her hands braced on the railing.

"Hey, Mom. Check what Mr. Fortuna put on for me. New skins ... " She didn't answer. Just kept looking down the road, so intently he found himself looking, too.

"He gone. No trace. Just up and just ... he took it all ... "

Now he saw her eyes; they were beaten, running black with mascara. She still wouldn't look at him. He'd never trusted Suggs and never liked him and she knew that. Hopper looked at the cracked driveway.

"Mom, where's your car?" She turned and cried without making any noise and Hopper watched the image of himself riding that new black Cannondale pedal itself out of his mind. "Sorry, Mama." He stood on the pedals, rocking back and forth, feet steady, balanced perfectly. There was turbid air between them, and it started to choke him. "I'm gonna practice. Need anything from Naji's?"

That made her laugh.

"What's funny?"

"Just thinking; save a lotta money on chocolate milk ... " Her face twisted up on that and she slumped down. He let the bike fall and walked up the stairs. Standing in front of her, she finally looked at him, then hugged his midsection, sobbing into his stomach. He felt awkward but placed his arms around her shoulders and bent at the waist to hold her awhile.

The air turned cold. He jerked his body up and held the rear tire high in the air. The bumpers of two cars hung over the blocks, so he waited for them to leave. Two crackheads—wiry, hollow-eyed men with grey skin—hugged themselves as they watched him hopping. He could smell them. They whispered to each other, clapping at him occasionally.

"Hopper, how come you ain't out getting laid, man?" one of them said. "If I looked like you I'd be gettin' some *strange* trim to treat me all nice. Some *snazzy* trim." He ignored them.

It was getting dark out. He was considering trying something he had imagined once but dismissed for the high probability of it being physically impossible. He wanted to ramp the bike up the wall of Naji's in an arc and touch the light at the top. It was twelve feet at least, and there wasn't enough room for a speedy start, but his legs were so strong he thought he may be able to resist gravity long enough to pull it off.

A red Econoline pulled into the parking lot. The two addicts seemed to recognize something hinky, because one said, "Hopper you better roll home *now!*" as they vanished into the alley. Two men got out of the van and walked briskly toward the party store. From behind, Hopper saw them pulling their collars up high.

He wouldn't have noticed them at all except their van blocked his way, right in front of the wall. The van's motor was still running.

As urgently as they walked in, he figured they'd be right out, so he hopped the blocks to pass the time. The blocks were clear now. He concentrated on the spot above the front tire, and after he'd done the circuit twice, he decided to see if the men might move the van anytime soon.

A Middle Eastern rapper covering an Eminem song played louder than normal from the speakers. The television snowed static. Hopper looked first at the dairy cooler, then the ones filled with pop that ran the length of the store. He peeked behind the empty counter.

"Hello?" he called out, aware of the hollowness his voice emitted in the store. Then he noticed something wasn't right; all the mobile phones were gone from the cases. He looked behind the long counter where the rows of alcohol were displayed, past the hanging ribbons of scratch-off tickets and saw the cash register drawer open and emptied. Then he looked to the very back of the store. Through the glass of the cooler where the high-end beer was stored, between cases of Heineken, Bells and Samuel Adams, he thought he saw movement. It was just a sliver, a small rectangle of flesh, the contrast of blue-black hair and tan skin through the glass.

George's cell phone was by the register, next to a flattened-out Kool carton. The phone was a really nice flip-type, the kind Hopper would buy for himself if he had that kind of money. He went behind the counter and picked it up. A green light on it blinked. He looked at the green letters of the Kool carton. Green means *go*, he thought.

George Rashid sat on a case of Heineken, two purple knots sprouting from the corners of his forehead like a satyr's horns. A trap door at his feet was open, and there was a metal safe just below the surface of a space in the hardwood floor. He squinted at his two tormentors through puffy slits. The one holding the gun was a skinny meth head. He was wired up tight, looking around the large cooler with scared eyes. He had pink skin, various parts of which were pierced with silver studs and loops. His orange hair was coiled like a scouring pad. The other man was Samir Rashid. He was big: six foot and sturdy, his goatee braided into three little ropes. He moved shiftily in the expansive space—part boxer, part ballroom dancer—gliding in a circle around George with a kind of goofy grace. He couldn't sit still.

"Georgey, no, no, no more playing now. Open it and give it. Then we're done."

"Let's just fly with what we got. He's not opening, man," the one holding the gun said. Samir looked at the guy—his name was Jake but he went by Frizz—and in a moment of semi-clarity, Samir slid across the floor, shadowboxing with punches that ripped the air.

He put an arm on Frizz's skinny neck and cocked his head, "You'll get your taste. Open it little brother. Open, open, open. Very sly, very sly, my lil' bro can be—changing the combination. He will give it up, though. Isn't that right, Georgey?"

"Now you rob me *this* way?" George said. "Always taking—all you've ever done to me. My big brother, my *akhuna!*" he spat at Samir's feet. "What would Pappy have said?"

Samir jumped at him with a punch that rocked his brother's jaw backward. He came across with another to the nose, exploding George's face down the middle. Blood poured freely from his nostrils. Samir flung his hand back and forth, stretching the sting from his fingers. He grabbed George by the back of the hair, yanking his head back.

"Oh baby! Oh *bay-bee*—that one was out of the park!" Samir barked.

"Come on, man. I didn't sign up for this," Frizz said.

"Open the safe or I swear my brother—*my akhuna*—on Pappy's grave— our dearly departed *baba,* who banged those *abeed* whores every Saturday night, making a fool of our mother—oh, he never told you about that? Open it now or I swear it's only going to get worse for you."

George spit blood, gagging on it. His face was marbled up with bruises, parts of it looking like port wine cheese. A metallic sliding sound *click-clicked* in the cooler. Samir—his hand still pulling George's hair—turned to it, as if someone had tapped him on the shoulder. Frizz wasn't as calm. He spun toward the sound, pointing the pistol, a scratched up Glock, the handle wrapped with duct tape.

Hopper had the shotgun pointed at Frizz's chest. He was standing in the doorway, having walked behind the long counter and slipped quietly inside, undetected. George thought he was dreaming upon seeing the kid. Samir took a moment, sized things up, and then laughed, like he'd just gotten the punch line to some cosmic joke.

"Who the *hell* is this? *Hello!* It's the little *abeed* on the bike. You don't want any of me, little monkey boy. Hop away home now, little sheeny. Go on—hop, hop."

"Let Mr. Rashid up," Hopper said, his eyes darting from Samir to Frizz. The shotgun shook in his hand. Frizz looked at Samir for a next move. His gun shook, too.

"Little brother, your guardian angel is a *spook?*" Samir wiped his nose. He was sniffing, detached now, as if performing a one-man play. He let go of George's hair.

"Samster, let's get out of this," Frizz said, the gun still shaking at Levan.

Samir looked at Hopper. "Little monkey, it's up to you. I know that gun; Pappy's Browning—he used to shoot sporting clays in Metamora. There's a plug in it, so if it's even loaded, it only has two shots in it. So now what, *abeed*?"

Hopper kept his eye on Frizz since he was his immediate concern. He stared down the barrel of the shotgun. He had already decided he would pull the trigger if he had to, and from what he'd seen in the movies, he'd have to quickly pump the stock to eject the spent shell. How did it come to this and what the hell was his mother going to think?

"I got nothing to lose, homes. Not a thing," Hopper told Frizz. "I ain't playin'. Drop it, OK?" He hoped it sounded sincere.

"Levan. Walk away from this … " George said quietly. Hopper glanced at him, surprised George knew him at all, much less his name. Strangely, it calmed his nerves.

"Don't do it, Frizz!" Samir yelled, "He's all blow. Cap the little shit."

Frizz looked at Samir, his eyes shifting from him to Hopper and down to the floor where the bag of cash and phones lay. His body wavered, twitching like an epileptic. Finally, the pistol went slack, spinning around his index finger. It dropped to the floor. George exhaled and slung his head.

"Now kick it," Hopper pointed, "this way." Samir bit his lip and clucked his tongue, squatting on his knees as Frizz punted the Glock across the floor to Hopper.

"Didn't sign up for this," Frizz muttered. He leaned against the wall and reached into a case of Michelob. He unscrewed one and chugged the bottle in two swallows.

Hopper knelt and put George's phone on the floor, sliding it to him. It stopped, resting against the trapdoor that concealed the safe. George smiled and started to laugh a little.

"Lady said about five minutes," Hopper said.

It happened quicker than that.

"Police. Drop the weapon. *Now!*" A voice boomed from just outside the cooler.

"Help! This shine's trying to kill us! Shoot him officer!" Samir yelled.

Hopper squinted at Samir. Frizz raised his hands and the bottle dropped, landing on the wood floor with a hollow thud, where it continued to spin.

"It's not the kid!" George screamed. "Don't shoot the kid. Don't shoot!" He got up and lunged at Samir with his shoulder, knocking his brother to the floor.

Everything slowed down right then. Hopper knew enough that it was all out of his hands now. He thought of his mother not having him around and all the things she'd lost in her life. A glimpse of what might have been poked its head in and he watched himself on television, on some obstacle course, hopping over all kinds of stuff, being interviewed. Maybe it was silly, but it was *his* life flashing before his eyes. He was on that black Cannondale Mr. Fortuna sold him for a nice discount. Presently, as Samir and George fought, he couldn't really hear anything except the droning knock of the Freon condensers mounted above the door. He remembered telling the female dispatcher when he called that he would be the young black kid with a shotgun.

Now he wondered if the lady had passed that information on to the police.

Al Fortuna hadn't seen Hopper since the whole thing went down. A month had passed, and the kid hadn't returned. He had been all over the news, interviewed by every station in town. Al read about it in the papers and followed the story closely. There was a picture of George handing Hopper a check. Mug shots of Frizz and Samir accompanied the articles, detailing the meth debts Samir had racked up and the robberies he'd committed.

Frizz rolled over on Samir to get his case pled down to a weapons charge. As a star witness for the prosecution, Frizz told them Samir had one other piece of "serious shit" on his resume they would be interested in.

Al smiled watching Fiona Chatman tell a reporter how proud she was of her son, her *"Sweet Potato Pie,"* she'd called him. The kid stood next to her, the whole time looking down, his large eyes not giving the viewers the satisfaction of seeing his pride; that it was *him* who'd given her something to smile about again. There were follow-up articles, like the town couldn't get enough of the kid. Al's favorite showed a picture of Fiona—tearful, her hand partially covering her face—posing with the CEO of a local medical supply firm who hired her with full benefits. The Detroit Chief of Police cited Hopper for his bravery.

Like Al told his friends; you never met *this* kid.

Al drove on Torrey Lake Road until he got to Whittier. Waiting at the light to turn left, he watched the clean street change into a littered highway where Grosse Pointe became Detroit. He waited, determined he would stick to his promise. Al Fortuna believed things happened for a reason; what was meant to be was meant to be. The Cannondale Chase 2 was in the back of the van. The tires were wet with Armor-all, and he'd lubed the sprockets and adjusted the derailleur, checked the gears—made sure everything was *just* right. Even brought along a matching helmet: wishful thinking probably. And still he promised—he would not stop unless he saw the kid *hopping*.

As he made the turn onto Whittier, he instinctively locked his doors. Packs of black kids walked around, roving groups of four and five. He passed a White Castle and a wig shop and, approaching Chandler Park Drive, got ahead of himself and looked, seeing Naji's parking lot. The kid was hopping the cement parking blocks all right—the back tire of his too-small bike set at that crazy, impossible angle. And it made Al laugh.

It was rush hour. Al waited, finally turning down the side street, parking adjacent to the lot. He stopped and watched. Hopper hadn't seen him, didn't notice anything near as Al could tell. The kid was focusing, hopping the concrete blocks like a gymnast working rows of balance beams. He kept the windows up and left the van running. George Rashid stood near the front of the store along with some young black kids, all watching Hopper, the kids deifying him like a local celebrity that had come home to the neighborhood.

A stunning black girl was there, too, maybe eighteen or so. She was straddling a moped. She looked like a girl Al had seen in one of those music videos.

A couple of the kids pointed at the wall of the store. They were shouting at him to do something. He looked at the girl and raised his chin at her. She shook her head no, putting her hands up, pleading. George pointed at the wall, too, as if in disbelief. He was smiling and laughing, waving his hands negatively. Hopper grinned at all of them with a *you-dare-me-to?* smile. Then he drove around the side of the lot, right past Al's van and pedaled as fast as he could. He aimed his bike at the wall. Al watched and held his breath.

Hopper made a looping turn off the sidewalk and started angling at the wall with powerful speed. He pulled the handlebars up like a jet pilot, letting the front tire ramp the wall on edge, cresting at the third row of cinder blocks. The bike rode a graceful arc—ten feet up—nearly to the top of the wall; Hopper was now practically parallel to the asphalt. When he neared the apex, he reached up and ticked the light at the top with his left hand. He rode down, completing a crescent-shaped path. The kids cheered, and the girl took her hands from her eyes and clapped, ran up to him and hugged him, kissing his face over and over. George rotated his index finger next to his ear at the kid. He started to walk back into the store but stopped, just for a moment. Then he laughed and went inside.

Al looked closely at the tires on the kid's blue bike. He watched as Hopper balanced on the cement parking block nearest the girl. Watched him as he bounced, inching forward down the length of it. Watched Hopper *hop, hop, hop*—hopping in a line down those remaining eight blocks, heading right toward him—and he saw the big smile on the kid's face, focusing over his front tire.

So Al Fortuna made a *new* promise; if the kid made eye contact with him—right now—*then* he'd get out and give him the bike. But Hopper never looked up, focusing on a spot—one only he could see—floating somewhere in front of him.

Al put the van in drive and proceeded down the side street. He kept an eye on Hopper; saw his silhouette getting smaller in the rearview mirror—still hopping. The kid's tires had looked like they were holding up pretty good. The new bike would be waiting for him, whenever he was ready to come back in.

Leaving Copper Corner

At Northern Michigan University in Marquette, nearly 500 miles from his Detroit home, Richie looked to make friends among the Upper Peninsula denizens who went home every weekend to nearby towns like Lantz, Munising, and Baraga. He walked by the study room in his dorm, hearing the Yoopers prattle on about nailing the last of the salmon that were running. They peppered their boasts with "dontcha knows" and "you betchas." He poked his head in. One guy, a freshman like Richie, noticed him.

"How's it going, eh?"

Richie nodded and walked in. It was the second week of school, and he was just trying to blend in. He watched the students getting their fishing tackle in order. As an artist, he was attracted to the lures; colorful spoons with airbrushed, lacquered-on finishes and nasty treble hooks attached to them lay scattered on tables. That's what started a life of fascination and frustration with fishing. Fishing led him to realize that if you don't pay attention, you could end up thinking the idea of fishing is merely to *catch fish*.

Richie bartered for a rod and reel with a guy down the hall for a painting of a wood duck he had done. He had no idea how to use it, of course. Growing up on Detroit's East Side in Copper Corner, he was ill-prepared to pursue salmon, or any species for that matter. He was a piss-poor fisherman living amongst born Master Anglers. And while his first year at NMU gave him a greater appreciation for the pursuit of fish and game, he learned quickly that living in God's Country alone didn't guarantee instant woodsman status. The Yoopers weren't fooled by the inept ways he handled his yellow Eagle rod and cumbersome Zebco reel. They only put up with him because he tried hard.

In that early fall of 1980, the salmon were at the end of their run, though some were still coming into Lake Superior near the breakwalls at Presque Isle and other inlets. The stronger fish—that is, the ones that didn't look like swimming death—were few, but pods of healthy fish, mostly cohos and kings, and even steelhead could still be caught. Richie's first sight of the game fish was seeing two students walking side-by-side holding a big tree limb between them, threaded through the gills of two kings they'd pulled from the Dead River. The tails dragged on the sidewalk three feet below, causing the limb to bounce as they walked. Glittering sunlight danced on the cheeks of the dead kings, the biggest fish Richie had ever seen. The image seemed primordial. He wanted to carry such a fish in the worst way; however, his fishing experience was limited to catching bluegills using earthworms and a bobber.

One big Yooper Richie became friends with—he once watched him eat forty pancakes at a sitting—was Andy Burley. Andy hailed from Kingsford and played right tackle for the NMU Wildcats. Inside Andy's dorm room, he schooled Richie on the machinations of his newly acquired angling equipment. Andy's own tackle was arranged on his desk. Richie lifted a four-ounce lead sinker with a huge treble hook soldered on it.

"What the hell do you catch with this? Orcas?" Richie asked.

"Salmon. Snagging spoon. Thing works," Andy said, without looking at it. Old spoons—chipped up red and white Daredevils—lay about.

He threaded the line from Richie's reel through a brass snap swivel and showed him how to tie a surgeon's knot. "What test is this?" Andy asked, holding the gossamer thread between his thick thumb and forefinger.

"Hell if I know. *Clear,* maybe?" Richie replied.

Andy threw him a look and studied the monofilament. His lips puckered and he continued taking him through the knot steps. After nine tries Richie got it. Andy hooked the swivel into an eyelet. He examined the rod and ran a finger across the surface of the reel, turning it over and feeling its weight.

"Nice setup. Try not to break it, eh?"

Richie looked at the striped spoon with the sly, smiling devil portrait stamped on the white stripe. It looked nothing like a worm.

"Is a salmon really going to hit this?"

"You piss them off enough, they'll hit anything. Besides, all you want to do is cast across the river and drag it back. Call that *'straight lining.'* " Andy made quotes in the air with his fingers when he said it. "Most times you'll snag 'em in the tail or the fin. When you feel a bump, pull as hard as you can and hold onto your dick."

"That's really not *fishing* then, is it? Aren't they supposed to *bite it?*"

"They're all going to die anyway. Fucking DNR, they're always getting their noses into shit where it don't belong. Reminds me, I want to check your drag." Andy fiddled with a knob, pulling line from the spool. He repeated the process, reeling in slack each time before turning the knob incrementally. "There, perfect."

"Yeah, that's better," Richie said.

Andy smirked at him. "So when are you going to try it out, Ishmael?"

"Tomorrow. Around seven thirty-ish. Want to come with?" Richie asked.

"Got Economics. How the hell are you able to go so early without skipping?"

"I'm an art major, remember? All my classes don't start until ten."

"Art major. Jeez Louise."

"Hey, it's not all drawing naked chicks, you know."

"You get to see *naked* girls? Lucky fucker."

Fishing alone actually suited Richie. Alone, no one could bear witness to his awful technique. A main branch of the Dead River was less than two miles from campus, and men often fished on either side of the cement bridge there.

Walking on Big Bay Road, he passed the Blue Link Party Store, his boots trudging through the ferns that framed the road. The wind, tipped with an Arctic chill, whispered in from Lake Superior, and the lighting was his favorite kind; saffron yellow with enough mist to let sunrays filter through in a diffused beauty. There were few homes between the Blue Link and the Dead River Bridge. The last one before the river was quaint, like a miniature log cabin with a roof of deep green shingles buried in pine needles. An old man leaned on his picket fence out front. Richie could see the steam from his coffee mug fifty yards away.

Richie's art box jingled as he walked, pencils mixing with the Daredevils Andy had given him. Being from Detroit, he found the friendliness of the Upper Peninsula's residents hard to get used to. Even things as mundane as asking directions became conversations. He could see his own breath as he neared the old man.

"Morning. Gonna do a little fishing, eh?" The old man spoke in the signature Yooper accent, a Scandanavian lilt latching onto the end of words and statements oftentimes taking on question form. He had a wisp of greying hair over a strong face and the most startlingly eyes—they were flashbulb blue—Richie had ever seen. The man was hunched over. Richie guessed his age at seventy-five. He had the look of a once powerful man. A tin of Copenhagen sat atop the fence post.

"Figured I'd give it a shot. Any left in the river?" Richie did not stop, choosing to continue on.

"Some kings still coming in. Saw a young fella with a coho yesterday, silver as a Mercury dime. Them's rare now, though. Should've been up here a month ago." The man worked his tongue. "Over at the school, eh?" He gave a little smile then leaned over to spit out a brown stream of tobacco juice before taking a sip of coffee.

"Yeah, first year. Got class so I have to hustle. Nice talking with you," Richie said, hurrying past. The man's expression didn't change. He smacked his lips.

"Good luck. Watch out for the DNR," he called out to Richie. "That a-hole, he hides in the woods sometimes, dontcha know?"

The old man's warning reminded Richie that while he did possess a fishing license, he hadn't ponied up the extra dough for a trout stamp. Back then you could still fish in salmon waters without one, but you were required to release any salmonids you might hook. He was really only going through the motions, with no reasonable expectations of catching a fish of any kind.

At the bridge, the Dead River had a moderate current depending on the output the power plant upstream was running. It was about fifty yards across there. The banks were rocky, and across the road a park was nestled in the deeper woods. Harlow Park was named after the lake in the center of it. Richie saw two men in waders making casts against the current, letting their lines drift before jerking their poles violently back. He leaned over the bridge and watched them a moment. During one of the older man's retrieves, a heavy lure flew from the water, similar to the chunk of lead Richie had seen in Andy's room.

They were hard-faced men who gave him dirty looks when he waved hello, emitting a territorial attitude. Richie found a spot downstream on the other side of the bridge. Standing at the river's edge, his Detroit neighborhood in Copper Corner seemed like a million miles away, and the boundary of his youth vaporized. Living outside the confines of his parent's home, he felt free to make his own adventures and mistakes.

He took a Daredevil out of the art box. It was covered in graphite dust. He brushed it off on his jeans and snapped it on. His finger went underneath the line, and he clicked the bail open, reaching back to make a long, smooth cast—just how Andy had instructed him. In his confident mind, Richie looked like he'd done it his whole life. On his follow through, he felt resistance and the pole flew from his hands into the river. He peeked behind to see the red and white spoon impaled into a low hanging alder branch.

"Dammit!" he said.

He felt his face go flush, and when he looked upstream between the open spaces of the bridge, the men dipped their heads and spoke to each other. He grabbed the loops of monofilament and walked downstream, relieved to see his pole hadn't gone in the drink. It was stuck in an eddy of boulders at the riverbank.

He gathered the loose monofilament hand-over-hand and traced his steps back to the lure. After he extracted the hooks from the limb, he reeled in the slack and walked the riverbank. Being more careful, he looked behind and made a much smoother, long flowing cast across the width of the river.

All the way across the river.

The Daredevil got lodged in a pile of rocks there, leaving him with a tight-rope of monofilament spanning a foot above the rushing water.

"Son of a bitch … " he muttered, peeking up at the wading fishermen. Their heads went down, bobbing into the collars of their coats like smug turtles. He exhaled and watched a pod of three silvery kings leap from the water like trained porpoises. He looked skyward. "What are you trying to do to me here?"

"Little snag, eh?" A crisp voice called from the woods.

Richie turned and saw a conservation officer in green uniform and hat. He seemed to appear from thin air.

"Mind showing me your fishing license?" the officer asked.

"Sure. Give me a second … " Richie replied, fumbling with the rod. He pulled, causing the tight line to hum. Finally he set it on the bank and it tugged toward the water.

"Quite a cast you made," the officer quipped.

Richie said nothing, resting his boot on the rod to keep it from going in. He removed his wallet and glanced up for the wading fishermen. They were gone.

"My partner's waiting for 'em," the officer said. "The older man snagged three kings and a brown trout. Not very big. Browns are native to these waters, and he knows that, see? That's why we don't like snagging. His buddy took two kings. His were submarines, twenty pounds each, eh? They threw them into the brush off the trail, but we saw the whole thing. Stubborn in their ways. They'll never learn."

Richie handed the officer his license.

"Will they get fined for it?"

The conservation officer laughed. "You're not from around here, are you?"

Richie shook his head. "No, Detroit."

The man's eyebrows rose. Richie read his silver nameplate: CO WALTER AHO. He reread the last name and laughed. Officer Walter Aho shot him a look.

"Something funny?" Officer Aho asked.

"Um, well, actually. Your name."

Officer Aho narrowed his eyes.

"No—it's just that, this older man I talked to warned me that an *Aho* from the DNR might be hiding, and—well, you know, *a-hole? A-hole, Aho.* They kind of sound … the same."

Aho's face flattened out. "Gee, to think it took a guy from Dee-troit city to come up with *that*? I never heard *that one* my whole *entire* life." The officer's jaw jutted forward, and just as quick, he relaxed. "That'd be old Knudsen. He's a kind old fellow." Officer Aho laughed a little when he said it and sighed. "Kind of funny I guess, seeing that you're not from around here … "

The officer's face tightened and he went back into business mode.

"Hell yes, it's *a fine*. Three bucks a pound. I'll fillet 'em up, drop 'em off over to Atwater's Mission on Front Street."

"They don't even get to keep them?" Richie asked as Officer Aho returned his license. He looked up in annoyance.

"Why should they?" He sounded as though his integrity had been questioned. "They know the rules just like *everyone else*. And you have no trout stamp, son."

"I couldn't afford it."

"Well, what are you fishing here for? These are salmon waters."

The officer had him there. Richie didn't say anything, the space filling with sounds of water and the breeze whistling through the cedars and alders.

"Maybe a smallmouth or a pike. A sucker or something," Richie said.

Officer Aho fixed a look at him. "Well, if you *happen* to catch a salmon or trout, release it. Without a stamp, you're not allowed to retain salmonids. And *anything* foul-hooked, release immediately."

"Foul hooked?" Richie asked.

"Fancy word for snagging. Fish not caught in the mouth."

Richie thought of Andy.

"Save up for a stamp. Might want to try Harlow Lake for bass. Deer Lake in Ishpeming's good for pike. I landed a forty-four-inch northern on a live frog there. It's hanging on the wall in my office. Ain't going to catch anything in these waters but salmon and steelies, so until you get a stamp, why bother?"

Richie stuffed his license into his pocket and watched Officer Aho disappear into the woods. He snapped his line, giving up on the Daredevil stuck on the other bank of the river. When he stepped on Big Bay Road, the two wading fishermen were by the patrol car, their poles leaning against it. Two big tackle boxes sat on the hood. The older man pled his case to Officer Aho while the other officer, a young, unsmiling block of human flesh, stared at the ground.

"You know what DNR means? *Damn Near Russian*, you betcha it does!"

Officer Aho rolled his eyes at the older man.

"I knew your father, Wally. He'd have been ashamed of you." The old man wagged an arthritic finger at him. The other fisherman played with his suspenders.

"I've given you three warnings, Mr. Tormondson. Three! It's just, well it's disrespectful."

As he passed the men, the younger fisherman snapped his suspenders and looked up. He didn't smile. The old fisherman saw Richie, too. He stayed on him with his little eyes. Richie so wanted to laugh but instead crossed the road to get to his Life Drawing class. He couldn't wait to show his sketches of naked women to Andy Burley.

His illustration teacher lent him the money, so Richie went to the sporting goods store and bought a trout stamp. The first thing he did upon returning to his dorm was visit the pay phone in the lobby. He opened the phone book and scanned the A's. He hadn't made it through three surnames when he hit the first "Aho."

"I'll be dipped!" Richie said. "The poor *bastards*."

The directory contained two pages full of Ahos, including Officer Walter, but it was the six Harrys that Richie felt sorriest for.

At 6:30 the next morning, he was secure in the comfort of the trout stamp in his pocket. He was the son of a Detroit cop, and the last thing he wanted was the wrath of Officer Aho on his ass. Aho. A-hole. It made him laugh as he walked. The weather had turned, and it was grey, a cooler day awaiting him. All the details went flat and a haze hung in the air from a light rain. Richie tightened his wool coat and continued down Big Bay Road. He saw the old man ahead.

"Up a bit earlier, eh?" the old man asked.

This time, Richie stopped.

"'Morning. Thought I'd try to give it another shot."

"Whatcha using?" The old man smiled and sipped his coffee. The rain pattered on the brim of his green wax-cloth hat.

Richie self-consciously held up the pole. "Daredevils."

"Naaaa," the old man frowned, spitting tobacco juice. "Wait here," he said. He ambled into his garage.

As Richie stared at the Copenhagen can on the fencepost, he wondered how many kids the old man had or what he did as a younger man. He turned and startled at the sight of a four-point buck walking across the road twenty yards away. In two leaps it disappeared into the dark woods.

The old man returned. "Try these," he said, and held out his hand.

"Did you see that? A deer—it was right *there*," Richie pointed.

"He visits our salt lick."

"We're only a *mile* from the school."

When his comment went unacknowledged, Richie looked into the man's palm. Aged fingers sifted through five lures, carved wooden folk art resembling dull orange minnows. The hooks were exceptionally small considering they had to land a fish as large as a salmon. An eyelet secured to the head of the minnow, attached to a small brad, was bored through the body of each lure. He held one up for Richie's inspection.

"My father made these. What you want to do is throw it out there, let it drift downstream, see? Put yourself parallel to the river, close to the bank so you got lots of room, dontcha know? If you latch onto one, don't horse him. Rod tip up. That's why that rod's eight feet, eh? Let the *rod* fight him."

"Thanks for the advice. Do these really work?"

"Unless them fish grew brains since I was younger," the old man said, suddenly exuding an erudite persona. "You're welcome to 'em."

Richie's face creased up. "I don't have any money, and based on my last attempt I can't guarantee I won't lose these ... are you sure? They were your father's."

"They can't catch fish hanging in my garage. Rather see 'em go to good use."

"That's really nice of you." Richie placed the lures in the art box. "I'm Richie by the way." He held his hand out and the old man shook it, the grip surprisingly firm.

"Leif Jon Knudsen." The old man pronounced it *Life Jahn Ka-NOOT-sen.*

"Man, that's a great name. Nice to talk to you, Mr. Knudsen."

"You, too. Maybe you'll bring me a fillet sometime."

"Only if I buy it in town at Thill's Fishery."

They both chuckled, and Richie waved goodbye.

He looked over his shoulder and watched the old man walk back to his house. He moved like older men who used to be athletes do when their bodies have given up on them.

Richie had been at the Dead for fifteen minutes when he got a solid hit on his fifth cast using the Knudsen Nailer (his name for it). As the lure submerged, an immediate jolt went through the line that made him think of Andy Burley's words: His hammer hadn't tingled like that since seventh grade, when the wind lifted Diana Licavelli's plaid skirt above her waist. The eight-foot yellow pole bent in half. The salmon made one majestic jump, looking like a two-foot-long chrome sculpture. The reel whined as the fish peeled off fifty yards of line.

"Holy shit, stay hooked," Richie muttered, just before the fish spit the lure.

"Oh, she was a nice coho, too!" Officer Aho said. "Getting the hang of things?"

"Yeah. New lures."

Officer Aho looked closely at the orange balsa minnow.

"Hey, this is a *good* one." He looked up, an eyebrow jumping. "Local, right?"

"Yeah ... " Richie stopped short of full disclosure. "Garage sale." He took his wallet out and showed the officer his license. "Check it out."

Officer Aho looked at the trout stamp affixed to it.

"Well lookee here; Mr. Dee-troit fisherman. Long as you don't get tempted to snag, we'll exchange nothing but pleasantries." Officer Aho smiled and vanished into the woods, no doubt in search of violators.

He never saw Officer Aho again. The CO was transferred to Ontonagon County for his own safety after six shots were fired into the old Airstream he slept in during weekend hunting trips.

Richie's fishing excursions lasted the rest of the late-season salmon run. And though he never did catch any fish that year, he became *really good* at looking capable of it. The days he walked to the Dead, his conversations with Knudsen revealed more of each man's past. Leif Jon had a way of speaking that was maudlin but authentic. Slowly their chats turned to family and career. Richie learned that Knudsen was an alternate for the U.S. bobsled team that won the gold at Lake Placid in 1932. That he had been a woodcutter for the U.S. Forest Service and built docks for the CCC in many of the surrounding lakes of the Superior National Forest. He had taught forestry at NMU, and later, a welding class. Leif Jon Knudsen had been married forty-three years to Heidi, a girl he fell in love with at a picnic for the families of the men who worked in the mines. They tried but weren't blessed with children. Heidi Knudsen never emerged from the cabin during Richie's freshman year. He saw the shade on the backdoor window move once, the only proof he had of her existence.

The day of his last visit, when both men knew the fish were gone, talk turned to Richie's father. Between sips of strong coffee, he told Knudsen his dad was a prosecutor's investigator for a county outside of Detroit, having retired from the Detroit Police Department. When the old man asked Richie what town he lived in, he answered the way any true Detroiter does, with a mix of pride and a little arrogance, knowing the tough reputation preceding their city.

"Detroit. They call my neighborhood Copper Corner. East Side."

"I've been to Copper *Harbor*, that's at the tip of the Keweenaw—"

"Copper *Corner*," Richie laughed. "Lots of policemen live there. *Cops?*"

"Ahhh, *Cop*-per *Corner*. Now I get it, dontcha know?"

"It's pretty safe. Used to be anyway, but it's getting bad around the edges. Drugs. Some blacks coming around—I mean, you know, the bad ones, breaking in for drug money and stuff to fence."

Knudsen stared vacuously at him. Richie looked away.

The old man picked a speck of Copenhagen from his tongue and squinted. His face sagged. His eyes squinted like he was letting a sneeze pass, or a migraine. He put a hand on Richie's shoulder.

"Can I ask you something?"

"Sure," Richie replied.

Knudsen took a breath. "Have you ever been to ... Bob-Lo?"

The question and the sincerity with which it was asked caught him so off guard that Richie nearly laughed.

"Bob-Lo *Island*?" he clucked. "Yeah, dozens of times. Why do you ask?"

The corners of Knudsen's eyes crinkled, and his mouth curled into a lipless smile. He squeezed Richie's arm and closed his eyes as if recalling a past lover.

The old man looked at him. "Is it as beautiful as they say?"

And as immature as Richie was at that time, he knew enough to not be flippant. It had been years since he'd visited Bob-Lo. The last time he was anywhere near it was the summer before. The amusement park was in decline, put up for sale in 1978, but an entrepreneur had refurbished the Bob-Lo boats and used them for midnight cruises. Richie joined his Detroit buddies on one such cruise. On a humid August night, they watched a friend blow his harp with a blues band. But standing next to Leif Jon Knudsen required a different memory of Bob-Lo Island. He remembered the excitement he felt in 1970, floating high above the Detroit River as his third-grade class headed there for a field trip. Thrilling amusement rides; eating snow cones and elephant ears; leaning over the top deck to dribble spit on the heads of kids below; all of it came rushing back. Here it was, now 1980, and this sweet old man was asking him about a place that had become infected with much of what was wrong with Detroit itself. As if by some sort of geographic osmosis, the neglect and indifference of keeping one's house in order had entered the Detroit River and spread onto the island.

Simply put, Bob-Lo had become kind of a shit hole.

"Yeah. It is. It's beautiful," Richie answered, keeping a straight face.

Knudsen nodded. "Always wanted to go there. Never did."

"To *Bob-Lo*? Really?" Richie cocked his head. "Why didn't you?"

"Heidi. We had plans to go to all kinds of fun places, but ... we'd been married two years when she didn't seem ... *right*. Kind of like walking 'round with the blues. Didn't start out that way. Allergies coming at weird times, crying for no reason. She'd miscarried twice. Still think that set it all off. She's never been below the bridge. Psychoso—what did the doctor call it ... *psycho*-something."

"Psycho*somatic*?" Richie offered.

"That's it. Poor thing. Hard life at times. She's never left the Upper. Something about that bridge. Get anywhere near it, she'd break down—nerves, hives, the crying. Farthest south I ever got her to was Blaney Park." Knudsen looked up and rubbed his chin. "Wait. That's not true. Made it to Brevort once, just north of St. Ignace. But the sight of that span, all the open water of The Straits ... ah well, least we've seen all the Upper," Knudsen said. "From Calumet to Copper Harbor ... " using his outstretched hand as a map, he pointed at parts of his palm and fingers, the thumb acting as the Keweenaw Peninsula, and continued giving

Richie a travelogue of the U.P. " ... Menominee to Christmas to Cedarville. Just never got her below that damn bridge."

Richie had heard of people like Heidi from other Yoopers, but figured it for urban legend. The Mackinac Bridge opened in '57. At the time, the bridge was the longest of its kind in the world, an expansion bridge spanning five miles across the blue Straits of Mackinac, an imaginary line dividing the freshwater oceans of Lakes Michigan and Huron. The Big Mac joined the state's mitten-shaped Lower Peninsula with the Upper Peninsula. Richie's mind did the routes allowing a person passage to Minneapolis, Chicago, Milwaukee, and other parts of the Midwest without crossing the bridge, but the old man had obviously become bound by other forces.

"That's really a shame," Richie said.

"Maybe, but you, Richie—you've *been there*. Can you tell me about it some?"

"Well ... it's hard to really do it justice ... "

He proceeded to lie about the amusement rides that shadowed its rolling green hills, gardens planted with rows of every color flower God ever invented. The zoo filled with beasts as varied as peacocks and snow leopards. Massive aquariums teeming with exotic sea life, and the cobblestone walkway that guided one through the island's interior, until finally at the peak of Bob-Lo's highest hill, the glorious view of the Detroit River's Windex-colored water stretched out for as far as you could see. From there the crown jewel of Detroit was visible, the dream of Mayor Coleman Young—five cylindrical towers called the Renaissance Center looming skyward, a chrome Phoenix rising from the riot-ravaged ashes of the city.

"Amazing ... " the venerable Leif Jon Knudsen whispered.

"Yeah. It really is something to see."

That summer took a weird turn. Thinking he was missing something being so far removed from Detroit, Richie left NMU and transferred to Wayne State University on a small rowing scholarship. He could live at home for free and be at ease in familiar waters. Knowing he wouldn't be going up to the Upper Peninsula for a while, he boxed up his flannel shirts and his salmon gear. Among the things he would miss about Marquette, besides his friends and the girls, was not seeing the daily beauty of the region, and of course, his chats with Leif Jon Knudsen.

Richie trained on Belle Isle at the Detroit Boat Club, and many times sitting in the eight-man shell, he could look out across the polluted Detroit River and know Bob-Lo was nearby. For work, he hooked up with two other Italian guys on a landscaping crew, working in the Grosse Pointes. Another guy joined them, a Lebanese kid whose parents owned a jewelry store in Grosse Pointe Farms. The four worked hard, rising at dawn to cut the lawns of rich people all day until they unloaded the clippings into a farmer's field each night. Richie would roll in around 10 p.m. and do it all over again the next day. He smelled of grass and dirt and was a walking zombie. It may have been the worst job he ever had in his life.

The four got so tanned that from afar they looked black, and if you spent any time in the Pointes back then, you know that attracted some attention. It wasn't unusual to see black people walking south on Mack—sanctuary in the form of Detroit lay south of Seven Mile Road—get harassed by the police. Even cleaning women, still in their uniforms, were sometimes pushed against a police car, made to spread their hands out for a frisking. As the cops embarrassed them, white patrons sat inside The Original House of Pancakes, watching while they noshed on the restaurant's famous apple pancakes.

Richie and his crew got pulled over, too, allegedly for non-working lights. It was ninety-five degrees and they wore bandannas to absorb the sweat. The four had just mowed the acre-wide front lawn of a local car dealer's mansion on Lakeshore Drive when police sirens whooped. Richie's boss pulled the truck over and two police cars parked behind them, lights flashing. One pink-skinned officer demanded licenses. His partner examined the interior, one hand on the butt of his revolver. The lone cop in the second car checked his computer to see if their faces matched any of the felons it displayed.

"What are you guys—" the cop stopped in mid-sentence. "Hey, you guys are *white*."

"No shit, Columbo," Richie's boss mumbled.

"You," the cop studied Richie's license and pointed. "Detroit?" The other lawn cutters were Grosse Pointe residents.

"So? My dad was a Detroit cop. He's in Macomb County now," Richie replied.

"Sure he is," the cop said. "Keep moving. OSM motherfucker. Get back to your side." Richie had heard it all his life when kids he met from the Pointes asked where exactly it was on Seven Mile Road that he lived. On his reply, they'd wink at each other and snort, "Ohhh, *OSM!*" It meant *Other Side of Mack*. Another dividing line.

Later, when they arrived at the farm, Richie's boss had them stand behind the trailer while he tapped the brakes. All the taillights lit up. The four unloaded the hay with unusual vigor that night, no one speaking as the methane gas from the rotting hill of lawn clippings belched its fetid odor and heated their bare torsos.

The next day at the end of the block they were cutting, Richie noticed a sign for an estate sale. The street was Middlesex, a road locally infamous for being packed with Dagos that were into all kinds of illegal shit. Being a dedicated garbage picker in his younger days, Richie told his boss he needed to see what the rich folks were selling. Most of it was antique furniture and Depression-Era fare. There were many vintage books too, and Richie grabbed a few—first printings by Hemingway and London—for only three bucks apiece.

He wandered to the back where the sun porch was located. Wealthy bargain hunters threw standoff looks at his filthy appearance as he scoured the tables. Blue-hairs rummaged through magazines and picked over salt-and-pepper shakers, collectible spoons, and Danbury Mint plates depicting dead presidents. A thin woman bickered with the owner of the house over the cost of a copper art deco ice bucket with embossed penguins around it. The bucket was labeled six dollars.

"This is dented," she complained. "Will you take four? Four is fair."

"It's handmade. That adds to its antiquity," the owner countered. "Six."

Richie watched, amused as the two went at it. The bickerer lifted the copper bucket to make her point, and that's when Richie saw *it*.

"No fucking *way*," he said.

A spinster nearby fingering a bowl of swirled marbles turned her nose up at him. "Do you kiss your mother with that mouth?" she asked.

He cautiously approached so as not to draw the attention of the bickerer. In the bright sunlight, the item radiated iridescence from its powder blue background. It wasn't very big, maybe fifteen inches across. He slid his hand over it, feeling the silky material, perhaps rayon or taffeta. It was old but in brand-new condition. The design was idyllic, evoking a grand importance and elegance belying the condition of the current state of the locale it depicted. On the day it was originally purchased, it was probably spot-on accurate, though he had no way of knowing. A braided, gold rope was sewn on the short side, a wooden dowel likely affixed there once. All of this inspirational beauty was his for a mere buck-fifty.

He didn't even try to talk the lady down.

Going to bed early sucked. Not drinking beer sucked. And jogging around Belle Isle sucked. So his rowing career lasted one miserable semester. He hated getting up at 4 a.m. only to have to drive to Belle Isle to row the island, then have to rush to classes just to get smacked in the face by the hyper-political atmosphere at Wayne State. He hated the traffic, the smarmy attitude of the professors. His heart wasn't in any of it. He had been wrong about Marquette. He longed for the woods, water, and laid-back quality of Upper Peninsula living. After the fall term at WSU, Richie dropped the scholarship, took his flannel shirts and fishing tackle out of storage and headed north.

The ice finally broke in May. Spring brought a bout of fishing fever as the steelheads were running hard at the Dead, so he packed up and made his way out onto Big Bay Road, but it wasn't the yellow pole he carried. This day, he had a special delivery to make, and so he clutched an ounces-light package wrapped in blue foil.

It was a little before 8 a.m. when Richie saw the steam rising from the coffee cup. A low-lying fog rose from the base of the trees on each side of the road, and melting snow piles were over six feet high. Leif Jon Knudsen leaned against the fence post, sipping his coffee and looking the way of the river.

Richie was excited. "Good morning," he called out to him.

It took Knudsen a moment to turn, and Richie could see from twenty yards away that something was wrong. The right side of the old man's face drooped. There was a coffee stain down his cotton duck coat and at his feet a melted spot of brown snow. The tin of Copenhagen was missing from the fence post.

"Hello. *Richie?* Hey, it is you … where've you been, eh? Get you some coffee?" His speech was grainy, slurred, and hearing Leif Jon Knudsen at that moment, Richie's stomach flipped at the recollection of the menagerie he'd painted for him a year-and-a-half earlier. "Did you miss my handsome face?"

It was a struggle for the old man to say the words with his lip sagging down. He placed the cup on the fence post, but it fell. Richie ignored it.

He shook the right hand, now frozen in a semi-claw, and the grip was gone.

"Well, I tried Wayne State but I didn't like it. Too pretty up here."

"I had a stroke, ya know."

"I'm sorry to hear that. I thought something wasn't quite … " Richie fumbled for the right words. "Anyway, you look great now. So how are you feeling *lately?*"

Knudsen didn't seem to hear the question.

"Steelies are running. Seen a guy … young kid walking by with one. Where's your pole?"

"Not fishing today. I came by to give you something."

"Me?"

Behind Knudsen, the cabin door opened. A small round woman shuffled to the fence. She was bundled up. She placed an arm on Leif Jon's shoulder and handed him a pill.

"This must be your wife," Richie said. "Hello, Mrs. Knudsen."

Heidi Knudsen flinched, dipping her head. Her eyebrows had been plucked bald, accentuating her dull green eyes. A tuft of white hair poked from under her hood. A beautiful girl lived in that face once.

"This is my Heidi. It's the fisherman, Heidi. Richie from Detroit."

"Morning," Heidi said, still looking down. "Time for your pill, Leif Jon," she whispered. "It's time … "

Heidi snapped her head to look at something that wasn't there. Richie looked too, but Mr. Knudsen's head never moved.

"For your pill," Heidi finished her thought.

"Glad you're here. I brought this for your husband," Richie said.

He handed Knudsen the blue foil triangle with two sides twice as long as the shortest. The old man's right hand didn't work well. Heidi set the pill atop the fence post. Knudsen's shaking left hand gripped the side of the package. He looked to Heidi for help. She took one side and pulled, him holding steady, letting her open it. When it was unwrapped, he stared at the light blue pennant and blinked. His eyes squinted, and he took his right hand and clawed the rest of the foil away. Heidi's eyes were wet, crescents of tears brimming over the lids. Leif Jon Knudsen's startling blue eyes dripped, too, and he was unabashed in his emotions.

"Oh my God, *look at it* Heidi, just look at it will ya? The scenery ... *beautiful.*"

His crooked fingers grazed the braided gold rope. Her small hand, too, found the raised white lettering like one reads Braille, caressing the embroidered bold letters made of shiny, stitched thread that spelled, "Bob-Lo Island." Elegant script proclaimed, "The Jewel On The River." It featured a silk-screened depiction of a Ferris wheel emerging from a pastoral landscape teeming with people in summer dress. Riverboats floated lazily on a calm Detroit River, and a setting sun painted fluffy clouds with Easter egg colors. Richie had to admit, if he hadn't been to the island himself, he'd have thought Currier & Ives commissioned the illustration for an East Coast resort.

"Where did you find such a thing?" Knudsen finally looked up at him, and Richie tried not to cry. Once again, he somehow couldn't bring himself to tell the truth to the honorable man.

"My father bought it for my mother on their honeymoon. I told them about you and Heidi, and how ... " Richie looked at Heidi Knudsen and she was staring at the snow, rubbing her husband's shoulder. "They insisted. My parents wanted you to have it."

The old couple broke down and Richie moved toward them. Knudsen's chest heaved as he draped his left arm around Richie. He could smell his body odor and the scent of Vitalis in the old man's thin hair, yet to him, a starlet's perfume wouldn't have been any sweeter. Heidi placed her hand on Richie's waist and patted him there. They stayed like that a moment, three people embracing, and him feeling conflicted for it. Yet in his confliction, he asked God's forgiveness; that He understand his intentions.

And as Leif Jon Knudsen's head lay in the crook of Richie's shoulder, a white-tailed buck and a large doe stepped out from the woods of the yard. The deer waited for a smaller deer to catch up. When it did, the three animals moved slowly, walking within twenty feet of them, never looking their way. Richie watched them cross the road, not saying a word, watched as they disappeared into the thick woods on the other side. The lie felt good then, and Richie knew leaving Copper Corner to return here, to see the old man once more, was a part of his own mythology.

Turtle Food

The mist came up off the water at the landing, and the sunlight hurt Richie's eyes as he lowered his glasses over his nose. The other boats were already out, and Dante, one of Richie's two partners in the contest, had just pushed them off the shore. Richie drove the boat with Vince in the middle seat and Dante handling the anchor at the bow. The engine whined, throwing a small roostertail behind it, though the route required him to be judicious in his speed. Dante leaned on the front rail, keeping lookout for stumps hidden below, as the 9,000-acre floodplain opened up around them. The other boats—ten or so—headed toward the dam. Richie went opposite to them.

The sky was a cloudless blue ocean. High above Fletcher's Floodwaters, flocks of waterfowl aimed their bodies south. From their vantage point, it must have looked like a swimming pool in the top knuckle of lower Michigan's mitten. Fletcher's was actually the Thunder Bay River, dammed up in 1930 by Alpena Power, creating a vast reservoir. The Floodwaters—or Pond—was named in honor of the company's president, Phillip Fletcher. When first ice came, the Department of Natural Resources sawed the trees off at the new lake's frozen surface, creating a fisherman's structural paradise. Sometimes the floodplain's beguiling habitat was so absorbing to the men seeking trophy fish, they ran afoul of the stumps, shearing the pins off their propellers. You had to respect Fletcher's submerged forest.

"You're good now, Rich. Where do you want to go?" Dante said, sitting down.

"It's all fishy. You tell me," Richie replied.

Vince and Dante looked across the far shore. Dante pointed. "Let's try that shoreline by the inlet."

Richie turned the boat and puttered across. The walkie-talkie crackled and Vince squelched it.

"Hello," Vince said into the receiver.

"Helloooo," a voice purred with a singsong lilt barely audible through the static.

"Damn it, you bastards—we ain't been out five minutes! How many?"

"Oh, just one." It was Richie's brother-in-law Nick, who could catch fish in a mud puddle with a safety pin. Nick and Mike Materra, Richie's father-in-law, always seemed to be in the running to smoke everybody at the tournament, year in and year out.

"Ask him if it's any big," Richie said.

"Nice size?" Vince asked.

"Maybe ..." Nick said.

Richie reached forward. "Give me that damn thing." Vince handed over the walkie-talkie and Richie spoke into it louder than he needed to. "You or Dad? Let me guess, purple worm."

"Me. And perhaps ... maybe the purple, maybe black ... Oh, got a hit—c'ya!"

"Nick? Shit." Richie put the walkie-talkie down next to him and brought the boat to a stop.

Dante dropped the anchor. "Lucky bastards," he said, feeling the rope run through his fingers. "Nick and Uncle Mike; plain lucky."

"Ain't luck if it happens every damn year. What are you guys using?" Richie asked.

He could tell Dante and Vince weren't overly excited to fish. Vince had been painting a condo complex in Rochester that had him working thirteen-hour days the last three weeks. His eyes looked ready to slam shut. Dante's listless cast was indicative of being somewhere else, too, but out of a desire to see his uncles and cousins, he made the four-hour trek north from Detroit. Despite his name, Dante had grown more even-tempered as he had gotten older. It took a great amount of jostling in life to get his needle to move. He was a surgeon, and the meticulous nature of his craft had pervaded his demeanor down to the way he carried himself, even the way he dressed. He was perhaps the neatest of the cousins.

"Whatever I see first," Vince said. He picked up a jig. "This. This looks good."

"Rapala," Dante said. "Jointed one. What's the difference?"

It was 7:50 a.m. Richie looked through his tackle box. His brother-in-law and all his wife's cousins had bought out every Kelly's worm on the East Side of Detroit, both the purple and black varieties. Bait shops on the West Side, where

Richie had migrated to, didn't carry them. Pride dictated not asking to borrow any, so he'd settled on an off-brand that looked promising. Maybe he'd catch lightning in a bottle with them. The new lures were clear with orange spots, a color called "crayfish." The rubber worm was a weedless setup with three snelled hooks woven through the pliable body of the worm. Spring-clips soldered to the hooks allowed the lure to swim snag-free among the vegetation, though nothing was truly "weedless" or "snag-free" in Fletcher's gnarly waters.

You had to go with a buried hook if you were fishing any depth below three feet. Adding to the acres of roots and stumps, submerged and emerging weeds grew in thick masses everywhere you cast. But the place was so loaded with fish that you put up with it. Monstrous northern pike and largemouth and small-mouth bass that flirted with state records swam here. Even the pan fish were huge, and hand-size crappies, bluegills, and perch of twelve inches were caught with regularity. Urban legend had it that the DNR once drained the pike breeding areas and found a northern that measured twelve inches between the eyes. Richie never believed it until a pike with a head the size of goat's swallowed a buzz-bait whole the first time he went fishing there in 1991.

The rules of the Bassmaster on the Floodwaters were simple. Like the pro tourneys, live bait was prohibited and the best five bass won the trophy and the all-important bragging rights. Each boat put in twenty bucks for Heaviest Stringer, with Big Fish being a separate payout. The cousins even used to award special champion T-shirts to the winning boat, but after the third year the practice was discontinued, deemed "too gay" by consensus. Now the names of the winners appeared on a "classy" gold trophy featuring a leaping largemouth above a two-handled chalice. The trophy had been backdated since the tournament's inaugural fifteen years earlier.

It had been ten years since Richie's name had been engraved on it, and that was only because he'd been paired with one of the many Nicks who carried most of the weight back then. Fishing had been particularly bad that day, and three "almost keepers" had been enough to wrest the trophy from Richie's brother- and father-in-law. Because of conflicting schedules with everyone's kids and their activities—football, soccer, volleyball and swimming—the contest was held in September when the fishing had started to wane. Still, there'd been some big-ass fish caught over the years, including a six-pound largemouth.

Richie's first cast settled next to a submerged log he could see through the polarized lenses. He'd become a decent fisherman since his college days in Marquette. He studied with diligence the habits of bass and favored working shade and structure like the stumps that were everywhere in Fletcher's, but especially the isolated ones. He felt the slightest twitch on his fingertips and pulled the rod straight back.

"All right Richie!" Dante came to life, seeing Richie's rod bend.

"Shit, get the net, Vince—he's a good one," Richie said. The drag on his rod whirred and he tried to keep his heart from splitting. Vince and Dante pulled their lines from the water. The fish went on a run past the nose of the boat and Dante let out a long whistle. He ducked his head as the taut line rubbed his hair. Richie turned to the right and started recovering line. He saw the wide green body swim past in the stained water.

"Easy! Don't horse him," Vince said. "He's a big bastard, look at his rod."

"He's coming up." Richie waited and saw a huge clump of weeds flopping on the surface. The weeds looked as though they'd been dropped in a washing machine's spin cycle, twisted into a circle. He reeled in the fish slowly and Vince worked the net underneath the hog just as it started shaking its massive head. It tried to swim off when it saw the boat.

"Holy shit, look at the eye on that thing—like a marble!" Vince said.

"Woo-*hoo!*" Richie shouted. "Thanks for netting him."

"Hopefully, you'll be returning the favor," Vince said.

Dante peeked over Vince's shoulder as Vince held up the net. The fish was green-black with thick white cheeks and a sagging belly. Richie reached in and lipped the bass and the weight of it made him pause. He hoisted it into the air and Vince slapped him on the back.

"Son of a bitch, Richie, you'll win Big Fish for sure," Vince said, and the thought of taking a few bills from every man in the contest felt sweet at that moment. "I'll get the stringer," Vince said.

Richie put a tape on the fish and it measured twenty-two inches. He hooked the digital scale under its gill and flickering red numbers registered the weight between four pounds, twelve ounces and five and a quarter. He turned the read-out toward Vince and Dante.

"Witness," he said. The two looked.

"Call it five. Fuckin' ay, Rich," Dante said, squinting at the scale.

Richie threaded the point of the stringer, a two-foot piece of heavy braided white nylon rope, through the gill and out of the fish's huge mouth. He carefully handed it over to Vince.

"You take care of the stringer," Richie said.

"I'm all over it, chief."

They fished there for another hour, and Richie couldn't miss. He caught eight more bass while Vince and Dante washed their lures. The fish weren't all keepers, but it was non-stop action. There was no explaining it. It got to the point where Richie didn't even celebrate for fear of pissing his partners off. He offered both of them the exact same crayfish-colored lure he was using. Dante refused, preferring the Kelly's purple. Vince had no luck using it.

"Not even using Kelly's," Dante said. "Not even purple. Yet Richie's slaying."

"They're crayfish-colored," Richie said, working the rod tip. "Bass eat crayfish."

"Crayfish color on a worm … genius. But he's still reeling 'em in," Dante said.

"What's the diff? *Worms* aren't purple. Maybe it's his presentation," Vince said.

"Maybe," Richie replied, just as a bass hit. "They seem to work—net Vince!"

"He's like Bill Dance," Dante said, shaking his head. "All right. Gimme one."

Richie reeled in the largemouth. It was just under legal, as had been the last eight fish he'd caught. "It's not like any were as big as that first monster," he said, letting the fish go. He looked into the water to the left and saw the bucket-mouth he'd caught with his first cast swimming lazily, the white stringer around its thick lip. It was the biggest bass he'd ever caught and, in Michigan waters, a true trophy. "Vince, lift the stringer, I'm going to take us to Stumpville."

Vince lifted the big bass from the water and it slapped its thick tail against the side of the boat. *"Maddon'!"* Vince said. "Thing's so big, its got a *dick*."

Richie chuckled and started the engine. He felt the prop hit some weeds, chugging as it shredded them into coleslaw. The average depth was around five feet unless you could locate the river channel. There it got up to ten, with gravel beds that the smallmouths preferred. He looked down at the wide body of his catch, its sides expanding and contracting like a jade accordion. Its eye really *was* as big as a marble, and its head was so much larger than anything he'd ever caught.

They planned to finish their morning working Stumpville—so named for a hundred or so cedar stumps that rose three feet above the waterline—for the morning's remaining two hours. The rule was you had to come in at noon for *the feast*—hard sesame seed rolls with every Italian lunch meat, cheese, produce, and olive medleys to be found at Nino Salvaggio's and Pete & Frank's, two of the best Italian markets on Detroit's East Side. There was always, it seemed, way too much food when you saw it all spread out on the picnic tables, but somehow at the end of the weekend there was little left but an unclaimed piece of *fontinella*. Some of the cousins could eat more than that little Japanese guy who won those hotdog-eating contests every year at Coney Island. Richie had seen his wife's cousins Peter and Sam go through six sandwiches and five sirloins in the course of two hours and still have room for a plate of brownies before bed.

But Richie didn't care about eating. He wanted to fish. They had one bass on the stringer, albeit a monster, and he wanted to find another to keep it company before the trio headed in.

The walkie-talkie crackled. *"Helllllooo … "* Vince picked it up.

"Yeah," he grumbled.

"Got another," Richie's father-in-law Mike said. Vince grinned at Richie, and he held his finger up and shook his head.

"Big?"

"Oh, he's a keeper ... what about you guys?"

"Nothing yet. Well, Richie did get ... one."

The silence was palpable among the random birds that played on the shoreline.

"Really. Good size?" The three laughed. *"Hello ... hey, come clean. How big—"*

Vince acted like his voice was breaking up. "We'll see you at lunch, fellas."

"I'm cutting the engine," Richie said, pushing the kill button.

"They're going to shit the bed. Vin, that was beautiful," Dante said. "I'm going to drop right here." He slid the anchor, a Folgers can full of cement, over the side.

"Monster returned, back in the water," Vince said as he carefully placed the stringer off the side of the boat. Richie watched the bass stretch the stringer to its full length. Vince secured it to the oarlock on Richie's port side, and as the stringer tightened all the way, the nose of the bass was even with his knee. The fish reversed position and went as deep as it could. They were in three feet of water and he saw the tip of the fish's tail break the surface like a tiny shark fin.

"OK, time to contribute, Vin," Dante said, tossing his lure out past the stumps. He had switched to a black Sluggo. As soon as Dante's Sluggo—a rubber lure meant to replicate the action of a dying baitfish—hit the water, it disappeared in a roiling splash. "Yes! Finally ... " he yelled.

It was over before it started. His line came back looking like a piranha had used it for dental floss. Dante held the frayed line up, his lure bitten clean off.

"Must've been a big northern," Vince mused.

"Gee, *you think?*" Dante said. "Dammit to hell. I would've liked to just seen it."

The three sat there for an hour and a half having caught nothing, when Vince looked at his watch. "Eleven forty-five. We should head in—"

"*Minchia*, not again ... " Dante said, watching Richie's pole bend in half.

"He's huge!" Richie said. "Get your line in, Vince."

Vince reeled in. He and Dante sat and watched Richie fight the bass. The fish had hit ten feet from the boat. It was stuck at the bottom under a stump.

"I can't move him." Richie's mouth clamped tight. "He went straight down."

"Don't horse him," Vince said.

Richie managed to look sideways at Vince. "Yeah, I know."

"Go easy, I'll row you over there. Take up the slack." Dante said.

He slowly rowed with one oar toward the spot where the fish had stopped moving. The only sounds were the lap of the oar in the water and the laborious cranks of Richie's reel. Right over the top of the stump, he could see the brass snap swivel of his leader wink at him, six inches below the surface, above a spread of roots that originated from a long-dead cedar. The top of the fish had to be just underneath, protected by the cage-like root structure. He swore he saw the black hump of its back, so close he could reach down and touch it. His arms were starting to ache as he fought off the tension of the rod.

"What the hell do I do? Any suggestions?"

"Don't horse him." Richie just stared at Vince. "I'm just saying—"

"Yeah, I know, don't horse him."

"He'll get tired. Be patient," Dante said, staring at the unmoving leader. They sat like that for two or three minutes, Richie holding the rod high in a graphite arc. An osprey screeched overhead and roosted atop the metal framework tower of its nest, set up by the DNR twenty years ago. Suddenly, Richie's line went limp and a V of water shot away from the obstruction. He quickly cranked on the handle to take up the slack.

"Oh, man, I hope I didn't just lose him," he said, searching his line for tautness. The bass leapt above the surface with a skirt of muddy seaweed trailing him and Richie felt the comforting tension of a taut line.

"Hoo-haaa!" Dante yelled. "You slick son of a bitch."

Richie let the drag tire the fish out before reeling it closer to the boat. Vince netted it. Richie lipped the fish out of the net and presented it to his partners.

"They're twins! Look at that." Richie laid the flopping fish across his feet and ran the tape: twenty-two inches nose to tail, on the button. He inserted the hook of the scale into the bass's gill and it bottomed out at five pounds. They were a matched set. "Grab that stringer, Vin," Richie said.

Vince lifted the stringer and Richie loaded the second largemouth onto the white braided line. Richie proudly held them up between his outstretched hands.

"Say cheese, asshole," Vince said, pointing a camera at him.

"Cheese asshole." The flash caught the scales of the fish, glittering green and gold in the noonday sun.

The uncles and cousins were waiting for them when Richie eased the boat into shore.

"One-ounce fine for every minute you're late, you no good sons-of-bitches," Uncle Sam chirped from the muddy bank.

"Easy, Unc. It's barely three after twelve," Dante said.

A dozen leopard frogs jumped out of the way as the sixteen-foot aluminum boat jammed into the shore. Some of the younger cousins—sons and nephews of the men present—crowded around the boat. Dante leapt off onto the grass and helped Vince from the middle seat. They pulled the boat up onto the muddy bank.

Mike and Nick walked up to their own boat and Nick lifted a chain-link, safety pin-style stringer from the water. Three bass hung from it, two largemouth and one smallie. They were hearty fish, good color with strong bodies. Collectively they weighed around six pounds.

"And to think it's only noon," Mike said, his voice all syrupy.

"Those are nice ones, guys," Richie said, holding back a smile.

"Yeah, lots of fishing left, brother-in-law." Nick smiled at Richie and giggled a little as he returned their stringer to the water.

"That's true," Dante said. "Hope those words taste as good going down as they did coming out. Show him your catch, Rich."

"*Your* catch? What do you got?" Nick asked.

"Just a couple ... " Richie pulled the white stringer from the side oarlock and there was a collective gasp followed by a "Ho!" that rang out amongst much swearing in both Italian and English. Mike's and Nick's eyes glazed over and the father and son walked toward Richie's stringer like zombies.

"You sandbagging son of a bitch ... my daughter married a slick son of a bitch," Mike told everyone.

"Look at the girth on them. They're a perfect set," Nick lamented, opening the jaws of one of the bass and staring down its gullet. "Check it out." Nick placed his closed fist into the fish's wide mouth. Another of the Nicks laughed.

Uncle Sam walked over, his hands benignly at his sides, but Richie saw his mind working.

"Think I should I get one of them mounted?" Richie asked the group.

Mark, one of the cousins-in-law, stepped forward. Of the group of avid outdoorsmen that were present, he'd caught and mounted more wildlife than any of them. His den looked like he'd looted Conservation Mountain at Cabela's.

"Mount *one?* Richie, you're joking. Bass in the north don't get to twenty-two very often. Those got to be twenty-two easy. Mount both. Get a nice piece of driftwood. Lombardi will do them up real nice. Twelve bucks an inch, worth every penny. Tell him I sent you." Mark was referring to the Dago taxidermist in Anchor Bay. "Put them on ice now, though. You don't want to be dragging those beauties around the lake the rest of the afternoon."

"Good idea. Mount both ... " Richie did the math in his head, trying to figure out how to justify to his wife laying out half a G-note on two dead fish. Especially since she'd only recently forgiven his impulse purchase of a great horned owl mount thirteen years earlier. "Maria will love having these hanging in the cabin."

"Women got no sense of humor about that shit. Take her to dinner then tell her. Gimme, I'll take them to the cooler for you," Vince said.

"Thanks. And hey—" Vince looked back. "Don't horse 'em."

Vince did a double take before fake laughing. He loaded them, stringer and all, into one of the big coolers, transferring pounds of *prosciutto* and *mortadella* and the clear quart containers of olives to the tailgate of one of the uncle's pickup trucks.

"Watch that lift gate, Vincent." Uncle Sam stared at Richie, a half-hidden smirk on his face as he spoke. He narrowed his eyes and there was a mischievous glint behind his glasses. Richie smiled back, knowing the ball busting, even in the presence of such contradictory evidence, was coming. "You probably think you got this thing wrapped up going away, don't you?"

"Nah. Lot of fishing left."

"Fill the stringer, might even win Big Fish *and* Heaviest Stringer," Uncle Sam went on.

"Hadn't crossed my mind," Richie lied. "Got lucky, Uncle Sam, that's all."

"Goddamn right, 'cuz we know it *sure as shit* wasn't skill!"

Hoots rained down from Sam's three sons and the other cousins. Richie smiled and Sam returned it.

They had prepared the night before, inside the old cabin on Starvation Lake, a few miles from Fletcher's. Roman's Nick owned the place now. It had been a year since Roman's passing, but his spirit lived everywhere, starting with the sturdy picnic table the beloved uncle had built, a pine epitaph stationed in the kitchen. There they displayed their tools of ignorance, spread across its worn, honey surface, comparing myriad lures, busting each other's balls on who would catch what, and who the better fisherman was. Richie's in-laws and his wife's cousins had surrounded him—the large family that he'd married into. Five of the Nicks were present—you couldn't swing a dead cat at a family function without hitting a Nick—along with some cousins not named Nick. There were so many Nicks, each had multiple "Nick-names" to help distinguish them. You had Hairy Nick, Really Hairy Nick, Roman's Nick, Nicky Eyes, Big Nick, Doctor Nick, Russ' Nick, Hammerhead Nick, and other lively aliases.

The Bassmasters on the Floodwaters had grown into an annual event that had evolved—or devolved—into bragging rights of the worst kind. Ball busting had never been so high as when that group of Dagos got together. If they gave out degrees in it, Uncle Sam would have a PhD. He spread it around with vigor and no one escaped his wrath. For some reason he always saved a little extra zing for Richie. Once, Richie asked Sam's kids about it. "That just means he likes you," they'd told him. Richie thought about that and replied, "Man, he must really love me, then."

Sorting out his tackle the night before the contest, separating rubber, spinner-baits, hooks, power-grubs, et. al., Uncle Sam had stood over him and watched.

"Wow, look at all the tackle your son-in-law has, Mike. He's like a tournament pro." Sarcasm not shrouded in the least. Richie looked up and saw the smile.

Richie felt good knowing Uncle Sam would be sucking hind tit at dinner that night. All his boat had to do was catch three more "insurance fish" to fill their stringer, thus assuring victory. He dared not think about the double whammy.

"Hey, our two probably will hold up over anyone's full stringer," Vince said.

"Careful. Don't jinx us," Dante said.

"What do you mean, 'our two'? You haven't caught shit," Uncle Sam retorted, getting one last dig in.

Vince was right, though. Richie's brother-in-law Nick, the other nephews named Nick and the nephews and cousins-in-law not named Nick, along with the uncles, had sparse stringers, some with no fish at all. Two of Sam's own sons had taken the one bass they caught and filled its mouth with three bluegills for added weight. It was an old trick, but it always made everyone laugh to see another fish's tail sticking out of the mouth of a bass.

"OK homos, back on the water," Vince called out.

"Everyone get back to shore at five o'clock sharp." Uncle Sam winked at Richie.

The afternoon was more of the same. They hadn't been anchored one minute when the tip of Richie's rod dipped down. He nailed fish after fish, while Vince and Dante held onto their poles with about as much action as sentries protecting ugly broads from stalkers. Finally at around 3 p.m., Richie got into a real beauty. It was a smallmouth, bronzish-green. The fish had made three acrobatic leaps before he brought it in. It weighed around two and a half pounds, taping out at eighteen inches.

"Don't worry ... I'll get you the fucking stringer," Vince said flatly. "Here." He handed Richie the stringer. Richie looked at it.

"What happened to the other stringer?"

"Still attached to those hogs you caught. That's a brand-new one." Vince said.

Richie felt a little bad for his teammates, but he had been on that side of the boat before, though never like this. He threaded the point of the new stringer—a braided yellow nylon model that was nearly five feet long, through the gill of the smallie. He gave the stringer back to Vince, who wove it through the oarlock and tied it off. Vince set the bass into the water. It splashed once and Richie watched it swim all the way past his knee to the back of the boat, the long yellow line disappearing behind the motor somewhere.

They all made a few more casts that produced nothing until Dante stood up. "There's one!"

"*Finally,*" Vince said. "The spell is broken."

"There you go!" Richie chipped in. He and Vince watched Dante reel in fast until a perch came skipping out of the water over their ducking heads.

"Mother ... sonofabitch. Can't buy a bass today." Dante grabbed the perch and pulled it from the hook, disemboweling it in his haste. He tossed it back. The perch floated sideways, flopping as it tried to right itself. The three watched as a largemouth came from below and swallowed the fish whole, its heavy white belly rolling on its side toward the men.

"Wow," Richie said.

"That had to be a four-pounder," Vince whispered.

They sat there a minute until the ripples disappeared.

Dante's rod clanged against the side of the boat, settling on the other oarlock next to Vince. "Anchor up," Dante said, yanking up the coffee can strewn with mud and cabbage weeds. "This is bullshit." He let the can slam on the floor of the boat.

Richie played with the throttle. "Vin, pull the stringer, I'm going to start it," he said. He had a hard time meeting their gaze, especially Dante's.

Vince complied, pulling the stringer hand-over-hand until the single bass finally appeared at the side of the boat. Richie looked at the sixty-inch pile of yellow line coiled on the floor at Vince's feet.

"Go 'head, lucky," Vince said. "You can start 'er up."

Richie started the engine and felt the prop hit the weeds below. It cleared up and they returned to the point of the channel where they had started. Dante sighed and cast his lure out. Vince had given up, keeping his hook attached to the bottom eyelet of his rod. He laid across the seat and covered his eyes with his hat. He was asleep before Richie cut the engine.

They drifted through the river channel and the boat ended up at the same spot where the bass had nailed the perch. Dante slid the anchor in. As if on cue, Richie felt his pole bend. It was getting ridiculous. Why the fishing gods had picked him, he had no idea. Dante kicked at Vince.

"Get the net. Fuckin' Jonah's at it again."

Vince woke up and netted it without even having to be asked, and reeled in the yellow stringer. Richie loaded the second fish on and handed it back to Vince. He placed the stringer back into the water and laid down. Before he had a chance to cover his eyes, Richie's quick cast to the same spot produced another hit. Vince lifted the fishing hat's wide brim and squinted at Richie. He laughed sardonically.

"Net this one yourself, fuckface."

Dante looked over Vince's shoulder. "You're *kidding* me. I mean, come the fuck on. Oh, this is bullshit," Dante said.

"Sorry guys." Richie reeled it in—a one and a half-pounder. He didn't bother netting the fish, lipping the bass instead.

"It's in the bag now. There's no way they catch us—well, catch *you*—now. No way," Dante said.

Vince sighed and reeled in the five-foot, yellow stringer. "Give it to me *masser*. I'll put it on the stringer for you *masser Rich*. That's an official five—all you. What did you do, sell your soul before we got on the water today?"

"Don't be a dick," Richie said.

"I'm only *busting your balls*," Vince said, slipping the smaller bass on the stringer. "You don't have to apologize for being *the man*."

"I'm not *the man*, just lucky."

"Once is luck. Twice maybe. This is just silly."

"Silly," Dante slapped at the water with his rod tip.

Vince tossed the stringer back into the water and Richie watched the yellow line spool out until it went taut over the side, the largest of the three bass at the end of the line.

"How many is that anyway?" Vince asked.

"Not sure."

"It's seventeen! *Not sure, your ass!* Same boat, same lures," Dante muttered.

They made several more casts in the shallow water.

It was 4:15 and the wind had picked up. Richie looked to his right and saw the three fish on the stringer, fanned out and floating all the way around the boat.

"Guys want to make one more pass?" Vince said.

"Why not?" Dante said. "Anchor up." He started lifting the coffee can.

"Wait, guys, hold on," Richie said. "We've drifted the river channel enough. We end up here and this spot has been productive as all get out. Let's just hang here the last half-hour—"

"Productive for you, maybe," Dante said, pulling the anchor up.

Dante pointed to the lily pads on the eastern shore, past Stumpville. The pads were inviting, and the wind was blowing toward the shore, lifting the edges of the pads. "The baitfish might be blowing in. If we're lucky, the bass will be stacked up feasting on them. What do you say?"

Richie felt like he was playing with the house's money now anyway. How could he sit there, after all the fish he'd caught all day long and now tell them no, he wanted to stay put because he was *en fuego*? He had his two monsters on ice, sitting in a cooler and the three insurance bass on the stringer. All told, probably fifteen pounds worth of fish, soft. He watched the anchor in Dante's hand, covered in zebra mussels and seaweed.

"OK, let's see if we can't replace the two runts with a couple bigger ones."

Richie started the engine, keeping his sights on the lily pads. He felt the engine chug on submerged weeds, the prop laboring. It sounded different than before. He stared at the pads, seeing them lift and he had to admit the possibility existed that minnows and fry may be getting forced into the shallows of that shoreline. Had God left another five-pounder there for him? That would propel his ranking into the stratosphere—and cost another $250 to Lombardi the taxidermist.

The engine churned hard and the prop struggled. Vince looked up at a flock of cormorants and proceeded to bead and lead them with an imaginary shotgun. "I ever tell you guys how I fucked up that turkey Roman's Nick called in? He'd been calling this huge tom for two hours—thing's beard was nine inches long. I had to cough. You know, gotta cough, you cough, right? The tom got spooked, ran off. Fucking Nicky didn't talk to me for three days after that." Vince laughed at the memory.

"What's going on with the motor?" Dante asked, peeking over Vince's shoulder.

"Weeds, I think," Richie said. He gave it the gas and the prop finally freed itself. "There we go."

He opened it up a bit and looked at his watch: 4:30. He stretched his neck and looked at the floodplain behind them, relieved to have finally won the contest on his own. And if pride and envy were truly green, the water behind him matched it with its murky cast. Richie looked wonderstruck at the verdant roostertail caused by the nine-horse Evinrude. Then seeing the water suddenly turn clear, he felt his balls retract and his stomach tingle as he put it all together.

"Vince," Richie said, gearing down to a slow idle. "The new stringer. Did you pull it in from the water?" It was a rhetorical question but Richie felt it needed asking.

"No, but so what?" Vince replied.

"Oh, *Richie!*" Dante started moaning. "Oh, I'm so sorry, Richie."

Vince was still puzzled. "What?"

"It was *longer* than the old one is *what.*"

"Richie ... " Vince said, his eyes closing and his hat falling into the bottom of the boat. He covered his face as the realization set in. "*Maddon',* I forgot."

"Oh, *Richie!* Oh, Richie! I'm *so* sorry. Oh, my *God!*" Dante hit the words hard.

Richie stared at the remnants of the five-foot long, empty yellow line trailing behind, still lashed to the oarlock, looking like a rhythmic gymnastics ribbon gyrating in the churn of the propeller.

Then the walkie-talkie crackled.

"This gets better every minute," Richie remarked.

Dante's brown eyes bulged. *"Don't answer it!"* he begged, and Richie couldn't remember ever seeing Dante act so animated about anything.

"Richie, I'm sorry," Vince kept saying with his head bowed.

"Guys, don't you see?" Richie laughed. They looked at him, and he laughed harder as he picked up the two-way radio. "What can you do? You have to fuckin' laugh ... " He pressed the talk button. "Yeah, Nick," he said.

"Guys get any more?" Nick's voice faded in and out.

Richie thought about the question, Vince's bulging eyes imploring silence.

"Yes, and no," he said. "How about you guys?"

"Couple nice two-pounders. Nothing like the hogs you caught this morning. Today was your day, brother-in-law. How many more you guys put on the stringer?"

"Right ... let me ask you—*technically speaking*, if the fish were *on* the stringer at one time, do they still count?"

There was silence accompanying the occasional crackle of the walkie-talkie.

"Richie!" Dante pleaded, his neck muscles straining.

"Why? What happened?" Nick asked.

Richie didn't answer.

"Richie, what happened?" Richie turned off the walkie-talkie.

"I'm so sorry," Vince murmured. "I just forgot to pull it. That one time ... "

"You can't tell *anyone* about this—especially Uncle Sam! He'll bust our balls! Promise me Richie, *promise me you won't say anything.*" Dante was standing in the boat, his hands on Vince's shoulders. He stared hard at Richie. "You'll be sorry. You don't know how my uncle can get. Trust me. He's ruthless, worse than ruthless ... he's *relentless!*"

They fished hard, casting fast and furious, even drifting, replicating their exact patterns, hoping to catch just a couple more to fill the stringer, but it was no use. It felt like someone had turned the power off. It was over and Richie knew it. He hooked the new lure that wasn't a Kelly's onto his bottom eyelet. As they puttered past stumps, Richie saw the other boats heading in. At the front of the boat, Dante sat ramrod straight, the tip of his pole in the water, skimming the surface. Acknowledging his dejected partners, Richie leaned back against the engine and started to laugh, maybe to keep from crying. And when Vince looked up at him, Richie laughed even harder. They headed to shore for the weigh-in.

Uncle Sam had been strangely silent during dinner. He even congratulated Richie on the trophy pair he'd caught in the morning. But Richie had seen this act before. The group had just finished eating their steaks, spiked with garlic slivers and smothered with Uncle Mike's zippy tomato *amogue*. Fifteen anglers who were so ravenous, they wiped out twenty-three sirloins and a ten-pound bag of potatoes that evening. Richie chugged a beer and saw his brother-in-law, Nick, looking at his father-in-law, Mike. They both started laughing. One of the other Nicks walked over and stacked three tin cans in front of Richie.

"What's this?" Richie asked.

"Take a look," the other Nick said. Everyone laughed.

"Ha-ha. I married into a family of comedians," Richie looked at the handmade labels wrapped around cans of white clam sauce. The labels were adorned with crude depictions of fish being chopped into pieces by a propeller. They read, *"Richie's Famous Turtle Food."* Xs drawn inside their eyeballs denoted death. Smiling turtles with open jaws floated below. "When did you guys go to art school?" Richie asked. And he laughed along with them.

It still hurt though. His *two* early-morning monsters had lost out to his brother- and father-in-law's stringer of five bass by two ounces. There was no credit among these guys. No mercy. It was going to be a long road to redemption, if it ever came again at all, for Richie to have a shot at getting his name on the trophy. He knew one thing; fishing days like that one came around as often as the Detroit Lions won playoff games.

Uncle Sam finally appeared before him, his official *Bassmasters on the Floodwaters 2006* baseball cap pushed up over the tangle of greying, curly hair. The eyes crinkled behind the big lenses of his glasses and the thick mustache disappeared into the corners of his broad smile. Richie looked up at him.

"Let's hear it," Richie said. There was a pregnant pause as the rest of the group quieted down. They had been waiting for this.

"Hey, all I wanted to say was … " Uncle Sam's voice was comforting before its tone did a complete 180. "You gotta be the stupidest sonofabitch I've ever known. First of all, as *capo* of the boat, manning the engine, it's your responsibility to make sure that stringer's been pulled in."

"Who am I, Captain-fucking-Stubing? I grew up in Copper Corner. I don't know dick about nautical protocol. Besides, whoever heard of a five-foot-long stringer? That's messed up."

"Listen, shit-for-brains. Messed up as it may be, that's not what makes you the stupidest SOB I've ever known. No, the fact that you would come back *here* and *tell everyone* that you churned up them fish in that prop—effectively turning them into chum—that's priceless. I mean, *minchia*, what kind of *mamaluke* did my niece marry?" Uncle Sam looked at Mike, his brother, and continued. "Bro, seriously. This big dumb ass, I mean, where did she find this guy?" He turned back to Richie. "I can't believe you'd be stupid enough to leave that stringer in the water, not to mention—and this is key—that you would try to shift blame to your partner."

"I'm not *blaming* anyone," Richie said.

"You're not exactly *embracing* your responsibility. I mean, poor Vincent here, who wouldn't say 'shit' if he had a mouthful, he feels terrible. You're making him a scapegoat. I'm not even sure you caught as many fish as Vince and Dante *claim* you did."

Everyone laughed their asses off. The Nicks had tears in their ten eyes.

"Wait—how many fish you catch, Uncle Sam?" Richie asked. The question elicited a *whooaaa!* from the group but Sam was resolute, putting a hand up.

"Irrelevant. That's irrelevant to the point."

"Come on, you gotta be able to laugh at yourself," Richie said. "Am I right?"

"No, you got us to do that," his brother-in-law Nick said, inciting more laughter.

"I fucked up. I'm sorry Richie," Vince said.

"Don't apologize, Vincent. You're not at fault," Uncle Sam grinned at Richie as he spoke. "Like the stupid sonofabitch who was Captain of the *Titanic*, the man at the wheel is *always* responsible. Richie. *You* fucked up."

Richie took out a cigar and put it in his mouth. Uncle Sam regarded him. "You know, all kidding aside, you're not a bad-looking kid. Matter of fact, that cigar makes you look like a movie star. Handsome, even. What's the name of that ... " Uncle Sam squinted in the act of recollecting.

"Come on," Richie replied. Everyone was crowding in, listening.

"Turn sideways for me a second," Uncle Sam commanded.

Richie played along, turning his head in profile with the long, dark brown cigar sticking out of his mouth. He spied Dante in the corner chair staring at him, slowly shaking his head. In his youth people told Richie he'd looked like Sylvester Stallone.

"Who is it, Unc?" one of the Nicks asked. "Who does he look like?"

"I got it!" Uncle Sam snapped his fingers. "Lassie. Taking a shit!"

The cousins named Nick and the uncles and brothers-in-law and all the others not blessed with the name Nick howled. This is what they came for: to go home with their ribs sore from laughing. Richie shook his head and laughed, too. He got up and turned to see Dante flick his fingers under his chin at him in the *va fungool* gesture. His brow was furrowed and he mouthed, *"Ruth-less."*

"I'll be outside," Richie said. "Man, Uncle Sam ... you are unreal."

Uncle Sam smiled at Richie and got close to his face. He gave him a hug and looked at him, his eyes and mouth all creases of smiles. He playfully slapped Richie on the cheek. "Next time nephew, *lie.* You'll sleep better. Trust me."

Richie went outside on the deck and looked at the low-setting sun on the western tree line of Starvation Lake, a rich fireball affecting his face with warmth and the pines in front of the cabin with golden light. He cut off the end of the big Monte Cristo given to him by a golfing buddy downstate. He'd been saving it as a victory cigar. He looked at it and lit it up anyway. Puffing quickly to get the smoke going, he heard the laughter inside the cabin, no doubt all at his expense. He would've probably done the same thing, though maybe with a bit less relish. He chuckled, spurting out a plume of smoke that hung in the air in front of him. Listening to all of them at that moment, as funny as the whole stringer mess had been, Richie had to admit that Dante and Uncle Sam had both made damn good points.

Bring the Noise

Vince had been driving all night long. Three hours straight through. After the weeks of long days he'd been putting in, sleep deprivation was catching up with him and the road trance was getting bad; he'd hit gravel twice already. Even cranking the Nugent CD wasn't working. He had left after putting a second coat on the ceiling of the great room for a Grosse Pointe socialite who had been calling him to come back for all kinds of bullshit touch-ups—niff-naw details on some other rooms he had painted a month earlier. She had twenty years on him and put away a bottle of vermouth a day, showing him a little thigh or bending over in her tennis skirt while he worked. Actually, he'd thought, she wasn't too bad for an older broad. He figured her for lonely, but that didn't change the pain in the ass she'd become. She paid in cash though, so if it meant putting up with her yakking and flirtations, it was worth it. He cleaned his last roller and got onto I-75 North, heading for Uncle Roman's cabin on Starvation Lake at a little after 11:30 p.m. that Friday night.

At 2:15 a.m. he entered the town of Glennie. He stopped at a little gas station/bait shop that still had its light on. The tiny store jutted out on the edge of a rock shelf hanging over a dam on the Au Sable River. Water thundered over the cement ledge of the dam. He walked inside. The door shut off the noise of the crashing water, replaced by the din of a scratchy transistor radio mixing with the gurgling aerators from four minnow tanks. An old man, his eyes shut tight, sat behind the counter with his arms crossed, a pink flyswatter clenched in his right hand.

"Hey," Vince said. He studied the guy closely.

The old man didn't respond as Vince walked by. He made his way toward a Bunn coffee maker, ducking underneath a maze of sticky brown fly strips covered with flies and moths. Some of the trapped insects were still wiggling their legs. He selected the largest of the styrofoam cups and filled it to the brim with coffee. It smelled old. The man still hadn't moved. Vince stared at the geezer. He had suspenders on, and his dingy T-shirt was peppered with holes, as if he wore it while welding. Vince waved his hand at the guy. Nothing. He drank down most of the cup, not caring that it was too hot, and casually filled it back up to the top.

At the counter, he tossed down a package of powdered donuts, purposely trying to be loud. Fluorescent lights cast a sallow hue across the man's sagging, unflinching face. Shadows created by moths flying overhead darted across the white laminate countertop, which was worn through to the plywood. Vince drummed his fingernails on the counter, his nail beds speckled with white latex paint.

"Hey there." Vince's voice came out weak.

The old man gave no reply. As Vince tried to determine if the guy was even breathing, the flyswatter came down next to his coffee cup with alarming speed. There was a *thwack,* and Vince saw what was left of a fly's green body, strained through a few of the tiny holes of the pink plastic square.

The next time Vince looked at him, the old man's eyes were open. He smiled and lifted the pink flyswatter and flicked the insect's body into a wastebasket. A smear of blood remained on the white counter next to the powdered donuts.

"Dirty sum gun. Finally gotcha," the man said, still looking at the trash can. He wiped his finger on the counter. "You was a stubborn sum gun." He turned back to Vince and smiled. "Hello. You look tired. This all? You didn't get any gas out there, did you?" The man waved the swatter over the food as if blessing it.

"Yeah, that's it. No gas."

"From downstate?"

"Detroit."

"Uh-huh. Where you heading?" The old man turned the donuts over.

"Fletcher's. Fishing trip. We do it every year."

The old man's head rose up. "Good fishing, there, in the floodwaters. Some big pike in there. Water wolf, what we call 'em. Water wolf." The man pushed the buttons on an old register and squinted at the receipt. "That'll be three-fifty. Includes tax."

"Three-fifty? Coffee's only a dollar."

"Right," the old man smiled at him. "Dollar *per* cup."

★　★　★

Vince sipped the rest of his coffee as he drove through Curran. He *tsked* at the recollection of being caught by the old coot. Later, up M-65 North, he saw the dim light of the County Depot restaurant on his left and felt a rush of relief knowing sleep would come soon. It was around 3:30 a.m. when he turned at the corner of M-65 onto Starvation Lake Road, a few miles from Uncle Roman's cabin. The County Depot's lot was empty.

The moon was new, and he could barely discern the dying sunflowers that covered acres of fields to the south. He remembered back to the summer before last when he'd brought his wife and daughters up there for a weekend with Roman's son, Nick, and his family. He and Nick—his best friend growing up—had stood by the road and watched as their wives and children walked through the tall green stalks. Vince had been mesmerized seeing the kids' small hands graze the plants, causing the flowers to sway, the golden tops seeming to float lazily in a strange rhythm.

Presently, his headlights hit the reflective eyes of a large doe at the end of the road. He stood on the brakes as it froze in front of him. It trotted in front of his truck. As the deer passed, his beams shined on the double arrowhead yellow sign warning the road ended in a T. Starvation Lake was beyond it. He took a right, gently steering around the hairpin curves toward the lake's eastern shore.

Vince parked his car at the end of Uncle Roman's two-track driveway, next to the rest of the vehicles. The cousins had already been up for two days to hunt partridge and woodcock. The family bass tournament—the Bassmasters on the Floodwaters—would be held the next day on nearby Fletcher's Pond, a 9,000-acre floodplain. They would rise at dawn—the fifteen or so nephews, uncles, and cousins—and Vince knew he'd have to garner up the strength to wake, shower, then eat the French toast and bacon Uncle Sam and Uncle Mike cooked. After that he'd sit his ass in a boat for eight hours of hard-core fishing, sleep-deprived or not. Otherwise they'd break his balls for being a pussy. If he didn't give it his best without complaint, Uncle Sam would especially eat his ass alive.

He got out of his truck with his duffel bag and stretched his legs. The urge to piss from the coffee was strong, so he stood there and urinated, staring at the blackness of the night. Walking toward the cabin, the songs of peepers and crickets was deafening, then it stopped, leaving only the trickling streams that fed the lake to break the silence. As his boot hit the first stair of the porch, something moved in the woods behind him. It snorted and crashed through saplings and brush. The sound of the frogs and insects returned. His neck tingled. Vince turned the doorknob. Uncle Roman had left it unlocked.

He shut the door behind him, still on edge from the animal outside. Walking as lightly as he could past the furnace room, he detected the faint scent of propane. The room was inky black, but he could make out the shapes of tackle boxes stacked atop the washer and dryer. His arm brushed against fishing poles leaning against the wall. Boots lined the low nap carpet at his feet. The air was muggy despite the open windows and the whirling blades of a ceiling fan at the peak in the living room.

Vince tiptoed around the corner hearing cacophonous, muffled snoring emanating from Uncle Roman's and Nick's bedrooms—they were side-by-side— even though both had their doors shut. Five or six nephews and cousins were draped over couches and cots in the living room, also emitting slightly differing, though similarly guttural, sleep arias. From the bedrooms stationed on the second floor he heard the echoes of yet more snoring coming from the mouths of at least six more men.

"Good God," he whispered.

Vince was in the dining area. He felt for the edge of the wall, and his hand touched the countertop. He made his way past the long sink and dual refrigerators. Delicious food aromas—salami, *mortadella*, *fontinella* cheese, and garlic—were especially redolent as he walked past, and the coolness of the refrigerators played at his cheek. He set his duffel onto the huge picnic table Uncle Roman had built and removed his hat.

As he ran his fingers through his damp hair, something the circumference of a small iron pipe, something very cold, was pressed to his forehead followed by a metallic click.

"Who the fuck are you and what are you doing in my cabin? Speak."

Vince's breath took a second to catch up to his shrinking ball sac.

"Uncle Roman, *no!* It's me—it's me, *Vince.*"

There was a palpable hesitation, strong enough to penetrate the symphony of sleep apnea that filled the dark void. Vince felt the cold metal pull away from his sweating forehead. His heart beat rapidly and he could hear Uncle Roman's raspy breathing. As his eyes adjusted, he caught the faint reflections in the aging man's crystal blue eyes. His pure white hair looked luminescent, even in the dark.

"*Minchia, Vincenza!* This is a *loud* cabin, Vincent. We don't walk *quietly* here. We make *noise* in this cabin. Noise equals my sense of *comfort.* And safety," Uncle Roman said, not whispering at all. He put the pistol at his side and returned the hammer. He scratched his thigh with the barrel. "Now go wipe your ass and find a place to sleep. Glad you made it here safe. Breakfast at six. Good night."

"Right. G'night." Vince was glad he'd urinated before walking in. He felt Uncle Roman's presence across the room. "Hey, Uncle Roman."

"What?"

"Thanks for not shooting me."

Uncle Roman paused at his bedroom door.

"You're welcome, Vincent."

Uncle Roman shut the bedroom door and was back to snoring within seconds.

Vince exhaled. He sat in a broken La-Z-Boy that smelled of cigar smoke and undid the laces on his boots. The tension left his feet as they slid off, clunking onto the floor. One of the men's snoring cut off violently at the sound, before resettling into a series of yips, only to return in sync with the chorus of the others. And Uncle Roman was right. Even with the logs being sawed and the chirping of peepers and crickets—all of it as loud as any rock concert he and Nick had ever attended in their youth—sitting in the old chair, Vince fell fast asleep.

Afterword

"It is the writer's first book in which are encapsulated the aggregate of his dreams from the entire life he has lived to this point."

— Jim Harrison, *Off to the Side: A Memoir*

The above passage helped me understand my own journey. When I started putting these stories to paper, I was partially attempting to write something one might bring along on vacation to northern Michigan, or "up north" as we downstaters refer to the forested, lake-punctuated region of the state. I wanted to write a book made up of grit, humor, and dramatic tension. I wanted it to feel like an escape—a mix of pulp, noir, adventure, dark humor, mystery—cinematic even, with an aim at entertaining. While most books like this are absent of pictures, I felt the drawings pulled the stories together. Besides, drawing is how I have expressed myself for most of my life.

I grew up in Detroit during the '60s, the son of first-generation Americans of Italian descent. They also grew up in the city, on the lower East Side—my mother on Mack and Chene, my father on Alexandrine and Elmwood, near the Coca-Cola bottling plant, maybe a mile from Eastern Market. Dad was a Detroit policeman and my mother a homemaker. They bought half a duplex on Seven Mile Road, a block west of St. Jude's Parish.

I was seven when I asked my dad why he became a cop. His reply was automatic: *"Because in my neighborhood, you were either a priest, a crook, or a cop. The first two weren't an option."*

His words stayed with me, my imagination filling in the gaps as to what his childhood was like. My dad being a cop *meant* something, the heroic affectation of his uniform only enhanced his stature in my eyes. Policemen and firemen—our neighborhood teemed with both—were true heroes to the kids I knew. As the kids of a policeman, we flew pretty straight, my siblings and I. Not angels, but pretty straight. Our parents taught us by example.

For my father, right was right, wrong was wrong—very little was grey. He was blessed with a huge presence—one that matched his mustache—and a personality that commanded the respect of sinners and saints—a disarming quality belying his dark exterior. He has a sublime sense of humor, an arsenal of jokes, and at eighty-three years old, can still kill the room when telling a story. Everything about him *made* me want to obey the rules. Don't get me wrong—I hit my share of detours, but he did a yeoman's job of setting me on the right path.

The six of us—I have two older sisters and an older brother who is deceased—lived in a northeast pocket of Detroit sometimes referred to as Copper Corner for the disproportionate number of policemen who resided there. It's a moniker I've grown to embrace. The neighborhood was crammed with well-maintained, modest brick homes and duplexes—our own was 800 square feet—filled largely with Italian, Polish, and Belgian families. It wasn't a tough part of town, but you definitely grew up street-smart. We were blue-collar families—many of our parents city employees, required by law to maintain Detroit residency. Everyone knew and looked out for one another.

Ours was also a segregated neighborhood, a mile south of Eight Mile Road. Before Eminem so eloquently touched upon that dividing line between Detroit and the 'burbs, we knew full well the invisible lines in *all* directions that separated blacks and whites—and the whites and *the whiter* when you consider the difficulty Italians had trying to move into the Grosse Pointes.

While I loved Copper Corner, at times I secretly wished I'd grown up in a different city, imagining a life without so much imprinted polarization. Everyone I knew felt it—they were all white like me. It was difficult not to feel it. I grew up hearing my father remark how he survived World War II without seeing action, only to nearly get his ticket punched during the riots of 1967, right in his hometown. Although I was only five during the riots, I have graphic memories of him returning home, weary and hollow-eyed, with puffed lips, bruised cheeks, and a nightstick painted with blood and hair. Those images went a long way toward coloring my adolescent views of the world outside Copper Corner. Dad's work *downtown* took him to a different Detroit than the place I was growing up.

When I left the city—finally settling in a West Side suburb—I like to think I left behind much of how its segregated ways affected me. I briefly toyed with naming this book *Leaving Copper Corner*, but in the end, it seemed too personal. "Leaving" took time and it *still* takes time, but leaving taught me that the East Side is very different from the West Side. I'll leave it at that.

And yet *living* there was full of adventure. So I choose to hang onto the very best qualities of that life, the essence of it. Those memories—the people, the incidents, the shops and their owners—covered me like the glazes used in oil paintings, subtly shading my attitudes and decisions through twelve years of parochial school, four years at Northern Michigan University in the Upper Peninsula, even during camping trips into northern Michigan, Canada, and Minnesota. The Corner rode shotgun with me to suburbia, renting space in my head during my bachelor years in Clinton Township, north of Detroit.

On June 1, 1985, my world collided with another when I "got hit with a lightning bolt" and met Maria. We married in 1990. Here I was, the son of a Detroit cop—of *Italian descent*, no less—wedding a girl of *Sicilian descent,* whose father grew up with a "strong dislike" for cops. The two men—now great friends—are similar, though each chose different paths. And yet both are so much alike, strong men of principle, guided by strict codes of right and wrong.

My father-in-law—to be sure, a second father to me—is a man I immediately respected and grew to love like my very own. I learned the importance of many things from my in-laws and their extended families, not limited to the generous use of garlic. My wife's heritage possessed the same deep love of family, friendship, and togetherness as my own household.

We're talking a big family. They have to rent halls for their Christmas parties. Our wedding party was so large that to get everyone in the picture, they had to take the photo from across the street. My wife has forty-one first cousins—*forty-one.*

I have two.

So now, embraced by this huge family, I've formed a unique outlook—how could I not? When you enter a family that big, there's bound to be some personalities in it and around it. There are some in mine, too. And while both my wife's father and my own insulated us from the more tangential members of our clans, the personalities in hers were slightly different than those in mine—similar, but way less ... *passive.*

In some of the stories in this book, the characters are composites of many in our families. While all are by and large fictitious, names were made up, mostly to avoid getting my legs broken or my anisette spiked with laxative. Hey, I *kid.* Sort of.

It's important to understand they're not in the *Mafia* or anything. They just have a different way of handling things. The same people who refer to Italians as *Eye-tallians* (think Olive Garden commercials) probably believe all of us are *mobbed up*, a belief no doubt embellished by *The Godfather Trilogy, Goodfellas,* and *The Sopranos.* Don't get me wrong: We *love* those movies—can even relate to them. Does that mean we *knew* someone in *La Cosa Nostra?* Nah, maybe. Were there *fringe* or "*wannabe*" *wise guys* in our families? Yeah, probably.

So within those Detroit and up north lives of mine, the seeds of these stories were sown. Coupled with my marriage, more were planted, sprouting slow-growing buds. During fishing trips with uncles, nephews, and cousins; at baptisms, funerals, first communions, and family reunions; a folk mythology steadily germinated. From the mouths of my father and my second father, the story stalks began to grow, staking roots deep in my subconscious, further watered by a passing joke or a seemingly insignificant snippet—an ancient anecdote, past event, or euphemism—retold as casually as one comments on the weather.

Now as a married man raising four kids, Copper Corner has melded into a kind of myth-world that I can't escape; a miasma of city and suburbia that taunts me as I recall the sweet and bittersweet, seen through the glasses of my own youthful naïveté. The tales, spawned by whispered hearsay and the aforementioned ingredients, led me to this book. I had the sensation of having gathered kindling for a kind of adult campfire story collection, paved in concrete and pine forests, populated with urban legends. Even if these wise guys and street gods still live among us, they are probably on the verge of extinction—or surely on the endangered species list.

All this leads to the end of my journey. Growing up, I wondered why certain people's mannerisms—their speech, habits, their walk—were so long lasting. They seemed to stand apart. Why, though? For me, it was resolved metaphorically through stories: They seemed to possess a kind of "inside animal" that they barely contained. Their spirit, filled with whatever it was that fueled their passion—be it religion, atheism, narcissism, love, sex, violence, revenge, compulsion, and/or compassion—lurked below the skin. There's a sports term for a related benefit: *controlled rage.* Good, bad, or ugly, it radiated from them. I believe it's a manifestation of the God-given soul, revealed through actions more than words. They overcame obstacles, conquered their fears, or died with honor. Heroes of all stories throughout time possess some component of it.

The theory isn't unique to me. It's been around forever, found within the myths of all cultures. Indian legends contain it. Characters in most movies must have it. Scholars, notably Joseph Campbell, wrote entire books about it. I'm no expert on any of it. Not even an original thought some may say, but one I believe. Strangely, I didn't realize until *just now* that my late brother, Douglas, personified the metaphor.

I was ten in September of 1972. On my first day of fourth grade, Douglas died from a rare form of lung cancer. He was twenty-two. And every September since begins a seasonal sadness I have no way of abating. The effect his passing had on my life was unquantifiable. Doug was *my hero*. A man-child—tall, dark, terrifyingly strong, at times funny but often brooding—he was a more raw version of myself. Doug backed down from no one, and there was knowledge in all who knew him that his animal—his soul—*truly* lived just below his skin. The stories of his actions feed his own myth even now. His life was a flame—a mist God breathed into our world then inhaled too soon—shattering us by his absence but whose brief existence remains strong thirty-five years after his passing. His memory is much of what feeds my soul.

Stories are the myths of our lives. They're the proof of what we are after we leave this Earth, of our one-time existence in it. And yet, they are still only *stories*—a chance to disappear into a dream-place and live there, if only for a little while. To crawl into someone else's skin and walk around—see what's going on in their neck of the woods. Ultimately, stories are here to entertain us, to be retold and passed down.

And so when I considered those writers whose books and movies inspired me and let me escape into their world, I have a hunch that on *their* journey they, too, discovered that one need search no further than one's own existence to find a story.

Joe Borri
2007

Acknowledgements

There's a Native American saying that goes, *"It takes a thousand voices to tell a single story."* My own took at least that many. Some I wish to acknowledge here, but first I thank God for putting them in my path.

Everyone at Momentum Books, especially Ed Peabody, Steve Wilke, and Leah Clark. Ed, I'm forever grateful to you for taking a flyer on me. Steve, your editing and input were key to streamlining the stories. You both helped tighten them while keeping my voice, and I truly appreciate that. Leah, thanks for the great design work and putting up with my "arty-ness."

Time is a most valued commodity, yet many gave freely of it: Marisa Miller, you're a gifted photographer but an even more wonderful person. Andrew Brown, getting advice from such a talented writer encouraged me. Rob Candor, you read *everything*, and in doing so you strengthened my resolve. Pamela Grath, my "up Northport" pal and owner of Dog Ears Books, our conversations left me stimulated, energized, and hopeful.

David Alexander, I'm fortunate to know you. You've imparted on me years of writing and life experience. Dear mentor and friend, thanks for trying to lay a solid foundation. The world would be a better place with more people like you in it.

Jack Epps Jr., between a busy schedule brimming with family, teaching at USC, workshops, and writing movies, you added yours truly to the mix. That you cared about me enough to do so is beyond humbling. You define the meaning of the word fellowship.

Pat Conroy, you're living proof of life's connectivity. Emerging from icy waters, you appeared as a flash of energy, imbibing me with a shot of humor. Over thirty years ago, when my soul ached from my brother's death, your talks started easing that weight, leaving me with indelible memories and the knowledge of how just *listening* can fortify a young mind. Thanks for being the man in the river, materializing when I least expected.

Patty LaNoue Stearns, you were my spark, the first one to take a chance on me as a writer and now, twenty years later, to convince me this book was in me. You write about food in ways that make folks laugh while their mouths water. But it's what emanates from your soul that I gained the most from. I'll never forget all you've done for me.

On to *All in the Famiglia* (hang on, dear reader—I swear I'm nearly done).

No disrespect, Matteo and Priscilla, but I'm ignoring our pre-marital agreement just this once, and calling you by your *first* names. In addition to the extended family you've graced me with, thank you for enriching my life with your love and acceptance.

Uncle Joe, Uncle Russ, and "Uncle" Jimmy M; gone but never forgotten.

My sisters Janet and Nancy for always being there. You, too, brother Doug.

My parents, Joe and Ardella. The artist's life is unconventional, made more puzzling when friends graduate to "normal" jobs. In art school, my peers told tales of unsupportive parents, their disinterest leaving many of them lacking confidence. I couldn't relate because of the unwavering belief you both had in me. Mom, your strength and faith shaped me, but it's your love of movies and ability to recall the names of every star in every film that ignited my passion for stories. Food-wise, your eggplant parmesan should be illegal! Dad, you're the best storyteller the world never met. And *nobody* tells a joke like you. Pat Cooper, that *mamaluke*, may have stolen your act, but trust me; you're the funniest man alive. More importantly, you're the benchmark of a father.

My four living dreams; Gino, Marina, Julia, and Ava. You fill my life with joy.

Finally, my Maria. Without you, none of this happens. You made the nights writing until 3 a.m. tolerable, keeping the coffee brewing and the laughter flowing. When I thought about quitting, you encouraged me. When I was ready to toss everything into a Kinko's box and bury it in the attic, you said, "Keep writing." You believed in me, and in the stories I wanted to tell. But you also challenged me to make them better—sharper, funnier, more entertaining. Along the way, I decided to listen. I discovered that your input not only made them better; they made me better, too.

I bought your engagement ring in 1989. The jeweler cautioned me to pick quality over quantity, saying, "Size and color sometimes clouds a diamond's clarity." As I wrote this book, some stuff read like real gems, some of it like an unpolished "lumpy." Still, just for me to get *here*, I'll bet I wrote a million words. In trying to find the right ones to express how much your support meant, I was tempted to write a million more, ransacking "Old Man Roget" of every ostentatiously Brobdingnagian jewel his thesaurus possessed.

Nah.

Heeding the jeweler's advice, I chose three clear diamonds:

We did it.